DISUNITED STATE OF AMERICA

A Charles Reynolds Novel

By

D.C. Reed

CBW Publishing, 2014

Thanks to my family and friends for all their support while
writing this novel.

Special thanks to Carolyn Wallock

No character in this novel is about or based upon any actual live
or deceased person. All characters are fictional in nature,
created from the imagination of the author. All descriptions of
agencies and organization portrayed in this novel are fictional
in nature and in no way represent the professional attention and
service provided by the actual agencies.

Front Cover Photo: ©.Arman Zhenikeyev | Dreamstime.com

Publisher – CBW Publishing San Antonio, Texas.
ISBN – 978-09823158-5-9

Prologue:

He was a young man in his twenties, dressed smartly in a pair of khakis complimented with a polo shirt with muted red stripes, courtesy of the one and only, Ralph Lauren. His haircut was of the fashionable variety, the kind that needed frequent swings of the head to keep in place. However, at the moment the brown locks mixed inharmoniously with the cashmere hues of a low-pile carpet. With one eye closed and the other searching frenetically through the underpass of his bathroom door, he was on the verge of crying. Rising up on his knees and then to his bare feet, he tried to calm himself. "Deep breaths, deep breaths," he whispered to himself. This mantra was followed by a shallow, "Must stay calm." Looking around the bathroom in an effort to conjure an escape plan which did not seem to be forthcoming, he shifted his thinking to that of places to hide. He could feel his heart accelerate its pumping and briefly wondered if it were possible to have a heart attack at his age.

A hard closing of a closet door echoing from downstairs signaled that the men who had breached his patio door only a few minutes ago were still searching for the presence of something, or more likely someone. The young man thought again about his split decision to race up the stairs to his room upon seeing the shadowy figures, weapons drawn, pass the sheer window dressing covering the glass rear patio door. It was now he realized that he should have detoured to the kitchen to collect his cell phone, which he had just plugged into charge on the kitchen counter. Fumbling through solutions to his immediate problem, he cursed himself for leaving his phone downstairs. Not just for the fact that there were no longer land lines in his parent's house, but also that the charging cell phone was one more clue for the invaders to gather when deciding whether anyone was home. No, he knew that they knew he was home. It was obvious they had followed him from the hospital. He knew that he should have been much more cautious.

Subtle worry lines inherited from his father were visible on his forehead as he gathered his courage. Putting his ear flat against the bathroom door, he listened. He could not hear anything, so he carefully opened the door to peak outside into his bedroom. He successfully ignored a trickle of sweat which quickly absorbed into the waistband of trousers, after undulating down the arch of his back. His thoughts were focused across his bedroom on the second-story window which overlooked the pool below. Curtains splayed with light streaming in, he determined the window was best chance of escape. He knew that if he could reach that window, it would be a short leap off a narrow roof ridge, which could lead to the safety of the deep end of the pool below. He and a couple friends had managed the feat in years past while in a drunken state, surely, he could do it while he was sober.

Taking a couple cautious steps toward the window, he held his breath, lightly stepping on the balls of his bare feet. Almost into the direct stream of the late morning sunlight brilliantly creasing the slats of the wooden blinds, a few more steps remained when his right foot stepped on a carpeted floorboard which squeaked a regrettable groan. The sound might as well have been a cymbal crashing for the men scouring the lower floor. If the intruders had any doubts about their prey's location in the house, there was none now. Thus, the search of the quarters, bottom to top concluded quickly, replaced with a stealthy climb up the stairs. Several doors at the top of the landing created the need for a decision of which to breach first.

With heightened clarity driven by fear's adrenalin, he threw caution aside. He yanked up the blinds, unlatched the window and easily raised the top sash. The bigger challenge was wrestling the window screen out of its groove with the intense glare of the sun causing one hand to instinctively rise as a visor. He gave a quick glance over his shoulder. The sunlight caused the flashes of light in his vision, but his hearing was fine which heard the echo created by the opening and closing the doors at the opposite end of the house. They were a couple rooms away, but they were making quick progress in their search which would eventually lead them to his bedroom door. Frantically, he used his foot to kick the stubborn window screen loose. Catching a bit of an updraft, the screen floated and spun, but finally landed with a clanking of aluminum on concrete. Shielding his eyes from the bright sunshine, he struggled to duck through a window which seemed to have shrunk since his last exit. Stilling a moment of panic that he would not fit, the young man turned to the sound of one of the men making short work of his bedroom door.

A punching shoe opened a fissure in the center of the door, but the frame, hinges and lock held the door closed. After removing his foot with some apparent effort, one of the men tried to gain a clear view to check down, up, left and then right. To the right was the bathroom which appeared to be empty. Angling his sightline completely to the left, he finally saw his quarry straddling an open window, with the cornered look of an escaping convict. The assailant nosed a silenced Walther PPK through the open hole, but the angle and lack of space did not allow a clear shot.

Seeing the silenced barrel of a handgun poke through the hole only confirmed the young man's worst fears and what was left of his self-control deserted him. Awkwardly, the young man crab-stepped backwards out the window opening while keeping his eyes trained on the hole in the door. He had done this before and his memory of leaping to the pool below raced through his mind. Extending outside, his bare feet found a shallow roofline which passed under his window, just as he had remembered. The asphalt shingles were hot from the late morning sun, but he hardly noticed the burn as he worked to squeeze the rest of his body out the opening, while gripping his last remnant of control, the one-inch aluminum metal frame of the window. Splinters of the door frame and pieces of the interior door erupted into his bedroom causing the young man to reactively recoil his face from the flying debris. Just as he felt his balance shift, and his grasp of the frame of the window slip, one of the assailants plunged entirely through door. The attacker ended in a heap just fifteen feet from the window.

Realizing that his descent off the side of the house was inevitable, the young man was able to simultaneously push off the frame at the last possible moment with his left foot and execute a double-quick backstroke in order to avoid an uncontrolled head over heal fall. He braced for the impact of the water from his second-story leap. Absent a glance, and assuming that the pool had not been re-located, he knew he was going to close to the edge of the pool even with his forceful push off backwards. The pool was, in fact, in the same place, but, unfortunately, the young man's parents had relocated a table with a protruding umbrella over the edge of the pool to provide some much-needed shade. As he descended, his right foot plunged through the fabric causing the umbrella to tip abruptly toward the pool and redirect his momentum back toward the house. The unexpected resistance of the umbrella caused his body to flatten just as he should have been entering the water. While the torso of his body did hit the water, it was his head that pancaked first on the concrete. No match for pool's edge, the collision killed the young man instantly.

From the second-story window, the nose of same PPK extended out, first pointing left, then right, and finally angled down toward the pool. This action was quickly followed by the slicked back brown hair head of a man poking out of the open window. Barely thirty years of age, the man's anger at the possibility of losing his prey, was replaced with a look of disbelief and then mild repulsion.

Like a loaded paint brush slowly sinking into a pan of water, the lifeless body emitted an ever-widening cloud of subdued red. A second, much older head pushed its way through the window to view the aftermath of the apparent death fall. The man's gray hair and cold blue eyes spoke volumes of his experience, but all he offered was a dispassionate, "Bummer."

DISUNITED STATE OF AMERICA

A Charles Reynolds Novel

By

D.C Reed

CBW Publishing, 2014

Chapter 1   Roanoke, Virginia Monday

In a combined ballroom at the Hotel Roanoke operated by Hilton's Doubletree, tables had been expertly arranged in front of a massive display screen, with a head table and podium. Registered as a historic structure, the Hotel Roanoke originally was built in 1882. Designed with a Tudor style, the hotel was a local favorite for meetings, weddings and family reunions. The clinking of fine stemware and an occasional laugh rose above the conversations at each table. Each place setting consisted of Westwood Celestial Gold tableware made from a combination of porcelain, bone ash, china clay and stone. The silverware was a lovely traditional Victorian pattern in gold. Toward the front, but a row of tables back, two young men, looking to be in their mid-twenties carried on a conversation too low for anyone to overhear. Trevor Whitworth was appropriately dressed for the event, with a trim fitting navy suit jacket with a mauve pinstripe embedded in the material. A silk yellow tie with a gray paisley pattern was complimented with a matching handkerchief in his breast pocket. A matching black belt and wing tip shoes completed the ensemble. His straight brown hair had just the right amount of muss to give Trevor a carefree look, which rebelled against his traditional business garb. He had brown eyes, but the tinted contacts he was wearing gave him the clear blue-eyed look that he wished he had been born with.

Trevor Whitworth commented offhand to his partner seated next to him, "This is lovely dinnerware. I overheard one of the aides say that it was the same brand as Franklin Roosevelt ordered for the White House."

In a bored air of condescension, Tyler Hansford commented, "Well, they are close. It was Teddy Roosevelt. They are straining to make a connection with F.D.R. and all."

"Yes, I suppose they are. Let's not burst their bubble." Tyler was also appropriately dressed for the occasion but decided his bit of rebellion would come in the form of a sports coat. Often mistaken as brothers, Tyler differed from Trevor only that his hair was neatly combed, and he would not stoop to change his brown eye color. His navy-blue jacket was graced with the silver striped requisite tie, tied with an expertly constructed Windsor knot.

Tyler said under his breath, "For $10,000 a plate, we should get to take it home."

"You act like you are upset that you came," Trevor said just loud enough for Tyler to hear.

Tyler just cocked an eyebrow with some expression that Trevor was unable to decipher. Tyler impatiently looked toward ceiling as if asking from help from above but said nothing. Trevor gave a little pout in response to the lack of answer. Tyler felt a sudden urge to punch Trevor. Why? Because he could be such a little toad, that was why.

"I just hate the fact that this bonehead of a President can collect $10,000 a head for a $10 meal and just walking through the door."

"Hey, don't rag on him. He is the only President, who has even been close to being on our side." This statement did not even receive the slightest of reactions from Tyler. Picking up a piece of sourdough bread and a butter knife, Trevor decided to try to provoke a response with a bit of needling, "I noticed that you were particularly enjoying the Secret Service pat down," Trevor said speaking softly.

Just below the hum of the crowd. Tyler said with no emotion, "Fuck you."

Trevor gave a slight smile at his successful goading. With his attention diverted, Trevor took a drink of chilled water. The rim of the glass did not quite make it to his lips allowing a steady stream of water to careen off his chin and into his lap. Immediately reacting, Trevor arched back, allowing the rebounding splash to land in his cloth napkin. Despite his quick action, the napkin was not absorbent enough to trap all of the water. Trevor felt a cold sensation along the inside of his thigh. Trevor let out a little curse under his breath, then dabbed at the wet spot while looking around to see if anyone had witnessed his slip. Tyler was mildly amused at Trevor's predicament, but other than a crooked smile, carried on as nothing had happened. With some urgency Trevor was dabbing at the side of his pants leg as discretely as possible. When satisfied that he could do no more, he turned his attention back to the crowd.

"I hate it when I do stuff like that."

"Don't worry, everyone will stop looking at you in a few minutes," Tyler deadpanned.

Trevor gave a brief conspicuous look around at the others at his table. Now it was Tyler's chance to smile. A devilish smile that Trevor did not notice as he was preoccupied with what he thought was a couple, which diverted their eyes when he looked up, but he could not be sure.

"I would go to the restroom, but I would probably miss the President coming in." There was pure anguish in Trevor's voice. He did, in fact, very much want to see every bit of the President. He continued to press a cloth napkin on his dampened slacks.

Looking bored again, Tyler took a swipe at an unruly strand of his light brown hair which had escaped the top crook of his ear. Hair length had always been an issue for Tyler's Dad, creating one of several areas of constant bickering. Tyler unconsciously pushed it back for the second time, successfully returning the wayward piece of hair to its holding position behind his ear. Most people said that Tyler reminded them of River Phoenix in one of the Indiana Jones movies. Quick-witted, handsome, and with a rueful air, Tyler could be ebullient and charismatic in one moment, distant and caustic the next.

Hearing a commotion toward the back of the room, Trevor excitedly said, "Oh look, he is coming in the back door now!" Moving his head around and at one point raising up out of his chair, he craned his neck to see over and around the others that were in attendance. The room erupted in applause as the President of the United States entered the room.

Trevor angled around to get a sight line, but now everyone was standing. Tyler continued to observe the table in front of him and was working his tongue around his back molar. A piece of bread or something was stuck, and he was determined to dislodge it. As he finally achieved some success with the wayward particle, the President made his way into the room with the usual entourage of praetorians and lackeys. Tyler reluctantly joined the enclave in standing and giving less than enthusiastic applause. The President was smiling broadly and waving as he made his way to the front table. Occasionally, he would give someone a point or a wink.

After about a five-minute descent toward the front, having arrived at the head table, he shook hands with those who appeared bold enough to approach him. Tyler knew from his father's political career that these were the ones that had made the appropriate contribution and each approach was choreographed ahead of time. Nevertheless, the Secret Service was on hyper-alert, watching each supplicant approach and then retreat. With the benefit of an advisor whispering the President's ear, each person received a warm welcome and was greeted by name. The crowd was still applauding as a belated and subdued version of "Hail to the Chief" had been piped in over the intercom.

The man next to Tyler said to no one in particular, "My God, it's the President of the United States, couldn't they at least have a live band or something?"

The uproar of the crowd at the sight of the President of the United States was enthusiastic and adoring. These people were the dedicated and steadfast supporters of this president. After a long period of waving and smiling, the President took a seat between an older couple after exchanging a friendly squeeze and a couple air kisses. The crowd settled back into their lunch, but the buzz of the crowd was like a juiced-up beehive.

"I wish I was up there!" Trevor said enthusiastically.

Referring to those "so lucky" as to be able to sit alongside the President, Tyler said under his breath disparagingly, "Those were the $50,000 spots."

Trevor leaned into Tyler to increase their privacy, and whispered, "I am not disappointed, Tyler. It is fun just being here. Your dad would be very upset if he knew you brought me." He gave a little mischievous giggle.

Blandly Tyler said, "I think he has come to grips with our relationship. Besides, gay is in. He has even been using me as some sort of political leverage with his constituents. You know, he is trying to seem in touch."

"Good luck in Virginia. Well," said Trevor, "I hope it gets him some votes, because this is really cool."

Trevor leaned back to allow the waiter to place the salad in front of him and he immediately started to eat.

"You think we can get a picture of us with the President?" asked Trevor through a bite of fresh spinach, topped with wine vinaigrette dressing.

"I doubt it. Dad is only a Senator, I think you have to be a big contributor to get that," Tyler answered.

"Too bad, I would look good with him."

4

Tyler shot Trevor an irritated look. Trevor knew it was not a jealous look but was not sure if Tyler was really just playing the impertinent youth part, or truly felt alienated by the whole event. Trevor knew firsthand Tyler could morph into the spoiled insolent brat as well as anyone. He thought that Tyler had gotten his perpetually dissatisfied nature from his mother. Ms. James Hansford, of course, fawned over Tyler. Trevor did not really like her too much and thought she needed to give the boy some space. Tyler certainly did not return the mother's adoration or any physical contact; he despised his mother as being weak and pulled away from her as soon as she released her grip. The harder she pressed, the more he pulled away. Then Ms. Hansford would go into the old "I'm terrible mom" routine and guilt Tyler into giving her hug or kiss. Tyler would always say begrudgingly, "No, you are not a terrible mom." "And" she would ask, "You love me dearly?" Tyler would always concede, "Yes, mother I love you," and then complain, "She is so God-awful dramatic." Bottom line, Tyler's mother had become a senator's wife and then a drunk; probably because the good senator was never around to give her any attention. Or perhaps she was a drunk before she married the future senator. She remained faithful to her husband, but only because she did not possess the guile to pursue other lovers and had no other means of support. So, she cast her neediness upon her son, looking for attention and affection.

Trevor found out how desperate Ms. Hansford really was two summers ago, when Tyler and Trevor had stayed over at the Hansford house after a family party. Tyler got absolutely lit on Sour Mash and crashed in his boyhood room. The room had been preserved as a shrine to Tyler's mediocre athletic prowess, and childhood interests: remnants of a time when everyone received an award. After Tyler had gone upstairs to pass out, Trevor was left lying on the basement couch watching the last of an MTV show. When Ms. Hansford unsteadily sauntered in, it was plain to see where Tyler got his pension for the drink. Trevor thought she was just going to confirm that it was okay for him to sleep over, or maybe offer him a midnight snack. Instead, she gave some cockeyed story about not being able to sleep and needed to talk. It was not like Trevor had never slept with a woman, but this was disgusting. She was slobbering drunk and when she made her move, a veined hand brushing across Trevor's zipper, he was able to slide off of the couch and avoid the cougar's reach. As he was going out of the room, he heard her say, "Oh yeah, I forgot you were a fag." Trevor replied back, "And I forgot you were a hag." It probably would not have mattered what he said as Ms. Hansford rarely remembered the previous night's drunk. But she might remember being called a hag, so Trevor just let himself out of the house without another word. He had never returned to the house, nor had he told Tyler.

Trevor knew Tyler equally reviled his father, but his crime was not showing enough attention to him. It would reason that Tyler sensed the lack of love between his parents as well. Tyler learned to treat his mother as his father did, with contempt. Perhaps that is the way of things, thought Trevor, sins of the father for three generations and all that. He mused that there would not likely be a seed from Tyler that would carry on to the next generation. So, there you have it. Not enough of his father's genes Trevor supposed, or too much of the mother's. He smiled at the thought. He was in love with Tyler, despite his pissy moods. Still on the whole, Trevor was growing tired of Tyler's indignant, chip on the shoulder, inferiority complex. What he did not realize was that Tyler was even more disgruntled with Trevor and would soon be casting off in a different direction.

The buzz of the well-healed supporters of the President reverberated throughout the largest meeting room of the Roanoke Doubletree. While making casual glances to the head table and maintaining polite conversations, the patrons happily ate the provided sustenance at their assigned tables while anxiously awaiting the President's address. Less concerned with conversation or proper decorum, Tyler Hansford took a bite of bread and surreptitiously continued to mentally eviscerate each of those sitting at the head table. Tyler supposed that his pithy attitude came from the fact that every single person at the head table had juicy skeletons in their closets, yet he the Senator's gay son was continually excoriated in the press for something that was much less harmless. Tyler realized that having money meant having a season pass for treating others poorly with immunity, but also meant that he was subject to the wrath of any bumpkin reporter looking to make a name for himself. The golden rule was never more evident to Tyler; those

6

that have the gold make the rules. He despised these sycophantic people, sitting at the head table in their best clothes, pretending to be so high and mighty. They reminded him so much of his father and mother it made him want to puke. Excuse me Mr. President; let me puke on the pretentious phlegm sitting beside you, pretending to have it all together. Those people were no different than his mother who was a drugged up drunk or his father, a philandering egotistical son of a bitch. And Tyler, meant son of a bitch, because his grandmother was certainly a bitch; albeit a rich bitch, but she was still a bitch. She at least would occasionally see to it that Tyler got his way. Like the time that his dad would not get him the car he really wanted. Grandma did. That really pissed the old man off, but he could not figure out a way to outmaneuver his mother once the deed was done. Tyler knew the whole mess really was a thorn in his father's side, so any time the two would get in a fight about this or that, Tyler would go out to the garage, fire up the McClaren M6 GT and peel out the front gates, just to really get him good.

Tyler could identify almost everyone at the head table, but one person's identity eluded Tyler. He guessed that the person might be a cabinet member, but he wasn't sure.

"Trevor, who is that seated, two seats down from the President?"

Turning almost entirely around, Trevor studied the person. He squinted and then reached in his pocket for a pair of glasses. He placed them on his face just long enough for the identification, then quickly took them off and returned them to his inside breast suit pocket. Trevor turned back around. Leaning across the table, he said, "That's *Senator* Mike Pemberton," with special emphasis on the title senator. "His daddy is a big donor to both parties and good friends with Senator Hart from Virginia, Summers, also from Virginia and Hutchins from Delaware. Daddy Pemberton had been trying to get Mikey in politics for quite some time, and finally did. When Mikey finally did run for office in South Carolina, he won easily by riding the coattails of the President, and spending the money of daddy, of course. In fact, he replaced the retiring Hart. Not very handsome, do you think?"

Unsuccessfully ignoring the last comment, Tyler gave Trevor contemptuous look, but trying to change the subject,

7

asked, "I thought you were wearing contacts. Why do you need the glasses?"

"Oh, the contacts are not prescription," Trevor said. He lifted and peered into his silver spoon to admire his fake blue eyes. Trevor was pleased with his new look and returned the spoon to its proper place on the table, but not before checking his smile.

Tyler gave an exasperated sigh. "How do you know all of this?"

"Know all what?" Trevor asked.

"All of this political stuff, you don't even hang out in Washington."

Obviously pleased with Tyler's question, Trevor said, "Well, for one I pay attention to the newspaper reports, and all the lobbyists are always name-dropping."

Under his breath Tyler said, "More likely you are reading *The Enquirer.*"

"Hey, *The Enquirer* has it right a lot more than you think," Trevor protested showing a slight pout.

The main course was served. Trevor had chosen the shrimp scampi over linguini, covered in a white creamy wine sauce. It was served with two crisp spears of asparagus, and rice pilaf. He thought the combination was a bit odd, linguini and rice seemed redundant, but nevertheless appetizing. Tyler had ordered the blackened Tilapia, which came with a similar assortment of side items.

"This looks divine," Trevor said loud enough for others to hear. He received the obligatory nods of agreement from around the table. A middle-aged man seated across the table looked at Trevor with a critical eye; then disapprovingly said something to his wife seated next to him that carried over faintly ended with a word that sounded like fag.

Oblivious to the man's reaction, Trevor asked Tyler, "Do you know the history of Roanoke?"

"Some," Tyler answered hesitantly. He did not really want to get into a trivia type discussion with Trevor.

"You know what the town was first called?"

"No," Tyler said with a slight exhale, "What?" His expression said you were going to tell me anyway, so go ahead.

"Big Lick," Trevor barely got out before busting into a hard laugh. "Big Lick," he repeated through his barely contained snort and chortle. He used his napkin to cover his mouth and then dab at his eyes. He deliberately slowed his breathing to get himself under control. After several moments and a couple deep breaths, he managed to compose himself.

Looking with a face devoid of expression, Tyler just stared at Trevor. "I am so glad you are enjoying yourself," mumbled a disconsolate Tyler. Trevor briefly looked up from his meal with a questioning look on his face but did not respond. Tyler rolled his eyes and announced, "I have to go to the restroom."

Standing, Tyler wiped his mouth and signaled to one of the attendants. Trevor looked on with a somewhat confused expression, then shrugged with a "what's bothering him" look and returned to his lunch. Nearby, an attendant nodded to a Secret Service agent, who quickly moved toward the table in need of an escort. The agent, Frank Lever was a well-proportioned man, six foot tall with alert eyes and a masculine jaw line. Despite a clean shave, the agent's beard shadow was visible, giving him a GI Joe look; the one with the permanent five o'clock shadow painted on at the factory. Tyler gave him an appraising stare, of which the agent either was either oblivious or chose to professionally ignore. Efficiently weaving between tables, placed uncomfortably close enough to maximize the room's donor potential, Agent Lever led Tyler to the exit with the nearest restroom. Lever handed off Tyler to a Senior Agent, Tim Kasich, at the door leading out into a common area. Tyler mused to himself that these guys were all business. Sighing, he accepted the fact that this was all part of the game of guarding the President.

Upon reaching the men's room, Agent Kasich turned to Tyler and said flatly, "I will need to search you before you can return to the dining room. Sorry for the intrusion."

Casually Tyler looked up and then down the agent. He thought to himself that the Secret Service might be an interesting place to work. "Don't apologize, agent," Tyler said giving a suggestive smile as he flamed through the exterior wood-grained bathroom door.

Agent Kasich's spine stiffened, but he said nothing as Tyler passed. The agent did wear an almost imperceptible frown on an otherwise placid face. *You deal with all kinds,* he thought to himself. Positioning himself where he could see the bathroom's outer entry door, as well as the doors leading to the dining room, Kasich settled into an alert stance: hands clasped in front, staring straight ahead. Keenly aware of his peripheral vision, the agent's mind could not help but puzzle over the strange young man. He began the age-old debate of born or bred while he waited for the young man to finish business and return.

Pushing through one door and then a second, Tyler entered the expansive restroom with three stalls preceded by a couple full length urinals. He glanced toward the mirror and let out dissatisfied sigh when he saw his aging profile. A weight program had trimmed his weight, but he still had a slight paunch. He wisped a hand through his thinning hair and cursed the genes that he had received from his mother's side of the family. He still had hair, but he could feel it slowly evaporating, and it would not be long before he was as bald as his maternal grandfather. He thought about the program that he watched on television the previous week about hair restoration. Feeling that he still looked reasonably attractive for being in his mid-twenties, he breathed out a sigh of resignation, followed by a slight pout. Drawing up to the mirror, he flashed a smile. Sure enough, he thought, it was a good thing he did have a winning smile. He wiped away a small piece of wayward salad on his bottom front tooth. Tyler entered the furthest of the three stalls and tried to lock the door unsuccessfully. The locking mechanism had been removed or perhaps it was never there in the first place. Tyler frowned and held the door in place with his forefinger. He waited a moment and withdrew the pressure. He thought about moving stalls, but this time the door stayed in the closed position. Problem solved but served as just one more little annoyance for Tyler. He gave an irritated sigh, shucked his jacket, placed it on the metal hook on the back of the door, carefully wiped the toilet with paper and dropped his pants.

As he sat down, the weight of his jacket caused the door to slowly swing open. Tyler let out a soft curse. Rolling his eyes, Tyler pushed it closed again. The door held for a moment, but slowly crept open again, eventually coming to rest against Tyler's knee. He resigned himself to the door being ajar. Tyler told himself to relax and stop being so easily upset. A thermostat, not a thermometer his psychiatrist had told him. Tyler thought angrily, *what did he know? He was a fraud that only used his position to take advantage of him. Like everyone he knew, people were always after something; even the ones that were supposed to be looking out for him.* Tyler wondered if it was his fate in life to be used and abused. And as far as Tyler was concerned, it was not just the males, it was females too. Whether it was his nanny – his "way too close in age to be in charge of an impressionable and seducible boy"- nanny or his pederast psychiatrist, they were all just after something. His dad wanted him to be this perfect little senator's son that he could never be. And his mother..., *Oh my God,* Tyler thought, *my mother. What the hell did she want me to be?* Tyler's body gave a little shiver. *Now the latest person looking to get something from me,* Tyler thought, *Trevor, the little shit.* But Tyler knew it was himself that had allowed Trevor to tag along for the ride. He could say no, Tyler knew he could, but often was too much of a "boyo." That's what his Puerto Rican boyfriend called him when Tyler refused to 'come out' to his father. Tyler missed Miguel. And down deep Tyler knew Miguel was right. Tyler did not have the guts to stand up for himself. Didn't he willingly and even eagerly allow the nanny to have her fun? Tyler mentally shrugged. *Well, twelve was probably a bit too young. No wonder I am so screwed up,* he thought. Then countered in his mind, *what was the harm? So, what if he got laid at an early age.* And Tyler could have stopped Dr. Mark – as his psychiatrist insisted that Tyler called him - if he had wanted to stop him. *But you didn't stop him, did you? And what effect did that have on my psyche?* Tyler wondered. No, he had not stopped the good doctor, because *duh, your gay. But again, what was the big deal? So, what if I gave the older putz a little thrill?* Tyler grimaced as his memory poured back through his consciousness. Part of him was mad and the other was ambivalent. Tyler wondered how many other boys Dr. Mark Clarke had convinced to "step out of their comfort zone" and to "explore their physicality" with him. *Wow,* Tyler thought, *what if just one came forward. Dr. Mark would be crucified, and just like the Catholic priests had been or even that football coach...* he could not remember his name. Tyler had thought about exposing Dr. Mark once when the doctor had pressed him particularly hard about opening up about how his parent's relationship was affecting him. Tyler responded crossly, "Maybe I should come clean about all my relationships." Dr.

11

Mark had quickly backed off. Now that Tyler thought about it, it was shortly thereafter that Dr. Mark suggested a reduction of their sessions to twice a year. It seemed all of a sudden that Tyler had achieved miraculously an emotional stability that no longer required Dr. Mark's extensive attention. Tyler gave a sarcastic laugh and said aloud, "Yeah right."

The bathroom was a quiet refuge, and Tyler was in no hurry to return to the insufferable lunch. He was so tired of the whole political game, and Trevor was such a bore. Tyler had introduced Trevor to his father for shock value. It had worked because his father had steered clear of the queer jokes from then on. The downside was that Trevor had interpreted introduction as a sign that their relationship was on a long-term course. Tyler knew that privately the Senator James Hansford was aghast that his son was gay and that he and Trevor were anything but a long-term relationship. However, at some point during the past few months, someone in the Senator Hansford political campaign must have somehow convinced Tyler's dad that having a gay son could be used to his advantage in certain circles. The Senator had not gone so far as to including any gay issues as part of his platform, but simply acted out the part of a caring, non-judgmental father. Which, Tyler figured his father had calculated, would appeal to both the conservative and liberal crowd. *What a political slut,* Tyler thought. Tyler did not like being used, but he guessed he was using his dad as well, so why should he get bent out of shape about it? For his old man, Tyler felt that just the acknowledgment that there were gay people out there was a big step in the right direction. And Tyler realized he was using Trevor. He would need to cut that boy loose, and soon. Tyler took in a couple handwritten notes on the stall. Reaching up into his suit coat pocket, he took out a pen and added some detail to a crudely drawn man's anatomy. He then cursed himself for the juvenile action. There it was again, even at his age, he could hear the voice of his disapproving father, "Tyler, stop that."

Outside the restroom, Kasich stood motionless while using his peripheral vision to fully take in the entire common area, including the doors leading into the dining room. While remaining diligently alert, this was still a break of sorts from monitoring the ebullient crowd. He checked his watch wondering what was taking the fruit so long in the bathroom, but he was unwilling to go inside to check. *No way I'm going in there!* Kasich thought. He adjusted the ear microphone which was just barely visible in his left ear. Two doors leading into the dining room pivoted open. Two men dispersed from the large banquet hall. One decidedly older than the other, they were being accompanied by the rookie of the Secret Service detail, Cyrus Straus. Kasich smiled at the thought of passing the current occupant in the restroom over to a rookie. Straus had always been a bit of a kiss up if you were to ask Kasich.

When Straus arrived with his two guests, Kasich took the lead and said, "Just to let you know gentlemen, you will have to be searched when you exit the bathroom, if you desire to go back into the dining room."

One of the men, older with graying brown, closely cut hair, and an aristocratic nose responded in a confident tone, "Sure, not a problem. Thank you, agent...," He paused for Kasich to say, "Kasich, sir." Kasich recognized him as a U.S. Senator but could not come up with the name. However, Kasich knew that the fact that the Senator did not wear a name tag meant that everyone already knew his name. No tag was necessary. The Senator nodded as if the name Kasich actually meant something important enough to pause and consider. The older man was dressed in a dark blue, moderately priced suit, which sported a burgundy tie emblazoned with the state crest of Virginia. Pushing sixty, his walk had exuded the energy of someone much his junior. The Senator's countenance was one of purpose and seriousness. Kasich immediately thought the search comment might have offended the Senator, but perhaps it was something else. Perhaps it was irritation at something that was said at the luncheon, Kasich was not sure. Maybe the Senator just really needed to go to the bathroom.

Not quite finished up with a conversation on his cell phone, the second, younger guest nodded to Agent Kasich, but slowed to finish up his call. Straightening his dark, three buttoned, Donatello suit jacket, he was listening to his caller with an impassive expression on his face. Everything about him was, well, average. Average height, gelled brown hair, average complexion, and average looking glasses framed an unremarkable face. Even his name, Mark Smith, scrawled on an adhesive tag stuck to his lapel, written with a black Sharpie marker was unmemorable. Perhaps Kasich was a little overly critical when it came to the looks of Smith, but he did look like an average "suit." Now to the fruit in the can, Smith was probably a real stopper, but to Kasich, just another suit. Kasich assumed Smith was part of the Senator's entourage and really did not pay him much attention as he had already passed muster on the way into the event.

To the Senator, Kasich said, "Let me get the door for you sir." Agent Kasich pushed open the first of two doors leading to the restroom, allowing the first guest to enter. He then moved swiftly through the first door and with some effort stretched his left arm to hold both doors at the same time. The Senator passed through both doors quickly and provided an audible "Thank you Agent Kasich."

Kasich then waited, stretched like a man on a torture device, allowing the second man, still engaged in his phone conversation, to enter into a small inner hallway leading to the restroom. As he passed through the doors, Smith nodded a thank you, but otherwise gave little indication that he was aware of anyone's predicament other than his own.

Allowing the doors to close, Kasich moved back outside the bathroom hallway. Trying to hide a smile, Kasich said to the junior in rank Strauss, "You stay with your guests. I am going to go back to the dining area. Everyone needs to be searched on the way back in."

Strauss, wanting to make a positive impression with a more senior agent, gave a quick nod and said, "Yes sir."

Kasich stopped abruptly. "Oh, you have a third guest in the restroom. A real prize," he said with a dry smile.

Straus cocked his head, first to the left and then to the right, mentally processing the statement. Kasich moved back to the dining room without further explanation leaving Strauss with the puzzled expression of someone who had missed the punch line to a joke. Straus assumed a position outside the entry of the bathroom which allowed him to see anyone coming or going from the dining area. Satisfied with his vantage point, he settled into his stance.

Seated in the stall, Tyler just was able to hear the outer door to the restroom open. Next, muted voices became audible as the inner door to the restroom opened with a slight moaning of hinges that Tyler had not noticed when he had entered earlier. That sound was followed by the echo of a pair of leather shoes on the marble floor. Tyler started to clear his throat, when he heard what must have been a second man entering the bathroom. Tyler remembered the broken latch on the door. With his coat still gracing the back of the door, he used one foot to gently push it closed and prevent it from swinging back open. As the second set of footsteps came through the door, Tyler realized the man must have been finishing up a call on a cell phone. It was a confident voice with no distinguishable accent, which said, "I will have to call you back, gotta go." Again, Tyler thought about clearing his throat. Maybe it was instinct, but for some reason, instead making a noise, he picked up his other foot, steadied it on the stall door and sat silently.

Chapter 2   Denver City, Texas Monday

Seventy miles south of Lubbock, Texas and ninety miles north of Midland, a flagstone entrance to a ranch called Brierfield, rested unperturbed. On the edge of 640 rustic acres of land, the only sign that graced a large metal gate entry was a straightforward "No Trespassing" sign, rusting at all four corners. A fence with vertical metal rods spanning its six-foot height bordered the property completely and was garlanded on top with a thin electrical wire passing through. The charge was substantial enough that it would give a "just south of lethal" shock to anyone trying to negotiate over the top. Discreetly placed behind a formidable stone entry were three-video cameras that fed live footage directly to the main house, almost a ½ mile deep into the property. A dirt road led into the property that was full of desert type animals. While some of the wildlife made for good hunting, one could suppose that there were also animals that would enjoy hunting people.

The vehicle Robby Young was captaining, rolled up alongside the Brierfield stone entry with its inconspicuous metal gate. His shaggy cut of hair protruded from under a John Deere baseball cap, which complimented a faded pair of old Wrangler jeans and a threadbare button-up plaid shirt. A mid-thigh hole in his jeans left a savvy observer the impression of someone in severe need of some sun. However, the face and hands of the thinly framed young man were deeply tanned, indicating a life of outside work. Robby's face was youthful, really more like the face of a teenager than his actual age of twenty-eight years. His face was angular with prominent cheekbones, his Cherokee heritage peeking through. Reaching down, Robby strained as he pulled the parking brake into the engaged position, producing a ratcheting sound followed by a final squeak. It was not his first delivery out here in the middle of nowhere, so the procedure was familiar to him, but it was the first Saturday delivery. Prior to leaving Midland this morning, he had placed two calls to concerned parties. He called the number to announce that he was leaving the warehouse, and then placed a second call providing approximate delivery and return times. As in the past, the trip was uneventful, mainly because there was no noticeable traffic this far out of any metropolitan area, even less on a Saturday. Two miles out from his destination, Robby opened a can of Skoal and put a dip in his lip. His body gave a slight shiver in reaction to the tobacco's nicotine entering his bloodstream and Robby gave a puny spit out the window. Within two minutes of his arrival, an old open bed truck approached from a distance inside the compound. The remote gate swung open allowing the dilapidated old truck to pass through. The 1950 pale green Ford pickup swung around into a loading position. Just as before, the truck was driven by what appeared to be a ranch hand, complete with worn ATS cowboy boots and an appropriately donned straw cowboy hat. Robby had immediately nicknamed the man Scrub, because of his unshaven face and his rough persona. A swollen cheek announced that the driver had a big ball of chewing tobacco in his mouth. Robby hopped out of the delivery truck, knowing that he was expected to help offload the delivery, just in time to see a long stream of brown juice being spat out from the old man's mouth. As before, Robby generously offered to continue on to the ultimate destination, which was sure to alleviate an extra unloading and loading. The answer he received was a quick, distrustful look and then a curt dismissing wave from the old man's age-spotted hand.

With both men lifting the ends of the crates, the transfer process from the delivery truck to the Ford only took a short couple of minutes. The process having been completed, Robby nimbly jumped down and recovered a clipboard from the cab of his truck. The old man hopped down from the bed of the old truck, but unlike Robby's youthful landing, his hefty landing was completed with a grunt and a slight groan. Straightening up with a grimacing effort, he gave a disgusted shake of his head. As Scrub opened the truck door and started the process of pulling himself in. Robby interrupted the ascent, "Just need your signature on the last open line."

After a moment staring away into the mid-afternoon sun, he gave Robby a dark look. The man's deeply lined face and tanned skin gave evidence of years of being part of the outdoors for the better part of his life. Robby might have described the man's face as having the qualities of a Shar-Pei puppy. Without a word, the old man reluctantly took the clipboard and scribbled a name using the pen secured to the clipboard with a piece of kite string. Robby happily accepted the clipboard back from the man, not even bothering to ask the man to clarify the signature. He already knew it would be illegible. Still looking at Robby, the man leaned to the left of the truck bed and spewed out a brown stream of juice, striking a large rock dead center. In response, Robby turned his head over his shoulder and gave a spit of his own. His expulsion was much lighter than the old cowboy's and it barely even reached the bottom of its intended target, a wooden post. A line of drool hung in the air and Robby had to use his shirt sleeve to arrest the embarrassing string of saliva. The old man gave him a pitying look and almost imperceptible shake of his head but said nothing. Robby tucked the clipboard under his arm and swung himself into the driver's seat.

Looking back out of the truck, Robby called out to the old man, "Bet I could win a pissing contest!"

Robbie could not be sure, but he thought the old man's head bobbed just bit, with a little laugh. His comment did, in fact, illicit a quiet chuckle from the old man, but there was no time to be encouraging conversation. He pulled himself into the truck and turned over a reluctant engine. Robbie had things to do also, even though this was his only delivery of the day. Checking in the side view mirror for any possible traffic, as unlikely as that was this far out in the boonies, Robbie fished his cell phone from his pocket. Next to the time, he noticed the message, no service. He truly was in the middle of nowhere. Turning the key and putting the truck into gear was accomplished in two quick motions. Pulling hard on the steering wheel, Robby executed a less than tight U-turn. A cloud of dust and dirt circled up into his window causing him to hold his breath and to wave his hand in front of his face in an effort to clear the air. Matching the sound of the delivery truck, Robbie let out a cough or two of his own. He completed his return to the pavement just in time to witness the old truck disappearing out of site, headed back in the direction from which it had come. The retractable gate had already returned to the closed position, and save for a swirl of road dust, the exchange point quickly belied the fact that any activity had ever taken place.

After driving long enough to receive a welcomed ping from his cell phone, he pulled over, and opened the creaky door to spit the Skoal out of his mouth. Robby took a swig from a bottle of water which had rested in the crook of the bench seat

18

with his right hand; with his left hand he removed a small wooden case from under the seat. He flipped up two-brass latches and lifted a wide mouth glass bottle full of dark powder as well as a pair of latex gloves. After pulling on the gloves, he carefully retrieved the clipboard with the manifest of fake deliveries and signatures. Robby expertly dusted the paper with the contents of the bottle. Having been alerted to observe where the recipient had placed his thumb scribbling a signature, Robby used a fine brush from his kit to gently sweep away the excess powder out the open door. What remained was a genuinely nice left thumbprint. He thought about retrieving the fingerprints from the back for the clipboard but decided that the thumb print was all that he needed. From his case, he removed a roll of clear tape, carefully pulled a strip and positioned it on top of the observable fingerprint. He put the clipboard in a clear oversized plastic bag retrieved from the case, pulled out his secure cell phone and placed a call.

Chapter 3   **Roanoke Virginia**   **Monday**

Both feet planted on the stall door, Tyler Hansford heard the distinctive drizzle of someone urinating. It was not a steady stream, possibly a prostate issue or maybe the man just did not need to go. Tyler suddenly felt the urge to pee but fought off the impulse. The need to pee subsided as his attention was drawn to the sound of footsteps moving in his direction. Tensing as he felt the interconnected stall vibrate a little, he thought he could hear a little groan. He felt sure the man had taken up a position in the first stall. Now it was Tyler's turn to look. With legs still braced against the door, this proved to be no easy task. Tyler leaned down between his legs, dropping his head low enough to see under the stall. He saw no feet in the two other stalls and feeling the muscles in his lower back scream in protest, straightened up catching a breath as silently as possible. His gut flinched as he realized that the person must have been checking to see if anyone else was in the stalls. Tyler's mind raced to put this puzzle together and felt a sense of panic overcoming him. Tyler thought, *Breath deep, breath deep.*

From outside the stalls a voice said, "Okay, you got me here."

It sounded like an older man with a Southern accent, who was quite irritated.

Tyler felt a vibration of the stalls again. Apparently, the stall checker had returned and was going to use the first stall. His voice echoed out of the enclosure, "Sir, we have some concerns about how you have been spending your time recently." Tyler thought he sounded like a younger man, perhaps in his thirties.

Leaning between his legs again, Tyler could see a pair of very nice black dress boots, Amedeo Testoni. Boots were not his style, but Tyler was impressed. Tyler noticed the man's boots were facing the wrong way to take a piss and he obviously was not sitting down. Tyler rose back up and took a relieving breath.

The older man, perhaps irritated by his weak stream, or the fact that he recognized the younger man's insolent tone said. "You have about 30 seconds to come to your point." *Yes, it was definitely a Southern accent, probably from Virginia,* thought Tyler.

The younger man continued, "You know, asking questions when you might not want to know the answers."

Tyler could hear the younger man messing with the toilet paper dispenser. Panic was rising inside of Tyler. If the first stall was out of toilet paper, he might eventually work his way down to Tyler's stall.

"I don't like your tone, Mr.., whatever your name is," the older man said in a defiant tone.

From inside the stall the man said, "You can call me Mr. Smith."

On the outside of the stall, the older man frowned and finished up his business with a shake and a demonstrative zipping up. He decided at that moment that he was not going to finish this conversation. He would just leave. He turned to the door to walk out. Unfortunately, his body had other intentions and he had to pee some more. Giving a frustrated sigh, he unzipped and again squared up to the urinal again.

Tyler's position, perhaps suitable for a gynecological exam, had started to become uncomfortable, but he did not dare move. Feeling his hamstrings starting to cramp, he looked toward the ceiling and deliberately slowed his breathing. What he could not know was that inside the first stall, Mr. Smith softly closed the toilet paper hatch after removing a Beretta M9 pistol. Reaching down inside his dress boot, he retrieved a cigar-sized cylinder from a small sleeve in the upper and quietly twisted it on the barrel.

Slipping the weapon into the waistband at the small of his back, Smith said with a congenial quality, "Not as clever as Rivers or Pepper, I will grant you, but Smith will do for now."

Having given up on the breathing technique, Tyler nervously cleaned the fingernails on his left hand with the manicured nail of his right forefinger, while wishing he could see who was in conversation. He did not know anyone named Rivers or Pepper. He thought *Rivers and Pepper, what the hell kind of names are those?*

The older man said crossly, "I have no idea what you are talking about."

The changing of the echo indicated to Tyler that Mr. Smith had poked his head from the stall before saying, "Oh come on now Senator, did AIG give you some tidbit of information, or is it the other way around. Perhaps it is you who is providing AIG with information." Tyler had heard of AIG but could not remember if it was a bank or insurance company.

Sounding agitated, but perhaps a little bit unsure of himself, the older man said, "I am not sure to what or to whom you are referring, but who I talk to and the questions for which I seek answers, are none of your business. And this conversation is over." He thought *this conversation would be over if it weren't for my damn prostate.* Giving one more jiggle with his hips, he zipped up for the final time. For emphasis, he added, "Who I speak with is not your concern. It's government business."

A flush of the urinal followed by a running faucet signaled that the older man had moved over to wash his hands. Mr. Smith had exited the stall and was no longer using his "nice" voice. Smith said with a trace of malice, "But it does concern us, doesn't it Senator?" Smith moved over to the sink standing just close enough to be uncomfortable for the Senator. A full four inches taller and at least thirty years younger, Mr. Smith's close proximity caught the Senator off-guard. The older man was determined not to show fear, but nonetheless, this man's threatening behavior was starting to permeate his countenance.

Tyler had heard the young man address the other as "Senator." The excitement of this revelation had caused goose bumps on his arms to form. He momentarily thought that Trevor should have been the one caught in here. The little gossip would love to be eavesdropping on this conversation. Tyler listened very intently but running water and the thickness of the stalls made it near impossible to determine what was being said. He realized if he was going to be able to hear more, he was going to have to get to a higher position. Remaining very quiet, Tyler allowed the door to swing silently open, and while squeezing the belt buckle tightly in one hand, gathered the waist of his pants. Carefully, Tyler raised himself up and adeptly stood, one foot at time on the toilet seat, being careful not to let his leather soles slip.

Now, placing his left foot on the plumbing, which extended out of the wall, he grasped the top of the stall, to carefully pull himself up with his one free hand. Upon clearing the stall wall, Tyler discovered the conversation became much clearer, and immediately realized the tone had grown surlier. Tyler could just see the tops of both men's head, one older and one younger, just as he suspected. The older man's face was partially visible, and Tyler could see that he was still washing his hands. Undoubtedly, this was the Senator, but that could mean any number of people. Tyler wanted to know who was being squeezed and who was doing the squeezing. The second man had slicked back, brown hair with what Tyler thought was styled with way too much gel. *Mr. Smith, I presume* thought Tyler. Tyler wished he could see more than the back of the younger man's head but did not dare to rise completely up above the stall. His footing was tenuous at best, and he felt a slight tremor in his legs caused by straining muscles.

Smith continued, "You must have received some erroneous information and evidently you have been in touch with someone in the press. And..," he added with some emphasis, "it has put you in a precarious situation with some of your benefactors, Senator."

The Senator bristled as he detected condescension in Mr. Smith's voice. He was thinking about whom he would call first when he got out this damn bathroom, and who was going to pay for this indignity. The Senator's corrosive glare eliminated the need for words.

"If you are able to tell me who you have been talking to, I can head it this off before it becomes a real problem...," Smith paused, "for all of us."

Tyler heard the older man say in a defiant, but controlled voice, "I don't like threats."

Tyler's curiosity had overcome his fear, causing him to rise up even further above the stall. With the new position, Tyler could see the partial face of the younger man, but now the older man was in full view and Tyler recognized him immediately. It was Hank Summers. An active workout schedule, a cautious diet, and occasional tanning had kept him looking much younger than many people his age. But today, weariness showed on his face. Perhaps his rugged schedule of late or the enormity of the issues of state had begun to wear him down. His profile featured a bit of gray hair starting to creep in around the temple, with visible laugh lines around the eyes. Not prone to overeating or drunkenness, this neatly fashioned man very much looked the part of a distinguished member of the U.S. Senate. A tough negotiator and respected by both sides of the political aisle, Summers was well on his way to a possible spot on the next presidential ticket. The only question was whether he would be on the ticket as President or Vice-President. If Summers had looked up at all, he would have had a clear shot of Tyler's head poking over the third stall. The fact that Summers did not see Tyler indicated how focused he was on the second man. Precariously perched, with one foot balanced on the paper dispenser and the other on the toilet plumbing extending out of the wall, Tyler's vision of the two men had improved dramatically, and he was going to be able to hear everything.

"You are right, Senator. We just need to back off. My fault."

Tyler thought the younger man sounded contrite, or was it sarcasm? He was not sure, but the excitement of catching this interchange gave Tyler, a little rush of adrenaline. Then he realized the young man was being patronizing and an inexplicable, sudden sick feeling rose in his stomach.

Having finished drying his hands and straightening his tie, the Senator turned to face his antagonist. Peering over the edge of the stall, Tyler could see the anger that flashed in the older man's face and heard it in his voice.

"You listen here. I am a United States Senator."

Seemingly undeterred by the Senator's outburst, the second man turned dismissively toward the sink. Using the back of his hand, Mr. Smith turned on the water.

Smith's conciliatory tone returned, "Senator, you should know by now whose bread you eat, is whose song you sing. You have been singing to the wrong person. Your 'friend' is not real happy."

Recognition at last shown on the Senator's face; his eyes narrowed, and the Senator's jaw line flexed. Having figured out who this guy was working for had an emboldening effect on the Senator. He was regaining some of his swagger. Everything seemed to fall in place, and he knew exactly who the players were and wondered why it had not occurred to him before now. He said resolutely, "Your boss should be worried if he has some involvement in what I am about to turn over to

Justice." His voice was not raised. It was intense and angry, but he was not yelling.

"Senator, you are drawing conclusion here that are one, incorrect, and two, very dangerous." The young man turned off the water and turned to the towel dispenser. Tyler got his first clear view of the man's profile. The guy could have been a model. Angular face, broad shoulders, and those full eyebrows gave him a sort of a pouty look that was so sensual. Sure, he needed to lay off the gel some, but he was practically a brunette Adonis.

Stepping between the younger man and the towel dispenser, the Senator said with steely conviction, "You can pass along that I am leaving this little meeting for boys over at Justice. And just in case your boss has some itch to try to shut this down, see how he deals with a Pulitzer Prize-winning investigative reporter when he gets his little file in the mail."

The older man had moved to square off with this impertinent man, but Mr. Smith seemed unperturbed. Instead of matching the Senator's anger, he disrespectfully reached across the Senator for a paper towel to dry his hands. Steadied once again in the best sustainable perch, Tyler peered and listened intently from above as the younger man wiped his hands, then put the paper towel in his coat pocket. He said in a firm tone, "And who would that be, Senator?"

Tyler had to adjust some because he felt his left hamstring starting to cramp up again. He steadied himself, but he felt his center of gravity shift. Momentarily he was able to use his forehead pressed against the stall to maintain his position. Regaining his balance, he was able to continue his surveillance.

"I am finished answering your questions. Friends ought to know better than to try this strong-arm bullshit. For Christ's sake, this is the United States, not Venezuela." Getting no reaction, he roughly straightened his suit coat and turned to leave.

It was then that Tyler witnessed the younger man's blur of activity. Reaching on top of the towel dispenser, Mr. Smith unlatched the catch. As the front panel dropped open, he adroitly reached inside the dispenser, withdrawing a syringe with one hand, and pushing the cover closed with the other. It was just like Tom Cruise in the *Mission Impossible* movies, moving in the extra-speed mode that could not be believed unless seen. In the next instant, Smith removed the plastic syringe cap with his teeth, and moved expertly behind the Senator, reaching the elder statesman just before he could grasp the door handle. Peeking over the stall, Tyler was afforded a full view of the young man plunging a needle into the Senator's neck and injecting a milky looking liquid. Placing a hand over the Senator's mouth, the attacker used his body to support the Senator's collapsing body.

Tyler let out a barely audible gasp just prior to losing his foothold on the plumbing. With a weight too significant to be held with his remaining grip, his hand was ripped free from the top edge of the stall. As he plummeted downward, he desperately extended his foot to try to regain firm footing. Instead, his ankle wrenched inside the toilet basin causing a rebound of water to splash up his leg and onto the bathroom floor. The pain of tearing ligaments in his ankle caused him to let out an unrestrained yelp of pain, which was followed by a different sound entirely. The solidness of Tyler's head was greeted by the unyielding metal, toilet paper encasement. Tyler's scalp split open; the blow knocked him unconscious. His torso landed with a thud and an audible crack of an indeterminable body part, probably a rib or arm, or perhaps his lower leg, finally giving way. Startled by the noise toward the rear of the restroom, the attacker awkwardly pulled his weapon, while supporting the Senator's collapsing body. The quivering spent syringe was left suspended in the Senator's neck like a dart having pierced a bull's-eye. Now with his gun brandished and head craning to see around and under the stall, the assailant attempted to lower the Senator slowly to the tile floor. However, the weight of the Senator's body was too much to be supported by one arm and the body dropped the last foot unabated. The plunge of the limp corpse was finalized with a slapping sound caused by the flesh of the Senator face meeting the cold, smooth, alabaster tile. Sprawled lifelessly on the floor, a dribble of saliva and a tear moved in tandem down the Senator's face and dripped to the tile.

The chemical injected into the neck of the Senator had caused an instantaneous paralytic shock which subdued its victim, caused death within thirty seconds, and then remarkably dissipated with nary of a trace for the examiners to find. An appreciation of the drug's remarkable efficiency and effectiveness did not escape the killer, but he stayed focused on the more immediate threat. Leaning over and with his weapon at the ready, the attacker could see the shadow of a collapsed body in the last stall. The killer let out a soft curse that he had not been more thorough in his earlier check of the stalls. He placed the M9 on the counter, removed the needle from the Senator's neck and carefully recapped it. He quickly wrapped the spent syringe with his used paper towel and returned the bundle to his pocket. Leaning down, the assassin looked again under the length of the stalls. Whoever it was, apparently was unconscious folded on the floor like a loaf of bread shoved in a cubby hole. Worried about someone entering the bathroom, the killer hastily dragged the Senator into the first stall and hoisted him onto the toilet. Wasting no time, he returned to get the gun and approached the last stall. He could see that the stall door was already ajar and gave it an additional nudge. The door slowly opened until it bumped up against the body. Peering around the door into the stall, the killer saw the interloper's face for the first time.

"What the hell?" the murderer angrily muttered under his breath.

The assassin did not recognize the young man who was bleeding profusely from a head wound and lay wedged with one foot in the bowl. The young man's body was squeezed between the toilet and the wall, and his pants were down around his knees, giving the situation almost a comical edge. The killer reached down to check for a pulse. He raised the silenced weapon to Tyler's head and fingered the trigger. This was a tough decision. Not wanting to risk leaving evidence, he decided not to disturb the scene. Besides, the kid may die anyway from the look of all the blood on the floor. A thought occurred to the killer. Smith quickly placed the weapon in the back of his waistband. He returned to the first stall, leaned over, grabbed the Senator by his lapels, and he wrangled the lifeless body out of the first stall and into the last. He then unceremoniously dumped the Senator on the top of the young man. Executing the final coup de 'grace, he reached around the Senator's waist, unfastened his pants and gave them a yank down. He said, "Let them try to figure this one out."

Chapter 4   **Houston, Texas Monday**

Dr. Sam Jackson, fresh off a weekend speaking engagement in San Antonio to a local Chamber of Commerce event, had returned to his home in the southwestern edge of Houston. Sam loved this 19th-century home. The front entry way, and the southern style staircase descending from the second story gave it a grand appeal from the moment you walked in from the mammoth front porch. One of his favorite features was a second-story balcony which wrapped around the front and sides of the structure. The back of the house featured a full screened in porch which overlooked the twelve acres of property. Sam saw the property listed on the city's auction list, while perusing for some other listing that was quickly forgotten, once he came across what was called the Canyon Creek Ranch. He had immediately called a realtor friend and then a lawyer. The property appeared to be somewhat dilapidated, but he felt that it would be salvaged with substantial renovation. Sam enlisted a builder friend as well to inspect the property, and to give him an estimate about the extent and cost of the repairs.

There were only a handful of bidders that showed, with even fewer having a true interest in Sam's prize. Several conversations included tearing down the house and dividing the land up into smaller parcels that could be developed. Perhaps they were confused by the fact the property had neither a canyon nor a creek, and yet was called Canyon Creek Ranch. Researching this apparent discrepancy was on Sam's to do list. Before he started entertaining, it might be a nice piece of the acquisition tale his guests would certainly be interested in hearing. Sam continued bidding until he was the last one standing. Not familiar with the auction process, he had brought along a colleague that was instrumental in the successful bid. Marley Thomas was a beautiful lady, but, unfortunately, from Sam's viewpoint, she was attached. They had been friends for several years and she was more than happy to assist. It was her advice and preparation that allowed Sam to place the winning bid, navigate the down payment process, and finalize the transaction. She and her boyfriend Greg would likely be the first ones that Sam asked over. Sam supposed that he liked Greg. He could not think of anything particular that bothered him about Greg, except for the fact that Greg was dating

Marley. Within forty-five days the property was in his name and the real fun began. Before starting the house renovations, Sam contracted to have a pool installed in the back, holding off on any other outside improvements until the construction was completed. Now, after almost a full year, the remodel and landscaping were finished, he had still not invited Marley and Greg.

Sam would have to wait till the spring to break in his swimming pool, but he could start entertaining whenever he wanted. Plus, in Texas, summer might begin in April, who knew. His new home was everything he had imagined it could be. Presently unattached, the professor seemed to be one of the most desirable and eligible bachelors in this small satellite community, just southwest of Houston and outside of Beltway 8. Far enough away and close enough to the big city, Sam also liked that he could be at Galveston Bay in under an hour. There was an airport nearby and Sam had always wanted to take up flying.

Unlucky in love it seemed, Sam Jackson's only steady companion for the past few months was Sylvester, who was currently curled in the edge of the sofa on the screened in patio. His black and white spots were similar to the markings one might see on a Holstein cow. The cat's size was also similar to that of a cow, making it a challenge for Sylvester to ascend any great heights, or even up on the sofa where he now rested quite comfortably. Sam had seen the cat move quickly, but typically it had something to do with securing a meal. Sylvester could in fact, move fast enough to catch a mouse if he chose to do so. Sam once watched Sylvester track a mouse moving across the back porch, only to decide it was not worth the effort and go back to sleep. Rotund and independent, Sylvester reminded Sam of the iconic fat cat named Garfield, but of the black and white variety.

Having just made a pot of coffee, Sam's morning routine was interrupted by the intrusion of a cell phone ring tone that mimicked Beethoven's 5th symphony. Not many people knew his cell phone number and Sam figured it was probably a wrong number. Then he thought about some colleagues that were traveling. *Maybe it was Dr. Sophia Busby. Um, that would be nice,* he thought. *Probably not,* but he decided to answer anyway.

"Sam Jackson."

"Mr. Jackson?" The man's voice was raspy and halting. His words sounded like a tremendous amount of effort was required with each syllable.

Sam did not bother to correct the caller and decided to ignore the temptation of reminding the person that he had already identified himself. It was one of those pet peeves of Sam when people really did not listen to what the other person was saying. Occasionally he would answer the phone, Sam Jackson knowing that it was a solicitation call. The caller would often reply, hello, may I speak with a Sam Jackson? To which Sam would answer, no I am sorry Sam Jackson is not here. Caller ID had solved those problems of yesterday, but he would have to admit, spoiled some of the fun too.

"Yes."

"I was given your number by a Bennie De Zavala."

Sam immediately flashed back to a convoluted phone call he had received from De Zavala just after his return from San Antonio on Sunday. He had not known who De Zavala was then and had been totally confused when the conversation had ended rather abruptly. Sam did recall that De Zavala mentioned that he would be giving his number to someone in an organization called the American Independence Group.

Sam said suspiciously, "Okay," and waited impatiently for the man to continue.

"Bennie said that you may be interested in speaking to a person who has some mutual areas of interest."

As the thought of hanging up crossed his mind, Sam hesitated while trying to decide how to handle this situation.

With a slight shaking of his head, Sam let out an irritated breath. "I did speak briefly to a Dr. De Zavala, but I really did not agree to anything. Can you tell me more about what you need?"

"I have someone that I think you will want to talk to."

Eyes with brows furrowed, Sam's bewilderment was further evidenced by his open mouth which mouth the words, what the hell? How many people was he supposed to talk to before he got to the bottom us this… whatever this was?

"Okay, well I am going to have some more to go on. Like to who am I speaking with?"

"I am sorry. I thought I identified myself. I am Charlie Rivers, and I am one of the board members for an organization that you might want to find out more about."

"Okay, Charlie." Sam found himself unconsciously slowing his delivery down so that the man would understand. He was trying to place the name but could only come up with the thought that his name sounded like a country music singer. "You are not helping me out much. What is this organization called?" Sam asked.

Undeterred by or oblivious to any slight, the man continued, "The name of the organization is the American Independence Group, but we shortened it bit and just call it the Independence Group. A colleague of mine would like to meet with you to give you an idea about the goals of the fellows that are involved. Evidently you spoke at a meeting in Houston," he paused. Sam's eyebrows raised in surprise and confusion. Sam lived in Houston and had spoken most recently in San Antonio. Rivers continued, "That highlighted some common interests. Would you be willing to meet with our representative? We could come to San Antonio on Wednesday. Would 5:30 p.m. work for you?

Sam was again shaking his head as if trying to clear up a fog of confusion. He was not sure if he wanted to tell Charley that he was, in fact, in Houston, not San Antonio. *If they are looking for him in the wrong city, that might not be a bad thing. Maybe Charley was just confused, but he did not seem stupid, just...* Sam thought, *vocally challenged.* Probably the man was a habitual smoker, who was losing the use of his vocal cords. He also seemed to be in a rush or something else. Sam just wasn't sure. Sam thought about the same urgency that Bennie had ended the previous call. He finally decided to try again to end this discussion maze.

"Charley, I appreciate the offer, but I think I am going to pass on this one. If you want to forward some literature to my office, I will be happy to take a look at it to see if there is something that I need more information about."

Interrupting Sam, he said, "Mr. Jackson, I have a very good friend that I would like you to meet with, He will be able to answer all your questions. I would meet with you, but, unfortunately, I am going to be out of pocket for the next few days. Can I pass along that Tuesday is a good day or would a different time work?

Undoubtedly ruffled, Sam said firmly, "Charley, it is Dr. Jackson. And I am not going to meet with anyone until I can get some more information. Send me a brochure, okay. Sorry to cut you off, but I have an appointment."

Sam flipped his phone shut and tossed it over the bar counter to a leather easy chair. He gave a little shake of his head while closing his eyes shut. Pulling himself up on a barstool, he proceeded to his Monday morning ritual of reading the paper, eating an onion bagel with cream cheese and drinking a cup of Millstone Hazelnut coffee with sugar and a shot of cream. He sprinkled a pinch of ground flax seed on his bagel, just to add some flavor and something to keep up his regularity. He opened up his laptop which went directly to his email. There were over fifty new emails. Most of the messages were from the online class that he was teaching, and he clicked on each of those and then moved them to a dedicated folder. He usually set aside Sunday afternoon to do all his grading and posting for the online course, but he had procrastinated this weekend and would have to make time today. The online students would be checking their grade book and if the grades were not posted in a timely manner, Sam would start receiving panic messages from students wanting to make sure that he had received their papers and scores. A new email arrived with the familiar "bing" sound. Sam said aloud, "Are you kidding me?" He sighed. Putting down his coffee, he clicked open the email realizing that this was not a student inquiry.

The email was from a GIJones@hotmail.com and read, Dr. Jackson, thanks for your willingness to meet me on Tuesday. I will be pleased to buy you dinner if you meet me at the 33 Ounce near your house. Perhaps we could meet for a drink at 5:30. Look forward to meeting you and discussing our shared interests. Best, George I. Jones.

Sam's eyes narrowed and his face began to turn a slight crimson. Standing abruptly, he rapped his open palm on the counter causing a boom loud enough to wake Sylvester from a morning snooze. With his voice escalating, "I did not agree to meet with you. I **did not** agree. I don't know who you are, and I have no intention of meeting you or anyone else from your... your, whatever the hell your group is called." He leaned into his computer, scrolling down in the message and said, "American Independence Group." He angrily read the name out loud again. He took two steps away from his computer and stopped. He closed his eyes and gritted his teeth. Taking in a deep breath, he calmed himself, but still had the look of a man ready to strangle someone. Instead, he massaged his face with both hands. Sylvester gave an annoyed look at having his nap disturbed, sighed and rolled over showing his back to Sam.

Sam sent a terse response to the George Jones email.

"Mr. Jones. Apparently, there has been a mistake. I did not agree to meet." Sam did not bother to sign with his usual Best Regards. He hit send with a satisfying punch of his index finger.

Glancing over at the Coo Coo clock on the wall that his parents had given him as a housewarming gift, Sam realized he was going to be late for class. "Dammit!"

Chapter 5   **Roanoke, Virginia**   **Monday**

Agent Tim Kasich leaned up against a fabric covered wall in the Doubletree Hotel, legs crossed at the feet and wearing a far faraway stare. Earlier the agent was guarding a harmless bathroom door. An hour later he was at the epicenter of an event which would be used for generations of future Secret Service training classes on how not to handle bathroom detail at a Presidential lunch. He and Straus would be forever linked to the Doubletree Debacle. Kasich could even imagine that instructors would tell young recruits: "Don't ever pull a Kasich." Straus was not far away. He too was reliving the last hour in his mind, perhaps his last in the employ of the Secret Service.

Straus had straightened a bit when a man with the name tag of Mark Smith exited the bathroom muffling his cell phone against his chest. A relaxed Mr. Smith said apologetically, "Hey, I have received an emergency call, can you take me to the nearest exit?" He added, "Unfortunately, I won't be going back to the lunch." Returning the phone to his ear, he began walking in the opposite direction of the dining room.

Caught somewhat off-guard, Straus recovered by touching his radio com saying, "This is 76. I am escorting number two guest from the men's restroom to an exit. Waiting for the remaining party to exit. Over."

Kasich responded, "10-4 76. This is Blue Blue. Copy two out. I am on the opposite side of the dining room, but I will be there to cover the remaining guest. Make sure the guest does exit." Kasich clicked off the com and sighed, "Fruit duty, no doubt."

Straus hesitated for a moment realizing that he should wait for Kasich, but Mr. Smith was already turning the corner, phone to his ear. Figuring this man was a bigger risk than the Senator, Straus said, "Excuse me sir, I need to escort you to the door." The man seemed to be distracted by the phone call. In that instant, Straus moved his hand to the butt of his Sig Saur P229, but Strauss did not really believe this guy was a threat. Regardless he needed to respect the protocol. "Excuse me sir." Straus had said just a little louder but with some urgency in his voice. Smith had not even looked back but had the nerve to signal with a hand gesture of a traffic cop that Straus needed to catch up. In a few strides, Straus pulled aside, but the exit could be seen just yards in front of him. The trip to the exit took only a matter of seconds, to the left and around the corner and then straight ahead. Badge out, Straus had opened the door and spoke briefly to soldier dressed in Army fatigues. "This guest is not returning." Mr. Smith exited, not even giving Straus a second glance. After making sure the door locked, Straus hustled back toward the bathroom. He had not run back but walked as fast as one could without it being considered running. When he turned the corner and arrived back at the bathroom, Kasich was not standing guard. Or, Straus pondered, had it been just enough time for the Senator and Kasich's guest to walk back into the dining area? He looked over to the dining room just as one of the doors closed shut. *That must have been it*, he thought. Or…, perhaps his trip was so quick that Kasich had not even appeared from the dining area and that was someone else going into the dining room. Which would mean the Senator was still in the bathroom. Or the worst-case scenario, the Senator had returned to the lunch without being frisked. He thumbed his communication device to check with Kasich. In a faint voice, Straus said into his wrist microphone, "Blue Blue, this is 76 outside the men's restroom. Do you copy?"

In Straus' ear bud, "I am almost there. We had a wheelchair exit to deal with."

Straus frowned. It sounded like Kasich had not come to cover. Straus again lifted his wrist to his mouth. "I have escorted one to the exit for a no-return and have resumed position." Straus did not want to ask about the status of the Senator over the radio.

Kasich's face had flushed with anger. There was a brief pause. "76, you should have waited for me." That awful feeling that something you did without much forethought was going to bite you in the butt flooded around Kasich. "Are the Senator and the guest one still in the restroom?"

This had confused Straus. "The Senator was guest one and I escorted guest two out. Over."

"Just stick you head in the bathroom and see who is there. I am 10 seconds out."

"10-4." Straus calmed himself with the thought: *Everything was going to be fine.* He entered into the anteroom of the restroom with a bit of trepidation. He listened with his ear to the entry door and a hand up ready to pad his head in case the door flew open unexpectedly. There were no sounds from inside, but Cyrus figured that even if there were any noises being made, the heavy door would be a significant sound barrier. Opening the interior door slowly, he stuck his head in and said, "Excuse me. Secret Service. Anyone in here?" The lack of response and the fact that he could not see anyone in the bathroom caused a moment of confusion. He thought the Senator must have left the bathroom when he escorted Mr. Smith to the exit. The repercussions of an unescorted guest to a Presidential lunch coursed through Straus' brain processes. Upon looking under the length of the stalls, this uneasy feeling was replaced with an immediate sense of horror.

Now, almost thirty minutes after a code red had been issued, Straus stood outside the restroom with one hand on his hip and the other massaging his forehead, standing just feet away from a pale-faced Kasich.

Speaking to a fellow agent, Straus said with an exasperated sigh. "He just walked out and said that he would not be returning, so I called in and escorted him to the exit around the corner."

The nausea had almost been too much as Straus realized that it was possible that he had unwittingly escorted a murder suspect out of the building. Of course, he could give a very good description, but he would be held responsible for the blunder. He felt a flash of anger towards Agent Kasich, who would almost certainly be thrown under the bus as well for his part in this ignominy. However, it was Straus who would be the one that would be the focal point of the heat, which was going to blister the Agency as well. A United States Senator was dead, and the son of a well-known politician was found unconscious in a bathroom which he was responsible for securing. This, of course, was complicated by the fact that the President of the United States had been speaking in the next room over. No, this was not going to be good anyway that he could figure. Straus could see the Detail Leader, John Stamos headed his way, and he closed his eyes trying to make it all go away. Stamos was of medium height, but with a large, confident gait. With a square jaw and deeply set eyes, the approaching Stamos sported an intimidating scowl. A crowd had gathered outside the hotel near the dining area, and the press had predictably set up shop outside the lobby, and just beyond the perimeter that the authorities had quickly established. With his stomach beginning to feel like an agitating washer drum, Straus thought, *this is not going to be pretty.*

Stamos approached Straus with an expression which bordered on disgust with a touch of malevolence. His pudgy face had a noticeable tint of crimson, and his stride told the rookie agent everything that he needed to know. Straus braced for the onslaught.

"Okay, Agent Straus, I want to know everything that happened, and from the beginning."

Straus noticed a condescending tone when Stamos pronounced the word agent. Well into Straus' story, the concealed body of the Senator emerged from the bathroom. Bagged and tagged, the Senator was being carried by four EMT's, emergency medical technicians, before being hefted up onto a gurney. Several officers, members of the Secret Service security team and medical personnel escorted the Senator's body to an idling ambulance. Another gurney arrived and Tyler Hansford was helped out of the crime scene by two additional EMT's lending support to his weight from both sides. Straus felt some relief that at least someone survived. He looked over at Kasich, who, one might have thought would also feel some relief of at least one survivor. But Straus did not think Kasich looked like he was feeling relief. Instead, it was a look of reproach that Kasich's face revealed. It was an expression of that slightly irrational thought process looking for someone, anyone to blame the misfortunes of life. It was a look which expressed, *"Why the hell did you get me into this damn mess, you little fag?"*

With a substantial wrap around his head and an air boot surrounding his left ankle, Tyler was assisted up onto the second gurney. Now conscious, but still dazed and confused, Tyler looked like he may have been in shock. The Emergency Medical Technicians, an EMT, had cut off Tyler's shirt enough to use strap tape for his bruised ribs. His coat and tie were draped over the foot of the gurney. Even at a distance, the stain of blood which paraded down the shoulder and arm of what was left of his shirt was visible through the hotel's floor to floor windows, causing a gasp among the sidewalk crowd. Others, made up primarily of attendees of the fundraiser, remained behind the banquet room door. A security officer was posted outside the door, preventing anyone from exiting, but each time an official entered or exited the banquet room, the holdovers were afforded a look. This time when the door opened, the dining room peepers were titillated by Tyler being wheeled to the lobby.

Somehow, Trevor managed to push his way through the door, calling out Tyler's name. Distracted by Trevor's beckoning, Stamos gave a disapproving look, but waved off the officers who started to restrain the young man. The investigation had already rocketed into full action, with a workup on all the attendees and their guests. Stamos had been briefed about Hansford's "friend" immediately upon his arrival and, as a result, Trevor was allowed to accompany his friend to the ambulance. Visibly anguished and making no effort to hide it, Trevor tried to ask questions, but Tyler was still too dazed to even speak. Trevor appeared to be suffering from the vapors and at one point successfully stopped the gurney's progress by stumbling slightly and appearing to be about to faint. A fast acting, female EMS technician diverted around the rolling bed to prop up Trevor, allowing the primary patient to be loaded up into the ambulance. Trevor, apparently having recovered, was chatting up the EMS lady and successfully talked his way into the ambulance as well. From the inside of the ambulance, Trevor helped to close the back door before it raced from the hotel, lights flashing and siren blaring.

Hands gripping on the rolling bed, Trevor sagged heavily to one knee next to Tyler. A teary-eyed Trevor looked up and said, "I wish I could switch places with him, even if he is going to die."

Staring somewhere in the middle distance, Stamos shook his head at all the commotion the boy had created, before turning his attention back to Straus. He grumbled, "I sure as hell glad that boy went with the Vic. If he flamed any more, the fire department would be in route." Face flushed, Stamos said. "Straus, this is a clusterfuck...," But, before he could resume his interrogation, his phone vibrated in his inside coat pocket. His screen displayed "Deputy Director." Stamos let out a frustrated sigh, pointed at Straus, and mouthed the words, "Don't leave." After Stamos had turned away, Straus gave an incredulous look,

39

thinking, *where am I going to go?* Straus stepped backwards and allowed the weight of the moment to be supported by the nearest wall.

Chapter 6   Houston, Texas Monday

Dr. Jackson's morning classes had been anxiously hoping that their tenured professor would arrive past the obligatory ten-minute waiting period. Sam thought he could feel a corporate groan when he walked in eight minutes late. He delivered a rousing lecture about the reasons why international trade had increased over the past half century and the impact on marketing and free markets. Though it took a while, the class eventually warmed up and began to enjoy the presentation. Sam concluded by showing a video that show the difficulties of operating a business in a foreign land which proved to be quite entertaining. He flashed a test review for the test which would be administered the following Monday.

Only three students visited his office during the required hours, and he quickly satisfied them with reassurance that they would do "just fine" on the upcoming exam. Sam's graduate assistant, Stan stuck his wiry-haired head in the door. He was a lanky fellow, inoffensive in nature and one of the better GA's that Sam had enjoyed over the past few years. Stan was certainly better than the last one, an attractive foreign student that took up the role of Sam's mother. She would follow behind Sam and clean, giving a soft, but disproving clucking sound with her tongue. She also did not limit herself to cleaning, but instead chose to interject herself into the appropriateness of Sam's professional and personal choices. The thought of that clucking sound made Sam actually cringe and shiver. Her feelings were hurt once when Sam became irritated at the young lady's constant mothering and had to become quite direct in addressing the issue. Then, of course, Sam felt bad that he had severely hurt the girl's feelings. Fortunately, the semester, and thus the assistantship was concluding. Mia did not reapply for the following semester and Stan did. Things were better now.

"Dr. Jackson, do you have anything for me?"

"Hey Stan. Not until the test next week. You can take off."

Stan gave a little salute and closed the door behind him.

The cell phone in Sam's pocket vibrated and he smiled when the screen showed, Penny Reed.

41

"Hey Penny. How are you?"

"Hello Sam. Have not heard from you in a while. What's going on in the world of a college professor?"

"Not much. Just the usual working papers, grading papers, and rolling papers," Sam quipped.

"Really?" Penny said with an interested tone. Stretching out the word, really.

"No. Not really, but wallpaper may be in my future. I am still trying to get the house in shape."

"It was looking great when I was there last. I bet you have done a lot since I last saw it."

Sam took the hint. "You will have to stop by and see it. I can wrestle up some steaks if you like."

"Sounds like a date."

"How about Saturday, say about 7:00?" Sam asked.

"Done. Look forward to it."

Sam gave a cheery goodbye and disconnected the call. Another call followed almost immediately, but this time it was his cell phone.

"Dr. Jackson," he answered.

"Dr. Jackson, I am glad I caught you. This is George Jones."

Sam scrunched his face with a pained expression.

"I love your music," Sam deadpanned.

A chuckle could be heard on the other end of the call. It was a deep laugh that made Sam smile. All the cloak and dagger did not set well with Sam, but at least whoever this was had a sense of humor.

As if reading Sam's mind, "I know that we have not been introduced and I apologize if this all seems a bit shrouded. I apologize for the confusion in my email."

Sam rolled his eyes. "George, I am sorry, but what in the world is this all about?"

There was a pause. "Again, I am sorry; I was under the assumption that Charlie had probably given you a run-through."

Sam just waited silently for the man to continue.

"I would like to meet you and pick your brain about economics and a little history." George said without apology.

"Okay, but you sound a little old for a college student and my next economics class won't start till next fall.

Again, the man gave a small but genuine laugh.

42

"I heard you have a good sense of humor. I wish I had had professors like you when I was in school. Might have done a little better than I did."

The man had a rich baritone voice that commanded respect, Like Donald Sutherland or Jason Robards. Even with no idea where this was leading, Sam was only mildly intrigued. Sam thought he detected a Texan accent, but it was refined, possibly showing some eastern schooling.

"Mr. Jones, I don't want to sound impertinent, but before I meet with anyone, I would need some additional information."

"Certainly, I understand that you don't want to waste your time. You have a lot of things on your plate, I am sure. I just want to share some ideas that have been bouncing around in my head and I would like someone play some mental gymnastics with me. I can promise you that it will not be boring and that you will be intellectually stimulated."

There was a long pause in the conversation. Sam waited for the man to speak and evidently Mr. Jones was comfortable with the silence. Sam knew that the first to speak in a negotiation was the loser, but he could not help himself.

"Could you give me a little more here, George," Sam said with a little more consternation than he intended. "I mean the offer is curious, but I am a little put off by the intrigue."

"I understand your reticence. But could you humor me if you get a good meal out of the deal, and I promise that I won't bother you again?

Sam recognized that he was dealing with an articulate and intelligent man. He was now curious, but still wary.

"This isn't timeshares or some investment opportunity, right?

Another chuckle from the other end.

"I promise."

Sam persisted, "Because I have all the investment advice I need. And, in fact, I have sunk all that I have in my recent house purchase."

"No, I promise. Just want to engage in some intellectual conversation."

Sam sighed and marveled at the persistence of this man.

"You don't seem to take no for an answer."

Another chuckle. Sam liked the man's laugh. He appreciated his confidence, and he was intrigued.

"I have been told that."

Resignedly, Sam said, "Okay. Where and when?"

Chapter 7   Washington, D.C.   Tuesday

The FBI Chief of Staff Shelly Van Aucken stood at a podium adjacent to a long conference table. Reading from notes which she had prepared for her boss, Russell Epstein, Interim Director of the Federal Bureau of Investigation, her naturally red hair was cut short emphasizing an angular face and attractive green eyes. Russell was running late due to a briefing at the White House, where he had severely been chewed up by the President for not moving fast enough to nix the recent domestic terrorist activities, as well as the death of a U.S. Senator. When he arrived, his shoulders looked as if his hands were attached to concrete blocks. He entered the conference room and immediately straightened and walked briskly to the podium. Hazel-eyed and of average height, Epstein combed his hair with a neat part on the left side, revealing the first stages of male pattern baldness. His casual manner belied a nervous nature which frequently required him to pop Rolaids to overcome an unsettled stomach and an occasional Xanax for the particularly difficult situations.

He looked quizzically at Shelly, who cleared her throat and said, "I was just going over the caterer's menu in case we had to order in."

Looking at his watch, Russell realized that his ass chewing session had been over two hours and his team had been waiting for almost an hour. Another thirty minutes and it would be lunch time. "Sorry guys. The President was particularly hungry this morning and it took a while for him to get his fill."

Everyone in the group of twelve, which included the Chief of Staff, Deputy Director, the Associate Director and Executive Assistant Directors, gave that "oh boy" look; each taking in great breaths or shaking their heads because they had heard about the President's famous, behind the door tirades. The fact that the current director was in fact, still an interim director, was an indication that life around 950 East Street Northwest, the FBI Headquarters, was not going to be comfortable for a while yet. The last director, Jeffrey Story, had resigned after being publicly humiliated by the President for using FBI resources to investigate several of the President's closest allies in the Senate and fundraisers. This misuse of power charge was lodged at a Congressional Intelligence hearing, which forced the previous director to admit that he had authorized wiretaps on several U.S. Senators. After Director Story has been railroaded out of town, Epstein seemed to be the favorite whipping boy, ironically for not being more aggressive in rooting out "unhealthy seeds before they were able to encourage other malcontents." The very action for which his predecessor was unceremoniously dumped was now what the President seemed to be requiring of Epstein, specifically surveillance and wiretaps without probable cause.

When he said as much to the President, he was given a stern look and reminded of his tentative position by the use of his current title. A crimson faced President had said, "Interim Director Epstein, the previous director was investigating my friends. The ones that helped get me elected...the ones that share the same vision that I have for this country." As he continued his invective, his voice rising, "If he had not been chasing after the wrong people, we would not be in the fucking situation we are now. A handful of anti-government wackos is causing social unrest and encouraging activity that may force us to have a national lockdown. If I do that, you know what they will say? They will say, 'See I told you so!' I want these people hunted down and I don't care what you have to do to catch them. It should not surprise you that we have some that have threatened my life. I do not intend to be a JFK or a Lincoln if it means that I die in the process. Waterboard their mothers if you have to...," he stopped and look to make sure that no one was writing this down. His voice and anger under control, placing his arm around Russell's shoulders he continued calmly, "Look Russell, this thing could be dealt with very effectively by isolating the instigators and the whole issue will die down. See what you can do, okay?"

Now addressing his task force, Russell pushed his glasses back up on his nose which now framed a pair of dark rings around his eyes and gazed out at the faces. "We have a delicate matter to attend to and I know that you are up for the task. We have an element in our country that is not happy with the current administration and apparently the direction of the country. Which is fine except they appear to be," he paused, "acting out as my wife would say."

46

Just in front of the short podium atop a conference table, sat the Executive Assistant Director of the National Security Branch James Leeper, who asked Epstein, "Are we talking about the threats on Federal buildings or is there more? Leeper was a tall man, early forties, brown hair parted on the right, with a significant nose protruding from an otherwise forgettable profile. He wore a perpetual look of mischievousness that pissed off many but was part of his sarcastic humor. Gripped in his right hand was a file folder which contained the latest copy of the threat condensation reports compiled by the Extremism and Radicalization Branch of Homeland Environment Threat Analysis Division, in coordination with the Federal Bureau of Investigation.

Epstein's right hand unconsciously reached for his temple and began a slow massage. "As you are aware, yesterday's death of the Senator has brought all of this to high alert status."

Leeper persisted, "So the President is saying the death of Senator Summers had something to do with the recent threats to the federal government?"

Epstein liked Leeper, but the man's impudence sometimes tested his patience. "James, as you know, the death of Senator Summers is still being investigated. We don't think Senator Summers engaged in some kind of lover's quarrel."

Almost everyone broke into small pockets of nervous laughter because of the absurdity of the press even throwing the idea out there. The quiet chuckles quickly died out because the death of the Senator was no laughing matter.

"The young man," Russell said thumbing through his notes to find the correct place. Shelly reached around his shoulder and pointed. "Yes, Tyler Hansford, son of Senator James Hansford, appears to have been in the wrong place at the wrong time. Rick, where does the investigation stand?"

Rick Uhler, the Assistant Director, was a career agent that had risen through the agency. Savvy, articulate and experienced, he was respected by the insiders of the agency, which was why he was a leading candidate for the Director's position but was passed over in favor of Epstein. Clean shaven including his head, Uhler was the Mr. Clean of the FBI. He was not inclined to worry about his ascent to the top. However, he was dedicated to the agency and would support whoever was in charge without playing the games which others would be tempted to engage in. That very quality was what people admired about him. Uhler was surprised when the file had been placed on his desk because he had been left out of almost all, but the most mundane cases since Epstein had been chosen by the President to head up the FBI as the Interim Director.

Rick began, "The Secret Service determined that the Summers' incident did not involve a direct threat to the President and turned the investigation over to our people. They, of course, want to be tapped into anything that investigation turns up. The President is expectedly torqued about the Senator's death, which he feels was carried out by one of the sedition groups." Uhler delivered this last bit of information with a tone which suggested that this was not what the facts actually meant.

Uhler's intonation was not lost on Epstein, who asked with raised eyebrows, "But you don't think that this was, in fact, the work of one of these groups?"

Sidestepping the question, Uhler gave a subtle shrug of his shoulders and returned to verbally reviewing his notes. "Following your instruction, Director, I have assigned the two agents you requested to work the Summers' death from the perspective of assuming there is a connection to the dissident groups.

Uhler looked to Epstein, who gave an uncomfortable nod of agreement. Uhler continued, "It is still early, but with regard to the Senator's death, the toxicology reports revealed that the Senator had no drugs in his system, but the heart attack was not due to normal causes. These two statements of course, are somewhat contradicting."

A general nodding of heads showed the group had the same thought.

He continued, "The fact that another man was in the bathroom prior to the attack makes the scene suspicious. Mr. Hansford suffered a blow to his head and was knocked unconscious. He claims to have no recall of what happened."

Epstein's eyebrows raised and several others began their own private discussions with their counterparts.

Uhler gave an indeterminable slight nod of his head acknowledging the inconsistency and continued with his report. "Mr. Hansford could not shed light on how he received a blow

48

to his head, but the agents determined from his wounds that he struck his head on a metal toilet paper dispenser. It is not clear whether his head was shoved down in a manner that caused his head to strike the corner of the dispenser or if something else happened."

Wilson Garcia, a Senior Intelligence Analyst, assigned to the Director's staff, gave an incredulous smile. A broad barrel-chested man, his dark complexion, had an oily look that gave the impression that he was in a perpetual sweat. He asked, "What are the other theories?"

Epstein nodded in agreement with the question, prompting Uhler to give a gesture with his face and hands, which indicated the only available theories, were best guess scenarios, and nothing on which to place a reputation. Letting out a breath, Uhler said, "Some have speculated that for some reason that Mr. Hansford may have been standing on the toilet looking over the stall and fell, striking his head on the way down."

This description of events caused another undercurrent of gasps, while others spilled muted laughter. Discretely the latter covered their mouths, while several others just looked down at the conference table, pretending to be studying their notes.

Epstein gave a stern look that caused the group to suspend the tittering. This situation, after all, involved the death of a U.S. Senator. Russell suppressed his own amusement managing to give an entirely convincing glare to those that were failing to regain their composure. He cleared his throat and said, "So it is possible that the young man witnessed the death of the Senator."

"Just speculation," responded Rick. "Until he fully recovers his memory or chooses to give additional information, whichever the case may be, we can only wait until more tests come back. There were no visible signs of assault on the Senator. He was found on top of Hansford in the last stall. The Senator and Hansford were found with...," he looked at Epstein as if asking for permission to proceed. Epstein gave him an expectant look, Uhler finished, "with their pants down."

This caused the room to break into another round of tittering, gasps and masked amusement. After a moment, they received another look of warning from Epstein. "Please, ladies and gentlemen. Please treat this with the professionalism that is required. This is not a laughing matter."

Sensing the Director's discomfort, Rick quickly injected, "Sometimes the details of a peculiar situation like this, does seem to be, well, oddly humorous."

"Yes, peculiar is a good word," Epstein said with an exhalation.

Not willing to let this apparent incongruity pass, Leeper said incredulously, "Let me get this straight. Hansford, a publicly known homosexual, is using the toilet. Hears a say...," grasping for a possible scenario, "hears a conversation. With his pants down, climbs up the stall to see what is going on."

The visual caused several to close their eyes, while others, as if praying for a reprieve from what was to come, bowed their heads, waiting for Leeper's indelicate summation. Leeper continued, "He slips and falls. Hitting his head on the toilet paper rack? He's found with a dead U.S. Senator lying on top of him, both with pants pulled down?"

The group erupted in discussions. It took a several moments, but Epstein successfully brought the room's focus back on track. "Okay, okay. Guys and gals, quiet, please!" Looking at Uhler, "Where do we stand now?"

Rick continued his report, "Hansford was taken to a hospital, and treated for his injuries. He is not under arrest but is being informally detained at the hospital. Once his memory returns, he is to be turned over to the Secret Service at which point he is supposed to be," he paused, "debriefed."

Chapter 8   Houston, Texas Tuesday

Tuesday had been a full day of classes, but Sam arrived at the Ounce Steakhouse just a little after the appointed time, but evidently still before Mr. George Jones. The outside décor was misleading as the inside was truly appointed in the style of a first-class steakhouse. Sam, greeted by an attractive young hostess was seated at a corner table and ordered a Shiner Bock. Sam wore his blue blazer with leather patches on the sleeves and a pair of Khaki Chinos. He looked over the menu while he enjoyed a piece of sourdough bread. The restaurant was filling up and Sam wondered about how the recession had affected this upscale eatery. After perusing the menu and the various prices, he decided that apparently there was still money flowing in some circles. The lowest price steak seemed to be in the fifty-dollar range. Sam momentarily panicked; *Surely, George Jones will pick up the tab.*

Sam thought how much he was looking forward to the weekend with Penny Reed. He reminisced about his last date with her that seemed quite a long time ago. He wondered why it had been so long since he had seen her. Sure, she traveled a lot, but they had seemed to enjoy each other quite nicely. Sam felt a little surge of physical excitement just thinking about Penny. Yes, he was looking forward to Saturday night.

Sam noticed a man entering the restaurant that he immediately knew was Mr. Jones just from the confidence the man exuded. The man's distinguished look matched the rich baritone voice Sam remembered from the phone conversation. Sam watched as the man, probably in his mid-sixties and dressed in a black sport coat, crisp blue button-down shirt, jeans, and a pair of cowboy boots, stopped once in the door of the restaurant. He was engaged in jovial conversation with the maître' d, ending the conversation with a friendly pat on the employee's shoulder. After surveying the dining room, Mr. Jones spotted Sam and gave a pleasant wave in the direction of the host, signaling that he did not need an escort. How Jones recognized Sam, the professor could only guess, but perhaps he was the only single man looking expectantly at the door. For Jones' part, he did not look much like his country music namesake, more like Caesar Romero. He made his way to Sam's table, but before he arrived, he was detained by another

51

diner, who slapped the table with an excited smile while rising from his seat. Mr. Jones caught Sam's eye and held up his forefinger to signal that he would be joining him in a moment. They two men shook hands and engaged in a manly embrace. Sam could just make out the other man's greeting of "George it is so good to see you. You remember my wife, Kim." Evidently George did because he moved around the table and gave the woman a kiss on the cheek. She was dressed in a very fashionable three-quarter dark maroon dress, accented with a herringbone necklace and matching earrings. Sam thought that the lady was probably a frequent customer of Saks Fifth Avenue or some other classy clothier. Sam straightened his sports coat and wondered if he should not have worn a tie.

After a short conversation, George joined Sam with an extended hand and a warm smile. Both provided a firm handshake. George was easily six foot four with gray hair trimmed neatly.

"Come here often?" Sam asked while sitting back down in his seat and returning his napkin to his lap.

"No, no, no, this is an occasional haunt of mine. Actually, it has only been open for a year or two. I get into Houston every now and again."

"Can I get you a drink?" the waiter had surreptitiously appeared unnoticed by Sam.

"Chivas on the rocks, please."

Sam looked self-consciously down at his beer.

"I appreciate you taking the time to meet with me, Dr. Jackson."

"Call me Sam, please."

George gave a nod of acknowledgement, glanced briefly at the menu and set it aside.

"Did you find something on the menu that looked appealing?"

"Several, but I think the rib eye will do."

Sam was determined to let George breach the reason for their visit, but his curiosity had gotten the better of him. "I must admit that I am a bit more than curious about your reasons for wanting to meet with me."

George smiled while unfolding his napkin and arranging his flatware in their proper spots. It appeared as if he was about to speak, but his drink arrived, and he allowed the waiter to retreat before re-focusing on Sam. Sam was struck by the dark blue color of the man's eyes; so deep that he wondered if the color was aided by contact lenses. At this close distance he could see the flecks of hazel, and knew immediately that the man was of a generation that did not feel the need to change one's appearance to fit in.

"Sam, I am sorry about the rush of this meeting, but I am going to be out of pocket over the next few days on business and I wanted to meet you before I left."

Sam was playing it cool now. He was just going to let this man talk. He took a sip from his beer. George Jones mirrored the action. George tested out his drink and showed a visible sign of enjoyment. He swirled the ice in a circular motion appreciating the color of the libation

"Sam, I was told that you delivered a persuasive message to the San Antonio Chamber of Commerce last week."

Sam just gave a slight smile and nod but used silence to indicate he needed further explanation. Very cool.

"You vocalized a point of view that is of interest to me."

Sam gave another sage nod. George gave an indeterminable smile. Sam wondered if this guy was in politics but dismissed the idea. He knew most of the politicians of consequence and whoever or whatever he was, he was a heavy hitter. His confidence was too indomitable to be someone's underling. Sam managed to remain silently satisfied that he was delivering the impression of intellect.

In a deliberate tone George said, "I have a real interest in the perils of government becoming a leviathan."

Sam gave a nod with as if everything was now becoming apparent, even though he still had no clue about what this man wanted from him. He took a pull on his beer and noticed that George was taking in his choice of drinks. Sam reconsidered ordering a different drink, but he really did not like liquor. He decided that he would order some wine when the waiter returned.

"Do you like dark beer?" Sam asked.

"I am more of a scotch person, but when I do drink beer, Shiner is one of my favorites."

Sam was reminded of the television commercial with the dignified man that says, "I don't often drink beer, but when I do, I drink Dos Equis."

Sam decided to add to the small talk.

"What about wine?"

"Yes, I developed a taste for wine because of my wife. She enjoyed Cabs and Merlots, I found myself ordering red wine when I ate beef and white with fish. But I am certainly no connoisseur. How about you?"

"No. I mean yes, I like wine, but I am no connoisseur."

"Well, I will get us a bottle when the sommelier comes around. We'll see what he recommends."

As it turned out, the sommelier did appear, but he was a she. *A quite good looking she,* thought Sam. Mr. Jones flashed the lady a warm smile and ordered a bottle of 2006 Simi Cabernet from the Alexander Valley in California.

"Alexander Valley, good choice." Sam said appreciatively and decided to get the conversation going again, "You were saying that you have an objection to government playing a bigger role in a free market?"

"Yes. I do. This brings me back to why I wanted to talk to you. I am interested in underwriting a..." he paused, "speaking tour of sorts."

Sam's head tilted slightly, and his left eyebrow arched.

"What I am thinking about is trying to get your message across in a variety of venues. Of course, I would seek your input, but I am considering getting you more of, shall we say, a national audience."

"I'm flattered, but I think you are talking about *your* message."

Another waiter appeared and left a basket of sliced bread and whipped honey butter.

"Your message and my message are very similar."

"And you know this how?" asked Sam.

George smiled and began slicing off a piece of the sourdough bread, adding a sliver of butter. The waitress appeared and the two men ordered. Sam, being the guest, ordered first which caused him some angst, but managed to request a 12-ounce Prime Rib eye, medium well, spinach and gorgonzola salad, roasted poblano au gratin potatoes, and rosemary roasted wild mushrooms. George started off with an appetizer, Norwegian Smoked Salmon and Bruschetta. He ordered the medium 10-ounce prime filet, with a loaded potato and grilled asparagus.

Showing no signs of aging and a mind like a trap, George returned to the conversation as if there were no interruptions. "I have a few contacts around that heard you speak in San Antonio."

"Dr. De Zavala?"

A smile permeated George's face and his eyes gave a little sparkle. Sam was not sure what to make out of the expression. Either he really admired Dr. De Zavala or was taking pleasure in the perplexity of the moment. A momentary thought crossed Sam's mind that maybe this man was just enjoying the fact that he knew something that Sam did not.

"Yes, Bennie is a friend of mine. But if the truth is told, I received a couple calls from friends that are privy to some of my interests."

"Really?" Sam said with some incredulity.

"You should realize that your talent couldn't go unnoticed if you go around speaking to audiences such as the San Antonio Chamber of Commerce. There are a lot of people in Texas that are somewhat independent by nature and would like to see the federal government choke off a bit on the throttle."

Remembering the initial uncomfortable feeling he had felt at the beginning of his talk in San Antonio, Sam relaxed and gave a short laugh, "I thought I was fairly conservative till I started speaking to that group. It occurred to me that they were going to string me up because I am too far left of Barry Goldwater."

"Barry was a good man and probably could have been elected as president had he not been matched up with a far shrewder politician."

"So, can I assume you are not a politician?"

"You can." Another smile.

With nothing else forthcoming, Sam decided to remain silent.

"Do you think you have an interest in politics?"

Sam about let out a guffaw, but managed to say with a broad smile, "The university life offers all the politics I can stand."

George gave a smile and a small chuckle. "Well, I have no interest in politics, but the reality of the situation is that we are all subjected to politics whether we like it or not."

The wine arrived and George nodded for Sam to complete a tasting. He gave it his best expert imitation and signaled his approval with a slight nod. The young lady gave a slight bow and poured into two oversized stems.

"Are you in a business that is being adversely affected by government?"

"I don't mind telling you what business I am in, but that is secondary to the bigger picture." Sam noticed that George did not tell him what business he was in. "As you so accurately identified in your speech, the government has grown past the point where it is beneficial and is becoming the biggest threat to our national security."

"What do you think should be done?"

"There are several directions possible, but I think the winning of the souls and minds is probably the least objectionable and the most prudent."

Sam smiled and said, "And you think a college professor can do that?"

The salmon and bruschetta arrived, presented by yet another server who Sam had not seen before. The returning waiter, a tall slender man in his early thirties, stayed long enough to fill water glasses, and replace the bread supply. Sam looked up to see a man who appeared in his mid-sixties make his way over to the table and apologetically tapped George on the shoulder. George placed his napkin on the table; stood and greeted the man with a shake and an embrace. They shared some friendly talk, agreed to call each other. The stranger departed to another part of the restaurant and George sat back down.

"Seems like you know quite a few people in Houston for not being from here," Sam said with an accusatory tone.

"Just some old friends. I used to get around a little more than I do now. Things have certainly changed over the years. When I was your age, the Democrats ruled Texas."

Sam was familiar the political landscape of the Texas, despite being from Florida, but decided to just listen.

"But...," George's face actually showed pain, "the Democratic Party deserted us."

56

Sam smiled with the knowledge that the Texas Democrats used to be a fiscal and social conservative voice.

George plunged in a bite of salmon mounted atop the bruschetta into his mouth. He gave a pleasurable sound and his head nodded slowly; eyes closed. In a moment, his attention returned to the conversation. "Strangely enough, we went over to Lincoln's party – the very party that came after the Southern states for trying to leave the party...so to speak."

"So now what is the party of choice?"

"Don't suppose there is a perfect solution to all of this, but you seem to be a student of history, Dr. Jackson. Tell me what has been the downfall of most civilizations?

Again, Sam smiled and gave a little nod. "Economics and you have been listening to my rhetoric."

The main course arrived, and the communication halted between the two men. Sam marveled at the food's perfection. He was a bit of a griller, but often burned what he was cooking. He would always start out with good intentions of vigilante observation, but inevitably become distracted only to return to a blazing grill, food in peril. Patience was not his virtue, and he would go inside to check on something else or try to catch a bit of a television show.

With about a quarter of the way to go, Sam had to take a break from his assault on the steak. George was down to his last bite, stopping only for an appreciative sip of wine. With the last few bites disappearing, both men's attention returned to their previous conversation. The thought occurred to Sam that he would need a nap to recover from this excellent meal.

Sam was anxious to bring this conversation around. "So let me just sum up what we have covered so far. You have a concern about the scope of government, and you want me to embark on a speaking tour in order to change the hearts and minds of the country."

George's lip slowly moved into a smile from the top right corner. The sparkle in his eyes caused Sam to break into a smile as well. Instead of responding, George cut the lone remaining piece of steak and filled his mouth. Sam gave an almost imperceptible shake of his head. There was something about this man that intrigued Sam and he had the feeling that George Jones was used to getting his way. It was more than that.

Sam felt the man's confidence in being able to persuade people to come around to his way of thinking.

"You seem quite adept in dealing with people."

George gave an indeterminable smile, but it caused Sam to inexplicably break into a laugh.

"I suppose, but I do better with one on one."

"Fear of speaking to large audiences?" Sam quipped.

Another smile.

"Sam, I am willing to fund your efforts. I have contacts that can facilitate a platform for you to become a recognizable authority on government's impact on business. I think your point of view will be well received from the audiences I have in mind, and I think that it is something that this country needs."

"Forgive me if I wonder aloud. Why me?"

"Right message, right place and the right time."

"At the right price?" Sam injected.

"I don't want to give you the negatives because I want you to take me up on this offer. However, as with anything, there are going to be some that don't appreciate your ideology."

"Goes without saying." Sam gave a wry smile, followed with a curious, "What business did you say are you in?"

Unfazed by the question, George smiled, then said contemplatively, "I have a variety of business interests, but have been out of pocket a while. If I read your question correctly: Why you? Which leads you to why not me?"

Sam's facial expression said, exactly.

George spread his hands as trying to allow an answer to fall in that would adequately explain a complex situation. "Our end game is much more attainable with me out of sight."

"Your motives could be too easily called into question?"

George countered, "You represent a much more objective voice."

Sam enjoyed another drink of wine and a sip of water. "Having no financial interest makes me less susceptible as being labeled as a charlatan or ideologue?"

George gave a slight shrug.

Sam pressed, "Doesn't your promise to fund this endeavor… this speaking tour, violate the principle of having no financial interest?"

"The funding would be modest, but it is your ideas that have a chance to receive the attention they deserve."

"Which just happens to work somehow, in a way, which helps your cause?" Sam's question elicited another smile from George.

"Sam if our ideological beliefs overlap then there is no deception and more importantly it is a message that the country needs to hear."

"George, I am not trying to be self-effacing when I say there are voices out there now. Rush Limbaugh, Bill O'Reilly, Glenn Beck, Sean Hannity, Van Susteren, just to name a few. I am not even in their league.

"True. They are out there, but what grassroots movements have they been able to generate?"

"Well, the tea parties have been getting a lot of attention."

"The problem is that these people are seen as homers for the Republican Party."

"Sure, Rush and Hannity, but what about Walter Williams and Thomas Sowell. Those two are personalities that would be able to reach far more people than I could ever hope to influence. I have a doctorate from Florida State, not from Harvard, MIT or the Chicago School of Economics."

George gave one of those transmittable grins. It reminded Sam of his father when he used to give him a patient smile when he knew more than he was divulging. Never forceful, his father always seemed to see possess a wisdom beyond Sam's own understanding and he had learned to quiet his protestations and think about what the man was saying. Despite that lingering memory, he decided this offer lacked transparency and there was something that he was missing. Maybe it was a doubt about his own shortcomings, but something just seemed out of place about this. Discretely, George pulled his pocket watch from his pocket to glance at the time.

George nodded his ascent and said, "I understand your hesitation, and maybe even should we say, reluctance."

Sam gave an affirming nod.

George continued, "But I want you to think about the possibilities of getting your views out there to the public. You're very good at making things simple for the everyday person. Right now, your reach is only for college students who will likely be re-indoctrinated in the next class they take, by some other professor who really does not have a grasp of what is happening in this country. I am interested expanding your audience, but I understand your reluctance."

Having finished their meal and turned down the offer of dessert, the waiter delivered the check in a leather-bound portfolio. George slipped a credit card in without looking at the bill. Sam would have liked to have stolen a glance at the name on the card but resisted the urge to reach over and open the portfolio.

"George, it was an excellent meal and the offer flattering. I just don't think that this is for me."

A small frown crossed George's face for just an instant, but quickly vanished. "You are welcome for the meal. I wish I had more time to convince you, but I am scheduled for flight in a couple hours."

"If you have flown recently, you know security is a bitch." Sam immediately grimaced at his choice of language. "I am just saying that you are going to be pressed for time. Unless, of course, the plane is going to wait for you," Sam said jokingly. He gave a little chuckle and expected one in return.

George gave that knowing smile again. "I think they will be willing to wait. Listen, it was a pleasure talking to you Sam, and I would like to do it again," he paused, "real soon if you can spare the time." The receipt arrived which George quickly scooped up; the two men shook hands and headed out of the restaurant. While moving out, George said, "Sam, I see someone over here that I need to say hello to, thanks so much for your time and have a good evening.

Chapter 9   Houston, Texas Wednesday

Wednesday, Sam returned to his office having finished his classes for the day by 11:00 am. He had several messages that needed to be answered. Sharon, the department's phenomenal secretary, had already sent every message to email. Sam dutifully responded to the first three, but it was the fourth which caused him to draw a blank. Sarah Adams of the Atlanta Business Cooperative had called at 9:00 a.m. *Another cooperative,* he absently thought. Sam did a quick search on the computer and found an unimpressive website, but was able to find a picture of Sarah Adams, Director. She was very attractive, and Sam thought this would be interesting. He flipped open his phone and dialed the number. It was evidently a direct number because Sarah answered the call.

"This is Sarah." Her voice sounded pleasant and vivacious.

"This is Sam Jackson, I am returning your call," Sam said trying to match the young woman's upbeat tone.

"Oh, Dr. Jackson thanks for calling me back." Her southern drawl was genuine, but some of her enthusiasm seemed to have dwindled, in fact, her tone indicated she was irritated about something. Sam mentally shrugged thinking it could not have been something he had done; after all she had called him.

She said, "I am sorry to approach you at the last minute, but we are hosting a conference in Miami." Sam noted that her tone seemed to have a sorrowful quality. She continued, "I have an unexpected opening for the closing session. I was hoping that you might be able to make a trip to South Florida."

Sam was trying to think who he knew in Florida or Georgia that may have volunteered his name. He did have several friends that were spread out across the nation that could be the culprit, but he was drawing a blank on the state of Georgia. Sam was also trying to figure out why the lady's voice seemed to be more obligatory than inviting.

Sam tried for amiable, in hopes to break through this icy layer. "I appreciate the offer, but how did I show up on your radar?"

There was a lengthy pause. Then Sarah said sharply, "Well, it was our organizational board members who provided your name as a possible replacement. I do apologize for the last-minute notice, but we had an unexpected cancellation. We would, of course, cover your travel costs."

Sam detected reluctance in her tone and wondered to himself. Maybe she was having a bad day he thought. Maybe she had some other names that she was more excited to invite. He momentarily thought that he should offer up some excuse. After all, if she was not convinced that this would be the best choice, why should he be so sure? Not sure of what else to say, Sam asked, "Can you give me an idea about the theme of the conference?"

After another pause, Sarah said, "Well, the name of the conference is called the American Business Summit. It will be primarily attended by businesspeople from the southeastern part of the United States. It is a business conference that will focus on marketing and management techniques, but **you**," again that attitude with the emphasis on the word '*you*' thought Sam, "were suggested as a speaker that would talk about the changes in the market that will affect business on an aggregate basis. From your bio, it looks like your research pertains to the economy and, how government impacts business in general."

Sam was impressed. He guessed that Sarah had pilfered his biography from the University's website. "Well, yes, that sounds about right. Excuse my curiosity, but is there someone on the board that knows me?"

There was another silence and Sam momentarily thought that he lost the connection. "Hello?"

"Yes, well, I am not sure. Evidently, your name was provided by one the board members so I could not say if you know that person or not. Because I am not sure which board member it was," Sarah said in an indeterminate tone. She was not apologetic and not evasive. Sam thought perhaps she really did not know. She may truly just be a Kelly girl. Sam realized Sarah was still speaking returning his attention to the conversation. "We have several successful business leaders on the board, and I was not given any background on their suggestion."

"Okay...," Sam drew out the word trying to determine why this invitation seemed like this lady was not particularly happy with having to make an offer. "I am sensing that you might have some others that might fit the bill a little better than me."

"Not at all," Sarah said in an unconvincing tone. With no further elaboration, she said, "You could fly in on Friday evening and speak on Saturday afternoon. You will certainly be welcome to fly in earlier on Thursday if you have an interest in attending the other sessions. The Summit begins midweek, but we would only need you for the closing session Saturday afternoon. We could schedule you a flight around 2:00 on Friday if that works for your schedule."

He thought her brisk redirection might indicate that he qualified because he was the only one who could arrive on such short notice. Sam was definitely confused by the mixed signals this lady's voice was intimating. He wished he could see her body language to give him a clue as to her real feelings. She had answered the phone so enthusiastically and now she seemed as if a gun were being pointed at her head. Her words were saying yes, but her tone was saying I think you are a piece of crap, and I am doing this because I was told to do it.

"Dr. Jackson?" Sarah prompted.

Not knowing what else to say and actually interested in the opportunity, he decided. "Friday at 2:00 o'clock would work. Will you just email me the flight and hotel information?" Before she could respond, he added, "What about the return flight?"

"That is up to you. I can book you for a return on Saturday evening, or Sunday; whichever you prefer. If you decide to stay Saturday, we will, of course, pick up the hotel bill."

Sam thought about the turn-around time and said, "Let's do a Sunday afternoon flight."

As if checking off a list Sarah said, "I will manage the details. I will send you an email confirmation of the flight and hotel information. I will also include a form that you fax back to me that will provide your preferred introduction information. I am afraid it is too late to publish it in the guide. I will also include a form that will allow us to properly pay you the honorarium. Will $5000 be satisfactory?"

Sam's expression changed from one of caution to one of pleasant surprise. He had not even thought of being paid. After exchanging email addresses, both thanked each other.

What should have been a mutually gratifying arrangement left Sam with the feeling that Sarah had performed her duty with the lack of enthusiasm that a whore might offer in concluding some unseemly transaction.

"Dr. Jackson?" Sarah prompted again.

"Yes, yes, that will be fine." As an afterthought Sam asked, "May I ask who was supposed to be the speaker?"

There was a long pause.

"Sarah?" Sam prompted, returning the favor.

"Yes of course. It was supposed to have been a U.S. Senator."

Sam's brow furrowed. "Well Sarah, not sure I can compete with that, but I will do my best to take his place."

Another long pause.

Again, Sam fumbled for something to say. "I am sorry did I say something wrong?"

"No, no, of course not. We look forward to having you as our guest Dr. Jackson."

Chapter 10   Washington, D.C.   Wednesday

The Deputy Under Secretary, Terrence Mitchell, sat at his desk at the Department of Homeland Security Office of Intelligence and Analysis - referred to as I&A. With a map of the United States spread in front of him, his shirt collar was spread open, graced by a loosely knotted burgundy tie with bright blue horizontal stripes. His dark closely cut black hair showed signs of graying at the temples. Because he had grown up primarily in the U.S., his Australian accent had dwindled away over the years and the only evidence of his heritage was only visible in the light brown color of his skin. In Australia, he would have been known as a Mulatto or Creamy, but in the U.S., no one seemed concerned about his racial makeup. He liked that lack of attention, but on occasion would break out his down under accent, which seemed to provide quite a bit of entertainment. A pair of wireless Calvin Klein glasses was perched upon the top of his head, momentarily freed from the gaze of his intelligent eyes.

Yesterday, Terrence's regular routine, as an expert in international terrorism, was interrupted when his boss' boss, Corey Weitzman, the Under Secretary of Intelligence and Analysis, entered Terrence's office with a stack of classified files under his arm. In an unusually cryptic delivery, Weitzman had said, "You know, that Mary...," referring to the Principal Under Secretary and Terrence's immediate supervisor, "is out on pregnancy leave." Terrence gave a tentative nod but said nothing. Weitzman continued, "I have an emergency meeting with the President in one hour. I received two sets of these," with some effort he elevated the stack of files he was carrying as proof, "by courier an hour ago."

Using a hip and the momentum from his approach, he had plopped the folders on Terrence's desk. Weitzman, obviously in need of a haircut, pushed his hair behind his ears with both hands. He was hoping to stop by the barber prior to coming in to work this morning, but his schedule had been unexpectedly changed by a new directive. He would make an effort to get it cut and was hoping that he would not be called in by any of the higher ups before getting a chance. That turned out not to be the case. Standing just a couple inches taller than the five foot eight Terrence, Weitzman had dark circles which were starting to develop beneath his eyes, signaling a need for sleep. It was the third time in the same week that his plans had been changed by the course of events, with each change causing an accumulated deprivation of sleep. Terrence gave a quizzical look and waited for the rest of the story.

Weitzman said, "You are be redirected to this immediately. I need you and your team to go through these files as quickly as possible and get up to speed with what is in them."

"Who sent 'em?" Terrence was nodding slowly and began thumbing through the top folder.

"We will have to talk about it later," Weitzman said pushing back his hair behind his ears and opening the door. "This is…," he paused. "I am not sure what it is really."

"It looks like domestic terrorism?" Terrence stated with a questioning tone.

Nodding his understanding of the confusion Terrence was experiencing, Weitzman responded, "I know that this is swerving out of your normal area, but I was informed by the powers that be, we will be assisting the FBI in this. So, you are now assisting the FBI in this…," he paused to look for an appropriate word, but settled on "situation." He gave a suffering sigh and said, "I need a threat report by the time I get back. The Secretary has already been in a meeting this morning and I got a call to go to the White House stat."

Terrence knew exactly how he ended up with this task. It was Russell Epstein who would have thrown his name into the mix, and he did not mind doing a favor for his former boss. He missed working for him over at the National Security Agency. He could have gone over to the FBI when Epstein was appointed Interim Director if he had wanted to but decided to take his current position at Homeland Security.

Corey continued, "I looked over them, but I need as much of the analysis as quickly as you can. When I get back, I will brief you about what the hell is going on. But this has something to do with Senator Summers' death." He stopped on his way out of the office. "Or it may be tied to the intel about an assassination plot."

Terrence's face registered surprise, "Assassination plot?"

Weitzman was almost completely out the door, with only his head remaining. "I don't know Terrence, what it is about, until I go to this meeting. I will let you know as soon as I know. If you can find anything that I might need although I don't know what I need.," he provided another look which might have been a pout, "call me. If I can take the call, I will. Otherwise, I will get with you when I return; if I return." He had thrown up his hands and hurriedly walked out.

Terrence had begun sifting through the data immediately. Now, after almost three stints of four hours each, devouring the files, a dozen or so circles had been drawn in red marker in various places around on the map of the United States. Maybe Weitzman had not been joking about not coming back. He had not returned on Tuesday and still had yet to show today, but Terrence was grateful for the extra prep time. Terrence knew that National Security meetings could go on for days, with brief breaks for a trip to the bathroom or more likely a smoke break. Terrence thought back on all of those meetings at NSA. He liked it when Epstein had been a smoker because he would have to call meetings to a halt after about an hour and one-half for a smoke. The worst-case scenario was for a smoker getting stuck with a non-smoker boss. Terrence had heard that Epstein had given up smoking when he moved over to FBI because the President was trying to quit. As it turned out the President just kept smoking, but Epstein was able to abstain for the long haul.

Terrence returned his thoughts to his maps. The majority of the circles were in the middle states, but the next greatest concentration of markings was in southeastern states of Florida, Georgia and South Carolina. Pictures of three men were laid neatly along the side of Terrence's desk, but were of such poor quality, offered little help. Twirling between in his fingers was a Morgan silver dollar, a gift from a distant aunt who had also made her way to America from Australia, years ago, but then returned down under. Terrence could move the coin effortlessly between fingers like gamblers fiddle with poker chips. It was an unconscious act signaling Terrence was in deep thought.

From the outer office, Maria Telfare brought a tray of drinks and several packets of peanuts and pretzels into the large conference room. Dressed in a sleek business suit, her mahogany brown hair was pulled back behind, held in place with a gold hair clip. At a full five foot ten, she was somewhat self-conscious of her height and tended to sit whenever the opportunity presented itself. Behind Maria, Clute Ahlstrom followed her in, taking the open chair next to Terrence. Having just turned thirty, Clute had recently returned from his native Ohio, thus missed the initial briefing and was still trying to catch up. His face resembled that of a teenager, which would make one wonder if he even needed to shave. Dressed in a single breasted, four-button suit, Clute allowed Terrence to continue his study of the map without interruption.

Maria was not as patient. "Either of you want some coffee or a soft drink?" Maria interjected.

Clute reached over and snagged a Coke. "Thanks Maria."

"Coffee, with cream and sugar, please," Terrence said without looking up.

Maria and Clute had been given some tasks to work on from the previous day and now they were ready to reassemble; perhaps to develop a report or plan of action, but they were not exactly sure. At this point, not having the benefit of the Weitzman brief, there were many more things that the team did not know than did know. Maria set the coffee cup bearing the insignia of the Department of Homeland Security within reach of Terrence but resisted the urge to take a seat. Looking over Terrence's shoulder, she spied a report from the Office of Domestic Preparedness entitled Automated Critical Assessment. In Clute's hand was another report with a cover page that read Assessment of Patriotic Protestors.

Having reached a couple conclusions, Terrence spoke to the assembled, "The intelligence report was short on details, other than we have several groups of particular interest. The report implies that the people involved are well placed and have the money to pull off a major operation. The Secret Service has been given an alert as well because there appears to be a possible threat to the President.

"And we discussed how we ended up with this?" Clute sought to clarify.

"Clute, I don't have a definitive answer on that, but it is probably because we just do such damn clever work." Terrence did not even break a smile. It was his dry sense of humor, that often left those around if guessing as to whether he was serious or not. New subordinates would often come to Maria on the side, just to ask, for the inside scoop on what Terrence was actually saying. Maria would simply say, "He has a really good sense of humor. You just have to get used to it. Dry as the Sahara." Other people did not like Terrence's stoic self-confidence, brutal frankness, or his apparent willingness to take apart about anybody in a debate. Terrence seemed to have a polarizing effect on the various peripheral offices. One could actually hear Terrence described as too self-assured by one person and too soft-spoken by another. Clute and Maria just knew that the man was fair, honest, determined and an absolute bulldog when it came to pursuing a case and meticulous when it came to keeping expenses to a minimum.

Terrence continued, "We have been honored to be included in on, well, what I think is the quieting of a little rebellion." This received no comments, just knowing smiles of disbelief. Terrence was not inclined to bullshit his team. They knew it was odd that they had this project dumped in their laps. He did not have a satisfactory answer and he was not going to pretend that he did. Terrence ignored the reactions of his team and continued, "It looks like the most likely location is north of Atlanta, east of Dalton, and just south of the Chattahoochee National Forest. The second location is in Texas."

"Where in Texas?" Clute asked without much intonation.

"Denver City," Terrence answered moving his finger across the map. "Not too far from Midland."

Maria moved around the table and asked, "These two are connected?" She was referring to Georgia and Texas.

"Maybe." Terrence added, "Loosely. These guys are likely lone wolves, but with the internet, a confederacy of sorts. They may be tied by only by obsession. There is someone who calls himself Charlie Rivers, also known as the commander-in-chief. He seems to be one link. The head rebel in Wyoming is a guy named Michael Thomas. This could be an alias, but there is a Michael Smith that has some substantial bucks. The same thing for Georgia, with a player named Alex Stephens. Could be an alias, since the former Vice President of the Confederate States of America was named Alexander Stephens. The actual Alex Stephens seems to spend his time in Florida rather than

69

Georgia, so we can't be sure. He does have ties to Georgia though and he has lots of money."

"So why doesn't the FBI roll them up?" Clute asked.

Terrence let out a breath, maybe in frustration or resignation. "The information is circumstantial and incomplete."

Clute said, "I thought with the NDAA, we could hold and detain just about anyone that posed a possible threat." He was referring to the controversial National Defense Authorization Act, which allowed anyone suspected of terrorism to be taken into custody and held without due process. Several states, including Texas and Georgia, had passed nullification acts which the federal government had promptly taken to court. But the issue was still hung up in litigation. Meanwhile, the states were threatening to arrest federal agents who did not abide by the protections of the Constitution.

"We can't just snag a millionaire or billionaire, no matter what the law says. We already catch heat when we pinch foreigners with no money. Snag a citizen that has lots of contacts and pull, you just can't get away with that." Terrence pulled another note page and added, "Another goes by George Jones. He also appears to be in Texas."

"George Jones? As in the singer?" Maria inquired with a smile.

Terrence smiled but did not respond.

"Aliases?" asked Clute.

"Probably, but we think Jones has some substantial connections to a South Carolina contingent. One name has also caught our attention, Casey Friends, also a likely alias." Terrence pointed up to a red circle near Charleston. "We don't know who he is, but he is well connected and has lots of money. He has been able to stay in the dark, but a secret source over at the FBI has squirted Mr. Friends' name into the mix."

"More angry white men?" Clute asked.

"Aren't they all?' interjected Maria.

"Except some of these we think are elected officials," Terrence said as he looked up for the first time. This caused both Clute and Maria to raise their eyebrows in astonishment. Terrence continued, "The report refers to a possible inside man who is a U.S. Senator."

"You said that Under-Secretary Weitzman mentioned the death of Hank Summers. Could this really be related to that?" asked Maria. She moved around to sit next to Clute.

"Back channels are saying that Summers' death was not of natural causes," Terrence said.

Clute said, "So maybe it is related."

"There was one memo that the NSA intercepted from Rivers that appeared to have been sent to Summers. The text was scrambled so we don't know what the message said. He was chairman of several major committees and may have somehow been a threat to this group," Terrence said.

Maria offered, "If Summers was the inside man, it does not make much sense that his own group would have him killed."

Terrence gave a nod of agreement.

Clute took a drink of his soda and asked, "What else do we have to connect the names in the reports?"

Terrence said, "We have a couple things. No direct money connections, but we have some email chatter."

"That's promising. How did we get that?" Maria asked Terrence.

"It was a by-fishing catch passed along by the NSA. Showed up in the email sweep by the APP guys," referring to the Assessment of Patriotic Protests report. "I think this is where this whole thing started, but it could have been part of an ongoing FBI investigation."

"I guess this sharing of information is paying some dividends," Maria said through a mouthful of pretzels.

"They were actually careless enough to mention the President and the words confederate and liquidation in the same email?" Clute asked rhetorically, studying the NSA Threat Report. "But again, this is inconclusive because there are probably a lot of people who email U.S. Senators," Clute reasoned aloud.

"And all of this has to do with assassinating the President?"
Maria asked.

"Whoever this group is seems committed to pushing this movement to the limit in any direction that is necessary," Clute said.

71

Terrence leaned back in a leather clad chair which offered a groaning sound. "I think there is some panic inside the White House and we are being thrown into this because they are scrambling to figure out what to do. Under-Secretary Weitzman wants a status report when he returns from his meeting at the White House. But that was more than 24 hours ago. I have not seen him since. Regardless, when he does return, he will expect a report."

"What do we put in it?" Clute asked.

"I think we cover our ass and concur that we have a possible plot to promote sedition and possibly a faction that is working to get rid of the President," Terrence said.

"Would that be crying wolf?" Maria asked.

"I don't think so Maria. That brings me to the other connection." Across his desk, Terrence handed a copy of shipping manifest to Clute. Maria stared at the report over Clute's shoulder.

Clute unfolded a copy of a shipping manifest to a rural address in Texas. "This says the shipment manifest says oil rigging equipment. What could this possibly have to do with a plot to kill the President?" Clute asked.

"Probably unrelated. As far as sedition, the FBI says that this is the third shipment to a remote location in Texas. The area came to their attention when they received a report from a delivery driver that became suspicious about delivering shipments out in the middle of nowhere. We are not sure, but sources believe this to be the location of Charlie Rivers. The local West Texas FBI office sat on the report, waiting for something more concrete. Just last week, another shipment was tracked and delivered," Terrence said.

"That seems to be a bit of a stretch," Maria said with doubting look.

"It would be a stretch if we had not already had some surveillance of the same location. The F.B.I. had identified several potential domestic terrorist threats emanating from West Texas. This is one of those locations. They substituted an undercover driver who was able to secure a fingerprint of one of the possible players. The database said it belonged to one Abel Thorton."

Abel Thorton is Charlie Rivers? Maria asked.

"Actually, the reports say no. Abel is Abel," Terrence said.

The two aids looked expectantly at Terrence.

"But Abel is supposed to be in Georgia. He was nicked for an altercation with a state trooper in 1998. He was eventually released under deferred adjudication, with the charges eventually being dropped."

Clute asked, "How does the Texas connection match up with the Georgia location?"

"Here is where it gets interesting." Terrence paused for dramatic affect. "A shell corporation whose officers include Charlie Rivers and George Jones."

"So, where does that leave us?" Maria asked.

Terrence said, "With a jittery White House, this falls into the 1% doctrine," referring to the working policy of the Bush 43 administration's reaction to 9-11 bombing of the trade towers. If there was a 1% chance of an attack it should be treated as if it were a 100% chance. As a candidate, the current president had made significant political hay out of this doctrine, calling it maniacal and a catastrophic threat to personal rights. Today, the second term President was coming under the same type of criticism for violation of civil rights but had managed to dissuade several private lawsuits challenging the federal government's right to monitor the public. The individual States, on the other hand, were in a legislative frenzy trying to roll back everything from federal surveillance, airport searches and healthcare to the work of the Environmental Protection Agency.

Terrence continued, "We suggest that a real threat exists and there is a likely confederation of the locations that I have identified here on the map. We recommend wiretaps, email monitoring... the works. That should cover our ass if things go sideways. I don't want to shoot a fly with a cannon, but I think that we are going to want the good guys to hit the ground running if this goes the direction that I think it is.

Clute said, "In other words we put together the CYA report, in case anything actually does happen, and we end up in front of some kind of Warren Commission or 911 Commission."

"Clute don't say that!" Maria exclaimed.

With an apologetic smile, Clute said, "Hey, just living in the real world."

Chapter 11   Washington D.C.   Wednesday

Charles Reynolds sat in one of the bright red booths offered inside of Ben's Chili Bowl. He had just finished the Bill Cosby Half Smoked Dog with the joint's famous homemade chili sauce, when his cell phone vibrated in his gray Dockers pants pocket. He was wearing a blue buttoned-down oxford shirt graced with a white cloth napkin, draped around his neck to prevent the inevitable spill of his chili dog. His blonde hair, with some unwelcome gray forcing its way in, was parted to left and in need of a trim. Charles studied the phone's display but did not immediately recognize the number. It was a 281-area code which he thought might have been Maryland or Ohio or maybe even Minnesota. No, he thought *Minnesota was 218.* He shrugged and flipped open his phone.

"Charles Reynolds." He always answered the phone this way. The emphasis on the Charles and then the Reynolds was drawn out as if added by the swoop of a paint brush. Charles intended for the greeting to be upbeat. He had practiced it different ways but had eventually decided that CHARLES REYNolds worked best.

"Chars! How's the hooded bandit doing?"

"Oh my goodness," Charles paused for a beat, the brain engaged, and he said, "Sam I am, what are you doing? Tell me you are in town."

Among other names that these two men chided each other with, Hooded Bandit and Sam I Am, were childhood nicknames. Charles could not remember when or where his nicknamed was fashioned. Maybe it was when they were teenagers commandeering golf carts in the early morning hours from a nearby golf course. Introduced to the sport of downhill golf cart racing at the age of 12 by an older set of friends, Charles was pleased to have Sam, usually a "stiffy" when it came to getting into trouble, advanced the sophistication of the sport with some inside knowledge. The golf course personnel were particularly grumpy to return the next day to find all of their golf carts at the bottom of a large clubhouse hill. When it became evident that this was a growing pastime for the juvenile delinquents, the course manager began a process of one-upmanship which included chains, a fence and finally a huge metal storage building. It was Sam that solved the storage building dilemma when he removed a two-foot metal pipe allowing a sliding door to be angled out. Moving to the lock side of the door, Sam had pulled out a crescent wrench which he expertly loosened the bolt. Once the heavy chain had been defeated the big sliding door was pushed open enough for the boys to enter. What they found was a regular supermarket of golf carts lined up like horses in a stable asking to be taken out.

Sam said, "No, I am not in town, but I am going to be! I was invited to speak at a conference, on Saturday."

"You're kidding, that is great! You can stay with me!"

"The hotel will be provided, but if you are interested in dinner, I will be flying into MIA Friday evening."

"MIA? Oh Sam, I don't what I was thinking, I thought you meant D.C.!

"I thought you were in Miami," Sam said in a confused tone.

"I am, well, I am home based out of Miami. I have been in D.C. on assignment off and on for about a year and a half. I keep an apartment up here, or I should say the newspaper does." Charles was referring to the Miami Express, which was part of a larger national company which owned multiple newspapers across the United States. Consolidation of the newspaper business had become the norm rather than the exception. With a readership and advertising revenue being siphoned off by the internet, newspapers were scrambling to remain relevant and more importantly profitable. "I was just in Miami, but I flew up Tuesday to DC to cover the death of a U.S. Senator. You probably heard about it in the news?

Eyes peering up, Sam said, "No. I don't think so. When did that happen?"

"On Monday at a Presidential fundraiser," Charles said solemnly.

Sam realized he had not watched the news for several days. His travel to San Antonio had squeezed his schedule. "I am sorry to hear that Chars, I have been scrambling around just trying to get my head above water. I spoke to a group in San Antonio on Saturday, and I have been playing catch up ever since. What happened?"

"It looks like a heart attack, but it is still being investigated."

Sam said solemnly, "That is too bad. I have not heard anything about it. How old was he?"

"Not sure, but I guess he was 60 or 65?" Charles answered thoughtfully.

"Well, that's a shame, but I guess you never know," said Sam, who was still seemingly processing the information and perhaps the inevitability of death.

"Yeah, but it gets more interesting because the inside skinny was that there was something odd about the whole heart attack scenario. The first leak was that a gay lover's triangle or tryst or something was to blame, but that was so flimsy that even the press equivocated when it came to reporting it."

"Equivocated but printed."

"Yeah," Charles laughed, "they certainly got it in as a possible juicy rumor, but quickly warned that what they had just said had not been substantiated."

"Which some other station will use as a source," Sam said derisively. "I have seen how that game works. Rumored, then unsubstantiated, then unconfirmed, the reported but not verified to everyone is talking about it. You really are in a nasty game."

"I cannot argue that." Removing the napkin from around his neck, Charles examined his clothing for any chili stains. He gave a satisfying nod of his own success and carefully swiped his lip with his napkin, removing the last remnants of the delicious lunch.

"What's your connection? Are you syndicated nationwide now?" asked Sam.

"I wish. I do get some national play. Miami is full of titillating power deals and of course, there are drugs and the Cubans and party life. It keeps me busy. Unfortunately, the Senator, who died, was sort of a friend of mine, well more of an acquaintance. Not close, but I interviewed him several times and went to a couple social events where we talked."

Sam said, "I am sorry to hear that, Charles. I had no idea."

"That's okay, just going to try to follow the story to see what actually happened."

Changing the direction some, Sam asked, "Still working for the same dick of a boss? What was his name Stanford, oh and his secretary Bitch Patti?" Sam laughed thinking about the all the stories that Charles had told and how much he despised the two. Thom Stanton seemed destined to torment Charles, and his scheming secretary Patti Juarez was always trying to catch Charles doing something.

"Well, it's Stanton and yes, well sort of – it has sort of gotten convoluted with the different assignments. But yeah, they still are quite the team and looking for any opportunity to shove a pole up my ass."

"But you are covering a story in D.C. about a U.S. Senator? That's impressive."

Sam thought Charles was being modest and had, in fact, been elevated in the newspaper world such that he was brought in to do a special report.

In a self-deprecating tone, "Yeah, yeah, it is no big deal. I did a story a few years ago on a Florida senator that was killed by a guy named Heinz Innsbruck, a Chicago mob boss."

Sam interrupted, "I called you. Remember? To congratulate you on your award. What was it, the Pulitzer?"

"No, no, not that one," Charles laughed brushing off the compliment. "It was some investigative something or another. It seems like when a politician turns up dead, they think of me."

"But you did win a Pulitzer for investigative reporting, I remember."

"Yeah, but that was for something else."

"Was that the mob guy that was taken out in the car?"

"Well, something like that. Say Sam, where are you staying?" Charles asked, successfully redirecting the conversation.

"I think I was told the Sonesto Bayfront Hotel."

"Great, exceptional hotel – real nice. If the convention is very big at all, it will usually be held it at the Miami Beach Convention Center. What audience?"

"Business summit of some kind, I assume it is a Chamber of Commerce type thing that everyone gets together to bitch and moan."

"Sounds exciting," Charles said with a bit of sarcasm. "How long are you going to be there?" Not stopping for an answer, he added. "If you stayed through the weekend, I might be able to finagle my schedule. I need to button up my house anyway. I left in a hurry and this story may take a while."

"That would be great! Would love to see you. Are you still dating Amanda?" asked Sam.

"No," his voice dropped into a bit of a sulk, "We stopped seeing each other when I started traveling so much. It just wasn't working out and she was looking to go back to her ex anyway. Charles momentarily had a quick vision of Amanda. She was the complete package, striking high cheekbones, dark complexion and perfectly taut backside. *Damn I miss that woman,* he thought. "How about you?" asked Charles, who now realized it probably, had been over a year since the two had even exchanged emails.

"After Lizzy and I separated, I have just been dating around. Playing the field, you know." The recounting of his breakup sounded much more pitiful than Sam had wanted, so he added, "Things are going well," but could not help but adding, "I guess."

"Well, you and Lizzy were together a long time. What was it, ten years?"

"Twelve," Sam corrected quickly.

"That is a long time. Think she wanted to get married?"

"I offered, but she just seemed to need a fresh start. You know her parents both died last summer?"

"Know? No, I didn't." Not that Charles would have. Now, Charles was trying to recall if he knew the two had separated. Charles had only met Lizzy once, when he traveled out to Texas almost four years earlier. He had a vague recollection of what she looked like. She was a brunette, thin, and about 5'10." He had not seen Sam since either, only talking occasionally on the phone when Sam would call or exchanging periodic emails. Charles said, "Hey, text me as soon as you know if you can stay for the weekend, and I will see what I can do. I have to go into an editing meeting, but it is good to hear from you."

Sam clipped off the call and considered whether he wanted to stay in Miami an extra couple days. Jerking his head up, he said aloud, "What are you thinking?" Of course, he would want a couple extra days in Miami. But he would have to do some prep work before leaving, Stan could manage the rest.

As if telepathic, Stan stuck his head in the door. The unruly eyebrows were probably Stan's most notable facial feature, but his rather large ears were a close second. "Did you call me?"

"Oh! Stan, I was not talking to you."

"Okay," and without another word, he shut the door.

"Stan," he called trying to catch him before he closed the door but did not.

The door opened again. "Yes?" Stan asked sticking his head back through the doorway.

Somehow the popping in and out of Stan's head so quickly was amusing to Sam, but he managed to keep a straight face. Stan was a good graduate assistant, but strange. Sam could not put a finger on it, but yes, Stan was sort of odd. His lanky frame of six foot three and unkempt hair reminded Sam of the pilot in the Mad Max named Jedidiah. Those goofy eyes were only missing the pilot goggles. And yes, the ears, which reminded Sam of a Cadillac with the front doors open, completed the eclectic appearance of the young man.

"Here is a phone number in Georgia. Talk to a lady named Sarah Adams and see if she has already made plane reservations for me to travel to Miami this Friday. I want to see if it is a problem to fly back to Houston on Monday instead of Sunday.

"You are going to Miami?"

"Nice Dr. J."

"Yeah, you will need to fill in for me on Monday, depending on the flight arrangements."

Stan gave a pensive smile, said slowly, "Okay'" and nothing else before closing the door to the office.

"Stan."

Back in came Stan's head.

"Just give the test as scheduled. It will be fine."

"Sure, Dr. J."

Sam gave a smile of his own, but his was one of bemusement. Stan ducked back out of the door like a puppet yanked from behind.

"Oh, and Stan!"

The door opened, Stan cocked an eyebrow this time, which said, 'seriously.'

"Can you take care of Sylvester this weekend?"

Stan gave an indeterminate smile, and said, "Sure Dr. J. Key in the same place as before?"

"Yes."

"Okay to take a swim?"

Sam's eyes narrowed.

"I heard you put a pool in," Stan said with a grin.

Sam sighed. "Yes. You can clean the pool when you're done."

"Wild orgy?"

"Uh, no."

"Had to try," Stan said with a smile.

"Yes, I am sure you did. And Stan…,"

"Yes Dr. J."

"Thanks."

This time Stan gave a little salute and slowly shut the door.

Chapter 12   **Washington D.C.**   **Thursday**

In less than an hour after the CYA report had been completed and printed, Heitzman called Terrence with a directive for the report to be couriered over to the FBI and White House. Within five hours of the courier's departure, Terrence Mitchell and his team were notified to reassemble. Instead of being passed off to someone else, the recommendations had been accepted and unpredictably been given back for Terrence to act as some kind of coordinator. Feeling like he was trying to shake off an annoying piece of tape from his fingers, Terrence was frustrated to have been drawn back into the process. He was determined to pass this action to the next person and was hopeful to uncover a rationale that would extricate his team.

However, Terrence has not figured a way to pass this off and had been going over the images provided by a drone. Seated at his desk, with fingers digging into his temples, Mitchell asked, "Maria, what have you got for me?"

"Clute got everything we need. All we have to do is give them the targets and FBI will do the dirty work," Maria answered.

"Anything else from Einstein?" Terrence asked Maria, referring to the internet traffic monitoring system. He twisted open water bottle and took a long drink.

With a look of trepidation accented by raised eyebrows, Maria said, "Well, they will use one of the surveillance programs. I am not sure how they do it. But it will help to give them internet provider information so they can narrow their collection. I have not been made aware that anything else has been added of consequence to the surveillance portfolio."

Terrence moved over to an exposed window which extended from the floor to the ceiling. He gazed out at the vast parking lot below. "I don't know that we will be able to do that unless we get a name to run billing inquiries against. Plus, these guys are using aliases to protect themselves. If we get close enough for that, we should be able to get their actual email addresses. I bet these guys are using Skype accounts to communicate, but if we can get those conversations as well, we can get closer to the leaders."

Maria sighed and said, "There is so much ground to cover and there may be nothing that we can see unless we uncover a definitive location." Taking a drink of coffee, Maria asked, "What about involving local authorities?"

Turning away from the window, Terrence said with a bit of frustration, "Not our call. That will be the FBI's call. If it were me, I would. But involving locals may just be tipping them off. Who knows if Sheriff Billy Bob is a friendly or even one of the players? Tell the Einstein people or whatever they are calling it now, to include in the dictionary the names we have so far and the word abolition to their search. I doubt that our rebels are stupid enough to throw out the more obvious words but include secession and assassination in there as well."

"Along with the usual tip words, maybe we will get lucky," Maria offered.

Terrence let out a long breath and said, "Yeah, maybe we will get lucky. What else have we got?"

"We have a couple dozen or so names to start paying attention to and a couple dozen organization names that have been identified as possible threats. But most of these groups are just wanna-bees that are probably just internet sites that don't pose any real threat," Maria stated flatly.

Terrence returned to the table to view the map again. "We will have to track down as many as we can. We will focus on the Texas and Georgia connections. The rumor is that these two locations may have some financial backing. The FBI has been tracking some shipments of guns and is keeping an eye on some of the more vocal groups. I do not think the ones we are looking for are going to be as visible as Don Black of Stormfront, referring to the man who had taken to the airwaves to unapologetically promote white supremacy.

"Okay, then should that be enough to pass this along?" asked Maria.

Terrence said, "I think we are almost ready. Let's try to turn this over to the FBI for the actual operation and we will remain as far in the background as possible."

In the outer office, two men in suits were making their way to the glassed-in office where Terrence and Maria were working. Earlier, Terrence had received word from his secretary that two agents from the Federal Bureau of Investigation would be joining them in their next meeting. Prior to his work at the NSA, Terrence, and one of the agents named Jeff Parrish, had worked together at the Department of Justice. Terrence remembered their relationship was professional but friendly.

The two agents had initially been directed to a temporary office on a different floor until Terrence was ready to meet them with his team. Just ahead of them was Clute, who had just returned carrying several folders and what looked like large black and white photos. Upon seeing the agents, Terrence rose to shake hands and greet the agents as they entered the conference room.

To his team, Terrence introduced the two agents. Of the two, Jeff Parrish was easily the more intimidating of the two men. Where his partner, Alex McQueen could turn heads of the women, Parrish projected a no-nonsense demeanor that intimidated even the most seasoned criminal. Both wore the expected dark suits, bright ties and polished shoes, but Parrish had a beer belly which required frequent tucking of his shirt tail. McQueen, junior in experience and rank, was a handsome man with a professional look. McQueen was the physical polar opposite of Parrish. However, Parrish had an intimidating presence which was accomplished with a keenly intelligent look through wireless glasses. His pocked face gave witness to a teenage bout with acne, giving him a look that any mobster would be pleased to possess. About the same height of six feet, Parrish and McQueen made an interesting pair. Upon arrival, Maria took in the odd couple and imagined that Parrish had put on his weight since his Quantico days. Perhaps his job involved more desk work now. He still had to be in good enough shape to pass the required physicals, but she suspected that maintaining an acceptable weight-height ratio was a challenge for Parrish. McQueen, on the other hand, was a hunk. She stole a glance down at his left hand and frowned. She glanced over at Parrish's left hand. *It figured,* Maria thought to herself, *no ring.*

After introductions of those in the room, Terrence said, "Agent Parrish, it has been a while."

Parrish's head cocked to the right, but then nodded that he remembered Terrence from Justice. "Right, right, it sure has been a while."

McQueen quickly hid his own confusion and as he looked away, he saw Maria gazing at him. A bit embarrassed, he smiled and looked back toward Parrish.

Terrence said, "I guess I lost track of you, with all the changes, but I thought you had left the FBI."

Parrish was nodding but said, "Just been toiling away. Meanwhile, you have been very busy, and very successful I might add."

Terrence gave a self-deprecating smile. "Well, thanks, but sometimes it seems like I have been promoted from the pan into the fire." There were smiles of agreement all the way around.

Terrence addressed the agents. "Well, let's see if we can get you up to date here. We have completed the action report which Under Secretary Weitzman initiated."

Both McQueen and Parrish looked at each other in a brief moment of confusion or perhaps it was apprehension. Parrish gave McQueen an imperceptible nod, and then returned his attention to Terrence, who was still speaking.

"The Charlie Rivers lead is probably the best thing we have going. From the information that we have it would seem that he is very well connected and may be behind the weapons that have been moving into Texas."

Addressing McQueen and Parrish, "Where would the weapons, I assume automatics is what we are talking about...," Maria waited for and received acknowledgement from Terrence, then continued, "where are they coming from?"

Terrence looked to Parrish, "You might have something on that right?"

Parrish hesitated then nodded. In his Boston accent that often came across as a bit pointed, he said, "Several possible sources. Our best guess is that they are coming from directly from Korea."

"This would indicate someone with a military background and connected globally," Terrence interjected but again deferred to Parrish.

The two F.B.I men just nodded, but neither commented.

Sensing the agents were holding back something, Terrence broadened the conversation, "Do you have any other activities that we should be doing groundwork on before we turn it over to the FBI?"

The two agents look at each other as if waiting for each other to speak or which one should answer. Maria was not sure if they were going to say anything for a moment. Finally, Parrish said, "There is just a lot of chatter. We have quite a few individuals that could be considered domestic terrorists. But these guys are just malcontents and for the most part harmless. They would like to get others motivated, but really are not crazy enough to actually do anything violent. They consider themselves patriotic but are really just terrorists."

Maria noticed that McQueen bristled but said nothing. She was not sure if it was the thought of the terrorists or the idea that his partner classified these people as terrorists. Maria felt reasonably sure it was the latter. She double checked his ring finger again, but alas, the token of commitment was still in its place. McQueen glanced over catching Maria looking at him. She quickly turned her attention back to Parrish's overview.

Parrish continued after stealing a glance toward his partner and then toward Maria, "We are focusing on these groups though because they usually have the resources to do something destructive. There have been numerous little individual protests, but, of course, the Tea Parties are stirring a lot of anti-government sentiment everywhere. We dispatched agents to each of them and we are using surveillance to record attendees. Those pictures are being fed into the new BAT program and if we have a match, it kicks out a report. In addition, we have begun a concentrated effort to infiltrate the Tea Party's leadership in hopes of ferreting out some of the extremists."

"What is BAT again?" Clute asked.

"Biometric Authentication Technology." Parrish said with the tone of slight irritation; not at being interrupted, but the fact that this information expert did not know something as essential as the meaning of BAT. Parrish scratched his forehead and then continued. "It can link up facial features, fingerprints, gate, wingspan, and eye recognition; it is quite the tool. In another year or two we will be able to tell the dick size of every terrorist in America!" he said with certain drollness.

All three of the other men gave discreet glances over to Maria. She pretended not to have heard the coarse comment or gave no indication that she had taken offense.

Parrish momentarily paused, gave a facial shrug and continued. "We have had several hits of frequent flyers, but most are just the curious and are of no real threat."

Clearing his throat, McQueen interjected for the first time and Maria's body tingled just a bit. "If the person's picture shows up at two of the tea parties, it is kicked out and we start a portfolio."

His voice was steady and confident. His lack of any accent indicated to Maria that he was probably from the Midwest somewhere, and for a moment flashed to a scene where this FBI agent bailing hay, shirtless and had to refocus. She took a drink from the cup in front of her.

"Does that stay with F.B.I.? Clute asked.

McQueen narrowed his eyes a bit, but patiently offered, "Well if you mean do we share it with DHS, not necessarily." Referring to tracking and recognition software programs, McQueen offered, "Not unless Einstein or CS6000 kicks something out. But just because we have face duplication at one of these rallies, does not mean we have a name. But, if a person is a government employee or contractor who has an existing picture or a convicted criminal, his name will pop out. Obviously not everyone is a match, but we can usually identify those that are getting into a habit. We would not normally send it over until there was a known risk and maybe not then because this is our normal area of operation."

Terrence picked up on a bit of discontent in Parrish's voice in this last comment.

Directing her question to McQueen, Maria asked, "And the email surveillance is done with Einstein or CS600?"

McQueen slowly weaved his head with a side-to-side motion indicated that the answer was either complicated or a little of both. "Since Carnivore was replaced or actually renamed CS 6000, we have incorporated several commercial programs that monitor emails and internet traffic."

Parrish added, "We are not going to be able to identify people that just all of sudden go off the reservation, like the guy who flew his plane into the I.R.S. building in Austin. But someone who is planning a more systematic or organized effort is probably going to poke his head up from his hole and we'll take a picture and he...or she," looking over and acknowledging Maria, he gave a smile, "will be on our radar."

When Parrish finished, he frowned. Terrence noticed the expression and asked, "What's up Agent Parrish, you look troubled?"

Parrish froze for a minute realizing that he must have unintentionally revealed his frustration with this meeting.

Parrish said, "Hey Alex, would you mind finding a snack machine somewhere. I think my blood sugar is dropping."

Maria volunteered, "Oh, I have some crackers in my desk."

"Thanks, but do you have, like a Snickers or something like that?"

"We have a snack area down a couple floors, that probably would," Maria offered helpfully.

"Maybe you could show Agent McQueen where that is."

Knowing that Parrish wanted to discuss something alone, Terrence waited for the two to go and then gave a nod to Clute to leave as well. As the Clute exited, Terrence stood and closed the door.

"Terrence, I know you are a straight shooter from working with you in the past. That is why I thought this meeting was a good thing. I am trying to find out what the hell is going on."

Terrence just looked confused. "What are you referring to – the mission, the., the..., what?"

"The everything." Parrish jumped in with a bit more emotion than he had intended. "I mean why, all of a sudden, are you guys in on this?"

Terrence's posture straightened a bit, but really did not take offense. "I would like to say that communication around this place has improved, but you know how things work. The story goes that we," he raised an open palm toward the outside offices, indicating he was referring to his team that was no longer in the room, "meaning my group, were pulled away from the international side after the President met with the Under Security's team and they were briefed on the increasing civil unrest. Specifically, the Secret Service was worried about direct threats to the President himself. Weitzman said that there may be some connection to the death of Senator Summers. He also said that there could be some connection with an assassination plot."

"Terrence, that is all you know?"

"I have to agree it is not much, but POTUS demanded that I&A step in to help the investigation."

Scratching his neck, Parish said, "Stepped in it, may be a good description. But you say this is all coming from the Oval Office? That does not make any sense."

"I thought it was odd that we were brought in, but I just figured that..., he stopped. Terrence smiled at his own comment and nodded. "Look, I want to hand this off as much as you want me to hand this off..., all I can tell you is that we were working on an international gig and the Under Secretary came in with a file and said mimicking his boss' nasal voice, "Start working on this immediately."

Parrish gave a little laugh and a shake of his head in bewilderment. "And you are sure that it is coming from the President?"

"Everything that I have been told seems like it has been coming from the White House." Trying to move this along, Terrence continued, "What I'd like to do is be able to open a line of communication between us. You give me what you have and then I give you some idea about information that we could feed you that might be of use. Then, I am able to say that we have cooperated, with us handling the information and you are the boots on the ground. I am going to focus on the threat to the President but will pass along information that might help you with your multitude of anarchy groups. It could be one in the same, but I need to be able to show that we are making some progress. You may have some information that fits, and we certainly have more leeway in obtaining information. You still have to worry about getting permission. We can practically wave the national security flag and do whatever the hell we want."

Candidly Parrish said, "No, I am not talking about that. This whole thing is fucked up. I need to know, who pushed this your way."

"Obviously, you know more than I do, or I am missing out on what the problem is." Terrence quickly added, "Well, I see the obvious problem, but is there something else I am missing?"

Still pacing, Parrish turned and said with no anger directed at Terrence, "We have agencies on top of agencies. No one knows what the hell is going on and we are stepping on each other. People have switched agencies and doing this and that. We are running around like chickens with our heads cut off."

"Weitzman told me it was the White House who was passing this along, but I can ask him when he comes back."

"If he thinks it was the White House, Weitzman must not know who sent it."

Terrence said with some exasperation, "If it wasn't the White House, why would someone else pass it along? I mean if someone were trying to harm the President, wouldn't that make it likely that they would be exposed?"

"I am not sure, maybe their intent was to muddy up the water," Parrish suggested.

Terrence said with a bit more accusation than he intended, "Surely you don't think that we are so inept that involving us would help someone do damage to the presidency."

Shaking his head slowly, Jeff said, "Not at all. If you could find out who sent this your way, I really think it would be important. I am really worried here Terrence."

Terrence shrugged not knowing what to say. Then a thought occurred to him. "Well, now that you mention it, how did you find out that we had been brought in on this?"

Parrish gave an initial look which indicated he was searching for an answer. "It must have been when a member of your team called over asking for some information."

Terrence looked confused. "I don't think anyone from here called the FBI."

"I am not sure, Parrish said dismissively. "I just got the message that your office had been brought in for support."

Terrence just looked at Parrish with a questioning face but said nothing.

"Look Terrence, we have a Senator that was killed."

"And that has to do with this?" Terrence asked.

"Wow...okay." Parrish was up pacing, with one hand rubbing a temple and the other on his hip. "I don't even know what I can tell you."

"Tell me what? What are you talking about?" Terrence stood up and placed both hands on the table.

Reluctantly, Parrish asked, "Do you trust Epstein?"

Terrence was a bit taken aback by this breach in protocol.

"Sure, I do. I probably should have gone with him over to the FBI. But I decided to come here. Why?"

"Look T, you worked for Epstein, right?" Parrish asked rhetorically, then continued his line of reasoning. "I think the President is in danger from the inside."

Terrence gave a disbelieving look, but Parrish continued, "It would really help if I knew who passed along this to your department."

"Why?" asked in a level questioning voice.

"If I know who sent it to the DHS, I can figure out why?"

"Why not just ask Epstein, surely he knows what is going on," Terrence asked.

Parrish exhaled. "I need you to be more subtle than that."

There was a long moment of silence, but neither Terrence Mitchell nor Jeff Parrish said anything. Jeff had basically insinuated the Parrish's current boss and Terrence's former boss, the head of the FBI, Russell Epstein was somehow involved in the...*what* thought Terrence, *a supposed assassination plot on the President or the death of a U.S. Senator.*

Terrence placed both hands on his desk and rose slowly as the reality of Jeff's inference that Epstein was the person of interest was sinking in. "I don't believe it Jeff." Nervously, Terrence went over to the door, opened it and then closed it again. He said with resolve, "No, you are barking up the wrong tree or you are on the wrong scent." Terrence looked the agent quizzically and the intently. Still, Parrish offered no comment or even facial expression from the agent. Frustrated at Parrish's unforthcoming stance, Terrence asked, "You must have something that you are going on, here, right?"

"I am not sure what I can say, other than to tell you that you would be doing me a big favor if you can figure out where this is coming from. That's all." Parrish said, fearing that he had unnecessarily put Terrence on hyper alert.

Terrence frowned. "I can tell you one thing. Russell Epstein is not someone you have to worry about." Terrence, still shaking his head said, "I mean after the first election the President cleared the table of anyone that he thought was not on the team and it looks like he is doing the same thing after this one. Only, I think he is a little more paranoid because of... well I am not sure why. I hope that is not what this is, you know, paranoia?"

Parrish let out a long breath. "It's not paranoia, Terrence. But I just need you to be careful who you go asking and how you ask it."

"Look, I assumed that Epstein sent you to me."

"You would naturally assume that" Parrish said without emotion.

"But you are inferring that Epstein, your boss, sent this request to involve the OAI, without the knowledge of the White House. And the White House would not have wanted this to happen."

"Something like that," Parrish answered blandly.

"So, it is not Epstein who wants to know who pushed this onto our plate?"

"No, that was my idea." Parrish was studying Terrence as closely as he could, trying to determine what the man was feeling.

Terrence looked back at Parrish with some combination of frustration, irritation, and yet, he still trusted the man and wanted to help if he could. McQueen and Maria had come back into the outer office and were headed to the meeting room. Terrence could see that Maria was infatuated with this young athletic guy. Turning his attention back to Parrish, he said resignedly, "Okay, let me see what I can find out. Are you going to be in D.C.?"

"No, we have to follow up a lead that came up. I will give you a secure number to call. I'd appreciate you not posting it on the restroom wall," Parrish said with a sly grin. He adjusted his glasses and gave a confident smile.

Terrence stopped before opening the door to let McQueen and Maria back in the conference room. "A lead that we have not discussed?"

Parrish was obviously uncomfortable with the question. "Oh, it is probably another goose chase."

Terrence noticed the deception in the way that Parrish looked away when he answered but decided to let it slide.

Maria and McQueen were laughing about something as they entered the room, but quickly removed the smiles when they crossed the threshold. It could have been that both had noticed the tension, or that they did not want to seem to be having too much fun, given the serious of the situation.

Parrish headed toward the door. He said, "Terrence, thank you for your help and I will look forward to hearing from you as soon as you have something.

After the two had left, Terrence sat on the edge of the conference table in thought.

Clute entered, giving a cordial goodbye to the two agents.

"What's wrong Terrence?" Maria asked.

"Did your boyfriend say anything about what they were doing here?" Terrence asked.

"What do you mean?"

Terrence let out a breath, raking his hand over his hair. "Parrish just said that he was off to follow up a clue but would not tell me what it was about."

Clute said, "The other guy, was it McGuire?"

"McQueen." Maria said.

Both men gave Maria knowing looks.

"What?"

"Nothing Maria. Clute what were you going to say?"

"McQueen," he paused to look at Maria, which earned him, her disapproving glare, "took a call in the hallway. He was talking to someone who evidently was sending them to Florida."

"Yeah, he did say something about Miami and getting some sun," Maria said. "Why?"

"I don't know, but it seems like there is something else going on here, and we seem to be out of the loop," Terrence said suspiciously. Terrence tried to clear his head with a deep breath.

"What's up boss?" asked Clute.

Terrence paused again before asking, "Did either of you call the FBI asking for information?"

Clute volunteered, "I didn't." Both men looked at Maria, who gave an innocent look and just shook her head that she had not.

Then putting up her finger to hold on a second, Maria said, "I didn't call the FBI. But I did call the White House."

Terrence frowned and picked up his phone to place a call to Epstein.

Chapter 13   Miami, Florida   Friday

Arriving at the Miami International Airport, Sam awaited the arrival of his suitcase at the baggage claim. He regularly tried to pack everything he needed in a carry on, but since he was staying a few extra days, plus the fact that his suit did fair well folded into a travel bag, he relented and packed a small suitcase. He used the time to call to Penny Reed, canceling their Saturday date. Sam promised to call her when he returned, feeling a sincere stab of regret. Sam thought about Penny and her long brown hair which stretch all the way down to the center of her back.

On the huge flat panel television next to the rotating baggage handler, a CNN report caught Sam's attention. The reporter was standing in front of the Liberty Bell in Philadelphia. Somehow the icon of the United States has been defaced. The tenor of the report was one of disgust as the reporter rhetorically was asking how this could have been done both ideologically and practically, considering the formidable glass case remained intact. The bell had been irreverently painted black topped with the letters D T O M, in white block letters. The correspondent speculated that these letters stood for some radical organization, but said officials were still trying to determine the meaning of the letters. At the bottom in smaller white letters were LOD. Sam gave an incredulous smirk wondering how they could not understand the meaning of the letters. Sam muttered, "Seriously?" Was History not being taught anymore? How could anyone not make the connection that the letters stood for Don't Tread on Me and Liberty or Death.

Sam claimed his luggage and took a cab to the Sonesto Bay Front Hotel. Charles was right in his assessment. The place was immaculate. Located South of Miami in Coconut Grove, it looked out on a bay created by Barnacle Island. He received directions to the convention center where he was to speak just in case, he needed to arrange his own transportation. He was pleased to find out that the convention center was within walking distance, just up South Bayshore Drive a couple of blocks.

When he was settled in his room, which featured a simple but modern tan décor, he turned on the television to hear about the hotel's feature and benefits. He quickly grew bored and switched over to the news. He decided to check out the room's bar; after all he was not paying the bill. In the background, a television news program was covering the death of Senator Hank Summers of Virginia. The death had gained national headlines, and the intrigue was hot fodder, particularly for the Beltway crowd. The consensus was that the Senator probably had a heart attack, but there were many conspiracy theories that attributed the death to foul play. The Senator was on several crucial committees and was a player in the Whitehouse entourage of support. The reporter alluded to a possible witness to the death but conceded that no official report had been provided. It gave the typical biography of the Senator, listing all of his accomplishments while in office.

Sam stopped in the middle of finishing the preparation of a Gordon's Gin and tonic, when the name on the report caused him to stop short of slicing a lime. "Summers, Summers," he said aloud. "Why does Senator Summers from Virginia sound familiar?" He listened more carefully now to the story, and finally concluded that must have been Charles' Senator friend. He puzzled, *"Was that where I heard the name?"* Sam could not conjure the memory. He concluded that must be it.

Turning his attention to his gin and tonic, he sliced a lime and dragged it around the rim of his glass, Sam took a satisfying drink and congratulated himself on a job well-done. He moved over the bed, taking the remote control in his hand, and turning the volume up. It was another report on this Summers guy. The reporter was saying that Summers was on the powerful House Way and Means Committee, and the committee that was responsible for overseeing Homeland Security. Sam already knew that this massive bureaucracy had become the lightning bolt for so many criticisms, from both of the extremes that composed the social and political landscape. The Libertarian crowd had been relentless in its rhetoric about civil liberties. That made for strange bedfellows when the ACLU began piping up that the Patriot Act was infringing on privacy and trampling the constitution. There was a whole plethora of organizations that were calling on the DHS to do more, and of course, just as many organizations that objected to the U.S. foreign military involvement. Any one of those groups,

Sam figured, could be the tie in. He was glad that he wasn't involved in all that politics. He winced at the thought of how hard the job of President of the United States must be trying to maneuver through a minefield like that. It really was a no-win situation. If you tried to be fiscally responsible you would be portrayed as uncaring and if you implemented programs, you would get hit over the head by the other side.

Sam thought about Charles Reynolds' assignment to the case and figured there must be more than just the usual myocardial infarction or blood clot to the brain. He unfolded a Miami Express that he picked up at the check-in desk and looked for Charles' column. He found it on page one of the newspaper's editorial section. It was a humorous piece about handicap parker stickers and the process that one could go through to secure a placard. His article was born out of the frustration of seeing drivers park in the restricted areas, then pop out like they did not have any kind of handicap. Sam read with enjoyment as he could just envision Charles getting more and more irritated.

His cell phone vibrated, and he answered the call from Sarah Adams.

Briefly fantasizing about a romantic interlude, he answered, "This is Sam!" he tried to give an extra positive note.

"Dr. Jackson, have you arrived in Miami?" she asked.
It seemed to Sam that she was almost brusque or at the very least, matter of fact. Sam had thought she had been a little prickly on the phone before, so he decided to try to ingratiate himself a little bit.

"Yes, thank you. The accommodations are very nice."

Not responding to his comment, Sarah said "There will be a driver to meet you tomorrow. The latest you probably should arrive is 3:00. What time would be good for you?"

Sam frowned at the lack of .... Well, it was not like she was rude. She was either detached or somehow uninvested in the conversation. "How about 1:30? That will give me time to look around and get oriented?"

"His name will be Frederick and he will meet you in the lobby at 1:30. Thank you for coming on such short notice."

Sam started to respond but realized the connection had been terminated. Again, Sam frowned. Not even a good-bye? What in the hell had he done to deserve such an abrupt treatment? *That was just rude*, he thought. Sarah was not worth his time and probably was not near as sexy as she sounded on the phone. Sam shrugged and decided to blow it off. Taking advantage of the Miami warmth, Sam took in several hours of water and sun.

The pool was a moderately luxurious amenity, with plush long towels at poolside and a cute little waitress who provided Sam with a rum cooler that really took the edge off his travels. He returned to his room and ordered room service so that he could practice his presentation. After his food had arrived, a salmon croquet with a hollandaise sauce, French style green beans wheat roll and iced tea. Sam hit the remote to catch the evening news on the 47-inch flat screen television perched on the dresser. An update about the death of the Senator from Virginia switched locations to Washington D.C. for a live correspondent interview. Amelia Amberton was reporting from the steps of the Congressional building. She was mildly attractive with a short blonde haircut, designer top and strong facial features that gave evidence to her longevity in the reporting business. She was interviewing the ranking Senator from Delaware, Brad Hutchins, who was evidently a colleague and friend of Summers. A close-up revealed the tears welling in Hutchins' left eye.

"Senator Hutchins, you were close friends with Senator Summers. What can you tell us of the circumstances surrounding his death?

"I was a close and personal friend of the Senator. I can tell you that we are all suffering from the loss of this well-respected legislature and statesman."

A seasoned reporter such as Amberton was not going to let him off that easy. She tried again, "What light can you shed on the circumstances of his death?"

"Not any more than you folks have reported in the news. I assume that he had a heart attack. It is really a tragic end to a great man's career."

"Senator, there are several rumors that a second man was in the restroom when the Senator died. Can you give us information about the person and what this means to the investigation?"

"I really can't comment on any on-going investigation. You would need to consult with the Secret Service or the F.B.I.

for that sort of information. I was told that he had a heart attack. We really need to keep Hank's family in our thoughts and prayers during this very difficult time. Thanks Amelia."

He turned and blended into a half-dozen of his entourage and was whisked away.

"Well, as you can see, everyone is very tight-lipped about the death of the Senator from Virginia."

The anchor responded, "Amelia, what are the rumors to which you are referring?"

"Well, of course, there are the really wild ones that cannot be substantiated, but several people that I have talked with say there was at least one person in the restroom during the Senator's death. Reportedly, this man was walked out to a waiting ambulance, and another said that he left just prior to the discovery of the Senator's body. We have been unable to get a response from the F.B.I., however, an autopsy is supposed to be released soon. That would give us a clue if there were any foul play involved."

"But the evidence so far does not include a gunshot or wound of any kind?" the anchor asked trying to get even a bit of a scoop.

Amberton almost sighed and said, "That is correct."
After the obligatory thank you, the anchor went on to another story. Sam flipped the channel to another station wondering if anyone else was sniffing around at the story. Sure enough, a competing station was talking about the death but was attacking it from another direction. This news television station showed a spokesperson from the White House in front of a lectern garnished with a presidential seal.

The man was saying, "We have no other official word from the F.B.I. as to the circumstances surrounding Senator Summers' unfortunate death. We, like you, are waiting for reports from the authorities."

Sam read a little line at the bottom of the television screen which identified the man at the podium as the Presidential Press Secretary Harlan Ford. Ford looked like a typical press secretary, inoffensive in appearance with intelligent eyes and perfect posture. He repositioned his glasses further back on his nose and gave the assembled reporters a warm smile. Ford pointed his finger to the left side of the room, granting some nameless reporter the permission to speak. Sam started to change the channel but held back for just a second.

A reporter stood and asked, "The Senator's death occurred on Monday. That seems like an inordinately long time to determine the cause of death. When can we expect an official cause to be announced?"

"Obviously that is in the hands of the FBI, but these things take time, and we must be patient if we want to get accurate information," Ford said swatting the question away like an errant dodge ball. He hoped that his curt tone would discourage further questions about particulars that were not his responsibilities. Ford loathed some of these idiots when they asked some of the stupidest questions. Some reporters were just dense as a rock, while others were just lazy. He pointed to one of the reporters raising her hand. This one Ford recalled specifically. She had made a move on him when he first got the Press Secretary's job. Ford had replaced a man who had been tossed aside because he was having an affair with one of the Press Corp. In a twist from the typical run of the mill relationships, this was a gay tryst. When the relationship inevitably made it to the Oval Office, the President was disgusted. His reaction was to simply fire the wayward Press Secretary and to blackball the reporter. *So much for gay rights* thought Ford. Gay tryst or hetero, Harlan had taken the firing to heart and successfully repelled the solicitation. "Yes, Michele."

"Has the President spoken the immediate family?"

"The President immediately reached out to Senator Summers' grown children. Of course, Senator Summers was a widower of 12 years. Next question?" Ford was two for two in his mental tally. This was not going to be as hard as he thought.

A reporter stood on the very front line and introduced herself. She announced her television station's call letters with a little more enthusiasm that was called if you asked Sam. He did not catch the question as he moved over to the window which afforded a nice view of the aqua blue water. When he returned by the television, Ford was again giving an answer with an attitude.

"I think everyone knows that Senator Summers served on several committees, the Finance Committee, Armed Services Committee. Obviously, the Senator's leadership will be missed."

The same reporter followed up with this question, "Can you confirm that to this point the authorities have no indication that the Senator's death was anything other than a heart attack?"

Ford took a moment to consider his answer and all the possible ways it might be interpreted, regurgitated, sliced and diced. He said, "Again, all I can say for certain is that the cause of death has not been determined." Pleased with his answer, Harland rewarded himself with a drink of water and pointed to the next reporter waiting in the queue to deliver the next question.

A new reporter introduced herself and asked, "Wasn't the Senator on the domestic terrorist committee that was looking into activities of some of the more out-spoken groups?"

Apparently expecting the question, Ford nodded gravely and said, "There are several Senators that are working with the Department of Homeland Security to try to identify those that would bring harm to this country, both domestic and foreign. But this is a possibility which will be deliberatively looked into to see if there is merit, should the Senator's death be ruled something other than natural causes."

Another reporter stood, and asked "Is there a possible connection to the dissident organization that might have been threatened by the Senator's investigation?"

Ford gave a less than polite sigh. "I am not willing to speculate on that. What I can tell you was that Senator Summers was one of several senators that were in the loop of information that is being collected on dissident groups. However, to speculate about something like that is not appropriate because we believe that the Senator died from a heart attack."

Another reporter stood and said, "Sorry sir, just one more question." He did not wait for Ford to respond. "Senator Summers was heading up several Congressional investigations, could that have ruffled some feathers?"

Sam had about lost interest, but this voice sounded familiar. He moved closer to the television for a closer look. Despite the seriousness of the Senator's death, this question caused a mild ripple of laughter.

Sam did recognize the voice and shouted. "I don't believe it. I just don't believe it." It was Charles Reynolds asking the question. Sam quickly pressed the volume button on the television. Ford was getting visibly irritated, which was not something which was easily achieved by reporters, but often tried. Ford exhaled and tried patiently to move to another reporter's question. But, apparently exasperating for Ford, no one was raising their hand, perhaps anticipating that the award-winning investigative reporter was headed somewhere with this line of questioning.

Trying to turn the tables back on Charles, Ford asked, "Mr. Charles, it was suggested that the Senator's unfortunate death might have been a terrorist attack and I can assure you that the FBI will look into that should the death be ruled something other than a heart attack. So, unless you have some knowledge that everyone else has, it is irresponsible to offer this type of conjecture."

Not bothering to correct Ford on his last name, Charles, countered, "I do have it from a well-placed source that the Senator's death was not due to a heart attack."

Interrupting in a forceful voice, Ford thundered, "That is just unfounded speculation and sensationalist reporting." Ford gave a horrid glare at the Reynolds but quickly regained his usual composure. "No government agency has issued a final report about the Senator's death."

This energized the press corps. Hands were waving frantically to get recognized. As if subconsciously looking for some way to end this exchange, the speaker turned his head toward the exit door. Ford said, with a bit more force than called for if you asked Sam, who was riveted by what he saw on the television. "The F.B.I. has a domain over that area and would be better in a position to comment on that. We will need to wait until we have further reports. When we have more, we will make that information available to you." Ford quickly folded up his notes and said curtly, "I have a briefing to attend, so that will have to be the last question. Thank you everyone." He turned and as evenly as possible walked to the exit.

The crowds of reporters shouted out additional questions to no avail. Harland Ford had left the building. The program shifted back to the studio and the anchor said, "Wow that was interesting." Turning to the guest sitting next to him, he asked, "Jim, was that Charles Reynolds who said the Senator did not die of a heart attack?"

"It was Reynolds, and that gave the statement some gravity. After all, he has broken a lot of stories and won a Pulitzer for his work on the terrorist attempt on MacDill Air Force Base and subsequent investigation into corruption in the Tampa Bay Authority."

"Not just a stab in the dark?"

"Could have been, but it looked like a punch to the solar plexus, rather than a low blow. I think the press secretary was taken a bit off guard."

"A stretch, but never underestimate Charles Reynolds. Perhaps, it is something to find out more about. We'll be right back. We will try to get Charles Reynolds on our next report to find out more about what he says he knows."

Sam fell back on his bed and said aloud, "Charles Reynolds, oh my goodness! What are you on to now?"

Chapter 14   **Washington, DC**   **Friday**

James Leeper entered into Rick Uhler's office with a computer printout gathered up in his oversized hand. Momentarily gone was the usual look of the Cheshire cat. James incessantly wore a look that intimated that he knew something that no one else did. He said, "Boss, you aren't going to like this."

"Tell me."

"First, have you heard of a reporter named Charles Reynolds?"

Uhler's eyes narrowed. "Yes, I know of Charles."

"He just claimed that he had an inside source that told him the Senator did not die of a heart attack at Harlan Ford's press conference."

Uhler said, "Hmm. Maybe I should have our team make contact with Mr. Reynolds to see how he came across this bit of information that no one else seems to have. They have been to DHS to see what's up over there already."

Leeper sat down in a chair in front of Uhler. "Okay and well, there is something else regarding Tyler Hansford."

Looking up from a desk littered with a mountain of files, books and reports, Rick asked, "What did Master Hansford have to say from himself?"

"Well, that's just it." Leeper paused with a look which often infuriated Uhler.

"James!" Uhler said sternly in a voice that signaled he was in no mood for the assistant's usual mischief.

James said, "They could not find him."

The hand which held Uhler's chin dropped heavy on his desk which accompanied a closing of his eyes. When Uhler's eyes opened, he gave Leeper a lethal stare. Leeper's hands up surrender sign seemed to communicate "don't kill me I am just the messenger." Deciding that he had better not continue his reticence, he handed the printout to a disbelieving Assistant Deputy Director.

Patience strained, "What does this say?" was all Uhler could muster.

"It says that Hansford snuck out of the hospital."

"He was being guarded!"

Leeper just held up is hands, palms up as if to say, I am just telling you what the report says.

Uhler leaned back in his chair and glowered at Leeper.

Clearing his throat, Leeper said, "It says that the local agents went to his townhouse in Richmond, but he was not there."

Angrily Uhler challenged, "Did they check to see if he was at this father's house?"

"They did. Senator Hansford lives just south of Roanoke on a thirty-acre ranch. Tyler was not there either."

Standing with both hands on his desk, Uhler asked, "Have they talked to the Senator?"

"They contacted him, but since he was in Washington, he thought his son had gone back to Richmond."

"What about his mother?"

"Evidently when she heard about Tyler, she checked herself into a clinic in Roanoke," James paused and that sly look returned, "not for the first time."

Uhler raised his eyebrows but did not comment. From his silence, James understood that he was to continue his report. "They tried to contact her, but the doctors said they would pass along the message. The agent did not get the impression that they would actually pass along the fact that now her son was missing."

"I am scared to ask why."

"I guess she is not emotionally strong enough to handle any more bad news," James said while trying to suppress a smile.

Uhler said, "So you are saying that Ms. Hansford is either mentally unstable or deliberately trying to avoid revealing her son's location."

Leeper said, "I think the former would describe the situation best." He paused, "I think she is a drunk sir."

Uhler sat back down. "This has just turned an unpleasant situation into a debacle. I want a message sent to Senator Hansford immediately."

"From you or the Director?"

"I will brief Director Epstein, but I know the Senator, so make it from me. When you get him on the phone, pass him through immediately."

"I am not done," James said.

Uhler sat back in his chair bracing for more bad news.

"The agents followed protocol by contacting significant others."

Uhler just gave a withering look. "The partner?"

"Trevor Whitworth." Leeper volunteered.

Despite being as game for intrigue as the next guy, Uhler was done with this game. "Okay, James. Go ahead and give it to me," he said crossly.

"They found him."

"And let me guess, he would not tell where the young Hansford was?"

"He couldn't."

"Because…?" Uhler said stretching the word.

"He was found dead in his parent's swimming pool at home."

Chapter 15   Miami, Florida   Saturday

Sam had concluded his presentation of about forty-five minutes. The crowd looked to be made up of businesspeople, just as was described to him by Sarah. He was curious whether she was in the audience. While dominated by men, there were a few women in the audience. The small auditorium had provided for an intimate venue, even though it held about two hundred people. Sam wondered if the people were required to come or were there voluntarily. With the lights dimmed, he had been able to just make out some of the faces in the front few rows, but the rest in the auditorium were obscured. At one point, Sam moved around the podium and walked down the steps and to the front. Here he felt better and more relaxed. He could get a better feel for his audience, and they seem to feel less like they were being lectured to and more like it was a discussion. Several of his jokes had hit home and received an appropriate level of response. By the end, Sam had thought that he had made his points and won them over. Afterwards, Sam stayed toward the front of the room shaking hands and answering questions. Most of the attendees were anxious to get on their way having been in attendance for the better part of the week. A few did come to the front to offer their appreciation for his efforts and lend some encouraging words.

A television crew had made its way down the side aisle. In less than a minute, the camera man had established his position directly in front of a reporter and had the camera rolling. A five-second-test bite was concluded, and the reporter quickly corralled Sam for a spot interview. Quite uncomfortable with an unexpected interview, Sam tried to beg off unsuccessfully.

An extremely tall female reporter, who introduced herself as Gwenivere, (or something like that, Sam did not exactly catch the name), was quickly up and running with a microphone to her lips. She was quite attractive in a handsome sort of way. Sam figured it was because she was so tall. She was at least six-foot, but if that were not enough, she had chosen a pair of three-inch heeled pumps In Sam's mind this added height caused her to tower over him. He felt like a schoolboy being questioned by a teacher, having to look up all the time for the next question.

107

After a quick introduction, which Sam did not really catch, he was standing next to the lady, momentarily distracted by a long slit in the reporter's dress. He caught himself and unconsciously adjusted his tie. "Dr. Jackson," she said in what Sam thought sound like a little bit of an accusatory tone. Hearing his name, he abruptly looked at the camera and had the look of someone who just got caught egging the neighbor's car. Sam stiffened and said, "Yes ma'am." Only the edge of the reporter's mouth hinted that she was mildly amused at Sam's discomfort. Or Sam mentally gasped when he realized, she was enjoying this, and it was about the get worse.

The reporter continued, "You are from Texas and a University of Houston professor?" Sam leaned in to say, "Yes, well, I am a professor in Houston, but...,"

She did not let him finish. "One of the points of your speech was to question whether the government has the right to involve itself in the economy. Do you feel that it is, in fact, unconstitutional?"

Sam seemed to gather himself for a moment, feeling that he was moving into an area that he was familiar with, but the lady almost seemed offended. "Well, I am not a constitutional expert, and I will leave that determination up to headier minds, but I do see the conflict of a federal government that involves itself in the business of the states. The Commerce clause excludes anything that does not have to do specifically with interstate commerce. This notion has been skirted by the federal government by their practice of coercing the states to abide be federal edicts with the threat of withholding funding."

"Dr. Jackson, what recourse do the states have?"

Sam laughed and said pleasantly, "Well short of secession, States can band together by passing push back legislation. This is, in fact, what is currently happening. The States also can convene a Constitutional Convention to add or change the Constitution. The Constitution was an agreement between the States, not between the States and an existing government. The States can also seek protection by the courts, but ultimately the Supreme Court would have to agree."

"How likely is that?" asked Gwenivere.

"Can't say, however I don't see the Supreme Court in its current state, particularly favorable to states' rights."

"No, I meant, how likely is secession?"

"Oh...," Sam was caught off-guard for a moment and then continued, "I think that is somewhat unlikely, but there does seem to be a growing concern about the encumbrances this administration has been perpetuating."

"Sounds like you are concluding that states will have little recourse other than to go it on their own."

"No, I think that is a rather radical approach, but I do think States will and should make a decision on a cost- benefit basis. There are some states that really take a hit when it comes to sending money in and getting very little back."

"Is Texas one of those?"

"No, actually, New Jersey and Minnesota have the biggest gripe. But if the defense spending drops, Texas and Florida could be on the short end of the stick. Regardless, States are going to have to fight back together against the federal government which seems perfectly willing to nullify the Constitution."

Gwenivere's eyebrows raised. "Usually, nullification is a term used to describe the states ignoring federal laws."

"I see it as a two-way street."

"Thank you, Dr. Jackson," she said as she turned to face the camera full on. Sam quickly retreated out of the realm of possibly be included in the shot. He heard her say, "I am live at a conference of concerned businessmen. The general consensus of those that I spoke to upon leaving was that the federal government has overstepped its boundaries and should be scaled back. Others were quite vehement about forcing the issue of states' rights even if it meant forcing the President out of office. We will continue this coverage of the right-wing backlash, which seems to be growing in America today as many worry that it grows to include even more radical groups, which may be willing to ratchet up this protest to the next level, terrorism. This is Gwenivere Dickson reporting."

Sam frowned at the thought of being lumped in with right wing terrorist organizations.

The camera's light died leaving only the hushed lighting of the auditorium, which caused Sam to squint.

"Pack up boys," the reporter said pleasantly. Then she turned to Sam. "Thanks Dr. Jackson. Not sure if this will run on the early or late edition. Can I contact you later if I need another quote or two?"

Sam meekly protested, "I sort of object to being included in the same sentence with domestic terrorists."

"Dr. Jackson, this stuff attracts viewers. If you are not planning a terrorist threat, you have nothing to worry about." Gwenivere said dismissively.

Sam eyes were still adjusting to the dim light but did manage a smile and not knowing what else to say, he said, "Of course, but still...," he did not get to finish his sentence.

Gwenivere was already on her way out. "I have your contact information," she said over her shoulder. She and the cameraman left as quickly as they had arrived.

Discretely, Sam looked around one more time for someone who might be Sarah. Initially, he had thought Gwenivere might have been Sarah, but when he saw the microphone, he knew that was not the case. Instead, Gwenivere had turned out to be Mike Wallace in a skirt. Now as Sam peered through the dark auditorium, there was a lone remaining woman off to the side. Surely the lady who had arranged his coming would want to stop by and meet him. He was certainly curious to meet her, because one, she sounded sexy on the phone and yet, she sounded like she was pissed off that Sam accepted her invitation. Sexy and saucy – Sam's imagination caused him to give a little sigh.

Charles Reynolds had entered the hall toward the end of Sam's speech and now stood at the back of the room patiently letting Sam meet and greet the last of the audience who had stuck around after the interview. As Sam surveyed the auditorium, he finally noticed Charles. He was excited and surprised to see his old high school friend. They had been really tight for his formative years growing up in the Tampa area. Sam had gone off to Florida State in Tallahassee and Charles or Chars to his close friends had attended the University of Miami.

Charles began walking up the aisle and said in an echoing voice, "Great job!" With big smiles, the two men shook hands and exchanged a heartfelt hug. "Looks like you are going to be on television!" Charles said jovially.

"Yeah, that was a surprise. I think I stammered through the whole interview. I am hoping that they will just scrap it. I think the lady may cause my name to be included on the Most Wanted list."

"That does not sound like a good thing. How was she when she interviewed?"

"Very cordial, at least I thought she was nice." Sam said cautiously.

Charles said, "They are the worst kind. They move in like a cuddly teddy bear, all smiles and then proceed to cut your nuts off."

"You are not helping," Sam said with an uncomfortable laugh. Then the obvious crossed Sam's mind, "I can't believe you are already here."

"Just an airline ticket away. Besides whom else can show you Miami like me?"

Sam gave a shake of the head and laugh. "I saw you on television last night!"

"You did?" Charles said with a mildly amused look.

"I did and you really put a zinger to the poor guy."

"Yeah, it seemed like a risky statement even to me, but I did have a credible source."

The comment caused Sam to cock his head a little in confusion, but he was distracted before he could follow up with a question. A woman who had been standing off to the side was moving toward Sam and Charles.

"Hey, hold on a second Chars, let me talk to this lady," Sam said.

Charles turned and gave the advancing woman an appraising look. His facial expression indicated that she definitely met with Charles' approval. He gave a pleasant smile and said to Sam, "I am going to get some water and will meet you in the lobby area when you are ready." As Charles passed, the lady, he paused, opened up his stance to clear a path.

The woman, who gave an appreciative nod at Charles as she passed, was impeccably dressed in an all-black outfit. Her modest dress was belted with a tasteful buckle. Each piece looked expertly tailored, or perhaps Charles thought she just had a great body, which made whatever she was wearing look good. A petite flowered brooch accented the lightweight sweater stylishly draped over her bare shoulders. Sam guessed that the lady had to be at least 40, but it was tough to tell. However old she was, she looked great, whatever age she was.

"Mr. Jackson?"

Her heavy Southern accent alerted Sam immediately that it was not Sarah as he had earlier suspected.

"Yes, I am."

"I hope I didn't chase your friend off," she said turning back to see Charles making his way up the aisle.

"No, no, no, don't worry about that, he's coming back." Sam said.

Looking somewhat expectantly, and then realizing that Sam was finished talking, the lady said, "I am Margaret Stephens. I really enjoyed your talk."

Her accent went perfectly with her graceful appearance. She seemed enchanting to Sam, as she did probably to every other man she came across. Sam was rigid as if under a magical spell.

Sam's brain kicked back in time to say, "Thank you very much. I was glad to be able to attend."

"My husband was the one who recommended that the Summit invite you."

Sam's eyebrows raised in interest, accompanied by a slightly confused tilting of his head. He was ready to say that he did not know any Mr. Stephens, but he did not get a chance.

Margaret continued, "Unfortunately he was not able to attend, but he wanted me to extend his appreciation."

Sam wanted to ask several questions of this elegant lady but forced himself to be patient. It would do no good to launch into a barrage of questions, which might be embarrassing or make Margaret uncomfortable. He decided that politeness was the best approach. After all, he was getting paid, and the only real problem was that he was not sure what or who he was dealing with. Sam corrected himself, he had been paid, He had checked his bank account when he arrived, and it was $5000 fatter. It still had not relieved him of the feeling that he was being played, but he could not figure out the possible harm. His red flags were up, but this woman sure added some credibility to the whole situation. She was pure class.

"Then I am in your debt. I was flattered to be asked and honored to be included."

"Mr. Jackson, my husband and I would like to invite you to dinner if you are not leaving right away."

Sam hesitated, cocked his head little to the left and back to the right giving away some of his thoughts. Ms.

Stephens' perfect smile was genuine and remained expectant at the same time. The twinkle in her eye was one of energy and confidence. Sam was mesmerized.

After that brief moment where each person was appraising the other, Sam offered, "I am staying, but I have committed to spending some time with an old friend. That was him who just left. I was not expecting him to be in today, but he flew in to see me..." his voice trailed off as he stared into Margaret's eyes. In the poorly lit auditorium, he could not tell if her eye color was green or hazel. Sam's curiosity was telling him to accept but was conflicted by the fact that Charles had taken the time to come see him. Sam chided himself for a momentary thought of a Miami beach and Sam with a beer, and Margaret sitting beside him. Sam's attention returned and Margaret had an amused look on her face. "I am sorry. Thank you so much anyway."

Sam thought he noticed Margaret glancing at his left hand. With no hesitation, she said, "What a great friend! Tell you what. Why don't you invite him to have dinner with us as well? We would certainly be honored to have you and your friend."

Sam tried to quickly think that through, but he still seemed to be in some kind of slow motion. Again, his mind drifted into a romantic interlude with this woman, and again Sam mentally slapped himself for what he was thinking. This lady was married and what he was thinking – well, he should not be thinking what he was thinking! *Had she really just checked to see if he was married?* He managed, "Okay, well... if you walk out with me, I will ask him to see if he already has plans."

The Master of Ceremonies was cleaning up leftover paperwork and bulletins at the head table. He shook Sam's hand, passed along some well wishes and congratulations, and with the other hand passed him an envelope.

"What is this?" Sam asked sincerely.

"It's an honorarium for taking the time to speak to us today."

"Well," Sam hesitated for an instant before saying, "but I the person who scheduled me has already taken care of that."

"That was probably just traveling money. Thanks again."

And that was it. The man turned and walked away, leaving Sam there, mouth open and the envelope still in his hand. He was tempted to peek inside, but instead just slid the envelope into his pocket.

Sam shook his head and turned back to Margaret.

"Everything okay?" Margaret asked.

"Well, yes. Seems like I am getting double paid."

"Sounds like a nice problem to have. Let's go talk to your friend," Margaret said while taking Sam's arm. Feeling a little jolt through his system, Sam smiled from ear to ear.

Once outside, Sam enthusiastically performed introductions.

"Charles, this is Margaret Stephens."

Charles' eyebrows raised, but whatever the look meant, it was gone as fast as it had appeared. Sam noticed the momentary reaction but could not quite decipher its meaning. Glancing toward Margaret to glean some meaning, he was rewarded with her perfect smile and Sam forgot about his confusion.

Charles said genuinely, "Miss Stephens it is a pleasure." He took her extended hand gently and gave a slight bow.

"Oh please, call me Margaret and I will call you Charles."

Charles gave another slight bow. Sam now wondered if he had somehow been transported back to Margaret Mitchell's Tara, and Rhett Butler was about to scoop up Miss Charlotte in his arms. It was the second time in this short span that Charles reaction had caused Sam to wonder if Charles knew this woman. It almost seemed that their words were rehearsed, and their actions were almost choreographed, and Sam was a bit jealous of whatever these two were sharing. Sam pushed his thoughts away and addressed Charles, "Margaret's husband...," Emphasizing the word husband, "I was just informed, was the person who arranged to have me come to Miami."

Sam saw that look again in Charles' expression and it again it disappeared as quickly as it came. The edge of Sam's mouth cracked into a questioning smile. But Charles had already shifted his focus to Margaret, who seemed to be studying Charles.

Margaret interjected, "My husband and I would be pleased if you and Mr. Jackson would join us for a dinner party at our house this evening if you don't have plans."

Charles gave another slight bow, "That is genuinely nice of you. I always enjoy a party. And was the good doctor agreeable to the invitation?"

Turning to Sam, she brought her hand to her mouth and said, "Oh Dr. Jackson, I am so sorry. How silly of me not to know that? Here I have been improperly addressing you the entire time."

Sam waved away the insignificant slight and said, "Yes the good doctor accepted, Charles," flashing a disapproving smile over toward Charles. "Please call me Sam."

"Oh, excellent," Margaret said with enthusiasm, "It is all settled. Shall I arrange for transportation?"

Sam looked to Charles for guidance.

"Just an address and I will have us to dinner on time," Charles answered.

She handed Charles a business card with the couple's address on it. "Let's say about eight, if that gives you enough time?" She looked at one and then the other. Both men nodded agreement. "If you get lost, just call the number on the card and we'll dispatch an escort!"

On cue, a dark sedan arrived, and Ms. Margaret Stephens was ushered into the back seat by the agile driver. With a wave of the hand, she was gone.

Sam looked at Charles. "This whole thing is just surreal."

Charles deadpanned, "Happens to me all the time."

115

Chapter 16   Miami, Florida   Saturday

After apologetically dismissing Frederick from his duties of returning Sam to the hotel, Charles distracted Sam with a pat on the left shoulder while slipping a Grant through the window for the man's wait. Up went the car's window and Frederick was motoring out of the parking lot.

"I hate that Frederick had to wait all this time," Sam said with a frown.

"He will be fine," Charles said enigmatically.

"I know, but he waited for several hours and then he did not even get to finish the job."

"Send a friendly note to his company saying what a great job he did," Charles said in an effort to get going.

"Yeah, but I still feel bad." Sam followed the car as it moved out of site.

"Sam, you are a good man."

Sam gave Charles a puzzled look, but Charles just smiled, and unlocked the doors to his automobile with his remote. He hopped in and said, "Let's go."

Having convinced Sam to stay overnight at his house rather than the hotel, Charles had taken Sam back to the Sonesto for a quick change of clothes and to grab his travel bag. They drove a congested thirty minutes to Charles' house which was modest in its outer appearance and located in what appeared to be an upper middle-class neighborhood. Sam had expected a penthouse or a rambling mansion, but the veranda style home was rather inconspicuous in Sam's estimation. While Charles unpacked his Washington D.C. "go" bag and changed into his clothes for the evening, Sam was sitting in the living room within earshot of the bedroom, nursing a cold beer.

From the living room Sam said, "I like your house. But seems rather domesticated or residential or something like that."

Emerging from the bedroom and moving over to the sidebar, Charles said, "Ordinary?"

Sam gave a shrug that said yes.

Charles said, "If you saw the prices on real estate down here you would know why I am all the way out here. Sure, I would love a place on the beach, but living in Washington part time and down here part-time; it is a killer.

116

"Well, what it lacks in Wow, it makes up for in charm," Sam said graciously.

"Thanks, old boy. And how's your house coming?"

"I am actually just about finished with all the renovations. I am really pleased with the result. You will have to come see it."

Glass raised, Charles said from the sidebar, "Absolutely would love to see it."

"Say, Charles, did you recognize Margaret when you met her?" Sam asked Charles, who was putting the finishing touches on his Tanqueray and tonic, specifically a lime wiped around the edge of the glass.

"No, but I know the name."

Sam frowned a bit and asked, "Should I have known the name?"

Charles sipped his drink, giving a satisfying lick of the lips. "Probably not unless you travel in the high-society circles in Miami. You are going to be dining with the Stephens family, who own one of the largest shipping companies in the eastern part of the United States. Alexander Stephens has put more people in public office than Cheerios has holes. And, if I have my history correct, the Stephens name goes all the way back to Georgia's Alexander Hamilton Stephens."

"Who was...someone famous I am guessing?"

Charles looked amused. "Jackson, you should really brush up on your history."

"Hey, I know a lot about history!" Sam contested. "I did notice that she did not seem to recognize you!" Sam said hoping to get in a friendly jab.

Chars gave a rueful smile and said, "No, but that is just because that damn picture they use for my newspaper column is about ten years old. And along those lines, if you would have introduced me as Charles Reynolds, she may have retracted the offer."

"That does not sound good. Should I leave you at home?"

"Would not miss it for the world."

"That is not what I was asking."

Charles laughed and said, "No, it will be all right. Southern manners would not permit them to treat a guest rudely."

117

"Now I am really worried."

Charles was dressed flawlessly as usual. His black, Just Cavalli jacket was perfectly combined with an open collar pinpoint oxford and dress slacks. Sam felt a bit underdressed until Charles lent him a sports coat to go with his khaki slacks and collarless dress t-shirt.

"We look pretty good," Sam said appraisingly in the mirror on the way out.

"Just be sure to use the correct fork at dinner, Clubbo," Charles jabbed with his nickname for Sam. Clubbo referred to Sam's occasional social flubs when they used to frequent clubs during their underage years.

"I will do my best to represent my family as they taught me to do," Sam said, acting out the poor Sam Jackson never got any respect routine.

"You will have to do better than that!" They both started laughing.

Sam offered, "I must admit I am a little nervous about this whole thing."

"Sam, you had a momentous day today. You picked up some cash and were interviewed for television. Enjoy the moment."

Sam partly conceded, "Yeah I know, but something up with all this."

"Sometimes you remind me of Eeyore," Charles said flatly. He was referring to gloomy character in the Winnie the Pooh cartoons.

"I am not like Eeyore." Sam looked over at Charles, who just looked back at him without saying a word. Rolling his eyes Sam said, "Let's just go before we are late."

In Eeyore's voice, Charles said, "Let's go before we are late."

Arriving right at 8:00 p.m., Charles parked his XK Jaguar Coupe on the circular drive.

As they pulled up close to an extended set of limestone steps, Sam said, "Amazing house," Craning his head to see the entire height of the structure through the car window. The trajectory caused Sam to almost bend in half at the waist.

"Yes, it is. I am surprised that we are not being met by servants."

The two exited the Jag and walked up the front walk the front step. Upon arrival to the front portico, they were, in fact, greeted by servants, three to be exact. All three looked rubbed and scrubbed and with eyebrows appropriately expectant.

An exceptionally large black man, dressed in a formal dinner jacket opened the door. "Good evening gentlemen." He stepped back slightly and extended his gloved hand inside. Just as Charles and Sam crossed the threshold, a small bony white man in a butler's uniform was queued next approaching Sam and Charles with a genuine smile. The skinny white man spoke in a low tone. "My name is Forbes. May I have your automobile keys sir? I will park your Jaguar." Though he drew out the syllables saying Jag u ar, Forbes had a surprisingly pedestrian accent.

Charles fished in his pocket for the Jag's key fob. Dropping it into Forbes outstretched hand, Charles said, "Thank you very much Forbes." Forbes gave a slight bow.

Under his breath Charles said, "All this bowing."

The third servant, a shapely woman in her early twenties, gave the arriving gentlemen a gracious smile, before ushering the guests through a short entry hall and into a large entrance room. Her white blouse was topped with a conservative short waist jacket over black slacks which Charles showed a brief peek of appreciation.

The house was truly remarkable with huge sweeping staircases on both sides of the entry room. Sam marveled aloud "This place could be featured in Home and Garden."

"It has been," Charles stated flatly.

"Dr. Jackson, I presume," said a voice from a hallway that presumably led to the back forty of rooms. It was a confident tone which was possessed refined quality of the upper class, but not of the haughty variety.

A man of diminutive stature entered the atrium with his hand extended to Sam. "Alex Stephens." His receding hairline featured curly graying hair. His face was angular with an intelligent look. Small dark eyes had a sparkle that engendered immediate trust.

"Please call me Sam."

"I was so pleased you could join us for dinner."

"The pleasure is mine." Sam turned to introduce Charles, but he was examining a portrait on the wall that appeared to be a gentleman from the Civil War era. A brass nameplate was inscribed Alexander Hamilton Stephens.

Stephens did not wait for an introduction, "You must be the famous Charles Reynolds."

Charles turned with that same look of surprise Sam remembered from earlier in the day, but this time it stayed in place for half beat longer. Nevertheless, he was not unnerved, offering a simple, "I am. Very pleased to meet you, Mr. Stephens."

The two men shook hands and held the grip a bit longer than seemed customary. Alex seemed to be sizing Charles up and Charles for his part had an inquisitive smile on his face. "Alex, please." Charles gave a nod and another bow.

Stephens broke eye contact, smiled warmly and said, "Margaret told me that you and Sam are old high school friends."

Sam puzzled; *Did I mention that?* It was those little comments that often threw Sam off his stride. Like when his father used to ask the young Sam unexpectedly, "Is there something you need to tell me?" It was like splash of chilly water that made Sam just freeze in place. Sam constantly wondered how his dad knew what he knew and here was this stranger with the same countenance as his father. While Sam stared with a puzzled look, Charles merely nodded an acknowledgement, but did steal a glance over at Sam and raised one querying eyebrow.

Turning back to Sam, Alex said enthusiastically, "I am sorry I did not make it over to hear your talk today, but I had several calls from friends congratulating me on my recommendation. They said you did an exceptional job, and I appreciate your effort to make me look so smart!"

Not sure how to answer, Sam just said, "Appreciate being asked,"

"I heard you were a bit modest about your abilities," Stephens said amiably.

Sam gave an appropriately modest smile, and a slight bow. *Dammit, now I am doing it.*

Charles piped up, "This house is amazing, but it looks like it should be in Georgia instead of Florida."

Alex said, "It is an excellent location for getting to the Caribbean or even South America. We do still maintain a home in Georgia, but this has become a second home to Margaret and me. In fact, some of our guests have just arrived from Georgia. Shall we go to the dining room?"

With an amused look of wonderment shared between them, Charles and Sam dutifully followed the diminutive man through an expansive hallway. When he reached a dark wood paneled door almost twice his size, Alex said to Sam, "I have placed you next to me at the table because I want to learn all I can from you. Margaret, on the other hand, is infatuated with Mr. Reynolds and wants to hear all the scuttlebutt about various Miami residents." He gave a sly smile over to Charles who was checking out another of the mural size paintings of a river lined with Georgian Oak trees. Charles had not been so absorbed in his admiration of the painting to have missed out on the conversation.

"Absolutely works for me, but I am afraid I am lacking when it comes to the gossip of the Floridian scene," he said without missing a beat.

"Yes, well perhaps the Washington scene will be just as stimulating," Alex said while pushing down a brush brass door handle. As the door opened a lively conversation with a mixture of voices from both women and men spilled through the doorway.

Alex led the way into a dining room could have doubled for a small gymnasium. Brass sconces spaced about eight feet apart emitted light in rays up to the ceiling which was decorated with elaborate wood crown molding. Heavy burgundy drapes blocked out any light that might have wanted in if it had been in the daylight hours. The long mahogany table was set for twelve, complete with bone china, crystal goblets and gold flatware. Surprising both Charles and Sam, the spots were taken with other guests who were engaged in active discussions. Sam instinctively checked his watch, but then wondered if they were late to this event. He wanted to ask Charles, but when the two latest additions to the dinner party entered, the crowd stopped their conversations and politely gave their attention to Alex.

"Friends, this is Dr. Sam Jackson and Charles Reynolds, our special guests this evening. You probably know of Mr. Reynolds, and we were just discussing Dr. Jackson's interview on the local news."

This caused Sam's eyes to jerk over towards Charles and then back to Alex. Looking at each of the guests, one by one, Sam tried to give each a nod and smile. He suffered a moment of panic when the thought crossed his mind that he might be expected to say something.

Charles gave another slight bow and said, "Good evening, everyone."

Sam managed a nod and a smile, determined not to bow. This was followed by a group greeting of "Good evening," and a couple who said "Welcome," in unison. It was not rehearsed, just nice people being, well, nice. Sam continued looking down the table, but after seeing that Charles was making his way down one side of the table greeting and shaking hands, he decided that was the socially acceptable thing to do and made his way down the other side, stopping for a short conversation or an introduction. Most of the men would rise and shake hands; the women stayed seated and simply extended a hand. Sam was beginning to enjoy the minor celebrity status. When he reached the other end, Sam's face went a bit flush. There was George Jones sitting there with that effervescent smile. Charles had moved around to the other side of the table greeting each of the dinner guests he had missed before, shaking hands and exchanging pleasantries. George stood and introduced the lady to his left. "Doctor Jackson, this is my wife, Esther." "Professor Jackson, good to see you! Excellent interview on TV." Sam smiled weakly "Thanks, I have not seen it yet."

Sam wanted to blurt out, *don't you mean, good to see you again or what a coincidence that we just dinner, or I sure pulled a fast one on you, ha ha.* But he did not say it. He did not say anything of the kind. No, he would just play along with this guy. Sam was trying not to show the irritation, he thought to himself, *let him pretend that this was all just a co-winky-dink. I got paid and paid well. I don't care if this, this, this..., nut thinks he is pulling a fast one or not.*

"Yes, George, good to see you and nice to meet you, Ms...., I'm sorry I did not catch your last name."

"Just call me Esther, you are among friends here."

Sam smiled acknowledging the lady's courtesy. He realized that he had done it again, a slight bow.

When the dinner, four courses in all, was finished, many of the guests engaged in more conversation as the party moved to a side parlor. Graced by volumes of vases of fresh flowers, the décor was something out of the French Rivera rather that the South. The drapes were drawn by a servant and the wall length glass doors had been retracted, allowing the night air to fill the room. Some of the guests sat on wicker furniture padded by thick floral pillows, while others leaned against a patio rail just outside, which overlooked a small courtyard and gave a slim view of the front circular drive. Light laughter could occasionally be heard following an animated story. Everyone seemed to thoroughly enjoy themselves, but obviously it was not going to be a late evening as some of the guests were already bidding good night to the hosts. Sam was determined to get back over to George and Esther, but was constantly engaged in one conversation after another, with each guest seeming to queue up, each time the other finished. Finally, he extricated himself, but George and Esther were telling the hosts good night. George said a quick "Good night, everybody!" to the group. The group responded in a staggered procession of "Good night!" Esther gave a smile and brief wave before the two exited. Through the patio door, Sam caught a glimpse of a dark Mercedes automobile which had been pulled around by Foster. After passing the keys to George, the old man spryly moved around to open the door for the lady.

Sam wasn't sure what to feel, but he definitely felt like he had been duped. His anger and frustration had subsided and now Sam was intrigued by the reach of this man. George had not insulted Sam's intelligence by pretending this meeting was a coincidence. It was like their meeting had never taken place. He had gotten what he wanted and did not seem in the least bit embarrassed about his methods. Nor did he seem to be self-satisfied. He was the same amiable man that he had dinner with just a couple weeks ago in Houston. He had so clearly outfoxed Sam but did not seem at all interested in pointing it out.

Throughout the evening, other guests dominated Charles' time, while Alex returned to Sam with another litany of inquiries which spanned economics, the government, history, and international relations. Sam and Charles had enjoyed an award worthy meal and been shown remarkable hospitality before the evening drew to a close. Cordial goodbyes and thanks were expressed. Sam followed Charles out to the Jag, which presumably Foster had returned along the circular drive, contemplating the night, the intrigue, the people and the extraordinary day.

Walking out to Charles' car, Sam asked, "Were we late?"

Chapter 17   **Miami. Florida**   **Saturday**

Driving back to Charles' home, Sam asked, "Chars, who were all those people?"

"Friends of Alex Stephens I presume."

"Oh, come on now," Sam said not to be denied.

"Well Sam, I don't know about everyone in the group, but in general you were dining with at least four of the wealthiest men in the United States. When that type of power gets together, I think someone is supposed to advise the Securities and Exchange Commission."

"So, it was just a dinner with friends?" Sam asked incredulously. "Wait, did you know it was going to be a dinner party?"

"It could have been just a dinner party. The rich and famous do have dinner with each other."

"Tell me about it, servants and the whole bit. Okay, so tell me, who did I just have dinner with?" asked Sam.

"Well, of course, the hosts were Alex and Margaret Stephens."

Shaking his head in frustration at Charles' apparent evasiveness, Sam asked, "Who else did you know?"

"Some I was not sure of, and some just went with first names. If you remember the man sitting next to Stephens and directly across from you, I think he introduced himself as Casey."

"Yeah, I remember him. He did not say much, and he may have been the only one without a date," Sam said.

"If memory serves me correct, I think he is Casey Friends. I think he is a hotel guy. He is probably worth about a billion or so. Wilbert Crenshaw may be from Texas or Oklahoma, but he brought his oil money to the Orlando area, buying up real estate. He is probably worth about a billion. The older gentleman with the suspenders was Howard Wallace. He goes by a nickname that I can't remember, but I know him because he is a big hitter with the Miami athletic department," Charles recalled.

Sam asked, "Who was the guy on the far corner? He introduced himself as George and his wife was Esther."

"He was one of the ones that I did not know."

"Great!"

"Why? Did you know him?"

Sam turned in his seat and gave that abbreviated touchdown signal that communicated that what he was about to say was important or if he had taken all he was going to and he was laying down the law. Charles got a kick at how easily Sam was thrown off stride. A little comment there or a little comment here could cause real panic in Sam. And now something was obviously up, as evidenced by the touchdown signal.

Speaking quickly and with his volume escalating, "I met with him back in Houston."

Charles gave a surprised look before returning his vision to the road. "Really?" He glanced over checking to see how serious Sam was being. Without a doubt, Sam was 100% serious.

"He called me after a speech in San Antonio. It was the weirdest thing. I started getting calls from people I had never heard of before." His voice dropped an octave and he said, mysteriously, "Real cryptic calls." His hands had come to rest at his side.

"You're kidding!" Charles was really becoming intrigued with this mystery and wondered if there was not a story somewhere in there. Still, he could not help but pulling Sam's chain a little more by acting nonplussed. "Got it, cryptic."

Sam continued with a left chop to make his point, "First it was some guy called Dr. De Zavala and then some other guy." He added a tarantula hand to the car's dash to emphasize his point. That was accomplished by stiffening all his fingers, taking the form of a tarantula and jabbing on the dash of the car, emphasizing each point. "Then there is this, George Jones. We ate dinner and he offered to set me up on a nationwide speaking tour."

Chars put a hand up, signaling for Sam to take it easy, "And he picked you because…?"

Realizing that his hands were chopping up and down as he was telling his story, he self-consciously retracted his hands and returned to the front forward position. Sam said, "He said that my speech in San Antonio had caught the attention of several of his friends."

Charles gave a laugh and said, "What was your speech on?"

Frustrated, Sam said, "Economics."

Charles looked over distracted momentarily from his driving. "Economics?" Chars' eyebrows raised and then scrunched into a pained furrow.

"Yes! I know, I know!" Sam gave a pleading look.

"And this guy said that your economics lecture was so riveting that he wanted you to go around the country enlightening the world?" Charles said incredulously.

"Well, the part that he was interested in was the part about the government getting too big and was creating the problems that it now was trying to correct."

"What else?" Chars asked figuring that Sam must be leaving something out.

"Well, Dr. De Zavala mentioned the part about defense contracts being reduced, and the fact that states were getting less money from the federal government than they were paying in."

"And you accepted?"

"No! I told him no!"

"And yet you are here, and your George Jones is here?"

Speaking quickly, Sam said, "I received an unrelated call; at least at the time I thought it was unrelated. I was supposed to be a last-minute substitution for the conference."

"That's convenient."

"I did not know that George had anything to do with it."

"Do you get lots of these invitations?" Charles asked with a little smile.

Sam gave a frustrated sigh.

"Yeah, I suppose I should have been susp...," Sam started but did not immediately finish. He frowned and then when he realized what had obviously happened his shoulders drooped. Sam and Charles traveled in silence back to Charles' house, each lost in his own thoughts.

Charles pulled into his driveway and clicked a button on his visor. A mass of spotlights blazed to life, illuminating his driveway and a beautiful front lawn.

Raising a hand that eclipsed the flood of light, Sam said, "Good Lord, are you expecting a 727 to land?"

Laughing heartily, Charles said, "Believe it or not old boy, Chars Reynolds is not on everybody's favorite reporters list."

"Those are your security lights? You're joking, right?"

"Afraid not. If you go knocking around rocks, there are always going to be some critters that are going to be disturbed."

He put the car in park and reached across to the glove box and removed a holstered Beretta Bobcat.

Sam hands raised and gave an astonished look. "You are serious! You carry a handgun?"

Charles countered, "You have concealed handgun laws in Texas."

"Yeah, but I don't know anybody that actually has one."

"You might, concealed means that you can't see it."

Sam checked his side view mirror.

"Sam, it is just a precaution. You are safe to get out."

Not entirely convinced, Sam took another look over his shoulder before opening the door and used the pull straps to extricate himself from the Jag. Charles stood up out of the car and started to stretch. "Get back in the car!" Charles yelled to Sam.

Sam looked over the top of the car but could not see Charles' face because of the blinding spotlights which sprayed from the corners of the house. He thought Charles may be joking with him, but a silenced pop-pop sound from the front porch area was instantly followed by the metallic ping of a bullet hitting the roof of the coupe confirmed that Charles was serious.

"Get in and get down!" Charles growled while ducking back into the car.

The back driver's side window of his Jaguar shattered as another shot was fired in their direction, the cartridge casing plinking on the front deck until it found a place to rest. Another incoming shot and glass shards from the rear-view mirror showered the inside of the car. Charles fumbled to get his weapon out of the holster and flipped off the safety while taking cover behind the front seat. Charles narrowly avoided another shot that blew out his door window. Lights from the nearby houses were turning on and indeterminable voices could be heard, along with a set of receding footfalls on the pavement. Cautiously rising up, Charles used the seat back to steady his aim, but did not shoot. Sam felt a burning sensation is his neck and when he touched the pain with his fingers, he winced. A voice down the street could be heard yelling, "Hey, what are you doing!" The only answer was the sound of an accelerating automobile and a slight squeal of rubber on asphalt.

Realizing they were no longer under attack, Charles deadpanned, "I guess someone did not like your speech."

Chapter 18   **Miami, Florida**   **Saturday**

Lieutenant Jerry Collins of the Miami-Dade Police Department, sat at Charles' kitchen table having completed a conversation with the investigating officers that were called to the scene. Collins had long succumbed to the battle of the bulge. His tummy lapped over a belt which sported a police badge competing for the light of day. His wiry brown hair was the only thin part of the career officer. Both elbows on the table, he was writing in a pocket size notebook. The investigating officers had gone outside to collect evidence, leaving the veteran officer with Sam and Charles. Jerry, a longtime friend of Charles, immediately responded when Charles called. Their friendship began almost a dozen years ago when two had been involved in a high-profile case in which Charles had showed metal that Jerry felt was uncommon in most reporters. The two had become solid friends and even shared family events. It was truly an uncommon friendship almost unheard of between a cop and a reporter. Charles counted Jerry as one of his most trustworthy friends and the feeling was mutual. The fact that Charles was again embroiled in a scrape was just a normal occurrence that Jerry had long ago accepted as part of the relationship. Now he was again sitting in Charles kitchen wondering what had precipitated this latest encounter.

Sam was sitting in the living room with a cold compress over a gauze bandage pressed against his neck. Still in the grasp of Sam's unsteady hand, an ice cold, half empty Sam Adams beer rested on a tile coaster. Jerry gave Sam an appraising look then looked over at Charles. Charles raised his hands in the air which was his signal that he had no idea of who the assailants were or why they had risked such a risky attack.

In his gravelly voice, strained by years of smoking, Jerry said, "So you two boys go to out to dinner; and return home; and without any provocation, some guy starts letting bullets fly?" He looked back and forth between the two men. Sam just stared at the lieutenant not knowing what to say. Charles just shook his head and gave a smile that caused Sam to doubt his friend's sanity.

"Okay, Sam you're a college professor in town to deliver a speech on what?"

"Economics," Sam managed to croak out.

130

Jerry gave a little laugh and joked, "Economics? I would probably take a shot at you as well if I had to listen to that."

The remark drew a small smile from Charles, but not Sam. Sam was used to the degrading remarks about his choice of careers, but the shooting had severely dampened his sense of humor. He took a deep breath and exhaled slowly.

"So, we can assume that they were after you Chars."

"Hey, what are you saying there Boudreaux?" Charles asked, pretending to be offended.

Sam flashed Charles a disbelieving look.

Seeing Sam's reaction Charles said, "Hey Sam, I am sorry that you got mixed up in this. It is just that..."

Jerry finished Charles' sentence with his usual gravelly voice that might have been a cross between Lee Marvin and Fled Flintstone, "you get used to being shot at, when it happens on a regular basis."

Sam had decided that Jerry definitely looked like a Fred Flintstone, with the only thing missing might have been the caveman's leotard.

Jerry was enjoying this and continued, "You see, your friend here is constantly sticking his nose in the business of real pearls of humanity. Plus, I would say that there is not a politician or bureaucrat that would have liked to have been pulling the trigger tonight. If the great Charles Reynolds, investigative reporter extraordinaire, had been the victim of the shooting, a celebration would have spilled out into the streets like the Miami Heat had won another championship."

"I take that as a compliment," Charles responded.

"I am sure you do," rejoined Jerry.

Sam just gave the two of them a slightly hostile scowl.

In a Jack Nicholson impression, Charles said, "Hey if you are going to make an omelet, you're going to have to break a few eggs."

Sam lifted his beer and said irritably, "My eggs are very important to me."

Both Jerry and Charles cracked up. Charles said with a laugh, "I told you I was sorry."

Sam's nerves were shot and with narrowed eyes he just cocked his head to the side which asked, seriously? He took a long drink of his beer.

"So, Charles, what are you working on that has you on the menu?" asked Jerry redirecting the conversation back to the matter at hand.

"Oh, I don't know. Could it be that I undressed the President's press secretary on national television?"

"Well, that could make a lady mad, but would she come all the way to Miami? Was she wearing anything underneath?"

Charles let out a chuckle. The Press Secretary is a man, you Gumba. His name is Harlan Ford."

"Actually, Melanie said she saw you on television." Melanie was Jerry's wife of twenty-three years and Charles had become one of her favorites of Jerry's friends.

"She did!" Charles stood looking pleased and went to the refrigerator to retrieve a cold beer. He grabbed three. He replaced Sam's now empty beer with a fresh one and then stabled another on the table next to Jerry.

Jerry gave an appreciative smile but moved it to the other side of the table. Nodding at the beer, he said, "Let's give the officers a chance to call it a night."

Right on cue, the door opened, and the two officers entered. Victor Ines, the more experienced of the two officers, said, "Lieutenant, from what witnesses tell us and what we have collected, the assailant used a silenced nine-millimeter. Three casings were found on the porch. There may be more in the bushes or grass, but we would have to look in daylight. If the fall pattern is what we think, he was moving left to right and then exited to a waiting car up the street on the far side of the house."

"Chars did you notice any cars parked on the street when you pulled up?" asked Jerry.

"Not really. No one is allowed to park on the street so I would have probably noticed."

"That means that they could have followed you from the restaurant," the second officer, Teddy Bishop interjected.

Sam looked up from his beer at Charles. Sam realized that Charles had evidently left out dinner with the Stephens when he gave his account of the night's events to the officers.

Charles said, "I was not paying attention, but I think they were already here when we got here. Or they may have been waiting. Did you notice a car parked on the street Sam?"

Sam gave a slight nod, no.

"What makes you think they were already here?" Jerry asked.

"They must have been inside when we arrived, or I would have seen them on the front porch."

Looking to one of the officers, Jerry asked, "Was the front door broken into?"

Ines walked over and looked. "Does not look like it. What about the back door?"

Charles walked to the rear of the kitchen to look. He stopped at the door leading to the driveway and said, "The rear entry door is fine." He continued over to the patio door, and called out over his shoulder, "but it looks like the patio door may have been jimmied open."

Jerry asked Charles, who was returning to the room, "We'll dust it for prints, but I imagine they were not that careless. Is there a way to get to the patio without going down the driveway?"

Charles gave a thoughtful look. "Yeah, I guess they could have come up on the other side and jumped the fence."

Jerry looked at the second officer, a large darkly complexioned man. "Bishop, check the far side of the house, the opposite side of the runway lights for some footprints."

Bishop gave an almost imperceptible nod and exited the front door.

"So, said Jerry, maybe they broke into the house and you guys pulled up interrupting their plans."

Sam said, "But the runway lights go on and scared them out the front door."

Jerry harrumphed. After a moment of thought, Jerry asked, "Chars, did you get a look at the shooter?"

Charles laughed. "No, not really, those lights are really bright."

Sam just rolled his eyes.

Ines interjected, "Your neighbor was out after the shooting and gave us a good description of the shooter."

Charles looked amused, "Let me guess, Ms. Wendell?

Ines said, "Yes, Ms. Wendell. What is she, like the neighborhood crime watch?"

With his head shaking, Charles said despondently, "Ms. Wendell. She will give me hell about this."

Jerry started laughing having encountered Ms. Wendell several times on his previous visits to Charles' house. "What did she say?"

"She said that the damn flood lights should be outlawed. Every time Mr. Reynolds pulls into his driveway, his floodlights light up her bedroom window like Joe Robbie stadium. She wanted to know if there was a light ordinance that we could enforce."

Both Charles and Jerry were laughing, and Sam said, "See, I told you that they were bright enough to light a runway."

"Yeah, she seems to be bit irritated by my security system," Charles said.

Jerry said, "Hey that's probably why the guy could not hit you. He was blinded...," breaking into a thick laugh until he started a hacking cough.

"Are you smoking again?' Charles asked.

Getting himself under control, Jerry said, "Yeah, yeah, I stopped." Refusing to engage in a conversation about his smoking he continued, "I can just imagine this guy pops around the corner and gets hit with these blinding spotlights. He is probably seeing spots but tries to carry out the hit on Charles anyway."

Even the two officers were enjoying the possible scenario.

Ines said, "Ms. Wendell did say the shooter had his hand shielding his face."

This caused another riff of laughter from everybody except Sam, who had moved over to the sink to check his neck wound. He was tempted to blurt out, hey there was a shooting here, could we just keep the funny down to a minimum, but said nothing since he was the outsider here. This was after all, Charles' problem.

Jerry said, "Actually the guy would have been shielded from the lights and you my friend would have been lit like a deer in headlights."

"So, you think they were trying to kill me?" Charles asked.

"No, but it does not make sense why he would shoot unless he was threatened," Jerry said.

"Could not have been because Charles whipped out his pistol when he got out of the car?" Sam interjected with sarcasm.

Jerry's eyebrows raised and he just looked at Charles, waiting for a response.

"Well, Sam is right. I did have a gun in my hand when I saw movement on the porch. And with the spotlights, the shooter would have had an unobstructed view."

Bishop returned through the door holstering his flashlight in his belt. We got two sets of footprints on the side of the house. They did not have to jump the fence because there is a gate."

Charles gave a shake of his head at his forgetfulness. "Yeah, I guess there is a gate over there."

Jerry rolled his eyes. To Ines he asked, "What else did Ms. Wendell see?"

Ines said, "She said that the bright light hampered her view, but the shooter was a very white male, six foot, 205 pounds, dark hair, and dark windbreaker with white athletic shoes."

"Sounds like the light really bothered her," Charles quipped.

Ines continued, "But the car was too far away for her to see clearly."

"Even with her binoculars?" asked Charles sarcastically.

"She must have not had time to get them out, with shots flying around." Jerry said with a humorous look over at Charles.

"Hell," Charles said, "she keeps them in her apron pocket!"

Sam said, "Hey, this lady should get some kind of award, instead of being ridiculed for being an observant neighbor."

Jerry gave Charles a conspiratorial smile but adopted a stern look. "Yes, Officer Ines, you were saying?"

"She says that Mr. Reynolds comes home late quite often and has had some suspicious visitors." The officer gave a crooked smile and paused to look up from his notes. Charles waved his hand in a keep going motion.

"She told me about the last time Mr. Reynolds had a break in and how she had to help you," pointing to the lieutenant, "solve the crime."

Jerry raised his eyebrows and broke into a smile.

Looking at Jerry, Charles said, "You are really enjoying this aren't you?"

"Wait!" Sam interrupted, "Someone already tried to break into your house?"

"Well, it has been several years," Charles said defensively. "That's why I put the lights in."

"You put the lights in when the Chicago mob was after you," Jerry interjected.

"The mob!" Sam almost yelled. "Charles, what the hell are you into?"

Jerry said, "Don't forget the councilman who came after you with a leg of the kitchen table."

Charles let out an exasperated sigh.

"Okay, okay...okay. Officer, could you go on?" Jerry said.

"Yes sir. The man shot three or four times and then the two assailants ran out to a dark sedan and got into the passenger side. And she says the dark sedan was in place before Charles arrived home."

"So much for my observation skills. She is a regular Ms. Kravitz," Charles mused.

Jerry smiled recalling the old television series, Bewitched. "Okay, thanks guys. You can take off, I will finish up any questions for Mr. Reynolds," he hesitated and looked over at Sam and gave him a thin smile, "and Mr. Jackson."

Thirty minutes later, and after finishing the beer that had been offered earlier, Jerry walked out to the front porch with Charles. "You two going to be all right, or do you want a patrol to stand watch?"

Charles said with a slight smile, "No, this is getting to be old hat."

Shaking his head slowly, Jerry said, "Well, don't try to take these guys on by yourself. Who do you really think it was?"

"I have no idea. I was covering the murder of that Senator up in Washington, but that could not have followed me all the way to Miami."

136

Jerry stepped off the front porch and parted with, "Well, someone has a hard on for you."

Chapter 19   Houston, Texas Sunday

George Love was back at his residence just south of Houston in the city of Bellaire. He had flown his 1993 Citation 525 Jet from the Miami airport, stopping at Biloxi to fuel up. The trip to Miami was prefaced by a meeting of the primary players of the American Independence Group in Georgia. It was there that the remaining parts of what Charlie Rivers, a.k.a. David Elliott had coined Operation Disunited State of America was finalized. George was tasked with assessing the pulse of the southeast partition and bringing them up to speed. He felt a kinship with fellow Texan David Elliott. Love respected Elliott and appreciated the former C.I.A. Director's particular skill set. Without him, the chance of Texas independence would not have gotten off the ground. Love had wrestled with the idea for years because of his enormous sense of American pride. It took the re-election of the current president to create a fissure that could not be repaired. It was like a levy finally breaking after holding back flooding waters after a hurricane.

In Love's mind, it was now clear that there were two Americas. It was a conservative America that was clearly against this leviathan called the federal government versus a liberal America which controlled the large population areas and the electoral votes necessary to elect their candidates to national office. Love found it interesting that the liberal of old was the one that was resisting the government, while the liberal of today was more than willing to have a massive government enforce the elitist will on the rest of the country. George felt in his bones that the federal government was gearing up for the inevitable conflict by passing the National Defense Authorization Act which allowed it to capture and detain without explanation or due process. And George Love had come to a conclusion after the re-election of the current president that the federal government rush to crush the 2nd Amendment was even more evidence of the crackdown.

He still felt a sense of lament over his final decision to implement a plan which would likely lead to the end of the United States as had existed for the past 200 some years. After all, George had been the beneficiary of the most powerful country in the world, and he would survive no matter who happened to be in the White House. After years of frustration with the continuing Washington debacle, George had reluctantly concluded that the country was ultimately not going to recover from the massive fraud that the federal government was perpetrating. He would tell the other members of his confederacy that he was not leaving his country; his country had left him years ago. And as he told his compatriots, it was no longer the United States but the Disunited State of America.

In the previous 12 months, his assignment had been to organize a campaign of information designed to create a grassroots awareness of the transgressions of the federal government. Elliott had the principal role of securing support within the State of Texas. It had been a masterful stroke of enlisting several of the top-ranking officials within the state government. Love's job was a campaign to educate and motivate the masses. Operation Disunited State of America was to be an incremental plan to put Texas in a position to exit, taking advantage of a pacifist and hopefully indifferent commander in chief. However, the reaction of the President to the initial efforts had been so precipitous; the plans had to be moved up. To one of his conspirators, Elliott had lamented, "I guess the commander is not as scared of getting his hands dirty as we thought." His efforts in his native Texas had to be expanded to include other states because of the highest nail theory. If there were a whole bunch of nails sticking up, slamming down the Texas nail would not be as easy.

There was the procedural issue of whether Texas could, in fact, legally extricate itself from the United States. Since that point of order had been a no with the War Between the States, the idea was floated amongst the confederates to use the right of dividing into five states, which might be used as a chip to bargain for a complete separation. The rationale was that the thought of five new conservative states added to the mix, might be enough of a scare tactic to them to blink. The thought of adding eight U.S. senators might tip the scale far enough to the right, that a Congress, teetering back and forth from Democratic to Republican one month to the next, would cause a knee-jerk reaction. Plus, if Texas were to secede, the idea of exfoliating 32 Congressman and two Senators from a primarily conservative voting state would also figure into the equation. In the end, several of the well-connected politicos of the movement predicted that it would come down to a political survival decision. Love's little dissident group was divided as to whether the answer would be don't let the door hit you on the way out or the Lincoln response. Surely the Liberals would fear a mass exodus. And they would try everything short of war to prevent Texas from going anywhere.

Several hot spots around the country gave an indication of the possible reaction of the President. George was genuinely concerned that other groups had been forming and they were much less subtle than his efforts. The authorities would be anxious to stamp out any trouble for fear of it spreading like a California wildfire. One group in Michigan had already been raided and the members herded up and arrested for being a right-wing militia group. The FBI has swooped in like it was the Davidian compound outside of Waco, years ago. Unlike that debacle, there were survivors in Michigan, but nonetheless, George worried that more of these types of groups were going to make his plans more difficult. If the President saw the Texas movement as isolated, he might be more willing to treat it as such and acquiesce. George thought this was highly unlikely and Elliott's efforts to galvanize the top Texas officials were critical.

After all this was no small game and the word treason was not a pleasant thought to deal with, realizing the consequence of being charged and convicted could be quite extreme. His mind drifted to William Travis and Sam Houston that were the treasonous ones the last time Texas took on the establishment. Their legacies had been that of heroes, but George knew that the odds were long that many, if any, would interpret their activity as anything other than incitement to rebellion. It could be that the President would react even more deliberately if there were many other movements around the country, but that could also work in his favor if the other groups served as a distraction. In a time where countries were coagulating together, the United States would be breaking apart. The Soviet Union had broken into all its current parts because the head of the government allowed them to do so. That would not likely be the case for the current President. The U.S. was moving toward more and more government control rather than to free markets. However, the breakup of the old Soviet Union was wrought because of financial demise, and that was very nearly where the United States was at this moment. If it were not for the Chinese funding the government, the United States would surely be on the precipice of bankruptcy.

George was a student of history and knew the likely risks to life if this plan were pursued. That was why his plan had been so carefully conceived and implemented. How these other events would play for or against his efforts, he did not know. But he still felt like the time had come and it was better to act now before the public was persuaded by the President and the liberal media that this was treasonous, rather than a state rights issue. He thought of his two children and the pain that may be forced upon them, even if his plans were successful. His wife had been against it at first, but even she became very despondent after the President's nefarious re-election. She had broken down in tears, but finally agreed that the time had come.

George sat back in a blonde wood rocker that had belonged to his grandmother. He was watching the news without the sound until the media runner at the bottom of the screen mentioned a special report on domestic violence alert. He fingered the remote and the sound sprung to life.

The anchor, a mid-forties man with the ubiquitous gray suit and red tie, was saying, "After several instances of violence, the Federal authorities are expanding their efforts to close in on several groups. An official from the FBI has released a statement that they were involved in a raid of right-wing extremist group in West Texas. The raid occurred in the early morning hours in a city near Midland-Odessa."

A large Texas map was flashed on the screen with an embossed star at the approximate location. George knew exactly where the star was pointing to on the map. He pulled out a cell phone but wanted to make his call after he heard all the report.

"According to the same spokesperson, six-deaths were attributed to the siege, two of which were federal officers attempting to serve a warrant, and the ensuing altercation between what the FBI is calling a highly dangerous right wing terror group."

George mumbled a disgusted, "They are the terrorists."

The news anchor said, "I am told we have a live report now from Sandy Crafton. Sandy, are you there?"

141

George was surprised to see that Sandy was a he, instead of a she, but he supposed he had met a male Sandy or two in his life. Sandy described the reporter's hair well, which was blowing like a sheet on a clothesline. Smoke filled the background, but a church steeple could still be seen rising up from the tree line.

Sandy quickly adjusted to the camera but still looked a bit startled. *Someone missed a cue*, George thought to himself.

"Yes, this is Sandy Crafton on the scene of an FBI raid."

It must have been extremely hard to hear because Sandy was practically yelling his report. Sandy stopped for a moment as if trying to decide whether he was actually on the air. Also, evident was a camera man's shadow whose arm was giving Sandy a swirling motion to indicate that the tape was running. George recognized the noise that was causing the confusion as helicopter's main rotor. Sandy gave a glance up confirming the bird's presence. West Texas rock and sand were dusted up enough to momentarily engulf the reporter causing him to stop in mid- sentence. He was now shielding his eyes from the debris and was drawing his hand across his throat signaling the camera operator to cut the connection, which he did. George's television picture was only blank for a moment, when the anchor popped back on apologizing for the lost report.

"We'll return to this rural location in West Texas where an FBI official has confirmed that the right-wing terrorist group site was raided, in just a moment. Our on the scene reporter, Sandy Crafton has reported that there are six confirmed casualties, two of which were government agents. Of course, it is too early to give any firm numbers. We will give you more details as they become available. We have been told that this is one of a dozen these types of efforts by authorities to eliminate these types of extreme groups around the country today. We must go to break, but we will return with this developing story."

George muted the television and punched a number by memory into his satellite phone. David Elliott's raspy voice answered on the first ring, but it was almost a whisper.

"Yeah."

"David, the ranch, it was on the news," George said.

"Should have been, the news crews are what tipped us off."

George was standing looking out his back window into a green belt which backed up to his property. The comment confused him, but he knew from the sound of David's voice that this would be a quick conversation.

"Is it safe to talk?" George asked.

"We are on the move and safe for the moment. I am afraid that we lost a couple men."

"The news said, four."

It sounded as if David was walking quickly or maybe running at this point. George wondered why he would even answer the phone, but just listened. A vehicle door could be heard opening and then slamming shut.

" George, hang on, I need to talk, but give me a sec."

An engine started and roar to life. In the distant, several more engines could be heard turning over and then there was a cacophony of grinding of gears. Voices on what sounded like a radio could be heard, but George could not distinguish what they were saying, only that there were rapid conversations taking place. He could hear a final door slam and David say, "Move out, but like nothing is wrong, got it?" He followed up with, "No idle talk from here on out."

George heard grinding of gears, the loud roar of a semi-truck's engine and finally, the squeaks and banging of the truck moving onto an asphalt road.

"Okay George! We are out of there and on the road. We are moving to the secondary site but will plan another move shortly after that. Do you copy?"

"Absolutely, I copy!" Trying to keep his emotions in check, he asked. "What did they get?"

"I don't think they will get anything. The drives were wiped, and all of our supplies had been stored in the vehicles that we are now in. My only worry is that they will spot us in a helicopter."

"David, there was a helicopter in the news report, can you get off the main road?'

"Actually, we are into to some traffic right now that works nicely to hide us."

George realized that David had made it through the escape tunnel and to a couple of semi-trailer trucks camouflaged at a distant edge of an adjacent property. Each semi was appropriately labeled with a nationally known distributor of grocery products.

"Who did you say tipped you off?" George asked.

"I did get a call from our friend, but what really saved us was that somebody must have told the news stations, because they were on scene thirty minutes before the black boots got there, if you can imagine that." David's breathing had returned to normal, and his voice had begun to go back to a more confident growl. "Our video cameras picked up the news crew that was setting up to film the take down!" David's anger was gushing up through his voice. George knew that it took a tremendous amount of push to get David Elliott off his game. He was one of the most completely controlled men that George had ever met. Twenty-eight years in the CIA would do that for you, George guessed.

"We would have all made it, but the bastards sent in an incendiary device that ignited a gas heater. That explosion caused the front edge of the tunnel to collapse and caught Billy and Cliff. They were last out..., guarding the rear."

"How did the FBI agents die?"

"Got me. Only way I could think of is if they shot each other and I don't think that happened. We did not fire a single shot or set off any explosions. They would have had to have done it to themselves. We got almost got out unscathed because of the damn news crews. Rich, don't you think."

"Very rich," George agreed.

"George, I have to disappear, but I will try to make contact later."

Love said, "Okay. No one better at disappearing than a spook. Be safe my friend."

"Let's hope!" Elliott said and ended the call.

George returned his attention to the television. On the TV, a live shot of the helicopter filled the screen. George moved in closer to the screen to make sure of what he was seeing. A dozen or more black-suited men were standing at the ready, while what had to be twelve men, hands behind their heads were being led out of a wooded area.

He quickly placed another call.

"Yes," a voice answered.

Not even bothering to say hello, George said, "Are you watching?"

Solemnly Alex Stephens said, "I am."

"Are you okay?"

"Yes. I have not seen any Feds or locals here."

"Do you expect to?"

"We have gone underground just in case. How is David?"

"I spoke with him. He was able to make an exit."

"Good deal. Hey, I gotta run, we are on full alert here and I have to go! We are still on target here and will continue to move forward. Get me a message with any news. Good luck."

The phone connection ended, and George was in deep concentration trying to figure out how the attack on Brierfield would play into his plan.

Chapter 20   Miami, Florida   Sunday

The next morning Ms. Wendell was at her side fence watering some of her beautiful begonias with a gentle almost silent stream of one of those sprayers attached to a bright blue hose. The color of the hose roughly matched her shutters which adorned her white stucco house. The fence was a standard pine slat fence that extended almost all the way to the street but was at only half height from the edge of Ms. Wendell's house to the end of her yard. Along the half fence, she had planted some high-profile plants which formed a barrier wall between her place and the miscreant, called Charles Reynolds, but not high enough to obstruct her view from her elevated front porch. This was her fifteenth year in this house, and she was eager to tell anyone who would listen how her life was much better before the arrival of the newspaper reporter. Her daily ritual included carefully managing the plant life with an expert care of an expert gardener. Her work was mostly confined to the front yard, which not coincidently, allowed for an unobstructed view of the goings on in the neighborhood. Standing at only five foot tall and with her colorful hat and cotton yard dress, she blended in into the vibrant flowers to the point she could not be seen. Returning from an early morning run, Sam approached from the other direction, completely oblivious to Ms. Wendell, who was standing amongst the flowers, not more than fifteen feet away watering away.

Sam had been somewhat reluctant to stay the night with Charles, but also did not feel like a long ride back to the hotel. Paying for hotel room closer in proximity did not seem to be a good idea either. So, he convinced himself that the assassins probably were done until the cover of darkness would allow their next assault. When the sun came up, he had felt like he had slept well. This really surprised him because he never slept well the first night of travel. Maybe it was the combination of alcohol and Tylenol PM that Chars had provided. He called Stan to check on the cat and the house. Stan sounded hung over but managed to give an "all-okay and squared away, Dr. Jackson" report. With light creeping in through the blinds, he decided that he would purge the previous evening with an early morning run. It would also be a good way to check out the neighborhood to see if anyone were lurking around. He zipped his cell phone in the back of his running shorts and headed out. Two miles and twenty minutes later, he was leaning over catching his breath and wiping his brow with his shirt in the sloping edge of Charles' driveway. When there was movement in the bushes next door, Sam about jumped out of his skin. His fight or flight instinct took over and he dropped into a crouch.

"Careful there young man, I have a water hose," Ms. Wendell cackled to herself sarcastically.

Sam quickly straightened up and tried to look as nonchalant as possible, after bolting up in the air like a goosed kangaroo and then dropping into some kind of quasi judo or ninja stance. He stole a look around the street to see who else might have witnessed his end of run routine and in fact, there was a young man begrudgingly retrieving a trash can, left out from the Friday pickup. He had stopped in stride and was just staring at Sam with a puzzled look. Sam gave a slight up nod of his head to acknowledge the kid. The boy gave a smirk and dragged his trash can up his driveway. Turning around at the top of the drive, he plopped down both elbows atop the trash can to watch the latest entertainment unfolding at the Charles Reynolds house. By now, Ms. Wendell had yanked her water hose far enough to the edge of the property in complete view. Sam gave an embarrassed smile and said, "Hello."

Without a word, she thumbed off the sprayer with the precision of a police officer flipping the safety on his service weapon. The spray of water stopped just inches from the tips of Sam's Adidas. Dressed in a thin house dress, one pocket openly sagged with what appeared to Sam to be a small set of binoculars. She gave him an appraising look. Sam let out a short breath saying, "I am sorry, you startled me."

Petulantly she asked, "You are sorry that I scared you?"

Sam corrected, "Well, I am sorry I reacted so... defensively."

The old lady cocked her head and a little laugh that came out as a short, "Humph."

She dried her trigger finger on her the hip of her dress, leaving small water mark. Looking back at Sam, she asked, "Take a hit in the neck?"

Sam unconsciously moved his hand to the small bandage that covered a small gash just above the collar line of his dress shirt. He was not sure whether it was caused by a grazing bullet or a piece of flying metal trim. Sam was planning to go with the bullet theory; it sounded much more impressive. All he knew for sure was that it stung furiously and bled like a stuck pig, not that he really knew how much a stuck pig would bleed. The med tech had wanted to take him to the hospital, but he had refused after the bleeding was under control. After all, it was not like his jugular that had been hit. He had decided to throw out the shirt but hoped he could save his slacks.

The lady was speaking again, "I said, did you take hit in the neck?'

"Oh, yes, I heard you. I think it was a piece of metal or something that flew off the car."

The little lady mocked, "Flew off the car! Flew off the car, he says. Why, yes ma'am it just flew off the car." She was shaking head her back and forth. "What do you think, I am blind and deaf and dumb? I am lucky that a stray bullet did not take me to my grave."

"So, you were watching when we came home," Sam asked hoping to get some more information.

The old woman's eyes narrowed as she perceived Sam's question as a personal insult. She crinkled her nose and looked like she might take her own shot at Sam. "Your friend there, that...Charles," she said with puckered lips and a disgusted tone, "Reynolds, big newspaper reporter, attracts a bad crowd, young man. Why just a few months ago, I had to help them solve a break in. Calls himself a reporter, he was drugged up so bad the police had to bring him home, that's how bad he was." She pointed a bony finger at Sam. "And when his friend the policeman comes around, you know there is trouble. You would be well not to be shackin' up with him. Bad for your reputation, hanging out with a man like that Charles Reynolds. Humph!"

Again, moving toward Sam, she was now gesturing with the point of her sprayer to make her point. Her face reminded Sam of a feisty dog and began to take a step back. He managed, "I will keep that in mind."

"If you had a mind, you would not have come in the first place."

She had come close enough and Sam stepped back again to give himself some space. She was an ornery old cuss, thought Sam. He thought about the wicked witch of the west, or was it the east? It did not matter. He could see her riding that flying bike and saying, "I'll show you, my pretty."

Ms. Wendell's was pulled to a stop as the hose gave a reluctant tug. She continued to give Sam the stink eye and pointed her sprayer to the ground. Turning to go, she gave one final yank of the hose and she flipped on the sprayer. For a full second, the water shot out catching Sam's feet with a full burst of water.

Quickly jumping back, Sam yelled out, "Hey, hey, hey!" He tried to jump out of the spray of the water. He was unsuccessful and he felt the water soaking into his socks.

He glared at the old woman who had turned away and was pretending not to have done that on purpose, but Sam knew she had done just that. Ms. Wendell retrained her water stream on a new bed of plants, going on about "the dam runway lights," or some other such thing.

Sam assessed the mud spatter damage on his shoes. He had just bought them a couple of weeks ago and been careful not to run through water to keep them new. He inwardly cursed when he saw two big splashes of mud were settling into the white mesh of the shoes. "Damn it," he said. Sam heard a noise that seemed like it was coming from where, across the street? Turning to look Sam could see the garbage boy draped on top of an empty can and hear him laughing uncontrollably. Still looking over at Sam, he was just able to straighten up so that he was no longer supported by the garbage can. Using the bottom of his shirt to wipe away tears that were clouding his vision, he calmed himself for only an instant before going into a hysterical laugh again. Sam glared at the boy while trying to shake off the errant water from his shoes. The boy straightened and retreated toward his home yelling into the house, "Mom! Mom! You should have seen it!"

All Sam could hear were the words trailing off, "old lady Wendell..." followed by what he thought sounded like "sprayed some jerk's feet," and the sound of a slamming door.

"Your neighbor is a real prize!" Sam announced while slamming closed the door as he entered Charles' house from the side.

Before he could continue, Charles put up a finger signaling that he was in conversation on his cell phone. Sam went to the sink, pulled a couple paper towels, wetted them from the hydrant and squirted thin line of dish washing detergent. Slipping off both shoes, he began to massage the splash streaks in hopes of saving the new look of his shoes.

"I am not sure that we can get there that quick, but I know we can be there by two o'clock. Is there anything that you can tell me now, that could help?" Charles asked.

Charles listened and to his amusement noticed that Sam was cleaning his running shoes. The memory of what a clean freak Sam was in high school flashed through his mind. He had always liked Sam, but often thought that he should loosen up a bit. Sam was always the one that was worried about getting caught, always the one that tried to talk the group out of what they were doing. He was the straight A, strait-laced schoolboy. Charles was the one that thought up ways to get in trouble. A third friend was the one that always seemed to get caught, but it was Sam who was always the one trying to talk them out of doing whatever it was they were going to do. Charles was again concentrating on what the caller was saying and writing notes in a small notebook as quickly as he could.

"Yes, I am still here, just taking notes. Do you think it safe for you to be meeting us like this, shouldn't you go to the cops or the FBI?

This caught Sam's attention and he stopped cleaning. Leaning toward the table, he peaked at Charles' notebook who gave him that 'just a second' sign again. Even looking upside down, Sam could make out a name, Tyler Hansford written in Chars' messy script. Charles was never a neat writer, unlike Sam, whose mother was an elementary teacher and insisted that his cursive be perfect. Now when his students turned in papers with illegible writing, he would immediately send those to his graduate assistant for grading. He knew that Stan always graded at least half a grade harder than he did. If Charles had been one of his students, Charles' work would have been passed to Stan for sure.

"Okay but stay out of sight and I will be there at two," Charles concluded the call.

Sam opened the refrigerator and removed a carton of orange juice.

"While you were out tangling with old lady Wendell, I was getting some really interesting calls. Pour me a glass, will you?"

Sam removed a couple glasses from the cabinet. "I see the name Tyler Hansford. I think I remember his name on one of the news reports."

"Exactly right Clubbo. The man for whom everyone is looking, and I have a meeting with him. Unfortunately, he is in Virginia Beach."

"How did he get there?"

"No idea. But I have to get there by two o'clock," Charles said checking the clock on the stove."

"And you can get to Virginia Beach by two?"

"Yes, so I guess I will have to get to the airport pretty quick. What have you got on your schedule today?"

"I was going to hit the beach…," he paused, "with you. But I suppose I could find my way around without a guide."

"Ms. Wendell might be a useful tag along!" he jabbed with a huge smile.

"Smart ass. She is one cranky old…"

Charles held up a hand to interrupt, "Yeah, but she really is just lonely. And she reads my column religiously. Not a day does goes by that she doesn't make some comment about what I wrote." Charles stopped and said, "Actually she is most often telling me what I did not write." He laughed and Sam nodded that he believed that.

"She sprayed me with water!" Sam protested, leaving his mouth slightly open showing a do you believe it expression.

Charles cracked up laughing. "She has hit me a couple times with her spray. She does it on purpose. She will wait till I am close to picking up the paper or something, and she will do a quick pivot sending a spray high in the air."

Sam was shaking his head in disbelief. "Do you call her on it?"

"Nah, it is usually after I have had some friends over from the night before and she's pissed about the noise."

"Payback, huh? The old goat is something."

151

"Okay, back to the beach idea. What are you looking for: water to swim in, white sand, scantily clad ladies?"

"All the above. I mean, is there a crummy beach in Miami?"

Charles gave a devilish smile and said, "Just some more crowded than others, and of course, you have the muscle beaches. I think Haulover Beach is the ticket for you, Sam Jackson."

Charles scribbled down some quick directions and handed them to Sam.

"Looks like it is easy to get to. Chair, towel and cooler?"

"I have all that and maybe some sunscreen for those areas that don't normally get sun. Get there before noon and you will beat the crowd."

"Haulover Beach it is! Any coffee?" Sam folded the directions and placed them on the counter.

"Yeah, just finished. Help yourself. Black?" Charles asked.

"Cream and sugar."

"Sugar is here, and you will have to use the milk in the frig." Charles retrieved two cups and poured.

"You said someone else called?"

"Yeah, some guy from the Senate called to give me some additional information on Senator Summers' committee assignments. Well, at least he said he was from the Senator Summers' office."

"Wow, does that often happen? I mean someone calling you to give you a background?"

"Never."

"What's up with that?"

"I don't know, but I am going to find out. Seemed like he was fishing for information – you know, how much I already knew? I have made a couple calls to check on the number and another to a friend of mine who has an inside on Washington politics. I have had thirteen other messages from papers and television stations wanting a statement. It makes me think I was set up at the press conference."

"I remember you said something about that."

"Yeah, I was about to go into the conference, when one of my old contacts at the Washington bureau started up a conversation. Her name was Ellen Cochran. I had sort of dated her, so I thought cool, maybe she had forgiven me."

"Forgiven you...for what?"

"Long story, but she left the paper." Charles was referring to the Miami Express, which also had operations across the country and was a subsidiary of the premier Washington D.C. rag. "I think she went to work in Washington. We started talking about the Senator's death and she volunteered that his murder may have had something to do with one the Senator's committee assignments."

"It was a murder?" Sam asked with a mix of surprise and intrigue.

"Exactly, what I asked. When she said that, I was like, whoa."

"Well, that seems a bit odd, doesn't it?"

"Yeah, because the Summers' death was only being reported as a natural cause death; it was still being called a heart attack. Then she says the word murder..." Charles paused, "I mean the comment stopped me cold.

A feeling of sadness overcame Charles as he flashed back to the last time, he actually spent time with Summers. It was the opening of an art gallery in Georgetown, not more than three months ago. Since they had a common interest in the artist Norman Pale, they had struck up a conversation. Charles had met the Senator a couple times before, but this was the only time that he had had a conversation with the man. Charles remembered how complimentary the Senator was of Charles' work and how surprised he was to receive any positive comments from a politician. Sam took a seat across from Charles and ventured a sip of the steaming coffee.

Charles continued, "She confirmed the word murder, but said don't use her name. Before I could even ask her about it, Ford walks in and starts the conference. When I turned back to her, she had vanished. Fresh in my mind I just threw it out there, but wow! I don't know if you could see the reaction to the question by the Press Secretary, but it was priceless."

"I saw how the other reporters reacted; it was like a frenzy. And now the people at the Whitehouse are calling you with more information."

"Very strange, right?" It was all stuff I already knew, but still...," Charles said thoughtfully.

"Can you get hold of your friend again?" asked Sam.

"I tried, but I have only been able to leave her a message. We weren't exactly on good terms, which make the whole situation even stranger. I am thinking now that she may have been setting me up, you know as payback or something."

"How did the Hansford guy get your name?"

"From the press conference, I am guessing, but I didn't ask. He said he wanted to meet with me. I suggested that the police were his first stop…"

Sam interrupted, "You suggested that he go to the police? Wow, you have scruples!"

"Wasn't much of a risk of that actually happening, he said that they were putting pressure on him to talk and that he did not want to cooperate."

"Don't supposed he said who 'they' were?"

"They, I guess meant the FBI or Secret Service or DHS, but I don't know. He sounded like he was in a hurry or very scared."

Sam asked, "Are they trying to hang the death, or I should say murder now…" Charles shrugged. Sam continued, "of the Senator on him?"

"I don't know, but I think that would be a stretch, I mean they supposedly found him knocked out in one of the stalls. This would eliminate him as a suspect and probably an accessory as well. He sounded genuinely scared, like someone was after him."

"This can't possibly fit with the guy that tried to take you out last night?"

"How do you know they weren't after you?"

Sam almost choked on a slurp of coffee. "Me?! Hey, I am not the one going around, pissing everyone off."

"I don't know, economics always aggravated me." Charles gave a little grin, then returned to Sam's question. "I don't see how, but if it were a pro and this sort of thing would involve a pro, neither one of us would be around to witness this beautiful morning. You would not have had the pleasure of discussing the evening events with Ms. Wendell."

Sam gave a sardonic smile.

Charles gave a nonchalant shrug, "Probably unrelated, now that I think about it."

154

Charles placed two more calls. One to arrange air, hotel and rental car; and the second to another old romance at the Washington Bureau Research Office.

Chapter 21   Washington, D.C.   Sunday

In what would have been normally a quiet Sunday, there was a moderate celebratory mood around the Washington FBI office. The raids that had taken place around the country were a success despite the lost agents in West Texas. The news reports were all positive relating the take downs as preemptive strikes against right wing fanatics who were planning to take out their frustrations in violent ways. The President had taped an upbeat message for the FBI director congratulating them, which was played for all the offices around the country.

In response the raids the President had said, "We will not be intimidated by threat of these malcontents; and the FBI, Homeland Security and the ATF have successfully thwarted attacks on innocent civilians, saved lives and upheld this great democracy."

Terrence tapped his pencil on the desk, thinking about the words that Weitzman has used 'assassination plot.' He thought to himself, *could it be true? Another plot?*   Terrence flashed back two months earlier to the first attempt on modern day president in over thirty years. Terrence and his team, Clute and Maria, had been in this very conference room watching a news conference live from the Rose Garden.

"Hey look," Maria said pointing at the television. "It is the President."

When the volume had been turned up, the President could be heard saying, "We will not allow our country to be threatened by extreme elements within our country. Our constitution allows for free speech, but not when it creates an inordinate danger to its citizens. You cannot yell fire in a theater and not expect to be arrested. Those that threaten to bring this nation down are sadly mistaken if they believe that the will of the American people can be broken or will be easily swayed into believing that this great nation is so weak that they can spread lies and make threats which will result in the downfall of this great nation."

Applause and shouts were loud and boisterous from the crowd in front with placards that read "It takes a Village" and "The U.S. is ONE."

"Where is this taking place? Clute asked.

"Looks like the Rose Garden, but there are so many people packed in and with the camera angle, I am not sure," Maria said studying the panel screen closely.

Clute asked, "Do they normally allow signs and all that in the Rose Garden?"

Just at that moment, a loud, rapid-fire popping sound could be heard joined by immediate screams. More dramatic than a Bolshoi ballet, a Secret Service agent leapt in front the President, while a second tackled the President to the ground. Several other agents piled on to cover up like a football team trying to cover a fumble. The screaming only intensified as no one could identify who was responsible. A gray smoky haze rose into the air causing more panic and coughing. A cloud of what was presumably gunpowder added to the sense that something dangerous had just occurred. Attendees were crying, having watched the Secret Service agents hustle the President out the back and begin to secure the area. It was impossible to tell if the President was badly hurt and no one could be seen being arrested.

Maria had her hand over her mouth and began cry. Clute watched the events unfold in disbelief sometimes turning in circles in a despondent sort of dance. Terrence was looking through the fingers on his hand, like a small child trying to hide from a scary movie. The murky haze on the television screen made it difficult to distinguish what was going on. Since the speech was on live television, the program directors had been caught off guard and it took a few moments to recover enough to get someone composed enough to go back live on the air.

Some on-air personality unfamiliar to Terrence, Maria and Clute, flashed up in a little box on the side of the television screen. "This is Fred Thompson, from the CTTV network and you are watching live a press conference that has been interrupted by what is presumed to be an assassination attempt on the President's life. We have no confirmation of that as it happened just seconds ago. We are checking to see if the President has been hurt, but again this is unfolding as we speak. No one was seen shooting and as the smoke clears..." his hand rose to his earpiece and intense look passed over Thompson's face. He said, "I see, yes, yes, thank you. The President was unharmed by the attack. Repeat the President was not harmed! No further details are available at this time."

"What the hell!" Terrence screamed.

"Oh, thank God!" Maria mouthed wiping tears away with a tissue.

Clute sat heavily into a nearby chair letting the wind flush out of his body. He closed his eyes and let the dread leave his body. All three looked as if they had just run a marathon, red faced and exhausted. The huge quantity of fear and angst exiting out of those watching the report was now being replaced with anger.

"What the hell is going on this country?" Terrence had yelled in total disgust and frustration.

In the days which followed, blame for the attack now referred to as the Rose Garden attack was assigned to a mysterious domestic group only known to a few insiders. In reflection, it seemed to Terrence that it was this single event which had propelled the current administration toward an obsession to eradicate the internal terror networks.

It had been just a few short days since Terrence and his team had put together a strategic threat analysis using the voluminous files that Weitzman had dumped on his desk. They had singled out connections and developed several hotspots which were high-value targets. They connected several names but could offer no definitive knowledge. What Terrence's team was able to do, was to utilize a report from the Office of Domestic Preparedness entitled Automated Critical Assessment and another report entitled Assessment of Patriotic Protestors. Concurring with previous FBI intelligence, Terrence and his team provided a final intelligence report which characterized the people involved as well placed and capable of a major destructive operation.

Earlier this morning Terrence had been told that it was his team's report which allowed the go ahead for the operation that had just occurred. Terrence and his team were back in the conference room, going over the latest intelligence gathered from the various raids and the enormous quantity of leads from the public that had poured in following the publicity of the takedowns. The majority of the circles for attacks had been in the middle states, but the next greatest concentration of markings was in southeastern states of Florida, Georgia and South Carolina. Pictures of three men were laid neatly along the side of Terrence's desk, but were of such poor quality, offered little help.

Once again, Terrence absently began moving a Morgan silver dollar between his fingers while reviewing the latest status report. In all, over a dozen militants had been killed, and fifteen were taken into custody, but regretfully two agents had been killed according to the reports.

In the corner, Clute was watching the news reports covering the operations which were being aired by all the major networks. The reporting was favorable apart from the Fox network who interviewed an equal number of people who said the federal government was to blame for these groups rising to stop a government, which was increasingly oppressive and overstepping its boundaries.

Maria came into the room and said, "Still watching the news?"

"Yeah, mostly positive," Terrence concluded.

Terrence looked up from the reports covering his desk and said, "You know that we really did not catch any big fish. The people captured were small-timers. The raid of Texas Militia group evidently missed the leader. Our intel said that they were well organized and probably were tipped off somehow."

"Really? Where could they have gone?" asked Maria.

Terrence said, "Satellite photos showed that two semi-trailers pulled out of nowhere just after the assault. Almost a half mile away, but there are several that believe that is how we missed the ringleader."

"Seriously, semi-trailers?" Clute asked skeptically.

"That is what I am told. They were far enough away that the helicopters did not identify their movement. There was no reason for the trucks to be out there in the middle of nowhere and they could have easily made it to the highway and blended in with traffic."

"What did the captives have to say?"

"The FBI would not release any information obtained from the prisoners, but I received a report back channel, that the captives were peripheral members. The information they did have was superficial at best. Seems like they either just arrived or were so far out of the decision-making process that they did not know anything."

"Maybe they were that good." Maria suggested.

"My contact said they were blabbering like a broken gumball machine, but all that was coming out was useless drivel."

Clute said, "Charlie Rivers or George Jones?"

Terrence said with a slight shake of his head, "No such luck."

Chapter 22   Miami, Florida Sunday

Sam had decided to hit the beach, in an effort to remedy his pale skin. He packed a cooler filled with a six pack of beer and a couple bottles of water, compliments of Charles' refrigerator. He decided to check the weather and flipped on the television.

Of course, the station was tuned to CNN, because that was what Charles would usually be watching. The news report was being presented with a divided screen of various talking heads. He almost switched it to the Weather Channel, but something caught his attention. They were discussing the death of Senator Summers, so he turned up the volume.

A field reporter was speaking, "That's correct Tom."

Tom Brandon was the host of the CNN news report. A white-haired man was giving a play-by-play recounting of the current investigation by the FBI.

With pictures of some condominium, which Sam assumed was that of the Hansford kid, the reporter continued, "Sources say that Tyler Hansford, a witness to the Senator's murder has disappeared."

Sam knew that they were, in fact, talking about Senator Summers of Virginia. He continued to listen in.

"Authorities have now listed Hansford as a person of interest and placed a BOLO report on the son of the Senator Hansford." Sam read along the bottom of the screen

"BOLO being a 'Be on the Lookout,' correct?" asked Brandon.

"That is correct, Tom."

Aloud, Sam asked derisively, "You have to ask that question? I even know what a BOLO is."

"And has the Senator made a comment on this?" Tom Brandon asked.

"By all reports, the Senator has dismissed all of the speculation as an overreaction and insists that the young Hansford had nothing to do with Senator Summers' death. Other than that answer, we have only received no comment."

The camera returned full screen to Brandon. "Of course, we will be following up with this breaking story and will update you as we have more to report. For now, Tyler Hansford is simply wanted for questioning."

161

A picture of what might have been a college yearbook picture of the perfect All-American boy flashed on the screen. Tyler Hansford had light to medium brown hair, cut short. His perfect complexion and teeth were replaced on the screen, with video of the emergency technicians placing a battered Tyler, head wrapped, and leg bandaged, onto a gurney following the murder of Senator Summers. Brandon was still yammering on, but Sam was concentrating on the video. He wondered; how could anyone think that he could have killed the Senator when he was that beat up? There was no way that kid had anything to do with it. Sam wondered how Charles' meeting would go with Tyler. He was feeling sorry for the young man when the news report changed stories and brought his conscious mind back to the television.

Brandon was still droning, but this time segueing into a new story. "In the other major story of the day, reporting on the attack on the President, Perry Salvatore is on the White House lawn."

Perry, a stocky man with an awful comb over and ruddy complexion, wore an ill-fitting suit with a bolo tie. "Yes, Tom. We are here at the White House where we have received the latest report that raids on the extremists' groups across the U.S. may have a connection with an unsuccessful attack on the President in the Rose Garden a couple months back."

"Perry, does the FBI have the suspects in custody?"

"They are not saying, Tom. But it is assumed that agents are working furiously, in conjunction with the other agencies, to ferret out everyone that may have been responsible. The President is scheduled to address the nation in a press conference within the hour. This is certainly perceived as good news and it is believed that he will initiate some broad steps to a broader crackdown on the dissident groups. What those actions will be, we will have to wait. It is this type of sweeping reform that the President's opponents have been warning against, but it seems with the recent events that the President has a mandate to pursue all options in clamping down on this uprising. Meanwhile, Democrats are calling for the immediate support of a crackdown by the Republican Party. Perry Salvatore, reporting at the White House."

"This is obviously a major news story, and we will be returning for an additional report. Thank you, Perry. We are up

162

against a hard break, but we will return after messages from our sponsors."

Sam skipped the weather report and decided to take his chances. He gave a look outside and the sky was clear enough for him. Earlier, Charles' Jaguar had been driven away by a local dealership employee. It had been scheduled for repair of the window and would remain out of service for a couple of days. Not wanting to infringe on Sam's trip to the beach, Charles had left the keys to a second vehicle parked in the garage. Earlier, with the sun barely visible, a Lincoln Towne Car picked up Charles for the trip to the airport, at the Miami Express' expense of course.

Having gathered all his equipment, Sam ventured out to see what his transportation would be. Sam reached down to lift on the handle of the garage door. The handle was the old fashion type that you had to raise by hand, the door springs groaned before finally lending assistance to the weight of the door. Sam made a note to recommend an automatic opener, but once the door was fully open, changed his mental note. There was already a garage door opener, just apparently one which did not work. Sam figured it had broken and Charles had never bothered to get it fixed. Through the dust particles meandering in the daylight, Sam was surprised to see an almost identical version of the first Jaguar, only a few years older, sitting in the dark recess of the garage. However, it was a convertible, and the top was already down. It was an excellent feature, unless of course, it started to rain. Sam thought about going back inside to check the forecast, but hadn't it been Charles that said he needed to wing it sometimes? Before getting into the car, Sam looked at his clearance on both sides and realized that it was tight, but there was still adequate room if he was careful. He took a gander at the driveway and decided that also, would not be a problem.

Across the street, the same teenage boy who had thought Ms. Wendell's water trick was such a hoot was raking leaves. Spying the boy busily at work, Sam thought about how he might make the little guy's life a little less funny. Justice would be served if someday the boy turned up as a student in his college class. Sam would be more than happy to "accidently" lose his paper. "Oh sorry, Mr. Think Soggy

Running Shoes was so Funny, I think you must have forgotten to turn in your paper." That would show the little prick.

After a successful starting of the engine, Sam pushed in the clutch. He gently geared into reverse without even a grind, this was going quite well. It had been many years since he had driven a manual. He gave it a little gas and the motor gave a healthy growl. Looking in the rearview mirror, he could see the kid had stopped raking and was looking his way. Letting off the clutch and other than the car dying, nothing happened. Sam had to think a moment, but eventually realized that the parking brake was preventing the car from moving. Finding the brake release, he started the car and again eased off the clutch but did not give the car enough gas and after a slight lurch backwards, the Jag died again. He checked the rear-view mirror and yes, he had the boy's full attention. Sam started the car again. This time he gave the car too much gas, let off the clutch and unintentionally gunned the car out of the garage so fast, a loud screeching of tires could have possibly been heard in an adjoining county. When the car's momentum had run out, in conjunction with Sam slamming on the brakes, the Jaguar lurched backward twice and died. A light breeze distributed a smell of burnt rubber and a light smoky haze over Sam's head.

"Good Lord, what is all the racket over there?" Ms. Wendell said from the elevated front porch, with a glare that reminded Sam of a snorting Brahma bull one might see at the rodeo. She even seemed to have a hump. Sam ignored her and rose up enough to see two long patches of rubber exiting out of the garage and disappearing from his vision under the car. What he could not ignore was a loud cackle from across the street. Refusing to turn around, Sam looked in his rear-view mirror and saw the boy was rolling on the ground with arms wrapped around his sides, presumably to keep his guts from busting out.

Refusing to even acknowledge these pests, Sam started the car again, backed out of the driveway smoothly and into the street with no problem. His maneuver was greeted by a blaring horn of someone that was traveling right at him. The huge SUV was able to swerve at the last second to avoid clipping the Jaguar. The woman did not stop, but did have time to give Sam, the finger out the driver's side window. The boy, still laughing, was now kicking the ground with the back of his heels, trying his best not to pass out. Looking straight ahead, refusing to be made the continual butt of jokes, he successfully let off the clutch, accelerating smoothly and under control. As he pulled away, he called over the top of the driver side window, "Good to see you so cheerful, Ms. Wendell," and gave her a little "la te da" wave, before moving down the street. Ms. Wendell responded with a gesture that would be used to swat away a nasty fly. What Sam wanted to do was to back over the little brat and flip the lady the bird, but he just drove away looking straight ahead.

Headed out to the beach, Sam made his way along I-95 to the beach that Charles had recommended. Haulover Beach was located off the Lehman Causeway and after such a harrowing start, Sam was pleased to find the going easy. He saw a sign which announced North Beach Parking and parked in the lot along with a good number of other cars. He gathered up his beach chair, towel and his small cooler. The beach did not appear to be crowded, in fact, Sam realized that it was entirely deserted. Sam looked back at the cars in the lot and then at his watch. He deduced the beach crowd did not normally arrive until after 12:00, but that still not account for the people who belonged with all those cars? It was a mystery that Sam would have to work out. He looked up at the sky and it did appear partly cloudy with the sun darting in between some grayish clouds. Sam cursed himself for not checking the weather report. It would be just his luck that a rainstorm would move in and him in the Jaguar, top down. Sam now guessed that was why there was not anyone around, or maybe there was a pavilion somewhere down the beach. The few people that he saw were shoulder deep out in the water, and he wondered if the water was warm. Further down in the surf, an older couple floated in tire tubes, feet sticking out and while holding hands. The entrance was almost thirty yards away, but Sam spotted a crossing in some hedges and decided to make use of the shortcut. Hopping through, Sam walked out on the beautiful sandy beach, plunked his equipment down and gave a gratifying stretch. No sense in agonizing about where because the beach was completely uninhabited.

Far down the beach, Sam could see some other big umbrellas, but really could not clearly see the people in the shadows. He did hear a faint sound of music riding in on an occasional wind, but the sound was indistinct. Sam thought surely that was where the scantily clad girls were that Charles had promised. Maybe in a little bit he would have to go check out his fellow sun worshippers. He spread out his towel on the folding chair just a dozen or so feet from the surf and settled in comfortably. Reaching for a beer, the chair was a little flimsy and he almost turned it overreaching the cooler. He readjusted his weight, placed a foot in the sand for support so as not to topple over into the sand, and was able to reach his cooler. Gratis from the refrigerator of the famous Charles Reynolds, Sam popped open one of the cans of Mickey's Fine Malt Liquor, figuring, why not, it was noon somewhere! The beer was cold and tasted good; different but good.

Sam squinted at the label. "I guess a little buzz would be nice," he said and now drank with some purpose. The warm breeze, the alcohol, and an emerging sun provided just the right combination for a second Mickey's. Enjoying "The Present" as doctor and world-famous author Spencer Johnson suggested, Sam toasted his green 16 ounce can to Dr. Johnson. This is exactly what the doctor ordered. As the ocean waters lapped soothingly, he soon drifted off into a restful sleep.

Chapter 23   Virginia Beach, Virginia Sunday

At Rudee's, Charles had waited almost twenty minutes, for the Hansford boy to arrive. On an inlet, less than a half mile inside Atlantic Boulevard sat the popular eatery, since 1983. Originally, Rudee's was designed to be a bait shop, but this only added to the rustic flair. With indoor and outdoor seating looking out onto Rudy's Inlet just a short distance from the Atlantic Ocean, it was one of the more popular Virginia Beach restaurants, featuring sea food and more of the standard American fare, such as sandwiches and libations.

Charles had flown from Miami to Norfolk on an early flight connecting through Atlanta. The early departure could not be avoided because Charles wanted to have plenty of slack time to arrive for his 2:00-o'clock meeting with Tyler Hansford. Charles had not checked any baggage, so he made it through security in record time. After grabbing some breakfast at the airport, he had rented a car for a short 18-mile drive to Virginia Beach. Upon arrival at Rudee's, Charles ordered a drink at the bar from a young man in his early twenties. His airline trip had been an uneventful jaunt, but a drink was just what he needed. His rented Ford Fusion had delivered him nicely to this lovely setting next to the inlet of water.

The bartender informed Charles that he was going off the clock but would start a tab. Charles tipped him a five and headed to a seat looking out on the dock. He was dressed in a lightweight navy-blue pullover sweater, on top of a white t-shirt and jeans. He had decided to leave his sport jacket in the car because the glorious sun had come out and it was a Chamber of Commerce Day in Virginia Beach. Charles was still young enough looking to fit the young and hip crowd but could no longer expect to be confused for a college student. His Key Lime Martini was delivered by the bartender and Charles relaxed long enough to take in his surroundings. Through the windows and large garage style sliding doors, beautiful yachts and sailboats were lined up along the docks, Charles figured that each one would easily cost a half million dollars. He liked the idea of owning a boat, but not necessarily taking care of one. His previous experience with boats in his last big case was still fresh on his mind, and the thought of being held captive on the open sea by terrorists, not to mention being blown off the back of the boat, sent a little zinger down his back. He did take a moment to relive his success of thwarting a terrorist attack and breaking the story.

Charles was waiting comfortably, but within a brief period of time he was wondering if Tyler had stood him up. Using his hand to swipe his windblown hair back in place, Charles used the back bar mirror to check out the other patrons just in case Tyler had come in without him noticing. But the late lunch crowd had dwindled to just two and their age ruled out any chance of them being Tyler. Deciding to assume a different position, Charles moved out into the Cabana covered with colorful green canvas. Taking a seat at a pub style table, he felt his stomach rumble, so he grabbed up a menu. Charles had not eaten on the plane, unless he counted the salted nuts and he had passed on the second half of a breakfast burrito that was clearly a product of a microwave oven. He was hungry and he wanted to give the second martini that he was about to order, some padding inside his stomach. It would not be good form to be smashed if the Hansford kid did show. Looking for a waiter, Charles looked back into the window of the restaurant which was fashioned as a replica of a Coast Guard station. A snapping red Rudee's flag which was announcing that a stiff breeze was blowing in from the east distracted Charles for a moment. Scanning the area, Charles did not see anyone that even came close to looking like Tyler Hansford. In fact, there were not a lot of people around at all. Other than some people working on the docked boats and a couple hand in hand walking, Charles was surprised at the lack of activity on such a beautiful day. Charles figured that the 2:00 o'clock hour may be a period of respite from the usual bustle.

The fact that Charles could not see Tyler did not mean that Tyler could not see Charles. In fact, Tyler had an excellent view of the reporter from inside a boat, docked along the inlet. About twenty minutes ago, with a pair of binoculars, Tyler had a perfect view of the canopied entrance of Rudee's and watched Charles arrive. Tyler was careful to survey the surrounding areas, the entrance, the front patio, as well as the front parking area. Keeping a watchful eye on Charles, Tyler almost panicked when it appeared that Charles was going to leave. Tyler was packing up and getting ready to head Charles off when Tyler saw Charles had simply moved outside the bar, taking up residence at a high profiled bar table on the patio.

Tyler settled back into his watch. He felt a rivulet of sweat making his way down the center of his back. It had to be nervous perspiration because the air conditioner of the trawler had cooled the room quite nicely. The bandage around his head covered a significant gash, which had been cleanly stitched. He grimaced as he removed the bandage and topped his head with a baseball cap. His ribs had been tightly wrapped and he had successfully killed the ache with some Darvon he located in the medicine cabinet aboard the boat. He briefly considered the expiration date of 2010, but decided it was probably okay. His ankle pain, however, would not relent from its throbbing ache, even though it had been splinted with an Air Cast. He adjusted his rib wrap and tested out his ankle without the brace. The ankle was swollen, but he could walk without too noticeable of a limp. He decided to leave the brace on and used his pant leg to hide the splint. But something in the splint was sticking his leg as he walked, so he returned to the bedroom, removed the brace and discarded it on the floor next to his head wrap. He looked at himself in the mirror, adjusted his ball cap and gathered his courage. He was ready to meet Charles Reynolds.

After his move from the bar area, Charles was approached by a nicely proportioned waitress. She placed a small water glass on the table which was dressed with a wedge of lime. Leaning over to retrieve his empty, just enough to give him appealing shot of cleavage.

Charles caught a faint whiff of a lovely perfume. He thought he recognized the brand as Giorgio Beverly Hills. Charles felt the young woman's breast brush up against his sleeve. Or at least he believed he did. Charles thought it was probably just wishful thinking, but she did appear like she was flirting a bit. Probably, she was just working for a nice tip. Charles could live with that. Charles thoughts returned to his stomach. Charles ordered a cup of She-Crab soup and an order of crab bites. She asked, "Do you want another Martini?"

"What else do you have?" he asked

"You could try our special drink called the Rudee's Ruckus."

"Sounds great. You wouldn't be trying to get me drunk, would you?" Charles gave a boyish grin.

"Of course not, but if you do," she paused, "my shift ends at 3:00. My name is Carly. If there is something else you need."

Charles for a moment was caught off guard but faked a confident smile. Inside, he was not nearly as calm. He searched her face for the slightest bit of humor or deception. To his surprise, there was none, at least that he could see. But he was not convinced. He rejoined, "Sounds interesting."

"But I can tell you are waiting for someone. Girlfriend?" Carly clicked a manicured forefinger to her front tooth.

Charles noticed the mannerism, wondering if someone taught that stuff or did it just come naturally? However, women learned the technique, he thought it was sexy as hell. "Well, I was supposed to meet someone. But actually..., no, no, unattached."

"Sounds interesting." She gave a lifted eyebrow, pivoted, smiled over her shoulder, and left without saying anything else. Charles narrowed his eyes wondering if he had badly misread that whole conversation. Then he concluded with much satisfaction, he was still attractive to the younger sex! Or maybe she was in fact, just angling for a bigger tip. Regardless, the attention was fun, and Charles began running some possible scenarios through his mind. Charles took a drink of the water and gave a little tip of the glass to Miss Carly, who had made his day. He checked his watch.

"That was worth the trip," Charles said aloud, "Mr. Hansford, you don't even have to show."

"Well, that's good to know." Tyler Hansford said.

Charles jerked around to see a man wearing an Orioles baseball cap pulled low, standing with his back to the sunlit harbor. Charles quickly recovered, "Tyler, I presume." Charles realized that the Carly had distracted him long enough to miss Tyler's approach, or perhaps it was the rigid feeling in his jeans. He inconspicuously as possible pulled his sweater to cover his bulge and decided he would remain seated. How unfair it was that men had this emotional flagpole that became aroused at the slightest provocation.

"Yes, Dr. Livingston, you are correct," Tyler said with a sardonic grin. He still had a sense of humor, but the overwhelming events had caused Tyler to be subdued even

170

when showing a glimmer of the wittiness he possessed. Without waiting for a response, he said, "You were able to make your flight from D.C.?"

Charles appraised the young man tip to toe. He noticed the cut on the Tyler's forehead sneaking out of the baseball cap, and his slight limp as he moved aside the table. "Actually, I flew in from Miami."

"Miami. I love Miami. It has so many...," he paused, "distractions."

Not sure what to say, Charles said nothing.

Tyler asked, "Why Miami? I thought you were in D.C."

Charles intuitively asked, "You saw the news conference?" It was a statement more than a question.

Tyler remained standing while doing a quick check around the bar and through the windows. "Saw the famous Pulitzer Prize winning investigative reporter throw a crotch shot at some poor slub of the White House."

"Ah yes, the little question to the Press Secretary, Charles said flatly. "Have a seat. You look like you are in pain."

Tyler reached across Charles and removed a lime from the edge of Charles' water glass. "I love limes," he said before clamping down with his teeth into the lime. A bemused look crossed Charles' face, but he said nothing. Lime still in his mouth, Tyler had to hoist himself up onto the elevated seat while trying to disguise any pain. Tyler could not help but grimace as swung his legs around to face Charles.

Charles gave a little shake of his head before asking, "How did you get my cell phone number?"

Ignoring the question, Tyler asked, "So why Miami?"

"I flew back to see a friend."

"Friend?" Tyler said suggestively. He placed the lime on a napkin.

"Yes, an old high school buddy was in town, so I flew back to see him,"

"Him?" Tyler asked.

"Well, yes," Charles said. Charles involuntarily blushed. This kid was starting to piss him off.

"Must be a good friend?" Tyler gave two little quick raises of his eyebrows.

171

Feeling a bit taken aback, Charles added, "It is not like that." Charles felt he was becoming defensive, which in of itself was strange.

"Maybe we all have a little gayness in us," Tyler said thoughtfully.

"It was really not like that," Charles said, again with a bit more volume than he intended. Charles gave a little shaking of his head as if to clear his thoughts.

The silence was filled by the waitress returning with a frosty drink and Charles' food order, setting them in front of Charles. Pulling a paper napkin with tableware neatly rolled inside, she looked directly at Charles and said, "I see your guest has arrived." She again grazed Charles arm with her breast as she placed the frosty mug in from of him.

Tyler volunteered, "Yes, we are together."

Normally never at a loss for words, Charles could barely muster an answer. Eyes wide, Charles said, "Tyler, Carly here is going to get the wrong idea." Then he quickly added, "What would you like to drink?"

With no hesitation, Tyler said cheerfully, "I will have a Mai Tai. And could you put a flower in it? I love it when it is served that way."

Carly gave a crooked smile of mild amusement. One that Charles was not at all comfortable with receiving. Charles looked Tyler with an exasperated look. He thought Tyler's voice had taken on a lilting quality that was not there before. Carly gazed over at Charles with a disappointed look. Charles tried to divert his eyes but could not help but agonize over the convicting expression of the waitress.

"Right away," Carly airily said and turned back to the bar.

After the waitress had left, Charles said glumly, "You totally ruined that for me." He took a drink from his mug and gave a gasp at its content of alcohol.

Tyler's head shot back and gave a hearty, yet feminine laugh.

"I guess it's your first Rudee's Ruckus."

Charles wiped a tear from his eye with a napkin. After a couple shallow coughs, he managed, "I take it you are a regular here?"

Ignoring the question, Tyler said, "She was interested in you."

"Hard to believe?" Charles challenged.

"I don't mean to be disrespectful. You are an extremely attractive...," he paused, "older man."

"I am not an older man. I am...,"

Tyler interrupted, "at least ten years older than her."

"Well, ten years is probably close, but maybe she likes older men."

Tyler gave a smile, but said nothing, rather choosing to stare out on the inlet. A deckhand of one of the boats, a large Hatteras 60 Motor yacht, was skillfully throwing a mooring line to the deckhand, then jumping to the deck to assist in the tie down of the craft.

Charles took another smaller sip of his drink. "This is superb. I can't really tell what is in it."

"Rum, vodka, gin, Blue Curacao, pineapple juice and sour mix topped with 151 Rum and shaken until frothy."

"You have been here before."

"Mr. Reynolds..."

"Call me Charles."

Tyler gave a devilish smile. "First names, you move fast."

Simultaneously, Carey was placing Tyler's drink on the table.

"I see you two are getting acquainted. Can I get you some food as well?"

Tyler looked over at Charles, gave an implying look and said, "I will just share what he ordered. I'll like whatever he likes, I am sure." Tyler covered Charles' hand with his hand.

Pulling his hand off the table, Charles felt a rush of embarrassment come over him and started to attempt a clarification. But it would not have done any good; Carly had already turned toward the kitchen, concealing her enjoyment of the Charles' obvious discomfort. She thought he was handsome and smart. Sure, he was a little older, but she liked the fact that she could get him off his game a little.

Charles said with genuine agitation, "Great. I may have had a chance to get laid and you are throwing down the gay act again."

Reaching across to snare a crab bite, Tyler said, "Not an act Charles, remember?" Tyler ignored the disapproving glare, "Besides, you are old enough to be her father."

Charles' eyes narrowed into a look that might have been coming close to the look of death.

Chewing the crab bite, Tyler continued, "See, I have seen that same look from my father."

Charles said nothing. His mouth was closed, but his tongue was moving around, probing his teeth, a nervous habit of his and a sure sign that Charles was about to say something in anger. Almost without exception Charles Reynolds was the one in control of any social situation. A cool customer, not easily rattled, Charles had grown up in the newspaper business. He was tough minded, and he knew it. But in a few short minutes, this impertinent young man had somehow been able to so discombobulate Charles so much that he was floundering around looking for something to say. Charles took a deep breath and to his relief several smart-ass remarks came to mind. But he remembered that this was a meal ticket in front of him and he needed to play nice. He tasted the She-Crab soup. It was delicious. Wiping his mouth with his napkin, Charles said, "Tyler, you look like you took a good hit on the head, and you have, what a sprained ankle?"

"Yes, ten stitches and a sprain. Compliments of a fall in a restroom stall. But the ankle is fine, now that the initial swelling has gone down. My ribs still hurt, but just a bruise."

Charles looked at the boy curiously, exhaled and took another sip of his Ruckus. Placing the drink, a little further away than usual he said, "I have got to slow down. This drink is going to have me tossed."

"Isn't that the point?"

Charles looked over at this young man with a sense of wonder. Tyler was a U.S. Senator's son and a person that was possibly worldlier than a hardened old reporter. He had to marvel at the kid's moxie. Trying to get back in control of this meeting, Charles ventured, "So, Tyler, you invited me here. What's the story?"

"Yes, the point of all of this." Tyler stopped as if to consider what he wanted or what he was willing to tell an investigative reporter. After a moment of contemplation, and a full swallow of his Mai Tai, "They are going to kill me."

Chapter 24   **Houston, Texas Sunday**

George Love sat in his living room continuing to watch television for the latest news of the FBI raids. Immediately upon hearing about the FBI raids, he had dispatched his wife Esther to their vacation home in the Jan Sofat area of Curacao. It was the first of two safe houses that the George and Esther had purchased in the last year. The second was in the Marshall Islands, which had no extradition agreement to the United States. George had moved most of his money to accounts that could be accessed anywhere in the world, with the bulk in Cayman. Of course, he had assured Esther that would make his exit if it became apparent that their efforts were going to fail. Esther had reluctantly left with their three grandkids and divorced daughter in tow. It was billed as an extended vacation, but from the amount of luggage, they were planning for the long term. George's daughter knew of her father's efforts and did not ask a lot of questions. The goodbye was emotional but approached with resolve and the promises to see each other soon.

George turned up the sound when the President made his way to the podium. The President's eyes were afire, and it was clear that he was going to speak to the press and citizens with the emotion that had won majority of electoral votes in the first election. His second presidential election, just a year ago, was fraught with controversy and vicious disagreement. With pre-election tactics, in which the party of the sitting President was able to register over a million new voters, the election came down to a slim electoral victory. The most contentious point was the electoral votes awarded to California via a particular piece of legislation that used the census to count both legal and illegal citizens for purposes of the electoral count. The same courtesy was not extended in Texas or Florida where the President was presumably going to lose. The accuracy of the census was called into question when it appeared that California somehow gained a million extra inhabitants and remarkably, Texas lost a million. The census was challenged in the Supreme Court, which voted 5-4 in favor of the official government count, just months prior to the election. The second tactic that infuriated most of the President's critics was the legislative goody bag delivered to Florida, which helped carry the

Sunshine state contradicting the polling numbers leading into the election. The incumbent won re-election despite only winning just seventeen of the fifty states, but still claimed that his re-election was a further indication of the mandate for change.

On the television screen, the President bellowed, "As you are aware, forces in this country have proven that they are intent on destroying our republic. Just a few hours ago, an attempt on my life was unsuccessful and has only increased my resolve to conduct the plans that you, true Americans elected me to do. I have tried with my presidency to bridge the divide of our nation. The vitriolic rhetoric that exists today calls for an immediate response. Otherwise, those that want to take us back to a country that is unwilling to take care of the least among us will be encouraged and yes, emboldened." The President was interrupted by raucous applause and had to wait till it died down. Nodding his head, he continued, "We cannot and will not sit by as a small group of extremists with racial biases, create a fissure in our country. Just this week, our Department of Homeland Security in cooperation with the FBI and local and state authorities have shut down two major cells of domestic terrorists." Applause broke out again.

Someone in the audience yelled, "Shut 'em down!"

The applause again reached a point where the President had to raise his hands to gain quiet.

"I feel that this level of animosity and violence must not only be dealt with in kind, but we must be aggressive in preventing these types of anti-American activity." More applause. "First, let me say that our media represents what is the best of our country. The opportunity for the various outlets to provide unbiased and accurate news is the foundation of the Constitution. I would never infringe on that fundamental right. I am requesting that all media outlets examine their level of inflammatory reporting in an honest evaluation of whether their reporting is perpetuating this anti-American sentiment. I ask that each of the major networks monitor themselves to ask the question does this build up this great nation or serve to tear it down."

Interrupted by applause, the President bobbed his head up and down in acknowledgement of the crowd's loyalty and support. "Secondly, in response to an escalation of violence and dissident activity, I have sent a letter to the Congress of these United States that will temporarily suspend these groups' ability to accumulate weapons which can only be used to try to destabilize local, state and federal governments." The camera flashed to a sign which read, "Only criminals need guns!" More applause.

"I am asking Congress for the authority to impose a registration program for all weaponry and encourage our law-abiding citizens to voluntarily turn in their weapons for safekeeping by local and state officials. I am asking all fifty governors to join us in an effort to rid our society of the dangerous weapons that are being used to kill our men and women, and especially our children." A loud explosion of cheers and clapping erupted in the audience. "With this program, we will finally be able to enjoy a level of peace which has escaped this great nation." The camera panned to the crowd which was now standing and applauding.

George Love, sitting on the edge of his couch, picked up a satellite phone and placed the first of three international calls.

Chapter 25   Miami, Florida   Sunday

Almost forty-five minutes or maybe it was an hour, had passed when Sam awoke from his ocean-side nap. It could have been his burning skin or the voices around him which roused Sam out of a deep sleep. He had been somewhere in the Caribbean with several beautiful girls answering his every beckoned call, before returning to where? Oh yes, Miami. His eyes cracked open, and he immediately knew that a crowd had arrived. Consciousness returning, Sam realized in fact, he was surrounded by beach goers in every direction. Thinking that his sunglasses were causing his vision to be blurry, he groped for the edge of his towel. Upon removing the sunglasses, he realized it was not the sunglasses causing his problem. Sam blinked rapidly, clearing his vision enough to make out an empty Mickey's can lying in the sand on his right. He wondered if he had finished it or if it had spilled when he dropped it. Then he noticed another empty can on the left side of his chair. Had he really drunk two of those sixteen-ounce beers? He could not have. As he sat up a little, he felt a swimming sensation in his head which indicated that he must have. He realized something else. He had fallen asleep without removing his contacts. That explained why he was looking through what seemed like a fogged-up shower door. Sam leaned over to open his bag, squinting in search of the bottle of saline he had thoughtfully included in his travel gear. He said with satisfaction, "Be prepared. Motto of the troop scout." As he reached inside, his weight tipped the chair making it necessary to plant a hand and foot in the sand to keep from falling in. He heard a giggle just a foot or so away but decided to ignore it.

Saddled properly back in the chair, gluey eyed Sam negotiated with the one hand that was now covered with sand, and one that held the bottle of saline. He switched the bottle to the sandy hand and used his fingers of the clean hand to pull back the lids. He squirted a generous amount of the refreshing liquid into each eye giving immediate relief. The excess saline ran down his face, but it didn't bother Sam as he allowed his eyes to gratefully rehydrate. He gave a sigh of satisfaction and pulled at a corner of his earlier vacated shirt to catch the overflow. Unfortunately, sand which had collected in the sleeve

179

of the shirt toppled into his left eye. Sam instantly recoiled letting out a muted "Shit, shit shit." With his effort to sit up, the rear support of his chair collapsed causing Sam to take a hard seat on the soft sand. He heard several more chuckles. Sam thought contemptuously, *Yeah, right I am the entertainment to the world; that's right ladies and gentlemen, step right up and see this clown embarrass himself for your entertainment pleasure.* Sam decided right there and then, he was going to ignore the idiots and not give them the pleasure of his embarrassment. He wrangled the chair back into place and used an extra towel from his bag to wipe the last remnant of sand from his eyes. He cleaned his sunglasses, brushed off excess sand from his chair and released a long cleansing breath before taking his seat again. Sunglasses in place, without turning his head Sam discreetly looked to his left for a look at his audience. To his surprise, the lady next to him had gone topless. Unfortunately, the lady's sagging breasts reminded Sam of two long sweet potatoes. Abandoning subtlety, Sam scanned the entire landscape to take in all the other sunbathers and finally grasped the completeness of Charles' recommendation. He said, "Charles Reynolds, I am going to get you."

"What was that you said, Honey?" croaked the old woman.

Both legs now planted in the sand on opposite sides of his chair, Sam bolted upright in his chair. He tried to stand, but in his haste or maybe it was the alcohol, his left foot just caught the edge of his chair, sending him sideways, headfirst into the sandy beach, looking directly up at the woman's bare breasts.

She gave him a smile laden with cigarette-stained teeth, and said with a pleasant but sultry voice, "Hi there, doll."

The large dark nipples stretched in an execrable effort to cover the sagging breasts, which may have at one time fit snuggly into a D cup. Now they looked in need of a tube sock. The woman, apparently enjoying a new rooster in the henhouse, gave Sam a little wink.

Sam grimaced. Mustering a weak, "Hello," He pushed up from the sand to his hands and knees, bringing her partner into view. He was a withered old man with his own set of shriveled breasts.

Meeting Sam's eyes, the old man gave a disinterested-up nod and said in a raspy Chicago accented voice, "How ya' doin'."

Sam forced a smile. He thought to himself, *don't look. Do not look*. But as if drawn to the gore of an auto accident on the side of the road, Sam's eyes inexorably panned down the man's torso. And there it was. A slong that was damn-near the size of a Kiolbassa sausage laid in repose between the man's tanned wiry legs. "Oh God." Sam quickly looked away managing to quell a small urge in his throat to vomit.

The woman said softly to her partner, "I think he's gonna get sick."

Snapping up a newspaper in front of his face he grumbled, "Dammit Helen, I told you we shouldn't have set up next to him."

Ignoring the reproof, the lady tried to engage Sam in conversation as he carefully returned the edge of his chair. "You missed the Jamboree up the beach this morning? You have been sleeping for a good hour or more. I was worried you were dead, so I checked your carotid artery. I used to be a nurse."

Unconsciously, Sam's hand went to his neck, and his eyes shifted to the woman's long painted nails. A small shudder ran though his body as he returned to a sitting position on the edge of his beach chair.

Helen gave a concerned look at Sam. Without turning to her partner, she said confidentially from the side of her mouth, "I think he's getting the chills." Now speaking to Sam, she asked, "Honey, are you alright, you don't look so good."

Turning his gaze out to the water, Sam said flatly, "I am fine. Thank you." He decided to just sit still for a moment and then he could get out of this hellish place. Trying to sit up straighter, Sam retracted the back of his chair. As Sam arrived at the full seated position, a lone man ambled by giving a disapproving look Sam's swimsuit. Sam willed himself to not let it happen again, but it did. He looked. This time it was a puny little dick, just barely…, and he mentally slapped himself, quickly averting his eyes. Realizing the lady had asked him a question, Sam said, "I am sorry, what did you ask?"

"I think I have my answer," she said. "This is your first time to Haulover Beach." Undeterred she continued, "Later, there will be some ladies here that would be very interested in meeting you. That is if you're not already taken." She gave a pathetic smile which showed tobacco-stained teeth again, but this time with an added smudge of red lipstick. As if seeing Sam's attention drawn to her teeth, she unconsciously dragged her tongue across the front and finished with a little smacking sound, which reminded Sam of his cat Sylvester's usual conclusion to the finish of Frisky Vittles.

Sam forced a smile but did not answer, then added just gave a slight raise of the chin which tried to convey his feeling of 'that's nice.'

"Don't worry honey; they will be a closer to your age." She gave a cackle of a laugh turning to the old man. He gave a little sarcastic "humph" and rolled his eyes.

Sam gave another effort to speak, but only was able to mouth "Oh" as if the prospect had been of interest to him. While he was looking around trying to locate all his personal items for an escape, the lady was still talking, "And you know, when in Rome, do as the Romans do. So, you will probably want to slip those trunks off. You know... show 'em, what you got." Sam gave a forced another smile and an embarrassed laugh. She continued, "But, you might lay off the Mickey's. Those will knock you for a loop and along with the heat... well you just might be falling down drunk. Just saying."

Her partner gave a little disgusted chuckle. "Yeah, falling down drunk."

Helen continued, "You know, it looks like you are getting sun burned. Do you need some lotion?" She pulled a plastic bottle from her beach bag like a gunfighter pulling pistol. She flipped the top, squirted a bit in her right hand before offering it to Sam.

She was right, Sam noticed. His legs were just starting to show a red tinge. Stuttering and gathering up his towel, he said in a clipped progression, "Yes, well, I guess... I have had enough sun. Sort of a burned white now. Don't want to get burned any..., more. Thanks. I guess I will, well..." Sam did not finish his sentence. His left sandal caught on one of the chairs rivets causing the entire side to rise up. Sam lost his footing and had to catch himself with his free hand and balanced in the sand precariously on one knee. Sand rebounded everywhere, invading every crack and crevice of Sam's clothes and body. One of his mostly emptied beer cans bounced up and tilted over, pouring its remaining contents of the can over Sam's ankle. The warm golden liquid soaked into Sam's right sandal. All of this falderal caused a giggle from Helen and earned a full belly laugh from the man. A middle-aged woman, with full melon breasts and a handful of seashells, passed in front of Sam. Her amusement was evident in her full moon smile and a shake of the head.

Covering her mouth, Helen said, "Norman, don't be laughing, it is not polite."

"Yeah well..., give him a paper towel or something," the man managed to say despite his laughing.

Sam accepted the paper towel which the lady extended, just making sure to graze Sam's hand with her nail extensions. Sam entire body stiffened which earned him another sly smile from Helen. After drying the beer, shaking off the sand, packing up, and an obligatory adieu to Helen and Norman, Sam headed back to his car. Within a few steps, Sam stopped hesitated and returned to pick up his two empty beer cans which he inadvertently left behind. The woman gave him a wink and said in her nasal tone, "Thanks Honey for keeping our beach clean!"

Chapter 26   Virginia Beach, Virginia Sunday

"When you say they are trying to kill you, who are they?" Charles asked while conspicuously looking around for the waitress, but also to see if anyone else was listening in on their conversation.

It was the territorial nature of the reporter that made him so cautious about anyone stealing his scoop, which caused him to covertly scan the restaurant. He even made a quick visual sweep of the parking lot trying to make sure that nothing suspicious, or out of the ordinary, was happening. Besides a couple businessmen at the bar, Charles saw nothing particularly out of place. But he did see Carly come from the kitchen with Tyler's food order and held his hand up to delay Tyler from answering.

"How is the drink kiddo?" asked Carly.

"Very strong," Charles said with a smile. "But the food helps."

Tyler gave a chuckle and said, "He is a bit of a lightweight."

"Maybe I could get some more water," Charles said while wiping his forehead with his napkin.

Giving a mischievous smile, Carly placed a gentle hand on Charles' shoulder and began a strange kneading that felt really great and yet it seemed very odd to Charles.

"What about another drink?"

Tyler raised a hand. "I will take one."

Charles was shaking his head and waiving an imaginary flag in a sign of surrender. "Just water, please."

Carly just gave a little giggle and said, "Okay kiddo, I will check back with you in just a moment." With a flip of her hair, she turned and retreated.

"I think she has got a thing for reporters," Tyler said with a sly look.

Charles rolled his eyes. "You saw that?" Charles cleared his throat, "Happens all the time," he said feigning nonchalance and sincerity.

Tyler gave a little harrumph.

Charles asked, "Tyler, what is going on here?"

Tyler gave him an inquisitive look, and answered, "You tell me, you are the Pulitzer Prize winning author."

184

Ignoring the jab, Charles said, "You are going to have to help me out here and give me some more details about what happened and what is happening."

"You knew about me before I called you right?"

"I am in the news business."

"But you knew about me, because it is still taboo in backwater Virginia to be anything but George and Barbara in the missionary position. And because I am a Senator's son it is big news to throw into the pot."

"Look, I understand, you have a beef with being ostracized. I get that. But you are spitting at the wrong dog."

Tyler's eyes grew wide in amusement.

"Tyler, I don't care if you're gay. You are what you are."

Tyler interrupted, "But, you would not want someone else thinking you were gay. Say like Carly?"

Charles sighed, "Look Tyler, you are a smart guy. You have to admit that being perceived as gay would not help me with the waitress. This rodeo is not getting us anywhere. What happened to you at the Presidential lunch?"

Tyler paused. Seeming to have organized his thoughts, he said, "Simple. I was in the wrong place at the wrong time, and I saw a U.S. Senator killed."

Even though Charles had already assumed this to be the case, the boy's frankness caused Charles to sit up in his seat. He stared at Tyler with a penetrating look. Reaching to pull out a notebook from his pocket, he remembered that he had left it in his jacket pocket which was in the car. *Amateur* he chided himself. "What did you see exactly?"

"Good looking man in his mid-thirties, gelled hair, big and broad shouldered, tailored suit, stuck a needle in the Senator's neck."

Charles' eyes narrowed. This was news. *Wow*, Charles thought, *the boy is just blurting out all the details that the police and every other law enforcement agency had to be dying to get.* "Have you told any of this to the police?"

"I did not tell them shit. I pretended to be confused and well, I did not have to pretend too much, I mean look at the cut on my head." He raised his ball cap.

Neatly spliced with stitches, the two-inch split had a rich blood red color. The swelling had receded some, leaving the preliminary stages of bruising. Charles had seen worse, but it did look painful, and he cringed for affect. Tyler returned the cap with a wary look around to see if anyone was watching. No one seemed particularly interested in them or their conversation. Turning almost all the way around, Tyler noticed a newly arrived, suited man with silver hair. The noticeably older gentlemen had saddled up to the bar next to the two businessmen, but all three, heads tilted up, seemed to be taking in the golf tournament showing on the big screen television above the bar. Charles had noticed the older man when he came in but had deduced that he did not look particularly suspicious. From the man's suit, Charles had pegged him as a traveling salesman or business owner, but not one of the yacht owners.

Tyler continued, "For all I know the police may be in on it. I mean the guy just walked in after the Senator into the bathroom at a Presidential luncheon no less. I've seen movies like this where the things go deep. You know, conspiracies and all that stuff." Tyler scanned the restaurant, and then glanced toward the boats and back to Charles. "He got past the Secret Service, and killed a U.S. Senator," he paused, "with a syringe! He was a professional assassin. Or maybe he was a rogue Secret Service agent. That is the point here. You don't know who it was or why. And he was fast. You know like you see in the movies where it is all speeded up and shit. One second this guy is washing his hands and within a second, he has opened a towel rack and shoves a needle into the neck of a US Senator. I am not exaggerating. It was like something that Jason Bourne does but in real life. And this guy was much better looking than Damon ever was. I mean if he weren't, you know, an assassin, I would like to meet up with him again."

Looking over Tyler's shoulder, Charles watched one of the men tap the bar, a sign that their imbibing was complete. Catching Carly's attention, the second man gave a circle the wagons signal, which Carly correctly interpreted as a desire to close out. Charles could barely decipher Carly's response, but he liked the tone of her voice, sweet, young, and enthusiastic. He watched as she as she momentarily positioned tray with a glass of water and umbrella garnished drink, presumably destined for Charles and Tyler, on the bar's edge. Charles wished he could see her lower half obscured by the bar as Carly turned back toward the cash register.

Charles relaxed and returned his attention to Tyler, who had a bewildered look on his face. Or perhaps he was wearing the face of resignation that he was going to be the next to get killed. Charles could tell the stress had gotten the best of this young man, but his upbringing had allowed him to put on a brave face. Charles said nothing, allowing Tyler to continue with the details that were pent up inside him. He seemed to be trying to make sense of the world that had once been held in reasonably good order. Probably held together by his parents or whatever overseer Tyler had been entrusted to at the time. Charles sensed that Tyler was the one who was used to being the one causing the chaos and now that his situation was so out of control, even his caustic wit had left him. The young man appeared to gather himself. It may have helped that Carly was delivering Tyler's drink and Charles' water.

"Great service," Charles said with a little wink and a smile. He felt confident around this girl and her attention was causing him to cock it up a bit.

"I am here to please." Carly said. "Here's your water and..," sliding Tyler's drink across the table, "yours's sir." Before leaving, she gave Charles another massaging grip again on his shoulder, which sent a pleasurable pulse through his body. Charles felt hornier than he could ever remember. The old emotional flagpole began to make its presence felt and once again, he quickly adjusted his sweater down.

Moving the umbrella to the side, Tyler took a large swallow of his drink, followed by a long breath. Carly had retreated to wait on a young couple who had entered the bar. Tyler blinked his eyes with an apparent dislike of the taste of his libation. He gave a strange look the glass, but decided it was okay and took another smaller swig.

"You okay?" Charles said while taking a sip of his water.

"Yeah, just the stress I guess."

"You were telling me about the Senator," Charles prodded.

With a quick look around, Tyler spoke in a faint voice. "This assassin...," Tyler seemed to have to conjure up the next words, "evidently walked as easy as you please out of the restroom, with all that going on; me busting my head and the Senator dead on the floor. Then he walked from the building

187

with no one asking any questions? And the police and Secret Service and the damn FBI seem to be coming up empty. Seems a bit strange don't you think and then who do you think killed my friend?"

Charles' face registered confusion. "Wait, your friend? Who are you talking about?" Charles was noticing that Tyler seemed to be slurring his words a bit. Charles figured that Tyler was probably a weepy drunk rather than a boisterous one. Charles, on the other hand, was a sleepy drunk. He would crawl into the nearest bed or just go to sleep on the floor. He would often say that his plane was landing and moments later, he would be asleep.

Tyler said resolutely, "Someone came looking for me and killed him. Trevor is dead. I think he tried to call me right before he died. I answered, but there was nothing."

"When was this?" Charles asked in amazement. His mouth was suddenly dry, and he took another drink of water.

"I don't know, it seems like it has been a lifetime ago, but I guess it was just the other day. How long has it been?" Tyler's face scrunched in contemplation.

Charles looked closely to see if he was serious. "Well, today is Sunday. The Senator was killed when last Monday?"

"Yeah, well a week or so." Tyler gave a visible shrug. "Seems like a month. I left the hospital like on Tuesday morning early. Trevor must have been killed on Wednesday or Thursday."

Charles questioned, "How do you know?"

"Another friend called me."

Sighing from this latest twist, Charles asked, "Another friend?" He was trying to sift through Tyler's story for crucial details. But hell, they were all important thought, Charles. Across the table Tyler gave Charles an 'are you shocked that I have friends?' look.

Exhaling Charles said, "Okay Tyler, the friend who was killed...," He paused until Tyler looked him in the eye. "How did he contact you in the hospital?"

Tyler held up his cell phone, giving it a little jiggle.

"And the friend that called you to tell you about...," he paused.

"Trevor," Tyler said. He turned away his moist eyes to the inlet.

Not without sympathy, Charles said, "Yes, Trevor. How did your other friend contact you about Trevor?"

Tyler could not speak, but again held up his cell phone as the answer. No jiggle this time.

"And I just bet you called me with that same cell phone." Charles pointed at the phone in Tyler's hand.

Tyler understood Charles' implied carelessness; Tyler frowned and slightly turned in his seat away from Charles.

Charles grabbed the young man's forearm and said, "Tyler, the police, the FBI, the Secret Service, I mean, could you have more people trying to find you? I saw a nationwide BOLO on you this morning before I left Miami. I can't believe no one has been able to track your phone."

"I don't think they knew about this phone." A tear glistened in his eyes again. "Trevor left it with me. The Secret Service confiscated my phone. He gave me his phone and said he would pick up another one so we could communicate. We were worried that investigators might stop Trevor from visiting once they realized that I was not talking."

"Is there any way they could be tracking Trevor's phone now?"

"I don't think they would because Trevor is dead. But, I suppose if whoever killed Trevor had picked up his spare phone the number would have been in the call log." Tyler did a quick glance around the restaurant. "I don't see anyone lurking around here, do you?"

"If these guys are as professional as you describe, we would not be able to see them. But yeah, I have been keeping an eye out and I don't think there is anyone here," said Charles with more conviction than he felt.

Tyler's carefree bravado had returned for a moment like a sidecar reattached to a motorcycle. Charles looked around the restaurant again and decided whether the 'paranoid' Tyler or the 'couldn't care less' Tyler was the better judge of the situation. It was still a light crowd as the happy hour and dinner crowd would not be here for another hour or so.

Tyler said with just a touch of a slur, "Trevor was probably stupid enough to try to hold out, thinking he was doing me a favor. Reality was, whatever he told them was wrong, because I went somewhere that he did not know about. His death was totally unnecessary, and I want to figure out how to punish these people…, and oh yeah, I want to live." Tyler paused and looked off into the inlet. "You know, I was going to break up with him."

Charles asked, "So you and…"

"Trevor," Tyler provided.

"Involved?"

Tyler smiled at the level of discomfort that asking this question caused this award-winning reporter.

"Come on Mr. Reynolds or should I call you Chars."

Tyler swung back into the gay persona and Charles bristled a little at both names. The first one because it sounded so old, and the second name because it was only used by close friends. He let it go and said, "How about Charles?"

Tyler gave an almost imperceptible nod but said nothing. The flaming act did not come natural to Tyler, but he could pull it off if it served his purposes. Trevor, on the other hand, could not help but flame. Tyler supposed that Trevor received some satisfaction from announcing to the world he was homosexual and proud of it. Charles looked at this young man who was probably given everything in life and it took losing a friend to make him realize the important thing in life was not things. Sometimes it was easy to criticize someone like Tyler, but Charles was impressed by his steel. A lesser man would have crumbled to pieces and run like a baby, but he was at least thinking it through. Not very smartly in Charles' opinion, but at least the kid had some moxie. But right now, Tyler looked like he was a small child just before nap time. He had a slight glazing over with droopy eyelids.

Carly returned to offer Charles another drink, but Charles put his hands up, signaling no thanks and saying, "No mas, no mas." He took a drink of his water.

"Well, if you change your mind let me know. I can call you a cab if you need me to or… she paused, "My shift is about up, and I could run you home. Your friend looks like he could use some coffee. You sure he is okay."

"Yeah, he recently lost a close friend. He will be okay," Charles gave her a big smile. "Hey Carly, do you have a pen I could borrow? I have left mine in the car."

Handing him a pen, Carly gave him a wink and returned back to the bar area. Charles was not sure what to make of that. Maybe this was all an act, after all there she was flirting with the two guys at the bar again. It took a moment, but he gathered himself, wiped his mouth and asked, "Tyler, are you doing all right?"

Tyler looked like he was going to heave, but it just turned out as a belch which he covered with fist. "No, I think I feel sick actually. I felt like this once before, but I can't seem to remember when that was."

Charles knew instinctively he needed to press on. "Tyler, you are going to have to start trusting someone or you will be playing right into these guys' hands. They have a lot more resources than you and they are probably professionals from what you say."

Tyler was unconsciously chewing on a straw that was unnecessarily included with his drink. He was obviously in thought and switched from the straw to a new lime for chewing. Charles deduced Tyler may have been reliving the murder of Senator Summers or contemplating the death of his friend or even perhaps the prospect of his death, who knows. Charles tried to organize his thoughts into questions that might get to the bottom of this monster of a story. Now he really wished he had his notebook. Charles asked, "How did you get here?"

"I just walked over from the boat. The Tyler Rose, remember? My friend named it after me." Tyler paused and looked in the distance. As if in some faraway place in his mind, Tyler was nodding his head in a moment of realization. "You know that is really sad because my friend is just using me. You know he has a video system on the boat which can record everything."

Charles volunteered, "Too bad there was not a video recording of the murder of Senator's murder." Both men gave an expression of *yeah if it were just that easy.*

Suddenly, Charles felt an uncomfortable sensation up and down his body. It was an odd feeling that crept over Charles which reminded him of times when he knew he was getting sick. He took a couple of deep breaths. Charles did his best to ignore this unsettling feeling which seemed to be permeating his senses. He asked Tyler, "How did you get out of the hospital?"

"I left" He giggled. "I just walked out. Actually, Trevor helped get me out. I had seen a murder that I was not supposed to see." Tyler asked distrustfully, "You don't think they were plotting to get to me in the hospital? Well, I have no doubt they were."

"I suppose they would," Charles said, still trying to get over the initial surprise that his own luck was so good. He practically had a golden goose dumping eggs right in front of him. But he was missing something here and needed to go back. He again chided himself for leaving his notebook in his jacket that he had left in the rental car and, he abstained from drinking anymore of that damn Ruckus or whatever it was. He felt like his plane was about to land and he needed to get this out. "Tyler, wait a minute. Start back when you left the presidential luncheon. Take me through what you remember."

"Trevor road in the ambulance to the hospital, but I was out of it. They stitched me up and Trevor left after a while. And, I remember the FBI would come in, and check on me, you know."

Charles nodded.

"I would pretend to be unconscious one time and then the next time would tell them I could not remember anything."

"Trevor left for several hours. Evidently, he had figured out a way to retrieve his car from the hotel. He showed up for the late evening visiting hours. I told him about the murder and that I needed to get out. He snuck me out after sending the guard on an errand. Not sure how he did it, but I think he like, grossed the guy out by coming on to him. Trevor was good at getting his way – one way or another if you know what I mean. Maybe he promised him a blowjob; he was good at that too."

Charles made a face while rolling his hand which was giving the 'you're giving too much detail here and get going with story' sign.

Tyler protested, "Hey, you wanted the story."

"I know, but just the important stuff okay. You can leave out the blow jobs."

Tyler shrugged as if to say, your loss. "Trevor lent me his car and he said he would wait to make sure I was away; and then take a cab to his parent's house. He was worried that I could not drive." Tyler looked away and discretely swiped a tear. "This is all going so wrong."

Charles prompted, "You took his car. He took a cab to his parents, who I am assuming live close to Roanoke." Tyler said nothing, just nodded. Charles asked, "But, you did not go to his parent's house?"

Tyler gave a pitiful gasp. "I blew him off and came here. A friend of mine owns that boat over there, the one with the Dixie Flag flying. The Tyler Rose." Evidently not remembering that he just mentioned this a few moments earlier, Tyler gestured grandly to what even Charles would readily acknowledge was an amazing vessel.

Looking closely at the young man across the table, he asked, "Tyler, are you taking meds?"

"Hell yes, wouldn't you be?" Tyler struggled a bit to straighten up, but still managed to look insulted.

"Actually, I feel a little like I am taking drugs." Charles blinked a couple times and looked suspiciously at the drink in his hand. "Tyler, I think we have to hurry," Charles said under his breath. Charles asked, "So you drove Trevor's car and he took a cab?"

Tyler gave a slightly irritated look at the fact that he had already covered this but nodded an affirmative. Charles thought a moment and asked. "Did you leave from the hospital?"

"Parking garage."

"And Trevor called a cab." Charles thought a moment. "Could Trevor have been mistaken for you when he got into the cab?"

"Well, his chin is a little different and, of course, the eyes are fake blue. No one could miss that. I told him to stop faking his eye color."

Charles again took a breath. "Tyler, stay focused here."

Tyler snapped to attention and gave Charles, a little salute.

"Hair color the same?" Charles asked.

"Yeah, I suppose. What of it?"

"About the same height and build, what about 5'8" 150 pounds?" Charles asked, trying to be patient.

Softly Tyler said, "You think they thought he was me?" Tyler's eyes glassed-up with tears again. He discretely wiped his right and then left eye with his edge of his hand, and then returned his gaze to the distance.

193

Afraid he was going to lose the moment, Charles continued, "It was possible that they mixed the two of you up, but they would have certainly figured it out if the police identified the body. Is there anyone else who knows that you saw the murder?"

Tyler shrugged. "Whoever the guy in the bathroom had to know I was there, but he may not know what I saw or heard. But I don't think these guys take chances."

"No, I don't think they are taking any chances," Charles said evenly.

Charles stretched his neck a little, to one side and then the other. He wiped his hands on a napkin and rubbed both of his eyes again. "Do you remember anything that was said that led up to the murder?"

"Not really. There was a conversation. I could not hear it all, but it sounded like the Senator was being coerced or something like that and he refused. He was incredibly angry. Well, not angry but irritated, you know? The man said something like...," Tyler switched into a deep man's voice, "You have been told the offer and you have refused." Switching back to his normal tenor, "Then the man stabbed him with a..," Tyler struggled with the word, hypodermic and gave up, "with a needle."

"With a needle?" said a disbelieving Charles.

Relieving the moment, with his hand covering his mouth, Tyler was nodding. vigorously signaling 'Oh yeah, you are starting to get it, right?'

Charles was just dumbstruck. "That was it? He said, you received the offer and you refused; then, the man stabbed him with a needle?"

"In the neck," Tyler said emphatically. Then quickly added, "Well, the Senator said something like, I don't know who you are working for, but I am going to bring Justice in on it. And friends ought to know better than this."

"Friends ought to know better than this?" Charles repeated.

Tyler shrugged, "I don't know. Something like that. Or friends ought to know better than this."

Charles let out a breath while trying to run through all the possibilities of what the conversation could mean. Nothing came to mind, and he scribbled on his napkin the phrase

Senator's friends ought to know better than this. He wrote: Summers knew about something that happened, and then added, Summers was being blackmailed to make a decision. After a quick thought he jotted, 'Was refusing to take a position?'. Charles tried to remember on which committees Senator Summers served, but the only one he could recall was the Armed Services Committee… or was it the Finance Committee? This was something that he should know but could not seem to come up with it. Again, Charles noticed that his mind seemed to be cloudy for some reason. He gave a little shake to try to clear his thoughts.

Charles asked urgently, "Is there anything else you can remember that they talked about?"

Tyler closed his eyes and with effort recalled, "Yeah, the younger guy said something about his name being Smith and not being as clever as Rivers and something. I can't remember the second name, but both were odd."

Charles asked, "Rivers and something. These were people's names?" Charles added this to his napkin which was quickly becoming filled with his scribbles.

"Yeah, but I can't remember the second one."

"Try and remember Tyler. This could be the reason why the Senator was killed," Charles prodded.

"Pepper and Rivers." Tyler gave a brief sign of satisfaction. "Rivers and Pepper, that was it. He said, 'you can call me Smith, not as clever as Rivers and Pepper."

Charles wrote Rivers and Pepper on his napkin followed by a question mark.

Shooting a finger in the air, Tyler slurred, "And something else. He said something about giving information to AIG."

Charles face showed confusion at this. "AIG as in the insurance company?"

AIG, a behemoth insurance company in the late 2000's with its origins in China, had been the poster child of government too big to fail bailouts. When faced with a collapsing asset base of mortgage-backed securities, AIG was rescued by the Federal Reserve.

Tyler shrugged. "Well, I guess so. How many AIG's can there be?"

Thinking aloud, Charles said, "AIG's problems happened years ago. I suppose there could be another scandal brewing with the bailout or something."

Tyler contorted as if he was bored with the conversation.

Charles asked, "What did the guy look like?"

"Handsome. Nice hair. But a little too much gel."

Charles gave a frustrated sigh. "What else can you remember?"

Tyler's nose scrunch began at the tip but seem to travel up to his forehead. "I don't know, six foot two, about thirty and nice dress boots. Amedeo Testoni."

Thinking this was another key name, Charles asked, "Amedeo Testoni?"

Tyler smiled. "He may have been a murderer, but he had good taste."

Charles massaged both sides of his head and then gave a clearing shake of his head. "Tyler, I have only had one of these drinks, right? I should not be this drunk." Looking at his napkin of notes, Charles tried to process what Tyler had been able to recall. Rivers and Pepper, where had he heard those names before? But his mind seemed to be a blur. Some sort of realization passed over his face. Charles said, "We have to get out of here."

Tyler's eyes widened up and he looked up to his left, giving an indication that he was looking for a thought somewhere up in the afternoon sky. He could not come up with it and shrugged the effort away.

Charles shoved the napkin into his back pants pocket and drew out a money clip. He dropped two twenties in the table and grasped Tyler by the arm.

"Hey, I have not even finished my drink. Or my food for that matter," Tyler complained in a tone that befitted a young child who was not getting his way at the grocery store candy aisle.

"Tyler, I am not messing around, we need to go to some place safe. Now!

Chapter 27   **Miami Florida**   **Sunday**

Relieved to be back on the road again, Sam was intermittently disparaging Charles and reliving his unexpected beach experience. He turned from the road leading away from the beach onto a two-lane road leading back to the interstate. A dark sedan flashed in his peripheral vision going way too fast, passed along his left side way too close and then appeared to lose control. The passing vehicle went into a slide and for a moment, Sam thought it was going to flip over sideways. Sam practically stood on the brake causing the anti-lock brakes to kick in and the Jaguar stopped with several feet to spare. He mentally patted himself on the back for being alert; the last thing he needed was to be in an accident after drinking all that beer. Sam wondered if the driver of the sideways car had suffered a heart attack or something. Or perhaps the driver had fallen asleep. Probably drunk he decided.

At a complete stop, Sam waited to see what was happening. He really did not want to get out; his day already had been a disaster. He decided to back up and go around, but when he put his car into reverse and checked his rear-view mirror, he realized that a second car had squeezed in very close to his rear bumper. He had not even noticed the car pull up, but he figured that the car behind him had been as surprised as he was and was barely able to come to a stop. The second car was so close that he could not even move an inch back and with the other car so close in front, he was effectively pinned in. Interestingly, both cars had tinted windows, which did not allow Sam to see inside, and the cars were almost identical. He waited for the car behind him to back up, but the idiot just sat there. Sam muttered, "Damn Florida drivers."

Finally, Sam had had enough. He was tired of having people laugh at him and this whole beach experience had just about sent him over the edge. "You know, I am just going to have to raise a little hell here," he yelled aloud. He made sure the car was not in gear and opened the door to give this pair of idiots a piece of his mind. As he stepped one foot out, a slight incline in the road and the fact that Sam had forgotten to engage the parking brake, caused the car to roll backward. Sam quickly sat back down and pushed the brake. But not before the Jaguar's rear bumper had ever so slightly bumped into the car

197

behind. Immediately, the driver side and the passenger side doors of the offended car opened. Sam gasped and gently pulled back up closer to the vehicle in the front. The driver of the car in front of him made a show of exiting his car, door flying open and moving quickly toward Sam. Looking alternatively forward and in the side view mirror, Sam noticed that the three men could have passed for brothers. All of them had the same short-cropped hair, wearing reflective sunglasses and dark business suits. *No, this was not looking good*, thought Sam. The inevitable confrontation created a queasy feeling in the pit of his stomach.

Behind on the driver side Sam heard, "Sir, could you place your hands on the steering wheel where we can see them?"

Sam's mind went to the gunman last night and the sounds of the bullets ricocheting off the car to the possibility that he had bumped a police car. From the rear-view mirror, Sam glimpsed the second man circling to the passenger's side of the Jaguar. Returning his attention forward, Sam was greeted with another of the brothers looking over the windshield from only a couple feet away. In a stern tone he said, "Sir, please turn off the engine."

"Well, uh…, who are you?" Sam weakly managed to squeak.

Ignoring the question, the man repeated, "Sir, please turn off the engine."

The circling man had just reached the passenger side door but found it was locked when he discreetly lifted the handle. In his side view mirror, Sam could see the man's hand resting on a handgun.

"We just need to ask you some questions," the man in front said, watching Sam very closely.

With a quavering voice Sam said, "Yeah, yeah, just let me put this in park." Sam let out on the clutch and cut the wheel to the left. The little roll backwards opened up the smallest of gap that he thought he get through. Sam jammed his foot down on the accelerator. The Jaguar leapt forward like an attacking animal, catching the front man in front about thigh high. The blow caused the man to stumble into the advancing rear guard, leveling both. The passenger-side man pulled his weapon, but evidently was unsure of whether to shoot or not, looking at the two on the ground and then back to the fleeing Sam. The Jaguar had cleared the front vehicle, fishtailing to its get away. Scrambling to separate themselves on the pavement, one of the men yelled, "Shoot him!" Dutifully, he took a few quick steps, and kneeled into a shooting position, calling "Stop or I will shoot!" He aimed at the fleeing driver and squeezed off a round. Sam instinctively ducked as the bullet pinged harmlessly off the corner of the metal frame of the front window.

From the highway and maybe even the beach, the echo of a shot could be heard, but all that was visible was a massive swirl of dust which rolled up eight feet in the air, clouding the entire road. A moment of stillness followed as the interested parties assessed the situation. From the cloud, the Jaguar emerged like a rocket launched from a torpedo hole with a wild-eyed Sam at the wheel.

Once out on the road and clear of being shot, Sam fumbled for his cell while accelerating and hit redial. It was Charles' voice, "Hello..."

Sam let out a sigh of relief. "Charles!" Sam yelled into the phone. The Jaguar quickly passed the 70 mile an hour mark on its way to 80.

"I am sorry, but I can't take your call right now, please leave a number and I will call as soon as possible.

"Answer the damn phone!" Sam screamed another obscenity and hit redial. Sam gave a glance in his mirrors and was relieved to see no cars behind him. He did not slow down, rather continued to accelerate, putting as much distance between him and his assailants as possible.

It was at that moment that Sam heard a siren behind him and looked in his rearview mirror. A Miami-Dade Patrol car, with like a Christmas tree on steroids, was quickly gaining on him. Sam felt a sense of relief and dread at the same time. He immediately left off the accelerator. Seeing an exit, Sam decided to get off the highway in preference of an access road. When Sam exited, the patrolman's squad car let loose with a "whoop, whoop" sound from his siren. For what purpose, Sam wondered. To let Sam know he was still there? Sam said aloud, but to himself, "I know you are still there asshole, I am getting off the road, okay?"

As suspected, Sam found ample room to pull over and coasted to edge of the access road. The patrol officer angled his car in behind so that if someone were to slam into his car from the rear, it would eliminate the possibility of taking out the officer while writing the infractions that this driver most certainly, sorely deserved.

From the rear of the car a slamming door could be heard, followed by an almost immediate command, "Sir I will need to see your license, insurance and registration."

Sam yelled out, "Thank God you are here." He started to get out of the Jag.

The officer moved his hand to his gun grip and said sternly, "Sir. Stay in the car!"

Sam immediately froze. "If you will just list…"

The officer was standing at the rear bumper, now with his weapon pointed at the ground. "Let me see your hands."

"Okay, you can see my hands, but will you listen…," Sam said while placing both hands on the steering wheel.

Holstering his weapon, "Sir, I need to see your license, right now!" the officer commanded.

Sam said patronizingly, "Okay sure officer, I have my license…, I don't suppose you saw the men who just tried to kill me, did you?" Sam stopped to think if he did, in fact, have his license.

Dubiously the officer said, "Let's start with the license and then we will listen to your story."

Sam's mind raced to think where his license was. "Yes, in the bag. I have my license in the bag," sounding quite relieved. He thought he remembered that the bag was in the trunk. "But it is in the trunk."

Suspiciously the officer asked, "In the trunk?"

"Yes, in the trunk, I can get it. No wait, I have it here." Now Sam remembered returning his wallet to his back pocket before getting into the car. "But the registration is…, I am sure it is in the glove box. But officer, I was being chased!"

Evidently convinced this erratic behavior was drug or alcohol related, the officer skeptically asked, "Chased?" While resting his right hand on the butt of his Glock 40, the officer signaled with his left hand to the second officer to back him up. Now his partner was easing up from the opposite side of the car.

Sensing the movement from Sam caused the second officer to draw his weapon. "Keep your hands where I can see them and no quick movements."

"Can I get my license, or do you want to see my hands?" Sam asked curtly.

"Is it in the bag?"

Sam sighed, "No, it is in my back pocket."

"Why did you say it was in the bag?" the officer asked.

Sam let out a frustrated breath. "I was rattled by the guys trying to kill me."

The second officer was quickly at the rear of the Jaguar with his service weapon in a two-fisted grip. He asked suspiciously, "What's in the bag?"

Sam exhaled with frustration. "My stuff for the beach."

The first officer asked, "Would that stuff include any illegal drugs?"

Now Sam understood, the officers suspected him of being under the influence. And why wouldn't they? He probably was a little drunk from the sun combining with the Mickey's malt liquor, and the smell. Hell, even Sam could smell the alcohol he spilled on is legs.

Calmer than he felt, Sam said, "No on the drugs, officer."

"Slowly give me your license," the first officer said. He slowly let go of his grip on his weapon after making eye contact with his partner.

Sam slipped the license out of his wallet and handed it to the officer whose name tag read, Beasley. With the situation apparently in hand, Beasley moved cautiously to the rear of the Jag, passing the license to the second officer, who immediately headed back to run the license through the system.

"Okay, Mr. Jackson, who was chasing you?" He asked in an incredulous tone.

"I don't know who it was, but they shot at me!"

"They shot at you?" Beasley questioned skeptically.

"Just like last night." Pointing to his neck, Sam said, "This is what they did last night."

Beasley said, "Okay, we will check that out. Were you or the car hit?"

"No, I wasn't hit, but it clipped the windshield. Here, right here."

Beasley's left hand fingered the minor scratch on top of the windshield. Pulling out a notebook, the officer began writing notes. Sam closed his eyes and tried to calm himself.

Beasley asked, "So where were you when these men shot at you?"

Sam said, "At the beach a couple miles back."

Apparently amused, Beasley asked, "Haulover Beach?"

"Yeah, that's the one."

Beasley stopped writing. "Haulover Beach. The clothing optional beach."

Sam sighed, "I didn't know it was clothing optional."

Beasley said, "I see." He began writing again.

Sam closed his eyes again. In a few short minutes, Officer Fuson returned to deliver a whispered message in Beasley's ear before returning to the patrol car.

Beasley asked, "So Mr. Jackson where did you get the car?"

Opening his eyes and taking a deep breath, Sam said, "Look, this is going to sound crazy... but this is not my car."

Beasley responded distrustfully, "I see. Where did you get it?"

Sam laughed nervously. "No, no, it is not my car, but the owner lent me the car."

"Uh huh," Officer Beasley grunted. "Was it the owner who was shooting at you?"

San brightened and said, "The glove box, I am sure the registration is in the glove box."

As Sam reached over, Officer Beasley said, "I don't need the registration; I ran the plates...,"

But Sam had already released the latch of the glove box. As the glove box opened a snub-nosed 38 fell onto the floor.

Drawing his service weapon, Beasley yelled, "Gun, partner!" He pulled his service weapon. "Sir, I will need you step out of the vehicle." He placed the barrel to Sam's left ear and with his left hand reached down to open the driver's door.

A moment later, handcuffed and with his face firmly planted on trunk of the car, Sam had given up on trying to

202

explain his situation. When the gun had fallen out of the glove box, he simply laid his head back on the headrest and said, "Just go ahead and kill me right here." He could only wonder how he was going to explain this. His mind envisioned an article in the University newspaper headline: Professor Jackson Arrested for Gun Possession following High Speed Chase – Suspended Indefinitely.

Out of the corner of his left eye, Sam could see the cars up on the highway slowing down to take a look at the entertainment and postulate what would cause the police to have a citizen laid out on the trunk of his car. Even cars which were up on the highway slowed in hopes of catching some of the action sure to be included on the next television version of "COPS." Closer to the access road, someone leaned out and yelled, "Police brutality!"

Sam responded as loud as he could with cheeks smashed on the trunk, "Thanks, but don't give them any ideas!"

"Sir, I am going to ask you to be quiet," Officer Beasley responded in a tone that Sam thought was unnecessarily derisive. Another police cruiser had pulled slowly by and parked in front of the Jag. Both officers popped out and as they walked up each gave Sam, a look deserving of a serial killer.

"Could you take your elbow off my neck? The metal is burning my face!"

"Sir...,"

Sam interrupted mimicking the officer's voice, "I know. I am going to ask you to be quiet," completing the officer's sentence for him. But the comment did get a slight chuckle from the assembled team from law enforcement.

Beasley responded with a harder push on Sam's neck. But then, he lifted Sam by his handcuffs and spun him around. The pain of the maneuver caused Sam to let out a demonstrative "Owww! I am not made of rubber!"

This caused one of the backup policemen to turn away and the other to cover a laugh with his hand. With reinforcements and the suspect cuffed, Officer Beasley relaxed some. "Don't move," Officer Beasley said with a menacing look.

Sam quickly said, "Fuck you," and instantly regretted saying it.

The officer turned back and moved toward Sam.

Sam offered contrition quickly, "I am sorry. I should not have said that." Sam turned around and laid face down on the truck. The two new officers broke into laughter. Beasley pulled Sam back to a standing position. This time Sam grunted but kept his pain to himself.

Returning to the Jag, Fuson said, "Got good news and bad news, Mr...." he looked at his clipboard, "Jackson."

"It is Dr. Jackson to you. Actually, it is Dr. Jackson to him," Sam said nodding at Officer Beasley. "You can call me Mr. Jackson." The two new officers again started laughing at their fellow officer.

"Yes, well, Dr. Jackson, I have good news and bad news."

"I am getting the death penalty, but it will be quick," Sam quipped, which garnered some more laughter. Beasley still had a scowl on his face, not appreciating the humor Sam was delivering.

Fuson continued, "We are going to have to give you a breath test...,"

"Okay, but I have had onions, so it won't be pretty."

"Cut the crap," Beasley said moving in once again. Sam quickly stepped so that Officer Fuson was in between him and the menacing Officer Beasley.

Beasley's right forefinger rocketed toward Sam's nose. Sam instinctively angled back.

Beasley growled, "I know you have been drinking, you smell like a keg of beer."

Another of the reinforcements moved closer to Officer Beasley and the prisoner, just in case there was a need to step in.

"Mr..," Fuson paused, "Dr. Jackson, if you will let me tell you what needs to happen then I think we can get you on your way."

Sam let his head fall back and mouthed a thank you to the sky. When he returned his attention to the officer, he saw one of the dark sedans pull to a stop up on the highway, a good fifty yards away. Officer Fuson was speaking, but Sam could only focus on the car, driven by the men that had tried to kill him. He started to tell the officers, but they already thought he was insane or drunk and a story about someone trying to kill him..., hell, he could hardly believe it.

Fuson was saying, "You are going to get a ticket for speeding, 80 in a 65 zone. You are going to get a ticket for distracted driving while using a cell phone. We have confirmed that the car has not been reported as stolen and will not charge you with possession of a handgun if we find that it has been properly registered. We will need to confiscate the weapon and the owner can claim it at the station. If you pass the Breathalyzer test, we will allow you to drive yourself to wherever it is that you need to go."

"I want to make a call," Sam interrupted.

"You are not under arrest," Fuson said somewhat confused.

Sam repeated, "I want to make a call."

"Dr. Jackson, you don't need a lawyer yet, and you will have to take the Breathalyzer regardless."

"I want to make a call."

Fuson gave a sigh of frustration. He asked with impatience, "Who is it that you want to call?"

"Lieutenant Jerry Collins."

Beasley chimed in, "He is **not** going to call the Lieutenant!"

Fuson shot his fellow officer a stare. In a very low voice, he said to Beasley, "You are not helping here."

"I want to call Lieutenant Jerry Collins. Then I will take your test and give you guys no further problems." Looking to each of the officers as if for approval, he said, "I promise."

The officers looked around at each other. One of the two late arriving officers was shaking his head with another laugh, said, "Brad, let him call. This can only get better."

One of the officers pulled out a phone and turned his back toward the scene and placed a call. In less than one minute, the officer handed the phone to Sam, who turned his shoulder showing that his hands were stilled cuffed. Fuson gave Beasley a long look before pulling his cuff keys from his belt. He unlocked the left cuff but decided to leave the right one in place.

Sam took the phone and said, "Hello."

In a growl that Sam recognized, a voice said loud enough for everyone within earshot could hear, "Who the hell is this?"

The two reinforcement officers both turned away so that their laughter would not be heard.

"This is Sam Jackson, Charles Reynolds' friend."

"Reynolds! That figures! What in the hell is going on?"

Fuson smiled and could only imagine what excoriation was going to follow. *Collins was going to rip this guy a new one, or else...*, a bad thought went through his mind. *I get shit canned by the Lieutenant for letting him make the call.* Fuson's hand began a steady massage of his left temple.

Sam took a breath and "It is a long story, but I need these officers to place me in protective custody."

Yelling, Jerry exclaimed "What?!"

Sam instantly moved the phone further from his ear. Then tried again.

"Jerry, there are people that tried to kill me, and they are parked just down the road."

Somewhat conciliatory, Jerry growled, "This had better be legit."

"They fired shots at me as I sped away!" Sam pleaded.

"Oh, all right, I should have known any friend of Reynolds would be able to get himself in as much trouble as he does. Let me talk to the officer in charge."

Sam handed the phone to the officer and gave a sideways glance to Beasley.

"This is Officer Brad Fuson."

"Fuson, do you see anybody suspicious parked nearby?"

Fuson looked across the road and then back over his shoulder.

"Hard to say Lieutenant. There are about two dozen rubber-neckers."

Sam said excitedly, "Look, right back there, the two dark sedans are turning in the opposite direction."

All the officers looked, but traffic was congested in both directions, thanks to the thrill of seeing a road bust.

"I don't know Lieutenant, there is a lot of traffic."

Collins barked, "Okay, tell him to drive to Charles Reynolds' house and give him an escort. I will meet you there."

Before the slam of a phone disconnecting the call, the officer heard his Lieutenant yell, "I am going to bust some heads!"

Since the police had not confiscated his phone, Sam had tried to call Charles on the way home with no success. It seemed as if the call was going straight to voice mail, which indicated that Charles had his phone turned off. He figured that it could also be that Charles was flying on his way back to Miami and thus was not able to receive calls. Whatever the reason, it was incredibly distressing and frustrating. It was just after five o'clock when Sam finally pulled the Jag into the Charles' driveway. They had not come straight home after the beach incident because the officers were in the area of an emergency call and had diverted to a breaking and entering in the opposite direction of Charles' house. Instead of letting Sam drive back to Charles' house, Sam was placed in the back of the cruiser. That police call had taken another couple of hours, all the while Sam was seated in the back of a police vehicle like a criminal. Once some of the onlookers had come around the cruiser and glared in at Sam to see if they could see who was being detained inside. Finally, the officers returned Sam to the Jag and followed him back to Charles' house.

Sam exited the Jag and went to pull up the garage door. He looked back over his shoulder to see the Officer Fuson and his dick of a partner had pulled into the driveway behind the Jag. A sound of a skidding tire caused Sam to freeze for a second, but it was only the neighbor boy on his bicycle coming to a skidding stop in front of Charles' house.

After assessing the situation, he turned to his house and yelled to his mother, "Hey Mom, the cops are back!"

Devin's mother who was apparently watching out the front window shouted back "I can see that, Devin."

Fuson and Beasley pushed open their car doors simultaneously, strapped on their utility belts and donned their caps. Fuson took a deep breath and glanced once around the perimeter.

Sam could hear a front screen door slam next door and out popped Ms. Wendell.

Sam muttered, "Shit."

Ms. Wendell moved to the edge of her raised porch and leaned against the railing. Her purchase gave her a full view of the entire street and, of course, the goings-on at the abode of Charles Reynolds. As a judge at the top of her bench, she could issue her edicts and pronouncements of the sorry state of the neighborhood. Today she decided to just be an observer, leaving the young boy to provide the verbal assault.

Racing across the street on his bicycle, Devin asked Officer Beasley, "What did he do?"

When he did not receive an answer, he persisted, "Are you going to arrest him?"

Officer Beasley started to begin a dialogue, but Fuson waved to his partner and signaled that they had other priorities more pressing. But Beasley could not resist. "The day is early."

The boy started laughing and yelled to his mom, "Mom, I think they are going to arrest the Huckleberry."

"Devin! I told you not to repeat that!"

"That is what you called him!"

"Devin! You need to come in!"

"Ah, Mom," he whined. "It is just starting to get interesting."

As if on cue, another police cruiser, the unmarked kind pulled up.

"See Mom, here comes more cops." Now addressing Sam, "Boy mister, you're in trouble now!"

"Devin! Now!" the mother shouted.

"Damn, I never get to see the really good stuff."

"Language!" sounded his mother's voice from inside.

Devin pushed, then pulled his bicycle into a 180-degree wheelie and pedaled back to his driveway and sped into the garage. Laying down a skid mark, he allowed the bike to drop to the ground and entered the house through the garage.

Fuson and Beasley were now headed toward the house, and it was time for Ms. Wendell to give her two cents. "You must be really proud of yourself, two days in a row! You are killing my resale value!"

This pushed Sam to the edge. "Woman! Go back in your house and work on your witches' brew!"

Ms. Wendell's mouth dropped open, and she gave one of the swatting the fly gestures but held her position.

"You are just making friends everywhere," Beasley said with a scornful smile.

Sam started to take on the officer but thought better of it when he glanced at Jerry Collins ambling up the front lawn.

Short of breath, Jerry croaked out, "Okay guys, I appreciate the escort. Send me any tickets that you wrote, and you can return to making the world a better place."

Beasley started to protest, but after seeing the demeanor of the Lieutenant, he just gave Sam a scowl, and returned to the patrol car. Fuson said, "Okay boss if you will handle the paperwork, he is all yours."

"Thanks," he glanced at the officer's name tag, "Fuson. I appreciate it." They shook hands and Fuson handed a copy of their report to Jerry.

"Do you want the weapon?" Fuson asked.

Jerry jerked his head toward Sam with a mix of anger and question.

Sam shrugged, "It was in the glover box."

"And you pulled it?" Jerry challenged.

"It just fell out when I open the glove box."

Jerry looked over at Officer Fuson who gave a 'yeah that is sort of how it happened' nod of the head.

Sweeping his meaty hand through his ever-decreasing head of hair, Jerry breathed out, "Yeah, thanks, give that to me too and I will take care of it." Glancing over the officer's notes quickly, he asked, "Is it in the report?"

Making eye contact with Collins, the officer conveyed his understanding. "Tell you what, I will put any other paperwork on your desk," Fuson said as he handed a plastic evidence bag with Charles' gun sealed inside, to Jerry.

Jerry accepted the bag. "Good man. Fuson right?"

Fuson nodded and accepted the implied, 'the Lieutenant owes me one' and turned toward the police cruiser. Sam was leaning on the Jag, head hanging down. If he had a tail, it would be buried between his legs.

In his scratchy tone, Jerry turned to Sam and asked, "What the hell were you doing at a nude beach?"

Chapter 28   Washington, D.C. Sunday

Russell Epstein sat in the Director's chair of the FBI across from Rick Uhler. Rick asked, "What did we get from the information from our anti-insurgent actions?"

"Not much," Epstein said with a sigh. He had come from yet another meeting with the President and the various heads of intelligence, let a deep breath that could have been interpreted as an indication of his frustration with the lack of progress. "Thanks for coming in on a Sunday."

"No problem," responded Uhler. "So where do we stand?"

Epstein loosened his tie and gave his face a thorough two-handed rub. "There are two issues that should be of concern to the FBI. You and I both know that these raids were a preemptive strike, but the success has been trumped up by the President in the press, to the point where if the truth comes out, there will be a huge blowback. Between you me and the fence post, this President is running scared."

Rick gave an affirmative nod.

"Then there is the second issue," Epstein said with resignation. "The disappearance of the Hansford kid. It has been almost an entire week with no real progress. Needless to say, the President wants constant updates and each time.... Well, let's just say he is becoming more volatile each time. This is where you come in. What has the Miami team found?"

Rick noticed that Russell looked like crap. With the dark circles under his eyes and the shadow of beard growth accenting his face, Rick thought his boss would be a good candidate for some of the sleep aid television advertisements. Rick was pleasantly surprised by the confidence that Epstein had shown in him. Considering that they had been both been considered for the position and therefore rivals, Epstein could have closed Rick out from the inner circle. Rather than excluding Rick, Russell had shared his frustration of dealing with this president who was condescending and disrespectful. Rick had been close to the previous director of the FBI and Russell had often asked what it was like with the previous administration, just to gain a barometer of the how things were progressing.

Rick thought that Epstein probably was qualified for the director's position on paper but lacked the experience necessary to really operate with confidence. It was the lack of experience that caused Epstein to grasp for any help possible, which actually Rick did not mind. Considering the current situation, Rick felt fortunate that he had been passed over for the position; particularly after seeing the type of 'scrotum vice' Epstein had been placed in by the President, and the way that the White House staff treated the Interim Director. Rick was grateful indeed to have been considered too close to the previous offending director, which saved him from being the next Director, who would be tossed under the White House bus. It was almost if the administrative staff despised the FBI or at least look upon them with some distaste. The investigation into the associates of the President had thoroughly established an adversarial relationship. That animosity continued even after the replacement of the spurned director with Russell Epstein. Epstein had also seen the barely veiled hostility filter down through the cabinet and into the staff. The fact that Epstein had kept Rick in the assistant's position may have been what hacked the President off. It was probably expected the Epstein would clean house. Instead, he actually delved into the records when making his appointments. This, of course, earned him some credit within the FBI and probably the sister agencies, but probably marked him as soft by the White House.

Uhler said, "We are in the process of tracking Charles Reynolds and the others on the list provided by White House, but as of yet it is a no go."

Epstein continued to massage his forehead with both hands, and then leaned back in his chair causing a groan of springs that was appropriate to the atmosphere in the room. He gazed at the ceiling with a disillusioned stare. Epstein's mind diverted for a moment to what his wife had told him when the previous FBI director had been unceremoniously booted out. "Russell, if you want this position, I will support you, but I have to tell you that every bone in my body tells me that you should run from this guy, stay low and fly below the radar." With some reluctance, he had submitted his application; feeling quite convinced that he would not be the choice of the new president anyway. He reasoned that if he did not apply it would be interpreted as a lack of ambition or that he did not want to be a part of the new administration. He was absolutely shocked when he had been chosen.

Epstein, who had a nervous habit of clicking pens, was busy clicking, said "The President is really putting the pressure on. People only know what the press reports. If his team puts out that it was an attempt on his life, then that is what it becomes." Click, click, click, click. "He is scared Rick. And he is a ruthless politician. If he thinks an attempt on his life makes him more popular or revered by the public, then I guess that is a justification. This all seems to be emanating from that and he has been quite belligerent."

Epstein noticed that Rick was staring at his pen before realizing that he was clicking again. He self-consciously put it to rest by the desk pad. He gave an apologetic smile.

Rick said, "I saw it before in a couple other administrations, where they believed that they could create reality. But this has a real chance of major blowback. This is not personal like getting a blow job in the Oval Office. This is a deception that will cause a significant distrust. Sometimes it is the little things that sink a President. Just ask Nixon. But people will find out there was no threat in the Rose Garden."

Epstein was slowly shaking his head in disbelief. "And there are so many people that have access to this report. I don't see how it will not come out. Someone is really drinking the Kool-Aid if they actually believe that the President was in any danger."

"I think they want to believe it. Part of his legacy," Rick said. Rick looked at Epstein with a penetrating stare. It was as if he was trying to read his mind, or he was trying to intuit real loyalties before making a tough decision. Russell gave Rick a quizzical look.

Rick finally said, "You look as if you want to say something but are trying to make up your mind whether you can trust me."

"Wow, I did not know that you were skilled in mind reading."

Rick smiled but did not respond.

"Rick, you have every reason not to help me. I know your boss was screwed. He was doing his job and when he stepped on the toes of the President's friends, he was drop

212

kicked out of here. That was almost the same thing that happened over at the CIA with David Elliott."

Rick unconsciously shifted in his chair. He was surprised at this man's candor, but not his intuitiveness. He hoped that Russell's internal detector did not pick it up his reaction to the mention of David Elliott. But sure enough, for an instant Epstein paused and looked deep into Rick's eyes searching for truth. Rick tried to look nonplussed.

"I got this job and I saw from the first day that you were equally qualified and the only reason you were not promoted was because you were part of the old guard. I was part of the old guard of the DHS. That's what made my appointment such a surprise."

Rick listened without acknowledging the fact that he was pleased that Epstein was in tuned with the reality. He was still cautious about what to say, but at least could feel comfortable that the new director's relationship with the White House was a topic that was on the table to discuss. That in of itself was remarkable. Usually, the loyalty to the one who appointed you to your position ran deeper than almost anything else. He decided to take a chance.

"Russell, I think there is more going on here than you realize.

Epstein cocked his head to one side.

Rick continued slowly, calculating the reaction of Epstein. "There are potential winners and losers here on a grand scale."

Now it was Epstein's turn to look confused but allowed Rick to continue.

"Have you felt the intensity." Rick added, "The tension rising to a new level?

"The election did seem to be a polarizing event, sure. What are you getting at?"

There was a knock on the door. A secretary poked her head through the door, "Director, the report that you wanted is here. Shall I wait?"

"No, no, I will take it. Thanks. This is what I have been waiting for to come through! I think we have a lead on the head honcho in Texas."

Rick just nodded his head.

"I want to hear what you are saying, but you will want to be read in on this."

Moving behind his desk, Russell pulled red folder from a larger documents bag. Several grainy pictures fell from the envelope onto the floor and buffeted by air fluttered down under the front of the desk, making a perfect landing in front of Rick's right big toe. Russell let out a little curse and bent under his desk to retrieve the photos.

Rick said, "Here I've got them." Reaching down, he saw a grainy image of a man exiting a medium size private plane, on the top of the assortment. The shot was not very clear because of destitute light and the distance. Rick placed the photos on Epstein's desk without going through them.

"What's in the packet?"

"These are the latest of the leads that we have on the domestic terror cells. These were taken by an operative in Atlanta. Supposedly there was a meeting of several of the leaders behind this movement outside of Atlanta, and a dinner meeting just outside of Miami. I don't know what you would call it, the secessionist movement, sedition, revolution, I am not sure. Anyway, everyone who attended this Georgia meeting and everyone who attended a little dinner party afterwards made our list. They are being sought for questioning as we speak." Epstein handed the list to Uhler.

"How did we get this?" asked Rick.

Epstein said, "We have a source inside the American Independence Group or AIG."

Reading off the top of the list, "Charlie Rivers and George Jones, I don't recognize any of them...," he fingered his way down the list, "...except Charles Reynolds."

Epstein said, "They are almost all aliases. Reynolds is probably just chasing a story, but that is why I had you send a team to Miami. He seems to know more than he should about the Summers' murder and he showed up at the dinner. Alex Stephens is on there and he is a real person. He hosted the dinner. He is very well-connected, and we don't want to stir up that beehive until the President gives his okay. I have seen that rodeo already and don't want to upset the President any more than he already is."

Rick asked, "Who is Dr. Sam Jackson?"

"Believe it or not, a college professor who the AIG brought in to speak to one of their conferences."

Uhler said, "Well, I remember that he was on the list I sent with the Miami team, but how did we get his name?"

"Let's just say that we have someone who is in charge of travel, in our pocket, which gave us the name of the college professor."

"College professor?" Uhler asked with disbelief.

"It takes all kinds." Epstein took back the list and handed Uhler, the photo he had noticed earlier. "And who is this?" asked Rick.

"The report says that the agent thought this guy getting off his plane in Atlanta is George Jones."

"As in the singer?"

"Yeah, the singer." Russell acknowledged the humor with a quick breath through his nose.

"Do you recognize him?"

Rick puzzled a moment. "Not a very clear picture. No, I don't think so. Did they get a tail number?"

"It was a fake number." Epstein followed with an obvious question. "How does someone land an airplane in a major airport and get away with having a fake tail number?"

"Was it fake or borrowed?" Rick asked.

"It was totally bogus," Russell said putting up his hand, "And there was no record of him landing. And...," he said with exaggerated expressions to make a point, "the car that picked him up had diplomatic plates."

"From where?" Uhler asked quizzically.

"Brazil."

"Brazil?" Uhler questioned. "What the hell does Brazil have to do with this?"

"No idea. We don't know why, and we don't know who picked him up."

"Why didn't the agents just arrest him when he landed?"

Epstein let out a breath. "There was no team in place. The agent wasn't sure who he was, and because he was hoping Jones would lead them to the rest of the leaders who came in for an emergency meeting."

"And do we know anyone in the rest of the pictures?" Rick asked.

Epstein suddenly looked uncomfortable. "Pretty much the same story. We think we are getting close, but don't really know."

Rick asked, "How did we know that it was an emergency meeting?"

"Because the communication traffic that the DHS was monitoring started pinging like a hailstorm on a metal roof. This monitoring was how we nailed down the locations of cells around the country."

Rick said, "I don't remember being in the line of communication for this. When did all this come down?"

"This came from DHS, an analyst report that was put together by a team of noodles that I know."

Noodles was Russell's nickname for those of actual superior intelligence, not the wan-a-be intellectuals that positioned themselves high up in the various agencies. Noodles were street smart and savvy when it came to deduction and reason. They were the few and far between that had the smarts and the common sense to see more than the obvious.

"The DHS stole several of the better ones, including a guy by the name of Terrence Mitchell." Rick knew of Terrence but did not interrupt. "He used to work for me at DHS and when he got the opportunity to go work directly for the Under Secretary Corey Heitzman, I told him go for it. What I did not expect was that he would take his whole team. Anyway, when I wanted an analysis, Terrence, Clute Ahlstrom and Maria Telfare were who I called. The report that they prepared was based on all the same data that everyone else had and yet they were able to put together all the locations that we hit."

"Amazing," Rick said genuinely. "How are the messages being intercepted?"

"We already knew the type of encryption device the leaders were using, and we have been able to record the transmission and then decrypt the data stream. Terrence and his group were able to make sense out of the reports."

"Sounds like we are one step ahead of them. And yet they got away. How did they know?" Uhler asked sincerely.

Epstein gave a self-deprecating laugh, Epstein said, "If we were ahead of them, we would have been walking out of those raids with the master-minds of this secessionist movement in handcuffs."

"Who did we miss?"

"That was just it. We did not get any of the ones that we thought were going to be at the various sites."

Rick stated, "Bad intelligence or a leak, it has to be one or the other."

"The intel was good all except that the leaders had decamped." Epstein sipped a glass of water, while moving around his desk to peer out of the floor to ceiling window. Below he watched as two nicely dressed women animatedly discussing something of obvious importance. From seven stories of above, he could see one of the ladies point a remote to an indistinguishable model sedan. Splitting at the trunk the two women opened the door of the auto. The driver was evidently still talking because her hands were flailing all over the place. Epstein did not think the ladies were having an argument, it just looked like the one lady was very excited about the information she was delivering. The car backed quickly out of the space into an empty lane. Epstein reasoned that it was a good thing the row was empty, because he bet the driver did not even look back, just gunned it backwards and slammed on the brakes when her front bumper cleared the neighboring car. With a side view to add to his overhead view, Epstein now could tell that the car was a BMW. He shook his head and was mildly amused as the car rapidly accelerated to the parking gate, barely slowing down and exited the parking lot.

Turning away from the window, Epstein wondered aloud what Rick had said. "Information exiting," Russell said to himself, but Rick heard him.

Taking it as a question, Rick answered. "Seems like it would be a tremendous coincidence that all the leaders just happened to be out." He was lightly tapping a pencil on his leather portfolio designed with the FBI logo by a company called You Name It Specialties.

Rick said, "I wish we would have been able to catch them at their big powwow in Georgia.

Or their dinner party in Miami," Epstein added.

"Why didn't we catch them?"

Epstein's face crinkled as if he was experiencing pain. Rick realized that Russell was deciding how much to reveal. Trust was not readily given to a person that competed for the very job that you possessed, and Rick could see the mental

217

struggle with which his boss was wrestling. Russ cocked his head to the right. Epstein felt that Rick sensed his indecision. This was a bit embarrassing and awkward, because inner office distrust was not something the Epstein had ever perpetuated, just the opposite. He was a consensus builder and a team player. Russell Epstein's reputation was for the trust he was able to establish, and he was not going to let the fact that he had been given a promotion over Rick cause a rift in the office. No, he would not do that, after all, this man was completely trustworthy by reputation and every sense that Russell had, was telling him that Rick was as solid as they come. Russell had felt a twinge of guilt about excluding Rick from the briefings to which he had been made privy.

"You asked how we knew what encryption device they were using. As I said, there is an infiltrator in this Secessionist movement," Russell said with a grim manner that implied this information was highly classified. Rick raised both eyebrows and nodded his head once indicating that this was a positive development. He did not say anything hoping the Russell would continue. He didn't, so using the apparent guilt of Epstein to his advantage Rick asked, "So are you going to let the Assistant Deputy Director in on anything else?"

Russell knew that Epstein's hesitation was the product of Russell not being considered in the inner circle. The President was not a very trusting man when it came to high-profile people that served other administrations. This had led to the cleaning of the top agencies, which, of course, was not entirely without precedent, but the manner in which the purification had occurred caused much consternation in not only the FBI and CIA, but also the Secret Service and Homeland Security. It was one thing to put your own people in the various power positions, but the impetus of the purging was presented as incompetence rather than preference which had led to some hard feelings. Russell figured that after the head of the FBI and CIA had been discredited and dumped in the first term, he would not be too far behind. However, that directive had not precipitated from on high and he was marked as a holdover that had been generously spared. It may have been hoped that Rick would quietly resign and fade into the sunset, which is exactly what most of Rick's counterparts had done in the other intelligence organizations, opting for lucrative consulting jobs with the various security and mercenary organizations that had become so ubiquitous in the last decade.

Rick had his offers for these types of positions as well but had decided to hang on until the most recent election, hoping that the American public would have had their fill of a president who obviously despised the previous uses of the U.S. military and the intelligence community in general. However, the election returned the President for another four years and regardless of the controversy which surrounded the election, a revitalized president felt even more entitled to pursue the redirection of U.S. policy. This had been a significant factor in Rick's recent decision regarding his career. He planned to retire at the end of the year. The domestic policy initiatives had created an undercurrent of distrust to turn into a surface squall or perhaps it had just caused an existing discontent to become more visible. It did seem that anyone who opposed the current administration became an immediate target of a highly active campaign of attack. If you happened to be part of the government, Rick had personally observed budget cuts and job reductions of any dissenters. The message had been sent early and often that you either get on board with the ideology of the President or you would be thrown under the bus. Intergovernmental discontent was nothing new either, but never had he witnessed such uneasiness.

Rick thought he knew the reason Senator Summers had been killed, but he was hoping to find out for sure before his tenure with the FBI was squelched or he exited on his own. His decision to stay on was based on the conclusion that he could be of more benefit within the beast, rather than on the outside. He believed there was a link between the Senator's death and the independence movement, but he did not think they were responsible. Especially, since Rick knew that Summers was a friend to David Elliott. But he had been surprised before and in fact he was being surprised right now. Not in a million years did he expect that Epstein to 'all of sudden' take him into his confidence, yet here he was, and Russell seemed to be ready to do just that.

Russell, let out a breath indicating that he had made a decision. He said, "As I mentioned earlier, we have a mole in the organizational side, you know travel and transportation, stuff. But we also have an informant who is in the inner circle of this group and has provided "us," he did the finger quote sign, then continued, "with the assumed names of each of the conspirators. He has not been willing to give up the actual names, but we have been tracking various groups and have put tentative names to the aliases. We think the travel records and financial connections give a better than average chance that we have the correct people. They are well connected and financially stout. We have several that are successful businessmen and a couple individuals who have some intelligence background."

"Who is the informant?" Rick asked.

"Strange at it sounds I don't know. The information makes its way through the President's staff; I can only surmise that it is a friend of the President."

"How many people are we talking about?" Rick asked referring to the Secessionist group. He shifted in his seat and resisted the urge to take notes.

"A half dozen or so, main players," Russell said while he studied the reaction of Rick. "We also think we have a leak in the White House."

"Why do you think there is a leak?"

Epstein continued to study the reactions of Rick as if trying to see inside his mind for the man's true barometer. "Well, with the last mission we really struck out."

"I could certainly put out some feelers and see what comes back, but my connections in this sort of thing are fairly limited to those that I know in the other agencies and there aren't very many of those contacts left."

Russell grimaced, knowing that Rick was alluding to the President's purging of various agencies. Rick saw that Russell was conflicted about the whole process but was not sure if the acting Director felt the actions were the product of necessity or simply paranoia. There may have been some question in Russell's mind whether the actions of the President had caused the seed of discontent in the various agencies or whether the President sensed disloyalty and had made the tough choices inherent with political survival. Regardless, Rick was pleased that he had been brought in on the briefing because it was a likely indication that he passed the vetting process having survived the first term and had stuck around for a second, rather than jumping ship.

Russell answered, "I realize that the last few years have been tough on you because all that has occurred. But we can use your insight and contacts now. I just want you to think about what and who you know that may be of use in undermining this sedition."

"From your meetings with DHS and Secret Service, is there the belief that Summers' death really has anything to do with the domestic terrorism?"

This caused Epstein, who was taking a drink from a water glass, to swallow prematurely and began a hacking cough. Rick was caught off guard and was reaching out as if to try to stop the man's coughing, but Russell stood and held up a hand indicating that he was going to be okay. It took several moments for him to regain control.

In a raspy voice, Russell said, "Sorry, it just went down the wrong pipe." He cleared his throat a couple times and sat back down in his chair. "No, no, no we are not any closer to finding that out."

Raising one hand again, he coughed a couple more times and retrieved a handkerchief from his pocket to dry tears that had leaked from his eyes. Rick tried to remove an amused look from his face as he waited for the man to stop coughing.

"Did not mean to choke you up," Rick said affably.

Giving Rick a quizzical look which would have translated if verbalized, are you telling me everything you know? Epstein said, "No, no, no. Not at all. What I provided in the earlier briefing is all we really know for sure. We are getting ready to roll up everyone on the list that was assembled by the domestic terrorism team. Quite frankly some of the people on the list are probably a waste of time. The team has been monitoring publications, Tea Party gatherings and speeches from any group or individuals that could be part of this secessionist movement. Most of it is just rhetoric, but we are getting ready to shake some trees and see what falls out. But the reason I have brought you in on this is because one of the people that we are looking at..., he paused, is someone you know."

Chapter 29   Springfield, Virginia   Sunday

Fueled by the Atlantic Ocean, a vigorous eastern wind was propelling the damp air of newly arriving cold front, over the water at Accotink Lake. It was as if the air conditioner had been switched on full blast in what had been an otherwise mild season for the Washington D.C. area. Two late model idling sedans rested next to each other as if conferring on their next destination. The only occupants that were evident from the outside were two sedentary drivers. In each car, the driver's profile could be deduced through the lighter tint on the driver's window, but identification would have been impossible since both windows remained sealed. The entirely dark rear windows showed a perfect reflection of the vibrant fall colors of the surrounding trees and foliage. The I-495 Capital Beltway traffic could be heard in the distance, but not seen. The undertone of traffic was overcrowded by an occasional airplane on its approach to Reagan National Airport. Otherwise, only an occasional call of birds disturbed the park's solace.

Absent of warm weather activities like canoeing, cycling and hiking, the park seemed deserted other than the two vehicles, and two conspicuously well-dressed men who sat on a conveniently located park bench. With their backs to the vehicles, one of the men was casually tossing small pebbles from where they sat, into a puddle of collected rainwater stranded from the lake's edge which had been undergoing a huge dredging project to return some of the lake's practicality. The breeze caused both men to pull their overcoats a little tighter. The older of the two, Brad Hutchins rewrapped his indigo blue mohair muffler around his neck, while taking in the beauty of the lake. Both men were of average height, but contrastingly, the older man would have been considered handsome by any passing female. His aging blonde hair gave him a look of distinction, but it was the hazel eyes that had drawn people to the five-term U.S. Senator from Delaware. Hutchins recently had undergone lens replacement, liberating him from the need for contacts and glasses. He was not necessarily youthful, but his energetic, suave style and baritone voice had served him well in his three-decade long political career. Close friends noticed that the age wrinkles, perhaps due to all the political battles fought, which had begun to invade the

222

lawmaker's features, had deftly been removed with some minor surgery. Of course, anything other than commenting how good the senior statesman looked would have been poor form. However, in private conversations, speculation about his age was common because the man was always in the center of controversy. Despite his high profile, Hutchins had the uncanny knack to always come out on the right side of any scrape. It paid to have a friend like Hutchins and the young man seating next to him knew it.

Twenty years his junior, Mike Pemberton, had an almost sallow complexion and an indeterminate gaze that left his U.S. Senate colleagues with an uneasy feeling. He was not downright ugly and even some said he had rugged attractiveness to him. His unframed glasses were almost invisible but contributed to a scholarly look and created an impression of credibility. Physical attractiveness aside, the junior senator was equal to the older man in most every other area, shrewdness, and charm notwithstanding. The older Senator was aware of his own good looks but seemed to appreciate the junior Senator's counterbalancing talents. Perhaps, he thought, lacking the good looks of his mentor forced the younger man to develop the Machiavellian skills which are needed in the climb of the political ladder. Certainly, South Carolina's political machine had recognized the young man's talent for strategic decision making, garnering the attention of a multitude of bandwagon supporters, Despite the trail of casualties, or maybe because of them, South Carolina had a new vibrant U.S. Senator that could seemingly wield the sword of power with the same wrath of the revered, James Strom Thurmond. It did not hurt that his daddy was a major player in the defense industry and good friends with many of the top-ranking senators and congressman.

Speaking with his native Delaware accent, the senior Senator asked, "What does your friend...," he paused, "the Senator from Texas say about all this secessionist garbage?" Hutchins turned to face Pemberton, as a poker player looking for a tell.

The younger man paused from his target practice with the small pebbles, and cleared his throat to say, "He says that unless these more outspoken people are shut down, this 'sedition movement' could propel itself into a national movement."

Hutchins gave a sly smile. "I would say that it already has become a national movement. But I can bet he gives no indication that he is aware of who the culprits might be?"

"If he knew would the FBI be all over it?" Pemberton asked.

Hutchins blew out a short burst of air causing a short vibration of his lips. "He knows exactly who the people are behind all this. Hell, this whole thing is being pushed by Texas, and it does not matter that he is on the same team as the President." He paused for a moment for Pemberton to say something, but when there appeared to be no answer forthcoming, he said solemnly, "They have no clue as to what they are bringing down upon themselves."

With mild exasperation, Pemberton said, "This President of yours shouldn't have pressed the states to assume the debt, socialized medicine, bailed out the banks, rolled Social Security in the income tax or unleashed the EPA on consumers and business."

Hutchins said nothing but turned back to face the lake.

Pemberton looked over at Hutchins, but now it was his turn to wait for a response. Instead, he continued to vent, "Let me count the ways this guy continues to shoot himself and the economy in the foot with all his socialistic ideas. What is he trying to do, turn us into fucking France?"

Holding up hands in surrender, Hutchins said, "Hey look, he's your president too. He wasn't my choice, but he did win back the White House and got re-elected."

"Yeah, but this guy is an unapologetic socialist," Pemberton grumbled.

"So was F.D.R. and look how he is revered today. People actually believe he saved us from the Great Depression. Hey, Lincoln got elected, and it led to the civil war, now he is rated as the best President of all time." Hutchins felt inside his outer coat to the pocket in his suit, retrieving a pack of Marlboro cigarettes. He pulled out a wooden match and struck it on his leather sole. Guarding the flame as if telling a secret to an old friend, he positioned the cigarette into the flame. Exhaling, the plume of smoke carried away with the breezes off the water, quickly dissipating.

"Thanks for the history lesson," the younger man said with a touch of sarcasm. "I would not be surprised to see South Carolina make a move. Hell, we were the ones that started the Civil War. Why should a hundred and eighty years make any difference?"

With his free hand, the senior man began massaging his eye sockets. "The F.B.I, Homeland Security, the NSA, the State Department, and the I.R.S. are all about the heat on those they think are behind the campaign. The President is apoplectic over the idea that he could be assassinated. Both the Republicans and Democrats have denounced any violent offenders as traitors and seditionists."

"But secretly hoping that someone does the country a favor?"

Hutchins said sternly, "That would not be a positive solution."

"So, what is your point?" the young senator asked.

Hutchins unconsciously looked around. "Don't underestimate the length to which this President is willing to go to stop this insurrection."

"Meaning that it is only going to get worse?" Pemberton asked with a bit of an edge to his voice and accented his question with another pebble throw which glanced off the bank into the shallow water of the lake.

In a confidential tone Hutchins said, "Meaning that the President will likely be able to get it under control and you..., hell what am I saying? I need to be on the right side of the issue."

Turning to Hutchins, Pemberton asked curtly, "And what side is that?"

The old Senator laughed and said, "The winning side."

A bird in the distance erupted into a chatter that caused both men to turn their attention away from their conversation. Flushed out of a nearby stand of thick trees, the bird loped out of a distant stand of dense trees and foliage. Both men paused to see what might have caused a disturbance, but wordlessly decided it was most likely just birds being birds.

In a quiet voice, Pemberton said, "You have been around this business a lot longer than I have and I want to be around as long as you have. There seems to be a whole new group of spokespeople coming out of the woodwork. What makes you think he is going to be able to calm the storm?"

Exhaling a stream of smoke, Hutchins stated unemotionally, "The President of the United States is still the most powerful man in the world, but I am not sure he can. But I can tell you three things. One, anyone you see on television, spouting out the rhetoric of secession will turn high tail and run once the full force of the U.S. government comes after them. Two, they are not the ones pulling the strings on this, they are just expendable agents."

Pemberton looked puzzled.

The venerable senator just gave a knowing smile. "Sun Tzu?" He was checking to see if there was any recognition. There was not. "Art of War?" The younger man gave a slight nod indicating that he had heard of the book, but it was clear from his lack of connection that he had not read it. "What do they teach in college these days? Who moved my cheese?" Hutchins was not irritated, just giving the younger generation a verbal poke. "This is being orchestrated by heavy hitters and I would not be surprised if the lineup does not go all the way to 1600 Pennsylvania." He gave a flick of his cigarette, sending a column of ash to the ground.

Pemberton mouth dropped in tandem with the rising of his eyebrows. "You're kidding of course?"

Hutchins gave Pemberton an 'oh come on now' look, and then said, "You just said the guy is an unapologetic socialist. Do you not think that there are other Democrats that were holding their noses when they voted for him?"

"Sure, me included, but I can't imagine that a coup is being organized by his own inner circle."

"Oh, there is much for you to learn grasshopper."

The younger man eyes rolled his eyes.

"The third thing is this President is in love with the European model of government and I don't even know what the end game is here. Besides being a ruthless politician, the President is an opportunist by nature. Take that little episode at the Rose Garden. You don't have access to the report, but you know what the real story was?"

The younger man leaned away taking in the full view of his mentor but waited patiently for the man to continue.

"Firecrackers." Hutchins dropped his cigarette to the ground and crush out its embers with the toe of his wingtips.

The junior senator's mouth opened like a bass sucking for air. "Firecrackers?" He paused, looking into the elder's eyes to see if this was a joke. He knew immediately the man was totally serious. "And the President set this up? I don't believe it."

"I did not say that he set it up. I am saying that he took advantage that someone did it. A protestor or someone set off firecrackers to disrupt the press conference. They were hoping the press would show the President diving for cover. Instead, it was reported as an assassination attempt. And the press bought it or played along."

The young senator fell back on the bench in disbelief.

"This guy is a… is a…" Words failed him.

The older senator just laughed and said, "Master politician."

"That is what you call him?" Pemberton said with disgust.

"This little insurrection is just what the doctor ordered as far as the President is concerned. Control of the internet, more gun regulation, and the push for regulation of business are just a few things that he would wiggle into place. It is amazing what can be accomplished when there is a threat to the sovereignty of the federal government. Gun laws won't seem radical if there is a real or perceive security threat. One might say a national state of emergency."

"I doubt that the independents and middle of the road voters would be too keen on all of this?"

"That does not matter because he had the backing of the money players. And even though the President has pissed some of them off, he is still a formidable figure." There was a pause, and then he continued, "So, we have to figure a way to stay close and distance ourselves at the same time."

Pemberton looked doubtful. "He can't pull all that off. The NRA will be on his ass like never before. He won't get it through Congress. Hell, these are exactly the types of things that fuel the nullification argument."

Hutchins smiled coyly, "Do you know the history of Caesar?"

"More history?"

227

"History is a great predictor of the future."

"Go ahead; tell me the history of Caesar."

"He was broke throughout most of his early years, and when he was elected to be the high priest of Roman..."

Pemberton interrupted, "Caesar was the high priest of Rome? Isn't that like Bill Clinton being elected pope?"

After a small laugh, the senator continued, "He was very popular with the common man because he was able to push through a welfare program that gave a daily allotment of bread. With the common man's support and by the death or imprisonment of anyone that got in his way, he rose to be proclaimed dictator perpetuo, dictator in perpetuity. He was able to convince the mainstream people that it was the Senate was to blame for their bad times. He was able to convince Joe Plumber that he was looking out for him. He was able to convince the masses that they could not succeed without the help of the government."

Pemberton asked, "This is supposed to make me feel better how?"

"It is just to give you a perspective and how the President operates."

"Well, I don't think anyone is ready to name him President for Life. Term limits put a little hitch in your history lesson."

Hutchins said evenly, "Google 'bills to eliminate presidential term limits' and see what you find."

Incredulously Pemberton said, "So you think the President is lining up support to eliminate term limits? I don't see that at all. For God's sake, that takes an amendment to the Constitution. It is not going to happen. Particularly if it is like you say that his own people are lining up against him."

Hutchins just gave a 'you never know' raise of the eyebrows.

Frustrated, Pemberton asked, "So what are you saying?"

Hutchins patted his coat for his cigarette pack, but then decided to wait for his next smoke. "I am just saying that it would not pay to be left standing when the music stops. This episode in the history books will have several chapters and your true allegiances will need to be masked quite well, until the opportunity presents itself. This revolution talk has no chance of gaining traction and anyone associated with it will be bulldozed over. If you want proof, just look at Hank Summers."

Pemberton's eyes narrowed and he turned entirely to face Hutchins. "If you are saying what I think you are saying, that is the most ridiculous thought I have ever heard."

"Summers knew something. I talked to him just last week. Now, he was not going to share the goods with me, but he did imply that he has something on the scale of an eight on the Richter scale."

"And why would he show his hand like that?"

"Hey, old guys like us still watch out for each other and Hank knew that I was not a big fan of the President."

"Hank Summers was killed because he knew the President was trying to eliminate term limits? Or was it because he was part of the secessionist effort?" Pemberton said incredulously. "Oh, come on, you have been reading too many Grisham novels."

Giving a shrug and raising his eyebrows, which said, 'you might be surprised at what this administration is willing to and how far they are willing to go.'

"You are saying that the President of the United States had Hank Summers killed?"

"Look, Mikey my boy, I don't know anything for sure. I don't know what Summers knew. I don't know who he told. What I do know is that there are dangerous people on both sides of this President and Hank Summers is dead. He was killed by a professional assassin. Hank walked into the bathroom with him, and the guy killed him. The FBI thinks the guy injected him with pancuronium bromide and potassium chloride. It paralyzed him and then caused massive cardiac arrest."

Mike Pemberton flashed back to the fundraiser. He had decided to leave early and did not find out about the Senator's death until later on in the afternoon. He had met Hank Summers through his dad. He also knew and trusted the man sitting next to him. Brad Hutchins had become his mentor and confidante. Hutchins was a savvy politician in the know and his cunning was legendary on Capitol Hill. However, this strained the man's credibility.

"Brad let's just say that Summers knew something explosive and someone, we don't know who, killed him.

Shouldn't you be worried? I mean after all, you said the two of you met just before he was killed."

Hutchins said nothing, but a thoughtful expression consumed his face. Pemberton began again this time with a hint of mockery, "Brad, why are you telling me this? I mean with your thinking, aren't you putting me in danger too?"

Ignoring the younger man's tone, Hutchins continued to gaze out over the lake. Hutchins thought about how peaceful it seemed at this very moment. "I think you know Mikey that the goal of any game is to come out a winner."

Another round of squawking drew the men's attention to the same grove of trees as before. Hutchins sat up straight and peered into the distance. To the short side of the lake about 50 yards away, two large herons evidently had entered into a disagreement about the ownership of a fish and were slapping water at each other.

"You need to understand that there are several games going on at once. You have to position yourself where you can take either side. And you," he paused for emphasis, "have to begin thinking in broader terms."

"So, what are you going to do?"

"I am going to see the President to find out what Summers knew that got him killed."

"Just like that?"

"Have you seen the show, Hillbilly Handfishing?"

Pemberton gave a little vibration of his head in confusion.

Hutchins smiled. They cover up the holes and wait for a bite. When the fish bites, the hillbilly pulls them from the hole."

"Yeah, but the fish you are after won't just bite, he will swallow you whole.

Chapter 30   Miami, Florida Sunday

Ms. Wendell still at her front porch perch said, "Nude beach! I knew he was some kind of pervert!"

Sam jerked around bellowing a guttural growl, "Uhhhhhhah!"

Jerry stiff-armed Sam's chest, halting his advance and cutting the air out of the verbal assault that was sure to have followed.

"Thank you, Ms. Wendell. We appreciate your conscientiousness of being the neighborhood watch person," Jerry said in a monotone.

Mockingly she said, "We appreciate your conscientiousness, Ms. Wendell." She made hissing sound with her mouth and teeth that reminded Sam of a barn cat. Before turning she croaked out, "Don't pretend like you are not part of the problem, Sergeant Collins."

Having regained his breath, Sam growled, "It's Lieutenant Collins and…" Sam did not finish his sentence.

Ms. Wendell cut him off, "Lieutenant! Hah! I'm surprised he is not Chief of Police. If Charles Reynolds can win a Pulitzer…," pointing at Sam, "This bozo friend of yours will probably win a Nobel Prize. It is a crooked world we live in; I can tell you that."

Jerry had a smirk on his face and said, "Let's go inside."

Looking back to get in one more retort, Sam started to say, "That lady is…, is…"

"Yeah well, let's go inside," Jerry interrupted, physically turned Sam around, and guided him toward the house by the shoulder.

It took about thirty minutes for Sam to give all the details of his beach adventure. Jerry was laughing so hard that he succumbed to a hacking fit that at one point caused him to lay his head down on the kitchen table.

"How is this so funny?" Sam asked while working on a Shiner Bock from Charles' fridge. He had not really wanted a beer, but Charles did not have any wine and the Maker's Mark seemed excessive. However, Jerry loved Maker's Mark and had poured himself two fingers worth on ice.

"Well, it is obvious that whoever it was, thought you were Charles. You were driving his car and they followed. They waited for you to finish your foray at the nudie beach." Collins began laughing again, culminating in another hacking cough.

Sam looked at him a bit disgusted and asked, "Still smoking?"

"Yeah, I but I am in the process of quitting."

"How's that working for you?"

Wiping his eyes and regaining control, Jerry said, "It is about the twentieth time I have quit. Every time we have some extended investigation seems like I just fall back on old habits."

Sam gave an understanding nod. His parents had been smokers and went through similar periods of cessations, only to fall back into the habit. Fortunately, Sam had never taken up the habit.

"Okay, so they thought you were Charles and tried to what kidnap you? I mean they only shot when you were trying to get away. Did they ever call you by name?"

"No, never."

"Maybe they realized that you weren't Charles after they pinned you in. Do you think the guy you ran over was okay?"

"I don't know, but there was only one car parked across the street, so maybe the other took the one I hit with the car to the hospital."

"I will put out an alert to the hospitals. And when they saw you take a cell phone from the officer, they disappeared?"

"I think so, I mean I saw them and that's when I insisted calling you. I saw them parked across the road and then that police officer started talking about releasing me and I just was grasping for a way out. I was actually scared at that point that they were going to let me go."

Jerry wrote down some notes, adding to the ones from the previous visit.

Sam said, "Jerry, I am worried. I have tried several times to call Charles, but it goes straight to voicemail."

Jerry gave a considered look, shrugged and said, "Well if it's one thing I have learned about Chars is that he is like a damn cat, with nine lives. He has been shot, run over, beat up and blown up."

"Yeah, what's up with that?" Sam asked with a mix of consternation and irritation.

"Hey, I wish I had that man's luck. The last go around he was blown off the back of a ship of explosives, carrying two Al Qaeda terrorists, headed to blow up a naval station in Tampa, being fired upon by snipers and within ten seconds of lit up by an F-15."

Sam was giving Jerry a look of, 'you have to be kidding'?

"Seriously, Chars has been through certain death at least four times since I have known him, and somehow, he always makes it out." Jerry started a gravelly laugh but was able to stop before breaking into another round of coughing.

"Honestly, I don't see how you think this is funny."

Jerry gave an unapologetic chuckle.

Sam sighed in frustration. "And you think this is another one of these times? For Charles, I mean."

"Oh hell, who knows, but maybe he has rubbed off on you, I mean you have been shot at twice in two days and a little nick on the neck is all you have to show for it."

Unconsciously, reaching for his neck, Sam's composure was starting to slip away.

"I am not used to getting shot at and when I see Charles again, I think I am going to tell him just that."

Returning the conversation, Jerry prompted, "So you say he went to Virginia Beach?"

Sam was hesitant to reveal about Charles' real purpose. "Well, yes."

"You say he is not answering his phone?"

Just at that moment, Jerry's phone beeped twice. He instinctively reached down, and one motion answered.

"Collins." He listened. "Yes, I am at the address now." Jerry gave a look of confusion. "Okay, thanks. No, I will handle it."

Sam was lost in thought so was not paying attention to Jerry's conversation. He was replaying in his mind the events of the day, and went from being mildly upset, to quite incensed. Yes, the nude beach joke that Charles had perpetuated was mildly amusing, but the fact that he had been drawn into Charles' scandal was not funny at all. Jerry had disconnected and was looking out the window.

"Seems Ms. Wendell has called in a Code 37."

"What is a code 37?"

"Suspicious vehicle. Probably my cruiser out front."

"That bitch!" Sam slammed down his hand on the table and said, "I am going to go over there and give her a piece of my mind!"

"Ah, let it go. She is just letting us know that she is not happy with all the excitement. You know she was the one that tipped us off that someone had broken into Charles' house and sort of helped us discover that the house had been bugged."

Unwilling or unable to let his anger subside, Sam ignored Jerry. "Can't you at least arrest her for making a false police report?"

Jerry laughed and began another coughing attack. "No, I don't think that would help. She would probably be right and then...," Jerry stopped in mid-sentence and abruptly went to the front door. He could only see a vacant driveway and small yard in front of the house but could not see down the street. "Sam, I am going to get in my car and leave. I want you to lock the door and stay put. I am to drive around the corner, but I won't be far away."

"What do you mean?!" Sam said becoming very concerned.

"Just hang tight. I just want to check something out."

"Wait, you think there may be someone out there?"

Jerry said, "Probably not, but Ms. Wendell has been right before and maybe she wasn't just being..., well, herself."

Sam rolled his eyes and saw Jerry to the door. Collins took another call. This time from the dispatcher and relayed that he was leaving. He disconnected and assured Sam that he was not leaving but would be back in a moment. After Jerry had exited, Sam angled his face up next to the window trying to gain a view of the driveway and the front of Charles' house but could not see much of anything. He heard Jerry accelerate off down the street and decided to go out on the front porch. Moving through the door, he checked his cell phone expecting to see a call from Charles, but the screen showed that he had not received any calls. As he looked up, he saw the tail end of Jerry's cruiser disappear around the corner. Glancing around, Sam became aware that he was very alone. He chided himself for being a chicken but headed back inside anyway. He almost forgot, but returned to lock the deadbolt, just in case. Returning his thoughts to Charles' disappearance, and his near abduction at the beach, Sam walked contemplatively into the kitchen. He stopped in mid-thought and returned to the living room. How did all this fit together? Sam figured that it could not fit together. It had to be a strange string of coincidences. Sam thought to himself that he needed to go get on an airplane and get his butt back to Texas. But then there was a feeling of guilt that he really should find out what happened to Charles before just turning tail and running. Deciding to give it one more try, Sam sighed and pushed the redial button and again was forwarded directly to Charles' voice mail. He thought *where in the hell is Charles, and why is he not answering.* The doorbell rang, startling Sam, causing him to fumble his phone. Frantically trying to grasp the falling phone, it careened off his hands, one after another, and finally rebounded off his toe under the couch.

"Shit!"

Now Sam was on his hands and knees, with one hand outstretched under the couch, trying to retrieve the errant phone. Fittingly, from under the couch, a muffled ring could be heard from the just out of reach communication device. The doorbell chimed again, and Sam said, "Dammit Jerry, hold on!"

The phone rang again. Sam dropped completely down on the floor and peered under the couch. The phone had slid on the carpet further back out of his reach under the couch. The doorbell chimed again, followed by the less than patient pounding of a fist on the door. Sam stood and grabbed the edge of the couch with both hands and gave the couch a lift. The phone discourteously stopped ringing just as Sam maneuvered one foot to scrape up the phone from under the breadth of the couch. Letting the sofa down with a clunk, he picked up the phone, but it was too late. The screen had changed to offer the message of Missed Call - Chars.

Sam cursed, "Damn it!"

Ignoring his visitor, Sam punched the redial. He could hear that the call was received, but the expected hello, did not follow, only silence. Sam said, "Hello." There was no response, only more silence.

Sam said, "Hello. Charles?"

A voice from outside the door angrily announced, "Open the door, FBI."

Sam grimaced. "FBI, what the hell." Now Sam's phone showed that he had a new message.

Sam yelled "Crap!" The doorbell rang for the again, and again, and again. This was followed by another round of pounding.

"Coming, I **am** coming!" Sam shouted angrily.

When Sam peeked through the door's peephole, he saw two suited men, one tall, young and athletic, and one older and slightly overweight. He hesitated before saying through the unopened door, "Yes, can I help you?"

The less bulky man said formally, "Mr. Reynolds, we need to speak with you. Could you open the door?"

Sam did not open the door. Wearily he shook his head and said, "Charles Reynolds is not here."

Removing his sunglasses the fit man asked through the door, "You are not Charles Reynolds?"

"No, no. I am not Charles Reynolds."

"Charles Reynolds does not live here?" The less athletically built man asked.

"Yes, he lives here. But he is not here."

"So, he does live here?" the younger man asked.

"I believe I just said that," Sam said smartly.

"If you are not Reynolds, who are you?" the older man asked with a scowl.

If they could have seen him, Sam gave the man defiant look which possessed much more resolve than he actually felt. But he was tired of being pushed around and was losing patience. He said irritably, "Who are you and what do you want?"

"I am sorry. Did we forget to identify ourselves?" The older man held up a badge to the peephole, said, "FBI."

The younger agent intervened, "Sir, could you open the door?"

Sam unlocked the deadbolt and cracked the door just an inch. Still trying to read the displayed badge through the crack of the open door, Sam said in a weary voice. "I am a friend of Charles. My name is Sam Jackson. What is this all about?"

The two suited men looked at each other in tandem. Now the older man took off his sunglasses and said disbelievingly, "You are Dr. Sam Jackson?"

Sam was taken aback by the man's question. Seeing the truth in Sam's face, and before he could answer, the older agent pushed through the door. Spinning Sam around, he pulled out cuffs, then slapped one of them on Sam's right wrist.

Sam let out, "Hey, hey, hey you are hurting me!"

Pushing past Sam into the house, the younger man said, "Who else is in the house?"

"No one else is in the house!" Sam said defiantly.

"We just happen to be looking for you in addition to your friend Charles Reynolds. Strangely, we come all the way from D.C., and you are in the house of another person of interest."

With the quarry now cuffed, the older man extended his arms giving Sam, a rough push toward the couch. Sam stumbled back and involuntarily sat down.

"A person of interest? Why in the hell would you be interested in me?"

Chapter 31   Miami. Florida   Sunday

Sam's eyes flashed a defiant look which was met by the visitors' looks of disgust by the older of the two and contempt by the younger one. The doorbell rang and Sam called out, "I am here, I am here, don't go away."

Sam bent forward and tried to stand. The older suit, gave Sam a little push back onto the couch, causing Sam to lose his footing. His cuffed hands slipped off the edge of the couch as he struggled to gain his balance. His outstretched foot caused the small area rug beneath feet to give ground. Sam's cheekbone caught the edge of a side table.

Unable to move fast enough to prevent a collision, the older suit just said, "Shit!"

The younger man moved to help Sam up and back onto the couch, but the older man waved him off saying, "Just go see who is at the door."

A slice in Sam's cheekbone presented a steady stream of blood down his cheek. The younger suit went quickly to the front window and angled his vision to look around but trying not to disturb the blinds.

"It is just a kid," the young suit said in a deep voice.

From the outside a voice called, "Hello, Mr. Huckleberry? Are you okay? Do you want me to call the police or something?"

"Badge him and tell him to get lost," the older suit said. He had been able to help Sam back up onto the couch and had reluctantly pulled his handkerchief from his pocket to stanch the bleeding from his cheek. Leaning askew on the couch, Sam winced as the folded handkerchief was pushed against the half inch width gap that dripped blood onto the arm of the sofa.

Opening the door slowly, the young suit, lifted his badge case and started to address the boy, but instead was greeted with the nose of a police issue, Smith and Wesson automatic.

Jerry growled in a loud command, "Hands where I can see 'em."

From the back of the room, the older suit was yelling, "Hey, hey, hey. FBI, FBI, Put that gun away!"

At the back of the house the door was busted open and three other police officers filed in, with their guns drawn.

238

Seeing that he was outnumbered and outgunned, both suits raised their hands. While both of the suits were yelling "FBI, FBI" the on-rushing policeman were equally as animated calling out, "Drop the guns!" and "Get on the floor!"

Refusing to get on the floor, both suits removed their guns from their holsters, handing them butt first to the nearest officers. Seeing the inside was contained, Jerry looked back over his shoulder to make sure the boy had moved back out of harm's way. He did not intend to use the boy, but the kid just appeared out of nowhere while Jerry's team was assembling, out of sight in the yard next to Charles house. As they maneuvered toward Charles' home for the assault, the boy was already stepping to the door and rang the bell. Then and now, Jerry wanted to yank the kid by the ear, but instead settled on giving him a death look.

Devin gave a sheepish smile, "Thought you could use the help!"

The kid took a quick retreat as the burly cop looked like he was going to come off the porch and strangle someone. Jerry scowled while saying, "You could have been shot! You little...," he stopped as he saw the mother come around the corner of the house across the street.

"Devin!" the mother screamed. It was an irritating, high-pitched yell which caused Jerry to cringe from the shoulders down. Devin also tensed before giving a cautious look over his shoulder. Again, she yelled, "Devin, you get home right now!"

The anger in Jerry quickly dissipated as he saw the boy shoulders sag. Jerry said, "Hey, thanks kid, we did need some help."

Devin's face showed surprise and then a huge smile erupted, showing a snaggle-toothed grin and sparkling green eyes. The boy gave a little wave and ran across the street toward his mother, waiting with hands on hips.

When Jerry turned his attention to the activity inside, the FBI agents were being patted down by two officers. Jerry walked in and took command of the situation. He took a look at the blood on Sam's face and asked, "Sam, which of these two men assaulted you?"

Slumped on the couch, with his hands still cuffed behind his back, Sam looked from one suit to the other and finally said, "Both." The bloodied handkerchief had fallen to the floor, leaving the wound to the right side of his face bleeding down Sam's neck.

"Sergeant, you have the IDs for these two?"

"Yes sir."

"Call in and verify that they are with the FBI."

The older suit said, "We are FBI, you have our badges. What more do you want?"

Jerry looked directly into the man's eyes. "Sergeant."

"I am on it, Lieutenant."

"Agent," Jerry paused for cueing by one of his officers.

"Parrish," said one of the uniforms.

"Agent Parrish, do you have keys to the handcuffs on this man?" He pointed to Sam, who awkwardly held out both hands from behind his back, for someone to uncuff him.

"This man is a detainee of the FBI. I am taking him in for questioning." Parrish said stiffly.

Jerry's eyebrows raised and he gave a little laugh. "Really? And what exactly is this professor, who is not even from this area, supposed to know that would require two of the Agency's finest to come in here and try to rough him up?"

Neither of the suits answered. Jerry growled, "If you are FBI and I am seriously wondering whether you are, you are so far off the reservation that I should arrest you myself."

"If you want to get into a pissing match Lieutenant, I have a big dick," Parrish said, and then gave a little frown as he thought that the boast might not have sounded right.

Jerry had taken about all he was going to take from this overstuffed suit. He said in a faint voice, "I am sure the word dick is often used in describing you, but in this case keep it in your pants, because I can assure you that this particular person has no information that could help you."

McQueen blasted, "Oh, I think he can. He is a suspect in a national investigation into domestic terrorism."

Sam blurted out, "Me?!" Sam tried to stand, but Jerry plunged out his hand catching Sam in the sternum, sending him back onto the couch.

Turning to face Sam, the older suit said accusingly, "Did you or did you not fly all the way from Texas to deliver a speech to a group that has been known to be subversive to the U.S. federal government?"

Sam was now on the defensive, but still defiant. "I spoke to a business group, you asshole."

"A business group, whose leaders have known ties to leaders of a dissident movement," jabbed McQueen accented with a pointed index finger.

"I was a paid speaker on economics, you boob." Sam spat through the blood dribbling over his lips.

Parrish shot back, "And I guess it was just a coincidence that you were the replacement speaker for the Senator who was killed by your dissident group?"

This new point gave Sam a moment of confusion. He finally only managed, "I was a replacement speaker, but I don't know who I was replacing, and I don't know any of these people you are talking about."

McQueen delivered the next verbal shot by practically spitting. "You don't know them? Then why did you attend a meeting of all their leaders and share a nice little dinner with them?"

Sam stammered, "Because one of the organizers invited me to eat dinner. I did not know any of the people there."

"Yes, now we are making some progress, organizers," spending some extra time pronouncing the word organizers. Gaining confidence, both McQueen and Parrish were visibly wresting control of this situation. Parrish sent out the next volley of accusatory shots, "We pulled your phone records Dr. Jackson, so you can stop playing the innocent game. You were in contact with a George Love."

"I don't know any George Love!" Sam protested.

"Also known as George Jones." Parrish added.

Hesitantly Sam said, "Oh, him."

Jerry saw where this was going and did not like it one bit. Adding to the change in momentum, Jerry's sergeant came back into the room and gave Jerry a subtle nod, which meant yes, the identity of these two suits had been confirmed.

"Okay, Agents Parrish and..," again waiting for a prompt.

One of the uniforms said, "McQueen."

"Yeah, McQueen. I am going to take custody of Dr. Jackson for now."

Parrish lashed out, "Like hell you are! He is either a participant or a material witness to a calculated attack on our President and the country. And if he is not directly involved, which I find highly unlikely, he most certainly knows some very important information that can help us track these malcontents down before they do any more damage." Spittle collected on his lower lip which Parrish used the back of one hand to wipe off.

"I tell you what agents, since I am assuming you don't have a warrant for Dr. Jackson, I will deliver Dr. Jackson to the Miami FBI field office, first thing in the morning. That will give you a chance to reconsider the assault on this man's person and the insult to his character."

The two agents did not look like they were going for it, but Parrish finally, said in a derisive tone, "You are going to wish you did not take us on, Lieutenant."

"Yeah, well we'll see. Don't forget to unlock the good doctor before you leave. I will see if I can talk him out of pressing assault charges."

With the agents gone, Sam was resting his head in his hands, while sitting on the couch where he had been held captive. A prominent bruise had already begun to develop, surrounding the split of skin covering the cheekbone. A makeshift ice pack had been assembled, using a sandwich bag and some crushed ice wrapped in a kitchen towel. Jerry was still on the phone with his boss at the police station. He was evidently catching some heat because of all the calls coming from one address. That address, belonging to the one and only Charles Reynolds, who everyone knew was close friends with Lieutenant Jerry Collins. After disconnecting the call, Jerry let out a blow of air and sat in a wing chair next to the couch.

"Were these the same guys that were at the beach?" Jerry asked.

Sam opened and closed his jaw, checking to see if everything was still functioning properly. "I don't know.

242

Maybe. I guess they could have been in the second car. I really never really got a good look at them."

"Who is this guy, George Jones?" Jerry asked.

Sam stammered, "Just a lunatic who tricked me into..., to..., to..., getting into this whole mess."

Sam explained the invitation to Jerry. After a couple Tylenol, Sam was leaning back on the couch with an ice pack resting on his cheek.

Sam said, "I need to get back to Houston."

Jerry took in a breath and let it out. "Normally I would say that is exactly what you should do, but I am not sure that is going to happen. I have to take you into the FBI tomorrow."

Sam just looked pitifully dejected. His left eye had started to puff up from the blow to his cheekbone. "How in the hell did I get into a mess like this. This has to be a mistake."

"I think you were in the wrong place at the wrong time. We could also have two different issues going here. The break in last night and the hit at the beach were likely aimed at something that Chars is involved with. They probably thought you were him at the beach. These FBI guys seemed legit, but I am really surprised that they gave up so quickly. Something was just a little off with their routine."

"You checked them out, right?"

"Their creds looked authentic, and I did not want to step in it any further than I already have. There is a Parrish and McQueen at the FBI, but something was off. In the meantime, we are going to an emergency clinic to have that cut stitched up."

Thinking about his return to the university and the endless questions, Sam placed his head in both hands and slumped down on the couch.

Chapter 32   Virginia Beach, Virginia Monday

Charles Reynolds was seated in a comfortable, easy chair as his eyes cracked open from a deep sleep. He was momentarily blinded by sunlight which he figured must have been coming in through his bedroom window. Waiting for his vision to adjust, he noticed a particularly dry throat and felt for the first time that his lips seemed glued together. In fact, his mouth tasted a little like glue. He must have really drunk too much because his tongue was thick, and a dull ache reverberated up the right side of his skull. The sound of an air-conditioning unit clambered on, and the breeze blew on his bare upper body causing a slight chill to run across his body. Looking down and with his vision coming into focus, Charles could see that in addition to not wearing a shirt, he was also not wearing any pants. But that seemed to be the least of his concerns. When he tried to move his hand to his cheek to determine why his lips felt so strange, his arms felt constricted. He thought that he must have slept in the wrong position because his arms felt numb. It was then that he realized that his hands were bound and the strange taste in his mouth was courtesy of a piece of duct tape. He took his first look around the room that was decorated in an unimaginable way, tan drapes, and hotel style furniture. There was a desk in the corner with several upholstered chairs evenly distributed throughout the room, and if Charles had not been bound, the room might have passed for a nice place for a business meeting. He looked around for any sign which would tell him the identity of the hotel, but there was nothing in sight. He tested out his legs only to find that they had been restrained as well.

As Charles began the process assessing his situation and the planning of an escape, an adjoining door opened permitting entrance into the room by a small gray-haired man. The same gray haired man Charles had seen at Rudy's slipped through the opening. Dressed in a tailored fitting suit, his face gave no indication of his purpose for being here, in this room, with a bound and gagged investigative reporter. After closing the adjoining room door, he did not even bother to make eye contact with Charles, instead, choosing to go over to a wet bar. Using a facial tissue, he retrieved a glass and then performed the same ritual when he removed a bottle of water from a

244

conveniently located mini-frig beneath the counter. Deliberately he poured the water into a glass, returning the partially emptied bottle back into the refrigerator. He then turned his attention to his captive. Not only was the man well-groomed, he smelled pleasant too. A whiff of Blue Water cologne wafted to Charles nostrils. It was cologne that Charles was quite familiar with and in fact he had a bottle in his own cabinet at home. Still trying to clear his head, Charles again puzzled to himself what particular set of circumstances had landed him in this particular situation. It had to be something to do with the Tyler Hansford meeting. Or maybe it was the news conference about the death of Senator Summers. Of course, it could be any number of other stories that had wrecked careers of some very unsavory characters. Charles dismissed the latter thought as he remembered that he was probably still in Virginia. Or maybe he wasn't.

The man deftly moved in his Italian loafers over to Charles. Gray hair perfectly in place, he reached quickly ripped the duct tape off of Charles' mouth. Charles grimaced at the pain of having the equivalent of a waxing strip applied to the face. Charles thought of the movie where the man had the hair on his back removed with one big rip but could not quite think of the title. Without a word, the man assisted Charles in taking a drink from the offered glass of water.

"Have any ice?" Charles quipped.

The gray-haired man gave a slightly amused smile but remained wordless. He went over to the television and retrieved a remote control from the top of the set. He studied the device and eventually pushed a button which brought the television to life. Charles now noticed a small camera resting on top of the television, pointed directly in his direction. The screen showed a view of a pitiful looking man tied to a chair. Just as the thought registered in his mind that the guy looks like shit, Charles realized that it was a video of himself. Shirtless and in drab blue boxers, Charles was beginning to fully appreciate his predicament. Charles tried to recall the events leading up to being tied here in what by all appearances was a hotel room. He thought back to his meeting at the restaurant. Charles struggled at any recollection of the details, but he concluded that his drink must have been drugged and the waitress was just too friendly. Wait, did he leave with the girl? His mood elevated, then fell again. He did not. Tyler and he decided to go to the boat. Charles remembered Carly's look of disappointment when he said that he was leaving with Tyler. That meant that his rental car was still at the restaurant. He wondered if that was of significance. Maybe the police would find it and come looking. Charles tried to clear his head. The thudding headache pain he felt was joined by his arms and legs. He could not seem to focus and struggled to think back. Gray Hair clicked off the television. Charles tried to force his mind to coagulate some thoughts. He could not. The pounding of his head was getting worse.

"Mr. Reynolds, I would like to get you back on your way, but I need your cooperation." The breaking of the silence was so abrupt that it caused Charles to startle.

Charles tried to decipher the man's accent and dialect. With his head throbbing, Charles managed to grumble, "Glad to hear that. I am sure that you grabbed me by mistake, so you can just let go and we can all just go back to our mundane lives."

The man laughed softly and returned the glass of water to the counter. "I think we can straighten this out very quickly, Mr. Reynolds."

Again, Charles noticed a slight foreign accent. It could have been Austrian, but Charles was not sure. The man sported cuff links, visible as his outstretch arm return the remote to the top of the television. "Very nice shoes are they Italian leather?' Gray Hair ignored the question.

"First, I am a little surprised you are here in Virginia Beach, when I expected you to be in Miami."

"You should not be surprised. Virginia Beach was on my bucket list of places to go, and Southwest Airlines was running a sale to Norfolk."

The Gray Man appeared not to be paying attention, instead concentrating on cleaning the fingernails on his left hand with his right forefinger. "And you just happen to be meeting with someone who the authorities are expending a lot of efforts to find." He looked up from is self-manicure to meet Charles' stare.

"Well, I can explain that," Charles said with a smile. "You see..." Frowning, Charles could not even concoct an explanation, nor a funny retort and just closed his mouth. The

246

look of the Gray Man turned to amusement for just an instant, but then returned to a more familiar steely-eyed gaze.

"Mr. Reynolds, I think you are a fairly savvy man. I understand you are quite the investigative reporter. Surely you realize the seriousness of your current predicament." Leaning against a low-profile dresser drawer, Gray Hair began lightly tapping his fingertips in an impatient rhythm.

"You made a peculiar statement at a press conference a couple days ago."

Charles thought, *now we are getting somewhere.* He said, "You can't take anything I say seriously. In fact, I am surprised anyone listens to me. I rarely have anything pertinent to say."

"Mr. Reynolds, please don't take my calm demeanor as an indication that your situation is not...," he paused, "a serious situation."

"Oh no, I think any time that I am kidnapped and tied up, as a serious situation. Say, you seem to know my name, but I don't seem to remember you mentioning yours."

Another smile, but this one did not seem as genuine as the ones that previously graced the older man's face. From his coat pocket, he removed a single glove, placing it on his left hand.

Charles said, "Say that's a good look for you."

"Mr. Reynolds, I am a busy man, and we have a limited amount of time."

"Please call me Charles. I can tell we are going to be friends. And your name is?" Charles had a look of feigned expectancy. He was not sure that provoking this man was a good idea, but his fate was probably not going to change much regardless.

"Back to your question at the conference, was that a spontaneous revelation or was it...," he paused, "prompted by some other piece of knowledge?"

"So, this is what this is all about? A random question at a random press conference? You said you were busy, but you know, I am starting to question your time management skills."

The man stepped toward Charles and executed a swift backhanded slap, knocking Charles sideways. The chair momentarily lifted on two legs, but did not tip over, falling back to all four. Using his tongue to check for damage, Charles almost immediately tasted blood in his mouth.

"Wow!" Charles growled, "That got my attention! Whatever time management skills you lack, you sure have a great backhand. Do you play tennis? Because I play on occasion and would welcome the opportunity to get you out on the court." Using his bare shoulder, he wiped the edge of his mouth and gave an impertinent smile. The result was that a thin stream of saliva strewn with blood traversed from his mouth to his shoulder. "Of course, I would have to get me one of those gloves."

"Charles?" He waited for Charles to make eye contact. "I want to know, what you know about the death of Senator Summers."

Charles mind flashed to the person who fed him the information about the Senator's death. She had simply told him that the Senator's death was not of natural causes. He weighed the consequences of giving up the person's name. He almost dared not think of the name for fear that it would somehow leak out of his mouth, but he could not help it. Ellen Cochran was after all a former newspaper co-worker and of course, a former romantic conquest for Charles. Perhaps that was why she primed him with such an explosive little detail. Charles mentally dismissed the notion that she had deliberately and knowingly put him danger. Would she? Charles thought she had taken a public relations job in Washington D.C. several years ago, but Charles had lost track of her. She had resurfaced once in a conversation when Charles was having lunch with Hank Summers, but that was almost two years ago. Charles scoured his memory that was as cloudy as small grease fire. Then she turns up at the White House press conference, working for who? Charles wondered. Was she working for Summers? His jaw joined the symphony of pain in his body causing his thoughts to be jumbled. He would have to investigate that when he got out of this latest predicament. In a serious tone Charles said, "You are going to be very disappointed at how little I know."

"I am used to disappointment," Gray Hair said tonelessly.

"But you don't seem to handle it very well," Charles rejoined.

Charles thought the man was going to strike him again, but instead watched as he headed out of the room. On his way out, he picked up the television remote and aimed at the television. With a push, the picture of Charles changed to what appeared to be a naked body lying unconscious or dead atop a king-sized bed. Gray Hair opened the door and entered the adjoining room. He immediately reappeared on the television, next to the body. Gray Hair looked directly at the camera and removed a silenced handgun from his jacket. Using the body's hair as a pull tab, Gray Hair lifted the head for the benefit of the camera. Charles immediately recognized Tyler Hansford. Aiming directly at Tyler's head, he said, "Mr. Reynolds, you can hear me, yes?"

"I hear you." His head's pounding had begun to improve, but the situation just seemed to be getting worse.

"I need your cooperation," called Gray Hair.

Charles gave a defeated sigh and said, "Okay, leave the kid alone."

The man reappeared in the doorway, his gun still drawn, but dropped to his side. With a menace that belies explanation, Gray Hair said, "I have some questions about Senator Summers."

Chapter 33   Washington D.C.   Monday

Confusion evident, the President of the United States said into the phone, "They have done what?"

Though not understandable, the volume of the response from the other end of the call could be heard by others in the room. Inside the Oval Office, the President, the Secretary of Interior and Chief of Staff were about to conclude an unremarkable meeting about the challenges of acquiring more land for preserves. From the flushness coming over the President, it appeared to be rather bad news. Katie Lang, the Interior Secretary, shifted uncomfortably in her seat and sat up straight.

"What does that mean to us exactly?" The President had a quizzical look on his face. Listening intently, he was slowly shaking his head as if trying to process what the caller was saying. He began pacing in a tight figure eight, switching the phone from hand to hand with each turn.

"Just tell them that we won't agree to it," the President returned to his seat behind the massive and intricately designed Resolute Desk. The same desk that had been in place for the previous three presidents was named so because it had been made from the wood of the English Artic explorer the HMS Resolute. Originally a seagoing sailing ship, Her Majesty's Ship the Resolute was refitted to explore the Artic as the flagship leading three others, the Assistance, the Pioneer and the Intrepid. Abandoned during the in-vain search and rescue efforts of the Sir Franklin expedition, the Resolute was successively frozen, abandoned, recovered, restored, and returned to England. The Resolute desk was one of three that were commissioned by Queen Victoria. The other two, a match to the Resolute Desk and a smaller lady's version both reside in museums. As a thank you for the return of the Resolute to Britain, the Resolute Desk was presented to President Rutherford Hayes.

"How can they just start dumping the Dollar? Don't they need our approval?"

He listened a bit longer, shifting uncomfortably from foot to foot.

"I don't care how much we owe them. They need us."

The President turned to the assembled. He pointed to Katie and signaled her to leave, which she promptly did leaving the Chief of Staff, Hassam Rashid shrinking into the upholstered side chair.

"What can we do to stop this?!" he yelled in the phone. He appeared to be ready to throw the phone across the room but instead returned the phone to his ear. "And no one knew this was going to happen?"

The President's face had turned a dark crimson and his eyes were wild with a fury that caused the Chief of Staff to stand. "I want an immediate conversation with those little fucking weasels, and I want it now." He made an about face pivot, turning to the window. "I don't give a shit if they have already refused contact. You get them on the phone now!" He shoved the phone towards its cradle and almost landed it home, but the entire set lost the battle of momentum and careened off the side of the desk.

Rashid was frozen by an outburst even more volatile than the explosions he had become accustomed to witnessing from the Commander in Chief.

Rashid, managed to ask, "Mr. President?"

The President advanced two steps toward the man causing him to take a stand and move around to the back of the chair, using it as a shield. Halting, the President bared his teeth like an attacking Grizzly. With spittle that would make a Thespian proud, the President stammered out "The fucking Russians, the fucking Chinese, the fucking Indians and the fucking Brazilians have submitted a formal plan to the IMF to end the Dollar as the world currency reserve!"

Rashid asked lamely, "Can they do that?" The look of confusion on his face indicated that the problem sounded serious, but he was not entirely sure why it was so serious. When the President turned to glare at him, Rashid instinctively reached to fiddle with the knot of his tie.

"Can they?!" the President yelled and then repeated, "Can they?!" He glared at his Chief of Staff. "They just fucking did it!"

Rashid asked, "Do you want me to get Harvey in here?"

Harvey Fleischauer was the Chairman of the Economic Council of Advisors.

251

"Yes, yes, I want him in my office within the hour and I want Tom on the phone right now!" He was referring to the Treasury Secretary. "And call an emergency cabinet meeting!"

"Should I let the Vice-President know?"

The President spun and shot the man a death stare. "Why, so he can pass it along to all his little spies and malcontents. Fuck no. Keep him in the dark as long as possible. Hell, for all I know, he could be behind this whole thing."

Rashid said nothing and turned to go.

"Hassam, I want an immediate damage report on this. I want to have an idea about what all this means and what we can do if anything, to prevent this from happening. The value of the dollar is going to nosedive, and the price of oil is going to skyrocket."

The President made another tight lap around the room, before slamming the backside of an adjacent side table with his open palm. "They are going to turn us into to Pakistan," the President picked up an ashtray and appeared to be ready to throw it across the room. Hassam instinctively ducked, raised and then quickly exited. Instead, he slumped back against the wall fabric and fished out a cigarette. Before Hassam could close the door, a staffer named Olivia DeMurr stuck her head in. "Mr. President, Senator Hutchins is here. As the President raised his face, anger apparent, the door was pushed open wider. Without an invitation, a head popped into view around the staffer and peeked around the corner of the door.

Hutchins said cheerfully, "Bad timing?"

Chapter 34   Virginia Beach, Virginia Monday

Returning from the other room, a chime from Gray Hair's pocket caused the man to holster his gun and to fish into his outside pocket for a cell phone. It was a notice that an incoming call had been missed. He studied the number and set it on a nearby desk.

Charles said, "You know we have a lot in common. I have a phone just like that."

"Yes, Charles you do. Were you expecting a call from someone named, Clubbo?"

Charles did not answer, but the question confirmed that it was, in fact, his phone. Sam would be checking in perhaps before he left Miami to return home.

Gray Hair said flatly, "He's called a couple times. He must be worried about you."

Again, Charles said nothing but figured it was a good thing that Sam was trying to contact him. He was the only one who knew he was headed to see Tyler in Virginia Beach.

Charles asked, "Think that mini bar has anything stronger than water? A good drink and I will tell you everything I know?"

Gray Hair smiled knowingly and moved gracefully over to the cabinet. However, after returning the silenced weapon inside his jacket, he did not reach into the mini bar. With a hand towel, he pulled up a large brown leather satchel from the floor onto the counter. After removing a partially filled bottle of Maker's Mark bourbon, the man tossed the towel on the counter. Charles noticed how careful the man was to avoid leaving any fingerprints. It was a satchel that looked remarkably familiar to Charles.

Charles said, "I don't often drink whiskey, but when I do, I prefer Maker's Mark."

Gray Hair said, "Yes, I have heard that you do." Using a manicured finger to knock off the hotel glass' protective cover, Gray Hair splashed in a bit of the amber liquid and returned the bottle to the satchel.

With a realization sinking in, Charles said, "Strange, I have a satchel just like that in my D.C. apartment. Must have forgotten that I brought it with me."

Gray turned for a moment to flash a malevolent smile at Charles and distractedly lowered the satchel to the ground, minus the towel.

Hoping that Gray Hair had not realized his mistake, Charles quickly continued his banter, "What is even stranger is that there is a half-bottle of Maker's Mark in there, just like I had at my apartment. No worries, I am happy to share."

Snapping a tissue from its box on the counter, Gray Hair said, "We are sharing now." Grasping the glass with a facial tissue, he moved over to Charles.

"But you don't seem to have a drink."

Ignoring the comment, Gray Hair said, "Mr. Reynolds, I have also heard that you have a penchant for driving and that you sometimes have trouble with driving drunk."

Charles said wryly, "Well that is where you were misinformed. I am strictly a designated driver kind of guy."

The man gave a sigh of disbelief at this man's uncanny ability to bullshit. "I am glad you are able to keep your sense of humor, Mr. Reynolds. However, if you are going to keep delaying, I am going to kill the boy and then I going to start cutting off your various body parts. Here, take a drink of this, it will help you talk, or..." he paused, "lessen your pain."

Charles attempted to sip the liquid slowly to allow for some time to think. Gray Hair had a different idea and sloshed the amber liquid into Charles mouth. The alcohol found the cut inside Charles' mouth and the pain riveted him back in his seat. Bourbon ran over his chin and onto his chest. Gray Hair gave Charles a moment to recover.

"There, Mr. Reynolds, that should loosen your tongue a little."

Charles gave an involuntary shiver and shake of his head. "Yeah, but you know alcohol makes me a bit of a smart ass, I just have to warn you!"

The man was clearly no longer amused, and said, "Were you bluffing at the press conference or was it conjecture based on some other piece of information?"

Charles was trying to place the man's accent but could not quite hear enough to fully decipher his origins. "I really don't know where to begin."

"Did you know Senator Summers? Gray Hair steepled his hands at his chin.

Seeing no reason to lie and realizing that the man probably already knew the truth, Charles said, "I did meet him, but I really did not know the man."

"Good." Gray pivoted and turned away. He moved toward the door and took a quick glance out of the entry door peephole. "The truth will improve your situation greatly. But I think you are shading the truth a bit." He relocated back over to Charles and asked, "When was the last time you heard from Senator Summers?"

Charles tried to remember the facts and decipher the best answer. He decided that the truth was innocent. "I was at a party three months back." He added, "In Washington."

"What did you discuss?"

Charles really did not remember but decided to ad lib with something lacking any detail. "We discussed the majority in the Senate, the state of the economy and..," he added, "the President's re-election. Just the usual stuff."

Gray Hair said, "Indeed."

Charles stiffened at this response, realizing that his chosen topic had been in the wrong direction. This whole thing did have something to do with the President of the United States.

"Have you received anything from the Senator..., say in the past few weeks?"

"What like a Christmas card," Charles quipped before he could hold the comment back.

Gray Hair gave a malevolent smile and then suddenly changed directions with his questioning. "You said that the Senator was killed. Do you know who killed the Senator?"

"I have no idea." Then quickly added, "Nor does Tyler."

"Give it a guess," the man said with an undisguised impatient tone.

"The one-armed man?"

Gray responded with another smack across Charles face, striking his cheekbone. A dribble of blood threatened to run down his face but held in place.

"Charles, you knew the Senator well, did you not?"

There was that accent again. Charles decided that it must be Austrian. Charles said, "As I said, I have met the

Senator on a couple occasions." He quickly added. "Social, not business,"

"Senator Summers was an acquaintance of yours and you are at a press conference where you imply that you have some detailed knowledge of the Senator's unfortunate death. You just happen to be the one that Mr. Hansford, the only eyewitness to the death of the Senator, contacts." Gray Hair slowly pivoted around with his free hand stroking his chin.

"Look, I have no clue. I was at the press conference because it was my job, which evidently touched a raw nerve with someone. Really sorry about that, but it was a coincidence. And, Tyler saw the press conference and contacted me."

"He contacted you? Why?"

Charles considered how to answer without making Tyler's situation any worse than it already was.

"Tyler was scared because he suspected the Senator had been killed. Then, his best friend was killed. I am sure that you had nothing to do with that," Charles said while carefully watching the man face for a reaction. But Charles did not even receive a raised eyebrow for his effort. The man simply looked at him without expression and waited for him to continue. Charles gave a little frown at his ineffective jab. Perhaps the man did not have anything to do with Trevor's death.

Charles continued, "He was looking for someone to get the word out that he did not know who the murderer was, only that he knew that the Senator probably did not die of a heart attack."

Now, Gray Hair did show some reaction. He took in a deep breath and let it out slowly. He adjusted his weapon inside his coat, giving Charles a good look at the silenced Walther PPK. Charles looked over at the screen and thought perhaps he saw Tyler's leg twitch.

"The Senator sent you a package. What was it?"

Utterly confused and not wanting to give up a bargaining chip, Charles said, "A package? I don't recall receiving a package from the Senator. Maybe I should check my apartment...," he paused. He thought but did not say, *or my house.* At that point, he realized that the two men were there to search his Miami house. He had returned too soon and caught them in the act. It was obvious that this man had already been through his apartment in DC, most likely looking for this package, whatever it was. "It seems you have been to my apartment more recently than I have. Perhaps you noticed a package on the stoop?" Charles gave an expectant look.

"No matter," said Gray Hair. "We will find it. Whether you help us or if you are unable to help us." The man straightened and smiled. His languid smile made Charles think that this man was enjoying the prospect of making Charles unable to help. Changing directions, Gray Hair asked, "Okay, what did the boy see?"

Charles resisted looking at the television. "He tried to see, but only heard the conversation. He fell and hit his head before he could actually see anyone. He was knocked unconscious. He really has truly little memory of what happened," Charles said with an almost pleading tone.

"What did he see?" the man insisted.

Charles glanced over at the television to see Tyler sitting up in the next room. This evidently escaped Gray Hair, who had moved to take another quick look out the hotel door peephole. Charles decided to distract the man a little longer.

"Okay, I only know he heard both men's voices…, and conversation that would indicate that the Senator did not know his killer."

The man was clearly intrigued and moved back closer to Charles. With his back now to the television and his attention on Charles, this juicy bit may give Tyler a chance to escape. Again, Charles willed himself not to take a peek at the television.

Before the suit could lose interest, Charles continued, "The conversation was very vague, but it was clearly the Senator was being threatened."

"What was he being threatened with?"

Charles noticed that same unfamiliar accent again. Perhaps the man was feeling stress and losing control. Perhaps he was very well trained not to have an accent and only occasionally fell back into the old more familiar tones. Charles had thought it was Austrian, but now he thought the accent must have been Ukrainian, or one of those Slavic countries. The man repeated the question with his pale eyes now two inches from Charles face. Charles was tempted to spit blood in this man's face but decided to refrain. "What was he being threatened with?"

"Tyler was not sure, but he thought the Senator was about to make public..., some information."

"What information?"

Charles clearly had the man's attention.

"Look, my hands are killing me. Could you just loosen this one on the left? The tape is cutting into my wrists."

Moving around the chair, the man peered over Charles' shoulder. Charles took the opportunity to glance at the television, but Tyler was no longer in the picture. Charles thought *At least the kid would survive.* A door slammed in the adjoining room. Charles thought irritably, *Really? Couldn't you have left a little more quietly?* The suited man wheeled, pulled the adjoining door open and in two quick strides was gone. Gun drawn; his image moved into the camera shot for which Charles had a front row seat. Charles saw and heard the man let out a curse as he moved out of the view of the camera. The door of the adjoining suite was opened and a moment later closed. Charles feverishly worked his hands and then his feet, but his effort was in vain.

Gray Hair, evidently unsure of what to do next, came back in to check on Charles. He was clearly out of sorts having just lost his prime detainee. Flushed with anger, he raised the gun and pointed directly at Charles' head. Charles closed his eyes knowing that his luck had finally run out.

Chapter 35   **Virginia Beach, Virginia Monday**

There was a bang, bang, bang knock on the door. Opening his eyes, Charles gave an incredulous look toward the door. Surely Tyler was not stupid enough to return. Maybe Tyler had somehow alerted the police. No, that did not seem possible this quickly. More likely that it was hotel security. Charles noticed just a bit of panic in the Gray Hair's eyes as he moved his aim to the door. Or maybe he was angry at himself for neglecting to make use of a Please Do Not Disturb sign. That would have seemed to be a little detail not to be overlooked. Gray Hair wordlessly retreated into the adjoining room with only the silenced weapon visible to Charles, which was aimed at whoever was going to come through that door. His movements seemed much less graceful, and Charles clearly knew the kidnapper was not expecting company.

"Probably just room service with my lunch." Charles volunteered with a little bit of blood bubbling from his breath.

Quickly, another round of bangs on the door followed this time by "Housekeeping!" It was a high voice with a Spanish accent.

Charles immediately thought: *Tyler, you stupid idiot. You should have just run when you had the chance.* And *that is the worst impression of a housekeeper I have ever heard.* But it did to seem to confound Gray Hair, who was torn between telling the person to leave and remaining quiet. His furrowed brow indicated that he was trying to decide whether it was Tyler or if this was, in fact, one of the staff. Or perhaps if he was from a foreign country, he did not know what the proper response would be. Charles was frantically working his hands to try to free himself, but progress was limited. The tape had ripped the last of his arm hair off. Despite pain, he was encouraged by a little space which began to present itself. However, to wiggle free, he would need much more time and probably even not then. Charles really did not want some poor maid walking and getting herself shot so he called out in a loud voice, "Can you come back? I am still getting dressed!"

There was no answer, just a brief moment of silence. Still standing in the adjoining room, Silver Hair lowered the weapon. A moment later, a bang, bang, bang could be heard coming from the adjoining room's entry door. Instinctively,

Gray Hair stepped back through into the room with Charles and closed the furthest adjoining door. The slightest of smiles crossed Charles' face.

"Housekeeping!" the same high voice crowed.

Charles wondered if this really was housekeeping, *where in the hell is Tyler?* He checked the television, still no Tyler, just an empty bed.

Clearly Gray Hair was also concerned about the whereabouts of Tyler. He started to re-enter the adjoining room, but when he heard the maid open the entry door, he quickly pulled the furthest door closed. Charles could hear the maid call out one more time, "Housekeeping!" before she the slight squeak of a wheel in need of a touch of oil, signaled her cart was being rolled into the room. A moment later Mexican Salsa could be heard coming from the other side of the door. Clearly frustrated, Gray Hair seemed to be regaining some of his lost composure and quickly moved to the door leading into the hallway. Gun ready, he yanked it open and peered down the hall. First right and then left, before moving back inside and closing the door. Gray hair moved around to the TV just in time to see a plump rear end in a white housekeeping dress bent over a vacuum cleaner unrolling an electric cord. Charles saw the maid's face close in on the camera with a goofy questioning look and then retreat back to her vacuum.

"Mr. Reynolds, I believe you, and you have told me everything that I need to know. So..," he made a looping motion with his silenced gun barrel while he mentally labored to come up with the correct phrase. He smiled, "I am sure you have heard this before; you are expendable."

Raising the weapon for the second time, he fingered the trigger. Charles could only stare at the business end of the silenced handgun. Next door the sound of the vacuum filled the morning. Gray hair smiled at his good fortune. He was not too worried about a silenced shot being heard, but the masking sound of a vacuum and the music, well that was just too perfect.

"DIOS MIO!" a wretched scream came from next door.

Gray Hair recoiled and momentarily froze. He hurriedly walked back to the adjoining door. The vacuum stopped, but the music played on. Gray hair cracked the adjoining door, leading with his weapon. The maid saw the door crack slowly open and the silenced weapon poke through.

She screamed a second even more blood-curdling scream and shoved the adjoining door on the intruder's hand, causing the gun to fall to the carpet. Gray Hair gasped in pain but managed to wedge his foot at the bottom of the frame. Still screaming like a siren, the maid released the pressure on the door. Amazingly agile for a plump woman, she managed to squeeze by her cleaning cart, but not without a couple sleeves of plastic cups tumbling to the floor. Still holding his injured hand, Gray Hair moved into the room, stooping to recover his gun. Unexpectedly the maid dropped into a pushing position that would have made an Olympic bobsled team proud. She rammed her cart into the man, just as he was reaching to retrieve his gun. The corner of the cart caught the man on the corner of Gray Hair's head. The man's momentum carried him into a second collision with the end of the bed. The plump maid scurried out of the room, leaving her intruder on his knees, grasping his head.

The music and the screams were loud enough to drown out much of the excitement. Charles could only imagine what was happening on the other side of that door as the television screen showed an empty hotel bed. On his side of the action, he saw Gray Hair wince when his gun hand had been slammed in the door and then heard the collisions. Charles let a little triumphant "Yes!"

Charles continued to struggle against his bindings but was enjoying every minute of imagining Gray Hair's pain. Behind Charles, the patio door slid open and in popped Tyler. He swayed a little from the right to the left; probably because he had not completely recovered from the drugs he had been given. Tyler's highlighted hair was matted with glistening blood where his original head wound had reopened slightly, and he was still naked. The "Dios Mio" of the maid now made perfect sense to Charles. Charles was craning his neck trying to figure out where Tyler had come from, but then it was obvious to Charles that Tyler did not leave the via the hall. He simply had retreated to the outer patio. Tyler quickly moved to the adjoining door, slammed it shut and locked the deadbolt.

"Charles, you alright?"

"You should have left."

Tyler bent down to undo the tape on Charles' feet.

"I couldn't leave you."

261

"We need to call the police!" Charles said.

Tyler froze and stood.

"What's wrong Tyler? Get me loose."

"Charles, I could have gotten out that door, but I did not want to leave you. And you can call the police if you want, but I am getting out of here. No police and no FBI. I don't trust 'em."

"Okay, just get me loose."

Tyler, standing like a modern version of Michelangelo's statue of David, crossed his arms in defiance.

"No police?" He evidently was not going to budge until he was certain Charles was serious.

Charles was to the point of exasperation but said, "Yes, just get this tape off."

Tyler analyzed the situation for a second, and then quickly, from a squatting position, peeled the tape, round and round until Charles' first foot was free; and then the second. The feet proved simpler than the hands because of the strange design of the chair. In addition, the cockeyed way Charles was taped to the chair and the way it was situated against the desk behind made reaching and unraveling the tape quite challenging. Alternatively, Tyler had to straddle Charles in order to get a half circle motion, and then move back behind chair to finish off the circle.

"If I had a knife or blade or something, this would be much easier," Tyler said with a strained voice.

Clearly uncomfortable with a naked man straddling him, Charles said irritably, "Tyler, how did you end up naked?"

Tyler stopped and looked directly at Charles. "You are saying you don't remember?"

Charles let out an audible gasp.

Rolling his eyes, Tyler said, "I am just kidding. Seriously, you worry about the stupidest things. There is a man who is going to kill you on the other side of the door, and you are here worried about why I am naked."

Charles frowned but said nothing.

Returning to his tedious peeling and tearing of the tape, Tyler said, "Here, I just have to get it around one more time. I just about have it."

The adjoining door careened open into the room. Expecting Gray Hair, Charles forced his hands free, and he raised them above his head. Tyler, in mid-straddle, could only look back over his bare bottom at a security cop with his gun drawn. Peeking around behind him the cleaning lady, poised to identify the pervert lurking outside the window.

"Well, Ms. Santos, I can see who the naked man was, but is that the man who pulled a weapon?"

In her broken English she said, "Jess, I tink it was!"

Chapter 36   **Virginia Beach, Virginia Monday**

It was not the first time that Charles Reynolds had been held overnight in jail. It was just the first time that he had been held overnight because he was a suspect in a sex-related crime. Earlier in his career he had been hauled in because his untimely entrance into a crime scene just before the police had arrived. The other time, Charles had been assaulted in a bar by an angry litigant of a criminal charge that resulted from a story he had written. Instead of arresting the guilty man, the police had just decided to arrest both parties as if it were a common bar brawl. Both times Charles had been forced to spend the night in lockup until his story was confirmed.

With his head leaning back against the wall of some type of exterior waiting room, Charles was sitting on a wooden bench inside the Virginia Beach police station. If anyone else had been in the room, he might have figured him to be the beating victim that he was, or maybe a homeless person, except that his leather satchel rested at his feet. It had been returned to Charles upon his release, minus the half empty bottle of Maker's Mark. But there was no one else in the waiting room to see how bad he looked. That was at least of some consolation because Charles knew he looked ragged and did not want to fend off inquiring eyes. Charles' injuries had been determined to be non-life threatening and were attended to by an EMS technician just before leaving the hotel. Most surprising was that Charles did not lose any teeth and had no broken facial bones. Early on, it had been decided that Charles was not injured seriously enough to be taken to the hospital, but now he wondered if that had been a wise decision. But Charles had concurred so as to expedite the process of capturing the menacing Gray Hair, but that had not seemed to be a priority for anyone but him. His cheek had stopped bleeding on its own, but the mouth wound required a small roll of sterilized gauze in Charles' cheek, which had given him a pitifully swollen look. The butterfly bandage on his swollen cheekbone made the Rocky Balboa look complete. His rolled-up clothes, rental car keys and wallet had been located in a laundry bag in the hotel room's closet and he was allowed to redress prior to his trip to the hoosegow. Those were the same clothes which graced his body now, minus his belt and shoelaces which had mysteriously disappeared. Charles was not exactly sure when or where that happened, but he vaguely recalled someone saying something about a suicide watch.

In spite of great effort, Charles could remember very little between his last drink at Rudy's and the time he woke up in a hotel room taped to a chair. Tyler's clothes had been located in the adjoining room, but the police just wrapped him in a blanket for his trip to the police station. Charles had hoped that Tyler might fill in some of the blanks; including the boy's complete nakedness, but the two of them had been separated at the hotel shortly after the cop had barged in. Each was delivered to the station in different cars. Charles was a bit concerned when they handcuffed him and not Tyler, but he figured it was part of the protocol.

After he had been transported to the station, Charles was locked up in a cell until a detective was contacted. After several hours, he was taken complete with handcuffs to a small interrogation room. This was also a point of concern for Charles. Not just because his claustrophobia had almost gotten the better of him in an earlier confinement experience, but because the police were either dubious of his tale of this mysterious gray-haired man or just did not give a shit. The latter troubled him most because when cops didn't care, Charles' experience had been that all kinds of bad things can happen. More likely the police were checking Tyler's identification in hopes that he was a minor so they could lock Charles the Pervert away for twenty years.

"So, Mr. Reynolds," a voice had announced upon entering the interrogation room. The sudden break in the silence had awoken Charles with a start.

The interrogation had been kicked off by a detective, named Bibi Peters sometime just before midnight. Charles quickly found out Detective Peters was not overly impressed by the reputation of the 'great' Charles Reynolds. When they read him his rights, Charles asked for a phone call. A call by VB police to Lieutenant Jerry Collins in Miami did help to establish some credibility for Charles, but even with the endorsement of a fellow officer, Peters still liked Charles for some crime. She was just not sure which crime to go after and seemed willing to throw through a variety of charges against the wall, just in case something might stick. While the crime ledger was not exactly weighing down her VBPD desk, in the end she was more annoyed than motivated. Virginia Beach was a nice town, and no one appreciated this big-time reporter causing a huge ruckus, much less the unwelcome revelation of a gay tryst of some sort. It was just unseemly and to what extent Peters planned to pursue this pervert would depend on how recalcitrant he was. Peters bet that Charles Reynolds was a spoiled little boy who would start calling a lawyer or throwing out how important he was as soon as the serious charges were woven into the conversation. Other than requesting the police call Jerry Collins, Charles did neither.

Peters' entrance had caused Charles' head to snap up from his folded arms resting on a metal clad table. He immediately wished he had not reacted so quickly. The pain rocketed to his frontal lobe.

Perhaps seeing Charles in pain sparked a moment of satisfaction in the detective, but she only wore a mirthless smile. "Drugs mixed with alcohol will do that to you Mr. Reynolds," Peters said with the appropriate level of disdain.

Still feeling the effects of whatever drugs, the Gray Man had delivered into his system and probably a hangover from the Rudy's Ruckus, Charles had felt in desperate need of sleep. Right hand to the forehead, his eyes struggled mightily to focus on the very attractive lady standing in front of him. But if body language was accurate, she stood like she was pissed. When his vision did clear, the hands on her hips were congruent with the lack of patience in her facial expression. When she received no immediate answer, she tried a different tact.

"Mr. Reynolds, what drugs have you been taking?"

Reynolds had regained his vision but was now trying to locate his voice. His pained facial expression irritated this detective, and she was tempted to slam her hand on the table.

Bibi tried again, "Mr. Reynolds, if you could just answer my questions, we can clear all this up and we can be on our way."

Charles noticed a water bottle had been sitting next to him. He untwisted the cap and took a long drink. In a voice which resembled the sound of a stick being dragged on a gravel drive, he asked, "Did you catch the man who attacked me?"

"Mr. Reynolds, I don't suffer fools very well."

Charles tried to make sense of this but thought he had missed part of the conversation or some other piece of this puzzle.

Charles asked, "Who are you are again?"

With a touch of derision, she answered, "Detective Peters."

Brow furrowed, he tried again. "I gave someone a description of the man, gray hair and steely blue eyes, five foot seven and thin, you know."

"Mr. Reynolds, can you tell me what drugs you have used in the past 48 hours?"

This caused a frown to form on Charles' face.

"I don't do drugs. Never have. Not at home and not in Vagina Beach."

This caused Bibi's eyebrows to rise in surprise and then in amusement, when she realized that Charles was not even aware that he had misspoke. Charles heard a chuckle from the corner of the room. It was now that Charles realized there was someone else in the interrogation room, but he could not quite grasp where exactly or who. Charles was starting to gather some clarity in his thoughts, but it was like his mouth was stuffed full of cotton and the ache. He took another drink and tried to decide where the pain was coming from? It seemed to be emanating from his left cheekbone, but Charles could not remember getting hit. *Oh wait, now I remember, Gray Hair did hit me.* Charles thought to himself.

"Mr. Reynolds, you know we did not find anyone. No, gray haired man. So why don't you just come clean, and we can work something out on the charges."

This caused Charles to focus on the woman intently. She was incredibly attractive and downright sexy, but she said something about charges. Charles was incredulous, "What charges? Getting drugged, kidnapped and beat to hell is a crime?"

Peters internally smiled. She wanted to bring Mr. Big Pants back to life and the word charges did just the trick. "Oh, I don't know Mr. Reynolds, how about public intoxication, under the influence of an illegal substance, illegal surveillance for sexual purposes. I am thinking there may be some charges along the lines of sexual deviancy. You know this is not

Washington DC or Miami, we have some standards around here."

Charles just kept going. "If you want to make some headlines, find the gray-haired man. He is very dangerous. He is very likely responsible for the murder of a very important U.S. Senator." Like a ball dropping in the roulette wheel, the question of what happened to Tyler landed in Charles' mind. "Where is Tyler?"

"Tyler is doing just fine. The FBI is very interested in questioning your *partner*." Bibi put a little more hold on the word partner than was necessary. It was clear she was still trying to provoke Charles. His story had too many holes in it for something not to be suspicious. She was certain that Reynolds was a famous guy who was used to getting off Scot free. And Bibi just did not like the look of this man who was enjoying some kind of kinky, tie up sex game with another man. No, she corrected herself, it was a young man. A boy practically, and this kinky reporter was probably doing the dirty with young men like this all over the country, a boy toy in every town. No, Bibi did not like Reynolds at all. "Mr. Reynolds. You are obviously on some kind of drugs. What is it, ecstasy, possibly some methamphetamine?"

Still groggy, Charles was jerked out of his memory lane when he heard his name.
He did not say anything, and this was more than mildly irritating to the detective. It was obvious to her that Charles was on some kind drug.

"Mr. Reynolds. Your toxicology report shows drug use in your system," she lied. The Tox Reports had not even come back and probably would not return for several days. Bibi was just fishing. "But which drug could not be immediately identified. In other words, it is not conclusive yet. From your injuries, it looks like you like to play your sex a little rough."

Again silence. Charles chose to disregard her recrimination, and just looked directly into the woman's beautiful green eyes, with brown flecks speckled in for a fascinating look. Those eyes seemed so deep, rich, and liquid.

Middle irritated, Bibi took in his reaction, saying "But the key word is conclusive. The techs are going to run it again."

Again, Charles did not say anything and appeared to be looking off in the middle distance.

"Mr. Reynolds, look at me."

And he did. Or at least Charles tried to look at the detective. But she was still a bit fuzzy and the pain in his head was mounting again. He adjusted a wad of gauze in his mouth to try to talk but was unsuccessful.

Bibi continued, "The fact that there was no gun and no evidence of another person in the room makes your story a little dubious."

That confirmed it for Charles, the police were dubious.

Charles groggily quipped, "I was just thinking that you sounded dubious."

Bibi wore an expectant look which appeared to anticipate an admission or confession or something. There was not. Instead, Charles was looking dreamily into her eyes. She thought, *What a putz!* And she had wasted enough time chasing this rabbit trail. She just decided to cut her losses and move on.

As she stood, she said with little emotion, "It seems that Mr. Hansford has bigger things on his plate than filing a sexual assault charge against you, and the hotel maid is not pressing charges. Seems that seeing a young naked man was of enough of a benefit which overrode the need to press any indecency charge."

Charles said, "I had my underwear on."

"Yes, you did Mr. Reynolds. Congratulations."

Charles just looked confused. Peters looked egregiously disgusted.

Bibi sighed and continued, "And since we could not locate the gun you pointed at the maid, we are just going to let you sleep the drugs and alcohol off tonight. In the morning, you can go in any direction you choose..., just as long as it is away from Virginia Beach."

Having been released after his night in lock up, Charles knew the call to Jerry had done the trick, or maybe they just did not want to do the paperwork. After being rousted from his jail cell, Charles' personal belongings had been returned, including his phone which had been reportedly recovered in the waste basket of the adjoining hotel room. Despite the blows to the head, Gray Hair had obviously had the presence of mind to dump the phone in the trash can on his way out. There were about a half dozen or so calls from Sam, another half dozen or so from his office, and a few scatterings of calls from other work-related contacts. Now the phone vibrated in Charles' pocket, and he immediately recognized the headquarters number of the Washington Bureau. He was hesitant to answer but decided it could be the call for which he had been waiting that would give some background on the Senator's committee assignments.

Standing up from the bench, he answered, "Charles Reynolds."

He projected his voice with as much enthusiasm as possible, but it was tough with a roll of gauze shoved in his mouth. The cell phone attracted the attention of the desk sergeant seated behind the reception counter, who gave a disapproving look at Charles, and then allowed his gaze to focus on a sign which read: NO CELL PHONES IN THE WAITING AREA. He was a large man, with reading glasses and a look that said he was another person who did not suffer fools. Ignoring the cell phone prohibition, Charles listened for several moments, gazing toward the windows which overlooked the main entry of the police station. He could see all the way out the front of the building where several trees and a set of steps led down to small access street. Charles could only listen as the voice harangued in his ear.

"Thank you so much for calling Patti. Your concern is duly noted."

He listened and quickly said, "No I do not have time to talk to him." But it was too late. Thom Stanton, his sometimes boss at the newspaper, came on the line.

"Charles, you need to give me some explanation about your behavior. One, you sound like you are on drugs right now. And two, I had a very disturbing call from the Police in Virginia Beach."

"So yeah, Thom, I am still sort of tied up with this, so what is it that you want?"

"Charles, I will tell you that I have already begun suspension paperwork. These are serious charges: public indecency, public disturbance of the peace, illegal video surveillance, and the officer even hinted that you were engaged in sexual activity witnessed by an employee of the hotel. You need to explain yourself or well..., well, I don't see how any explanation could..., explain this," Stanton stammered.

"That's 'cause you don't want to see, Thom. The charges were dropped. I was the one who was kidnapped. I was the one who was beaten. I was working on a story."

Charles' mouth wound sent a little charge of pain through causing him to grimace. He really loathed this man and his damn busybody secretary too.

"Let me stop you right there. I was not advised of any story that you were working on with regards to the Tyler Hansford boy, which is clearly required in the employee handbook. So, I was not able to confirm that to the police."

"Thanks for that Thom, probably why they gave me an extra inner cavity search. And tell that bitch of a secretary that I can hear her breathing on the extension phone."

There was a barely audible click on the other end of the phone line.

"Charles – not informing us a story is a violation of company policy and along with this sex charge, I am sorry to inform you that I have no choice, but to let you go."

"Screw you Thom, you can't fire me."

The desk sergeant looked up crossly. Charles recognized the warning glare. Charles gave an apologetic shrug and the officer returned to his report.

"Charles Reynolds, you are officially no longer an employee of the Miami Express or the Washington Bureau. I would request that you discontinue any projects which are in the works, and mail in your Amex and company door keys. I have already sent you a copy of the termination by Fed Ex and it will be at the Miami address we have on file for you by 10:30 in the morning. You will need to move out of the apartment in the next two days. I would ask that you sign the no-contest letter and severance agreement. Then return both in the envelope provided. I feel the offer is very generous considering the embarrassment you have caused the paper. We are boxing up all non-company materials and shipping them to Miami."

"Thom, you asshole, I don't work for you. I have not worked for you for over a year." Charles growled.

"Well Charles, you have not checked in, for what about a month now? Which is also a violation of company policy." Evidently turning to Pattie, he said, "Did we include that in the due cause?" A pause. "Well good. Thank you, Patti, for being on top of things."

Charles narrowed his eyes, and he did not like where this was going. It had been a couple of weeks since he checked in. He had received a memo from someone at the Miami Express, Charles could not remember who, stating that all full-time reporters were required to call in for messages and check in on a 48-hour basis. Charles figured that since he was in Washington, working more on the Washington Bureau stories, the memo was not probably meant for him. Granted his paycheck still came from the Miami Express, but that was just a weekly column. He had emailed in all of his stories on time, hadn't he? Sure, he missed a few staff meetings and the morning group hash out sessions, but he was on the road. His job was fairly narrowly defined, and those meetings were a waste of time anyway. He sat back down on the bench.

Stanton continued, "You see Charles, I have taken Sam Orenstein's job. Charles, I am the new East Coast General Manager, which puts me in charge of...," there was an appreciable pause, "you."

Charles swore to himself silently. He could see Stanton standing there with the phone in his hand with that smug look on his face. But Charles' usual brazen attitude had a crack in it because Orenstein had always been his ace in the hole, his trump card, and now he was gone.

"Well congratulations, Thom. You have the persistence of a turd that just won't flush."

"Nice, real professional Charles. Goodbye."

The call ended, and his battery indicator light of the phone blinked once signaling the need for recharging. Shoulders turned, Charles cocked his arm to throw the phone across the front reception area, but instead brought thumb and forefinger to the bridge of his nose. This was not the first time Stanton tried to fire Charles. In fact, Charles was hoping that the asshole did actually fire him. He would sign the severance package and then he'd have a job within a week at one of the DC's other top papers. He would miss Miami, but with the money that he was going to be making, he might be able to pay off the mortgage and keep a small apartment in DC. Stanton would be the one that comes out on the cutting floor for this. *You cannot get away with firing a Pulitzer-winning author just because...,* his phone vibrated again. The caller was identified

272

as the Miami Police Department, and Charles knew it was his long-time friend Jerry Collins.

"Hey Jerry, thanks for the vote of confidence. It really helped get me out of this mess."

Jerry's gravelly voice came through the phone, "What in the hell were you doing entwined with a naked boy?"

"I believe I was intertwined."

"What's the difference?"

"Not sure, but he was trying to untwine me, when the police busted in."

Jerry started laughing and ended it all with a hacking cough that made his eyes start watering. Jerry managed, "I just wish I could have been there for that."

"I am sure you received the play by play from the Virginia Beach finest."

This earned a quick glare from the Desk Sergeant. Charles quickly turned a little in his seat, shielding his view of the officer.

"As a matter of fact, they did. They wanted me to 'out' you from the closet."

"Great," Charles said derisively.

"And you don't know who kidnapped you or how you got to the hotel?" Jerry asked.

"No clue. The last thing I remember is a young waitress making a pass at me at the restaurant."

"That should have been your first clue that something was wrong."

Charles rolled his eyes. "Okay, so everyone is a comedian now. Look, I am waiting around to see Tyler Hansford. He's the...," but before he could finish Jerry interrupted.

"I know who he is. You think I am living under a rock?"

"Yes, I suppose he is a regular household name."

"You forget that I work in a police department. If he had not been on the BOLO wire, I would have heard about it anyway through the grapevine. I mean a Pulitzer Prize Reporter being intertwined with a young gay boy. I will be surprised if there is not a front-page picture of the two of you on one of the gossip rags,"

Charles' battery light blinked twice.

273

"Yes, well I guess I can always go to work for the Enquirer. Anyway, I am waiting for Tyler to see if there was something else, he can tell me."

"I can tell you something. You won't see him." Jerry said matter of fact.

Brow furrowed, Charles asked, "Why not?"

"Because I am reasonably sure the Feds have already picked him up. They were going to take him to the Norfolk FBI field office."

"Damn it! That can't be right." Charles was looking for a window or some glass to look through as if the boy might be seen, walking out of the hall right then.

"Hell Charles, you are right there, and I am in Miami, so why don't you ask around?"

"I am not exactly in line for Citizen of the Year here. The Desk Sergeant may just book me for violating the cell phone policy."

Another blank look from the Desk Sergeant, but he returned to his demanding paperwork.

"Tell you what. Put the Desk Sergeant on the phone."

"You know Jerry. I appreciate that, but if I bothered these rubes again, I might not be coming out again."

Now the Desk Sergeant stared directly at Charles.

Charles noticed the malevolent look but continued his conversation. "But I did not get what I needed to go to print," Charles said with a tone mixed with anger and despondency. Looking back toward the Desk Sergeant, he said loudly, "Looks like the cops could have told me that Tyler had already been picked up, instead of making me wait around." His voice was escalating, and Charles could not help but sneak a peek over his shoulder at the desk sergeant. Fortunately, he had stepped into the back of the office to file paperwork. *You know what. I wish he had heard me,* Charles thought to himself.

Jerry interrupted his little mind dream, "Well, otherwise you are okay?"

"Yeah, just a cut or two. I don't suppose you received the picture of the man who was hitting me?"

Interrupting Charles' question, Jerry said, "You sound like you are on drugs."

"I am not on drugs!"

Having come back into the front area, the Desk Sergeant stopped what he was doing and gave an indeterminable look of disbelief or amusement. He stood with one hand on his hip and gave a slight shake of his head. Frustrated, Charles reached in his mouth and grasped the bloody gauze. Pulling it out caused a ripple of pain causing Charles to gasp.

Jerry said, "I did get a copy of the drawing from the VBPD sketch artist. And you say that the guy just slipped out without you guys seeing him?"

"Well, yeah, I guess we were busy trying to get me loose."

"And this is when the kid got naked?" Jerry asked.

"NO! Charles said indignantly, "He got naked earlier. I guess. I don't really know when he got naked."

The Desk Sergeant gave Charles a sideways look. Charles frowned and said, "Hold on just a second, Lieutenant." He said the Lieutenant part loud enough for to be overheard. Turning to the officer, Charles asked, "Did the FBI collect Hansford?"

The Desk Sergeant gave an annoyed look. "What am I Match.com?"

Charles glowered at the man. "Am I free to go?"

The officer removed some reading glasses, "You have been free to go for the past hour. I have been hoping you would go. And yet, here you are." He started to turn back to his desk, but decided to finish up in a matronly tone, "And make sure to throw that bloody gauze in the trash over there before you leave. Don't want have to be cleaning up no AIDS waste."

Charles smirked, picked up his satchel, rose and began walking toward a glass enclosure. He felt like giving the man a little verbal brush up, but decided it was not worth it. He tossed the bloody gauze into a nearby waste basket and looked for the exit. Arriving at the glass partition, which looked like it should open, Charles was forced to an abrupt stop. He turned to glare back at the sergeant. The officer pretended not to notice, keeping his eyes focused on some incredibly important file on his desk. Charles made disgusted grunt and asked not so politely, "Excuse me. Could you open the door?"

Now giving his full attention to Charles, he said, "That's for people entering." Raising his arm and pointing in the opposite direction, he continued, "This rube would suggest using the door marked exit." He was pointing toward a gray, nondescript door which was marked with an exit sign at the top.

"Charles, are you still there?" Jerry asked.

"Yes. I am getting directions on how to get the hell of here."

"Good. I thought you might have been arrested again," Jerry jabbed.

Upon exiting the gray door, Charles pushed his way through two more sets of doors, all graced by cameras. He continued down a series of short hallways, which finally emptied to the outside of the station. Popping out from yet another unmarked steel door with only an exit sign above, Charles heard the door close with an audible locking device. Looking up the side of the building, Charles noticed another camera which seemed to be eyeing him like a wary dog expecting a bone thief. As he exited, Charles deduced he was at the front right corner of the police station, and he was correct. Turning back to admire the deep red brick building, Charles made a mental note to include this building in the story he was going to write. For whom the story would be written, Charles was not sure, but what was sure was that it would be a scathing indictment of the entire Virginia Beach Police Department. Except that is for Bibi. She was an exquisite exception to the shoddy work of the VBPD. He reluctantly pulled his mind from a very nice vision of him, and Bibi being served drinks on a yacht just like the one that Tyler was hiding out on. Charles began walking front and center of the police station, balancing the phone to his ear and fiddling inside his front pocket for his rental car keys.

Charles said, "I have got to identify the gray-haired man."

"Can't help you on that one. I already ran the sketch with no hits."

Thinking back, Charles said, "I remember now. Gray Hair had my briefcase, so they have been in my DC apartment. They must have been the ones who shot at me at my house." It was then that it hit him. Looking down at his satchel, he remembered that Gray Hair had touched the satchel without the tissue. "Jerry, I think I have a print on the satchel."

Jerry said, "You need to get that to the FBI."

Without responding, Charles continued through his murky memory. "The Gray Man asked me what package the Senator sent me."

"So, they were looking for a package. How does the package tie in with Summers' murder?"

"I don't know, but I think Summers found out something while working on a committee. He's on the Defense committee and the Appropriations committee and a bunch of others. I have a call into the Research Department at the paper to find out what the Senator was working on, but I have not heard back. From what Tyler told me Summers was about to head to Justice and then probably to enjoin a Congressional investigation of some sort. Somehow, the Gray Man or whoever employs him gets wind of the Senator's intentions. They send a hit squad to Virginia to either talk sense into Summers or they kill him. Not very elegant, but during the murder there are a couple hitches. One, Tyler happens to be in the bathroom and sees a murder. And two, Summers lets on he put together a packet which would blast whatever he found out to the press.

"Why did they tie it to you?"

"Because of the press conference: I said that I had a source which told me the Senator died of unnatural causes."

"Someone told you the Senator was murdered?"

"Yes, just as I was headed into the press conference." Charles mind was racing now. "But I am sure that was what the Miami team was looking for and whether I still had it. I bet my DC apartment has been ransacked as well. This all must tie in with the Senator's murder and the Virginia PD just let the guy slip out of town."

"Yeah, you are probably right, but Charles you need to give the VBFD a break. No gun, no bodies, this is not a big deal to them, and they probably think they are doing you a favor."

Charles blurted, "A favor!"

"Charles, there were cameras. You were entwined with a naked young man."

Charles corrected, "Intertwined."

Jerry said, "Yeah, intertwined?"

Charles said, "Never mind."

Jerry continued, "And you were practically naked yourself. The FBI has taken the Hansford boy off their hands, and you are the only detail which has not been swept up."

277

Charles said irritably, "Yes, yes, I got that part."

Jerry continued, "They would have told me if they had found anything suspicious, but I don't think they saw this as anything other than a domestic dispute."

"What!?" Charles bellowed "I told them there was a man holding us hostage." His sudden reaction startled a nearby grackle, causing the large black bird to scurry to the safety of a bus bench. Charles caught another movement out of the corner of his eye and turned. It was a woman, he had not noticed before, reading a newspaper returning her attention to whatever Charles' outburst interrupted.

Despite being out of hearing distance, Charles covered his mouth and his phone and began speaking quietly. Charles blurted, "And, Tyler said that someone killed his friend."

"What was his friend's name?" Jerry asked.

"I don't remember. Terry or Devin or River, no it was Trevor." Charles felt relieved that his memory was coming back. "Surely this is all related to the death of Summers."

Jerry was thinking about that but said nothing.

In an exasperated voice, Charles said, "Look Jerry, this kid is in big trouble. He saw who murdered the Senator and can identify him. He said it had to do with some piece of legislation or something that Summers was going to go to Justice with."

Charles could hear Jerry typing on the computer. "But you have no idea what that might have been?"

Charles just weakly said, "No."

Jerry said, "Here we go. A Trevor Whitworth was found dead in his parent's swimming pool. The police reported the death as an accidental death with suspicious circumstances. Seems as there was no forced entry, and it appeared that the boy jumped from his bedroom window. He missed the pool, and his head struck the side of the pool, killing him instantly.

"See, that's not right. He would have hit feet first, not head first," Charles said.

"Yeah, it seems like. Only an idiot would dive out the window."

Charles offered, "More like he was thrown out of the window head first."

"Let's see here," Jerry said as he was paging down the report. "No, they report says he leapt out, but it likely he snagged himself on an umbrella which caused his momentum to alter his path."

"How could they know all that?" asked Charles.

"Because there was no blood on the edge of the pool. It was on the umbrella."

"Yeah, but that is still suspicious."

"Like the report says, with suspicious circumstances. These guys are good. They don't miss a lot. I mean you know when they pull out those CSI flashlights, they are picking up all kinds of stuff."

Charles was not sure if Jerry was joking or not, but just listened.

"This is odd. There was a new bedroom door recently installed, but the CSI team found splinters of what was likely what remained of the previous door in a nearby closet. It says the room had been recently vacuumed, but no signs of blood or other evidence. The body had no signs of struggle or assault. Robbery was not eliminated as a possibility, but they could not locate his cell phone. Like the report says, accidental with suspicious circumstances."

"Trevor's cell phone, that's probably how they started tracking Tyler!" said Charles excited that something was starting to make sense. "Jerry, this kid is in big trouble."

Jerry continued to try to appease Charles. "The kid will be safe with the FBI. This is on a big- time scale. They are going to wring every last ounce of information out of this kid, and they are not going to let anything happen to him. We'll keep an ear to the ground and if anything shakes loose, I will get in touch. Now, go give the FBI the satchel; maybe they can pull a print."

Charles gave a little sigh and said earnestly, "Thanks for your help, Jerry. I am sorry to drag you in on this stuff."

"Hey, my life is so boring, and I can just live vicariously through you, Chars."

"Yeah, yeah. But I do want you to know that I appreciate your help."

Not a problem, I will need a favor one day."

"You know what they say, Favors between friends are never owed, they are a freely given."

"Say Charles, speaking of friends, did you happen to recommend Haulover Beach to Sam?"

There was a pause, and then Charles laughed for the first time in two days. "Yeah, did he go?"

"Yeah, he went."

In the first bit of humor that had come Charles way in a long while, he began laughing and eventually calmed himself enough to say, "Oh, is he going to give me hell about that. I just wish I could have been there!"

"Lucky you weren't. Somebody tried to kill him."

Chapter 37   Washington D.C.   Monday

"Mr. President," Walter Freeman said unapologetically from a partially open door leading into the Oval Office.

Angrily, the President's face snapped up from an emergency monetary action plan prepared by one of the staffers. The President had summoned all his advisors and economic leaders to one emergency meeting after another. With the US Dollar being openly discarded in favor of other currencies, the stock market had taken a drastic drop. Alone in his office following a contentious meeting, the President was trying to fully comprehend the scope of the potential desecration of the U.S. economy. When he saw who had interrupted, his anger vanished, and he dismissed three other people who were in the room. Once the staffers had cleared the door, the President closed the door behind him, and motioned to the sharply dressed man to step toward a short hall which attached to the Oval Office to a kitchen and the President's study. When both men were inside, he took one more look around and closed the door.

"Did you find him?" The President closed his hands around his mouth pressing his fingertips into the inside corners of his eyes.

The man with steel gray hair looked around suspiciously and asked, "Are we clean in here?"

"Yeah, yeah, we're good. Tell me."

"Virginia Beach," Freeman said with the reluctance one has when holding back on some atrocious news.

This brought a smile to the President's face which then became expectant.

The President asked with trepidation, "And you found out what he saw? How much did he know?"

Intuitively knowing what the President was asking, Walter said, "I am sure that he only got a quick glimpse and did not hear enough of the conversation to be a problem." Rather than use conjecture, Freeman decided that this situation called for reassuring confidence, even if it was not necessarily the certain truth. "He heard a very sterile conversation. The Senator gave nothing away and the assassin only made suggestive comments that he knew the Senator was up to no good."

Grasping his forehead with his hand, the President asked, "And how much did he see?" then added, "from the stall?"

Looking at the floor, Freeman said quietly, "Enough to know the Senator did not suffer a heart attack."

"Stupid putz. What the hell was the homo doing in the bathroom anyway?"

Walter was not sure if it was a rhetorical question but decided to answer just in case. "Not sure what all he was doing in there, but it was a coincidence as far as him being in there when the Senator entered."

Loosening his beige and navy necktie, the President grumbled, "But he saw the...," he paused to come up with an appropriate description, "the killer."

Freeman shrugged an affirmative, more than likely.

"He heard the conversation about what Summers was working on, and he saw enough to know the Senator was killed." It was more a question than a statement. The man was nodding in agreement, The President continued placing his right hand over his brow and asked, "And he can possibly identify the attacker?"

"I suppose he could give a sketch artist a description that would yield good rendering or might be able to pick a face out of a line-up."

Turning like a recalcitrant teenager, the President stammered, "Fuck. This is a complete abortion!" One of his hands moved to his temple. "But you have him, right?"

Unwilling to show his own anxiety, Freeman breathed evenly before saying, "Actually we don't have him. The FBI does."

In a trembling rage, the President uttered, "How in the hell did that happen?"

Changing details, he preferred not to divulge, Freeman said, "The Virginia Beach police department arrested Hansford for a public disturbance."

The president gave a disbelieving look of astonishment. The President had a very suspicious look on his face. He knew something did not add up, but Freeman often did not tell him all the details as a form of protection. Sometimes not knowing was a much better option. "Wait, I am confused. If they arrested him, how did you find out what he knew?"

"I was able to question Hansford?" Freeman said. Hoping to bullshit through the story, he continued before the President could interject a question. "The interrogation was over, but we were interrupted at the hotel before we could dispose of the Hansford kid. Someone from the hotel must have tipped the police. We had to get out." Freeman was optimistically counting on the details of the incident not ending up in any newspaper.

"So, what happened to Hansford?'

"The Virginia Beach police found him in a hotel room and arrested him for indecency."

The President made an impatient 'and then what happened' motion with his hand.

Freeman took a breath and continued, "Hansford was taken to the Virginia Beach station. When the police ran Hansford's name, they likely hit the BOLO. They notified the FBI, who claimed him before we could get him and took him to the Norfolk office. He will be eventually transferred to the D.C. office."

"But you are sure he does not know anything that could hurt us?"

Patiently Freeman repeated the story he had rehearsed. "He was in a bathroom stall. He heard some non-descriptive conversation. He likely witnessed the Senator being killed and can possibly give an identification. Although that is not a given."

The President caressed both sides of his head as if it was about to explode. He sighed and said wearily, "Okay so where do we go from here?"

Freeman said reluctantly, "There is another complication."

The President's head jerked up with disbelief which quickly turned to anger.

For the first time, Freeman showed a glimpse an uncomfortable feeling tingling in his body. He was not scared of this man, but the fact that so many cards were dislodged from the deck, the whole mess could become toxic. Walter shifted to lean against the counter. He said, "There was a reporter who was with the Hansford boy." Freeman saw no sense in volunteering that he had also lost him in the hotel falderal.

"But if the boy did not know anything, he could not have told him anything."

"Hansford confirmed that Summers said he had given a package to a reporter."

"Oh my God!" the President said in a stifled roar of anger. Anything louder would have caused the Secret Service to bust into the room. Right hand grasping his face he asked, "Who!"

"Charles Reynolds."

The President slammed his hand on the counter causing a soap dish to rebound into the sink, then regretted it as the sound echoed and the pain ratcheted through his hand. "I knew it. I knew it. From the press conference. I told you guys he was a problem. Remember? Remember?"

Freeman nodded. "And we followed up on that immediately. I personally checked his apartment in D.C. for any sign of information that Summers may have given him. There was none. One team followed him down to Miami. We were in the process of combing his Miami home...,"

The President interrupted, "How the hell does a fucking reporter have a Miami home and a D.C. apartment?"

Figuring this was a rhetorical question, he continued, "We were in the process of searching Reynolds' Miami home when we were interrupted."

"What you are saying is that your people fucked up again." The President angrily swatted the water cup off the counter causing a splash of water along the baseboard of the nearby wall.

Refusing to address the statement, but somewhat defensively, Freeman said evenly, "We were already short on time, and he came home unexpectedly early. We had tracked Hansford to Virginia Beach, so I went there. We were about to snatch Hansford when Reynolds showed up."

"I thought he was in Miami," the President said frenziedly.

Freeman almost grimaced, but managed to calmly answer, "My team in Miami says he must have slipped out in the early morning hours. One of his friends pretended to be Reynolds and led them on a wild goose chase the next morning to a nude beach."

"A nude beach?! All of these people are perverts." The President continued, "Well losing Reynolds was just shoddy work on their part." Taking a glass from the overhead cabinet, the president filled it from the water cooler. Fishing pain relievers from a bottle in a nearby drawer, he emptied four pills into his hand and swallowed them down with a gulp. "So, he knew he was being followed."

Freeman just shrugged a 'must have' answer. He said, "We are still trying to get back into the Miami house, but we also have to consider that the information could have been sent to either his office in Miami or in D.C."

Leaning heavily on the counter, the President's shoulder slumped. "Where is he now?"

"We think he will head back to Washington or to Miami to retrieve the package."

"Let's just review. You and your people missed the kid but managed to kill his gay boyfriend. You catch the kid and then let him get arrested. The kid spills his guts to some Pulitzer-winning reporter who has some unknown package from a Senator, who was trying to bring my presidency down. Now the only witness to the Summers' murder is in FBI custody and a damn reporter has enough details to turn this into Whitewater or Watergate. Does that about cover it?"

Freeman did not bother to correct the President's synopsis to include himself in the story. He did not figure that would do any good. Nor would excuses or details of how everything had thwarted their plans.

It had been a dizzying set of unfortunate miscalculations. Deep in thought, the President seemed to come to a decision. The rage had turned to disconsolation. He wondered if he could survive this. It was not the first time that his political career had been threatened. There were the usual sexual transgressions that had come out and a couple minor funding controversies. But most of that was a lifetime away and since becoming the President of the United States, he felt like the Teflon Man. Of course, that did not stop people from trying. Oh no, there were people lined up to shovel shit his way, big bags of it. But that was what was so great about the Office of the President. He had people that could deflect and defend him from every direction. There were dozens and dozens of people that their only job was to anticipate, react and spin any situation.

He also had the attack dogs waiting for their orders from the White House staff. In fact, Freeman and his crew were attack dogs.

The President said in a whisper, "We need to find out what the boy is telling the FBI and the reporter needs to be dealt with." The President raised one forefinger in the air, obviously enjoying a moment of brilliance. "And..., he paused, they need to be tied to the Independence group!"

"Actually, there may be a way to do that," Freeman said but did not elaborate. "We can find out what the kid tells the FBI?"

"Lucky for us Epstein is running a circus over there in an otherwise fucked up calamity. Epstein is a moron. I would like to get rid of him, but he is so damn malleable."

Shaking his hands and arms as if trying to rid them of water, the President suddenly turned to do some pacing. "Wouldn't it be better if the Hansford kid disappeared; just disappeared? I mean, how hard would that be?"

Even though a few hours earlier Freeman was primed to do this very thing, he cautioned, "I would advise against that, Mr. President. Tyler is after all a U.S. Senator's son, and he is in the custody of the FBI."

"I know. I know." The President slipped into the old habit of nibbling on one of his fingernails but caught himself when he tasted the enamel of his manicure. The President sighed heavily, pouted and asked, "I will find out what the FBI knows. What about the reporter?"

"I think it would a mistake to do anything to the boy. The reporter on the other hand we probably just cut our losses. He has clearly some inside information, but he is not sure what it all means. He was questioning Hansford trying to piece this all together."

The President said. "Let the kid go and bury the reporter. I know about Reynolds. He is like a wolverine. He won't stop until he has turned up every tater and turnip."

Freeman's cold blue eyes just stared. The President thought Freeman looked akin to a shark. Freeman, on the other hand, was wondering how this idiot ever received enough votes to be president. Then he remembered – he didn't. "Tater and turnip. Got it." Freeman said dryly.

"Okay, but don't screw this one up," The President said dismissively.

Freeman bristled at the comment but decided that arguing or excuse making would not serve any useful purpose. Instead, he switched topics, "Our mutual friend wants to know about what is going on with the domestic terrorist situation."

This comment caused the President to straighten, and then he narrowed his eyes. "What does that mean?"

The man did not even flinch at the rebuke. "Just that there is some concern with you are stirring up a wasp nest putting the hammer down on this so-called Secessionist movement. He has some friends that could drag him down as well. Don't forget that is where you have been getting all that intel and..."

Flushed in the face, the President moved closer to Walter. Walter's expression changed into what seemed to be an amused look on his face. Perhaps it was the look of someone who had already known he had the winning hand.

"Walter, it was you guys that became careless. You were the ones that somehow let Summers find out about the...," he hesitated even saying it. No, he could not even bring himself to say it.

"Mr. President," the man said almost in a patronizing tone, "do you want me to finish that sentence for you or shall we move on to the present. Because there is nothing that we can do about the past, and dredging up what if's and might of's, doesn't seem real productive. Summers had an inside source, but he is gone, and I feel confident that your secret is safe."

The President again looked like he might attempt to backhand the man, but instead asked angrily, "Who was the source?"

"We think it was someone in the FBI. We will narrow it down and take care of the problem."

Another Presidential sigh and he asked, "What does he want me to do? Does he want me to sit back and watch, while these otherwise insignificant fringe groups gather confidence and these, these, little insignificant malcontents...,"

"If you cannot strike surgically, then I would wait until you have more information. These people are not going anywhere unless you overreact. Announcing martial law just plays into their hands."

This obviously startled the President. Seeing the shot hit home, Walter decided to shoot another volley. "Are you planning to get rid of the two-term limit?"

The President laughed and said, "Yeah, Walter, I am going to install myself as the fucking Premier of the United States of America. How in the hell I am I supposed to get that by the Congress, the Supreme Court, and the media? They would roast me alive!"

"Not if you had it setup for Congress and the media, to beg you to accept. Not if the prospect of Civil War loomed ahead. Maybe they suspend it for a while at first, but then you just go ahead and call it permanent." Walter was not exactly fishing because he and his boss had discussed what the President was trying to accomplish with his recent moves to restrict ammunition, increase regulation on light arms and an outright ban of any automatic and semi-automatic weapons. This, of course, caused a glut in supply and the criminals were able to arm up with an excess supply and lower prices in the underground market.

The President's face was indignant, but he managed to keep his temper in check. "What could this possibly have to do with our mutual friend?"

"Everything and I mean everything, impacts business, Mr. President. You know that."

Voice rising, the President said, "Don't lecture me, Walter. You guys screwed up and you need to clean up the mess. I can only assume that you were the one that took care of Summers, but I don't want to know. I have a world financial crisis to handle."

Hands in his pockets, Walter's face was cast down at the carpet. He was trying to decide how to best direct this impulsive man. How he became the leader of the free world had confounded Walter when it happened the first time, but then he realized with big bucks anyone could be elected. Of course, the second time it was accomplished with the help of Walter's boss. It was not the first election that the fourth richest man in the world had swayed, bought or stolen. His influence was enormous, and his vindictive nature made him intimidating and irresistible. Walter's boss was the head of a mega global conglomerate which controlled information, technology and natural resources. This giant in the business world could call any leader, democratic or despot, and obtain immediate audience. Business and political leaders across the globe coveted and pursued his blessing, influence, and most of all his money. What additionally confounded Walter was why his boss had backed this man at all? This President had proven to be a left leaning idealist. *Hell,* thought Walter, *saying that this President was left-leaning Socialist was a like saying Bill Clinton took an interest in the intern program.* But Walter's job did not include assessing the talent or ideology of the sitting President. Now, he had to assess how far off the reservation this President planned to go.

"Walter, Walter. I am speaking to you. Are you listening?"

Walter gave a smile that could have been interpreted as polite. From the other room a voice from an intercom said, "Mr. President?" Then silence. The President stopped what he was saying and moved back into the main room. He said with a rather rough tone, "Yes Doris, what is it?"

"Oh yes, Mr. President, I am so sorry to interrupt, but you have another meeting with the Council of Economic Advisors. They have been waiting for about thirty minutes. I just wanted to make sure you were aware of it. Shall I tell them to wait or go ahead without you?"

Politely but clearly annoyed by the interruption, the President said, "Five minutes, Doris."

Doris replied on the intercom, "Yes, Mr. President."

Returning to the anti-room, he said, in a low but stern voice, "Look Walter, this reporter is a threat to this office. We need the package. I need this taken care of, got it." He had one index finger aimed at Walter. "How you do that, well, I don't want to know. But I am not willing to take the chance that this is going to come back to bite me."

"Okay, Mr. President. I will work on a permanent solution."

The President was now nodding, but still looking deeply into Walter's eyes as if trying to see if he really meant what he was saying. His eye contact was also meant to convey how serious he was about his directive and that he did not want to be misunderstood. Walter's expression did not change from the emotionless facade that was ever-present and had often aggravated the President over the last couple of years. The man was unreadable and that bothered the President. He reminded the President of a shark.

"And Walter, take the back elevator. I have managed to keep you off the log, so let's not have any slip ups."

Walter gave a slight nod of assent and moved toward the rear exit. When he had cleared the White House grounds and turned onto Constitution Avenue, he poked a number from memory on a disposable phone.

When the person answered "Yes," Walter said, "He's not going to back off on the domestic crackdown. And I would say that he definitely was working on removing the two-term limit."

The voice on the other end said, "What a fucking moron. After the announcement about the currency reserve, he will be lucky to finish out his term. If the stuff Summers was working on comes out, he won't last the year."

Walter said blandly, "He wants to eliminate the reporter."

This received a terse response, "He definitely represents a loose end. Get it done."

Freeman asked, "And the boy?"

"Can you get him as well?"

"It will take some finesse, but yes."

"And the boy as well."

There was a short pause. Freeman patiently listened until the man said solemnly, "I made a very poor calculation; one that may have to be corrected."

Intuitively understanding what his boss meant, "The press would make him out to be a hero, but if you decide it needs to be done, it will be my pleasure," Freeman said as he disconnected the call.

Chapter 38   **Virginia Beach, Virginia Monday**

Jerry had given Charles the full accounting of Sam's trip to Haulover Beach, the men who tried to capture or kill him, the visit of the FBI, and the resulting slash on Sam's face. Charles was having a hard time putting all the pieces of the puzzle together realizing that it would take some serious think time. Again, Charles noticed his battery demanding attention with a tiny red light that had progressed from an occasional flash to a constant red warning sign, when it showed a call coming in. It was a Washington Bureau number. If it was Thom Stanton again, Charles was not much in the mood for another throw-down. He chanced it. "Hello."

"Not the usual enthusiastic Charles Reynolds?"

It was not Stanton. It was Priscilla White from the Washington Bureau Research Department.

"Priscilla, thank you for calling me back."

"I am not sure why I should be helping you, Charles. Are you even working for the paper anymore? I heard Stanton fired you. You are supposed to be persona non grata."

"Word travels fast," Charles said.

"Stanton dispatched a companywide memo."

"Figures," groused Charles.

"I never liked him or that skunk haired secretary of his anyway. So, I decided to let our personal past not get in the way of me helping out." Priscilla said flatly.

"I really appreciate it, Prissy."

"Charles," Priscilla said in a warning tone.

"Sorry. Priscilla," Charles said quickly and apologetically. The passion they had shared while Charles was temporarily posted to Washington was a short one. Priscilla took on the jilted lover persona anytime Charles asked for research. Then Charles began spending more time in Washington and when he showed little inclination to rekindle the romance, Priscilla became quite prickly. But each time, she eventually acquiesced and helped out with what Charles needed. Which was her job, Charles had often thought, but never said. Now that he was no longer employed, that duty was no longer an obligation, but an indulgence. It was clear that she was going to reorder the relationship beginning with Charles not using her nickname of Prissy.

After a short silence, Charles ventured, "Did you find anything?"

After another short silence and in a conspiratorial voice, Priscilla said, "The Senator was on several committees. The most notable was the Appropriations Committee. He was also on the Homeland Security and Rules Committee, and the Senate Rules and Administration Committee."

"Well," Charles said, "I have heard of the first one, but not the other two. What else?"

"There are always ongoing controversies regarding money and homeland security as you might imagine, but I can't imagine anything serious enough to kill a US senator over. The Homeland Security is your best bet. If one of the domestic terror groups thought Summers was behind the recent crackdown, it could have targeted him."

"Seriously?" Charles asked. "Are they sophisticated enough to pull off the murder of a US Senator?"

"If you believe the President's circle, the rebels were the ones that tried unsuccessfully to assassinate him. They weren't successful so maybe they went after the next best thing."

Lightly scratching his brow, Charles said, "I suppose that is possible."

"I also found out that Summers was looking into the assassination attempt on the President. Of course, the Whitehouse denies playing up the actual level of threat, but then continually refers to it as the 'Attempt on the President's life' and the mainstream press seems to be ignoring any of the tabloids' claims that there was no real attempt. So maybe it was revenge for trying to finger them for something they didn't do."

"What do the tabloids say?"

"The regular run of the mill ones say that there were no shots involved and just small explosives, similar to what you could get for Fourth of July. The wackos say that the President orchestrated the entire thing, and he is using it as justification for his squash of domestic terror groups, buying up of ammunition and new gun reform."

"Why does the story not have legs?" Charles asked.

"Well, I don't even think this President is bright enough to come up with a plan, but the main reason was that all the suspects have been detained under the National Defense

Authorization Act. No charges have been filed and no due process. DHS is apparently just holding them. No information, no story."

"Why isn't the ACLU all over that?"

"The President is their man. You would be surprised what they are willing to overlook. I mean they are hardly going after him on all the wiretaps and NSA surveillance."

Charles cell phone bleeped this time with a warning that his battery was at critical level. Charles cursed under his breath. His charger was in his rental car. He would have to call a cab or thumb it back to Rudy's.

"Okay, if I lose the call, it is because my battery is about dead. I will call you back if we get disconnected. Real quick, is there anything other controversial stuff the Senator was working on?"

"Not really anything else that stands out. The Rules committee, I mean how boring is that? Elections and procedures are not really something that people kill over."

Charles started walking with his thumb in the air. He was not sure if people even thumbed for rides anymore. One car passed being driven by a young man who returned an enthusiastic thumbs-up response. Charles just frowned.

"Yeah, I don't see that either. Priscilla, you have been a star for doing this." Charles waited for a response. There was none. His phone was dead.

Chapter 39   Houston, Texas Monday

"Thank you so very much Alexei. It was a masterful stroke." George Love was seated in a large, leather recliner with a satellite phone to his ear. He listened for a moment, said goodbye and disconnected. There were two others in the room who were politely waiting for the conversation to end, each seated nearby with a glass of sweet, iced tea. George had already contacted the finance minister in India and his former oil partner in Brazil to thank them for their cooperation. He would not be able to contact his Chinese collaborator because it was too risky. Even though the plan had been amenable to the various central committee members, it would not go over well if China's leaders thought that they might have been duped or herded into the decision. China was holding one trillion dollars and the drop in the value of the dollar would reduce the worth to half within a month or two. Or maybe they had been successful in dumping all those dollars, buying large commercial entities, factories and property, George really did not care either way.

Sitting across from George was Todd Wallace (aka Casey Friends), dressed in a white cowboy sports coat, open-collared shirt, jeans and an Atlanta Braves baseball cap. To look at him one would have thought he was lost in thought, but he was deciphering the conversation that Love just completed.

Wallace asked, "So what will happen now?"

Love stretched his arms over his head, letting out a long 'you're guessing is as good as mine' breath. It was nervous energy that he was trying to deal with as he developed an answer to the question. "I am not sure. But the President has to know that prices for crude oil are going to skyrocket. Gold will likely initially go up. I assume that you two purchased the appropriate options?" He looked over at Todd Wallace (aka Casey Friends) and Howard Reasons (aka Howard Pepper Wallace).

Pepper gave a broad smile, "I did. I sold everything I had in the stock market. I bought contracts on sweet crude oil, and I bought options on the UAE Dirham."

Friends was nodding his concurrence but did not seem nearly as excited as Pepper. Wallace was a sixty-something with thinning white hair covered with a straw cowboy hat

294

adorned with small pins. From George's view, the pin collection included a Mobil 66 pin, silver spur and a pewter cactus. A Florida native, his suspenders, were bright red, finishing up an ensemble that would never make any fashion magazine, but may fit nicely in a Texas Highways magazine. Pepper was a robust character with a gregarious nature. He had made his money in textiles, investing in multiple overseas ventures. His unrivaled passion was his alma mater's University of Miami football program. He was one of the biggest fundraisers and even had a training facility named after him. He was almost the opposite of the man sitting next to him. Wallace could be volatile and irritable when someone crossed him, but people did not often take a chance to get crossways with the powerful Wallace. With a doubtful look on his face, Wallace asked, "And this one event is going to put the U.S. on the verge of financial collapse?"

"How can that be good for the nation?" Wallace asked.

George said gravely, "I am sorry to see it happen, but that jackass in the White House driving the country into the abyss anyway. It was just a matter of time before the national debt and massive expansion of the federal government caught up with us. It is just going to happen a little quicker now, and we will be off the sinking ship."

"Wait," interrupted Wallace, where did you hear he stole the election?"

Pepper spoke up, "Charlie Rivers told him."

Wallace sighed, "And do you mind telling me who told him?"

"Unfortunately, he is dead." Pepper said gravely.

Shifting in his seat uncomfortably, Friends sighed, "Summers."

Referring to the legislation which would in effect be a shot across the bow of the US federal government, Pepper asked Love, "When is he receiving the Division Accord?"

"Should be soon. The bill will be introduced on the House floor in Austin near the close of the session today. It won't take long for it to makes it way to Washington."

"You don't think they will let it be voted on do you?"

"I would be surprised if it were, either in Texas or in Washington. It will be tabled, but then the real negotiations begin." George gave a little chuckle.

"How will you ever even get it read in the US Senate?"

"It will be presented as a simple resolution by Lindsay Thomas of Texas." Charlie was referring to the two-term Senator from Tyler, Texas. "She will receive the balance of time from someone, I forget who, and she is going to introduce it as a non-binding resolution."

"Procedurally, that works?" Todd asked.

"No. It is not designed to do anything other than to start the ball rolling." Charlie said. He reached for his iced tea with one hand, and a napkin to wipe off the condensation with the other.

"And the Governor has already bought in?" Pepper asked.

Nodding slightly, George said solemnly, "I am sorry that I have kept the committee out of the last minute details, but you guys told me what you wanted to be done, and the fewer ears to hear, the more likely it would be that the FBI and all the rest of the soup bowl agencies would not find out David Elliott has been in secret, but frequent contact with the Governor and he has given it his blessing. No one will be expecting it and while it will have no force of law, even if it is passed, it will make the national news."

"Then what?" asked Pepper moving up the edge of his seat.

"The announcement that the US dollar is no longer going to be the world reserve currency will keep the President off-balance.

"And what exactly is the resolution going to say?" Todd asked.

"It will recognize the right of the State of Texas to subdivide into 5 states. Each state will have two more Senators, giving us a total of ten. The Congressional count will stay the same, but the way we have divided up the state, we should get a few extra Congressmen on our side of the aisle."

"Which side of the aisle is that? Hell, I have been voting Libertarian now for years. As soon as W," referring the George W. Bush, "started acting like a D.C. native, I could not take it anymore." Pepper said with a sour look on his face.

George gave a slight sigh acknowledging the current reality of politics in the US.

"If the President believes the threat is real, even if it isn't, we think he will make a mistake. We will pull the Lawyer's Coin on him." George said.

Todd gave a little puzzled look.

Pepper noticed and feeling that he knew exactly what Love had cooked up, he said, "It is like this Todd. If the President were to acknowledge the right for Texas to sub-divide, we would move ahead to do it and he will be excoriated by his own people. But he won't because he does not want to risk the chance of losing control of the Senate and losing even more ground in Congress."

George finished, "If the President denounces the right of Texas to divide, we will rally the call for Secession, using the justification that we have been denied our rights. A Lawyer's Coin is when it does not matter whether it flips heads or tails. The flip only tells you which way you are going to skin a cat. Either way, the cat, gets skinned."

Todd was nodding his head now, recognizing the logic of the Lawyer's Coin, but gave a disconcerted look. "What about the rest of the states, Georgia, Florida and Oklahoma.?"

"I would expect if the economic collapse happened, those states won't be too far behind." Pepper paused, and then continued, "I don't think it will come to that. I think this President will look to save face. We just have to offer him a way out that works for us.

Charlie said, "More like a deal that he can't refuse."

Pepper said, "Charlie, you can't back him into a corner with no way out. You will be asking for more trouble than you can imagine."

Todd looked disbelievingly at the two men. They were discussing revolution as if it was going to happen. The fact that they were who they were, and their casual demeanor was suddenly alarming to Todd. Sure, he knew what they had been planning, but that was when the possibility seemed far away. When it was not too likely to happen, it was easy to be committed. But now, that the possibility seemed actually achievable, well, Todd was having second thoughts. After all, they were speaking of treason. "And what does this look like when we are all done?" Todd asked.

Both Pepper and George looked introspectively for a moment and then George said, "It will be like starting over in many ways. If it is just Texas and the rest of the United States, I think we will have a lot of people wanting to come to Texas."

"Seriously, you think Congress will go for that?" Todd asked.

"No, but we are also going to push for a referendum concession, and I think we could get the term limits on the ballot."

"George, if the current President were not the president, would this discussion even be happening?" Todd asked.

"If Abraham Lincoln had not been elected, would we have ever fought the Civil War?"

Not giving up on his question and suddenly feeling the need to find an alternative solution, Todd asked, "What if the President was to resign."

"Todd," Pepper said, "He isn't going to resign. He is trying to get the two-term limit removed so he can run again."

Again shocked, Friends asked, "Where did you hear that?"

George was nodding. "I think Summers found out that was exactly what the President was doing. But the President would not kill over that, he could just deny it and the press would go along. It had to be something else."

Todd again looked extremely uncomfortable. "You two think the President had Hank killed?"

Throwing up his hands, "Well, it was not us and they blamed us. So, it is either them or they are completely clueless." George said.

Pepper gave a harrumph, sitting up on the edge of the couch, "I don't get what Hank could have possibly known that would get him killed, except that this President is a lunatic."

Looking at Friends, George said. "Casey, do you have any idea why Summers was killed?"

Friends' head shot up with his full attention. He quickly took on a confused look. "I never met the man."

George said, "But you heard of him in our meetings. So, you knew who he was."

Friends shifted in his chair and adjusted his baseball cap on his head. "Yeah, I remember that we talked about him, but why would that mean I would know why he was killed?"

Pepper said, "It was just after our meeting that Summers was killed."

Palms out, Friends contested, "But the timing does not mean anything. And why would you think that I had anything to gain from Summers being killed? I mean, this whole thing created a real mess for us all. Granted I have not been in favor of the Secessionist thing, but it does not mean I would betray this group. I have more to lose than anyone here."

George cleared his throat after a long swill of the drink in his hand. "I received a call from an old friend of mine just before you arrived. Is there any reason that your name would have come up when it came to some type of election fraud in the last presidential election?"

Friends' countenance still was one of confusion but said nothing.

George shrugged and continued. "Senator Brad Hutchins called. He met with the President and your name came up.

Friends tilted his head slightly to the left and his eyes had narrowed. "The President?" He repeated, "THE President used my name?"

Pepper fished out a cigarette from the pack in his shirt pocket and reached for a lighter resting on the table. Lighting up and taking deep intake, was followed by an intense stream of smoke which was dissipated with by the brisk motion of a ceiling fan,

George gave a stoic smile. "Hutchins called another friend of ours in the FBI to check how that might be related and turns out our FBI contact connected the dots with something that he had been working on."

Friends was slowly shaking his head as if he was trying to process all the intricacies of the revelations. Resigned to some scenario working its way out, he asked, "And your inside man at the FBI, what did he say?"

Momentarily ignoring the question, Peppers injected, "It is probably good that we never mentioned Rick Uhler's name in our meetings because he might have been on a kill list as well."

Friends breathed out. "I don't know what you guys know or more important what you think you know, but I did not have anything to do with the murder of Summers."

Still maintaining a placid look, George said, "Our FBI contact was feeding information to Summers on the elections committee but was stumped on how the election results had been corrupted, That was until the President let your name slip. Hutchins and Summers were friends and they both served on the Elections Oversight Committee. He knew that Summers had been getting information all along from Uhler. Once your name popped up, it was a quick study that allowed him to uncover that you surreptitiously owned the company that produced electronic voting machines."

Friends objected, "If this has just been uncovered, and I am not saying that it has any element of truth to it, why did Summers need to die?"

George said, "Summers must have somehow already figured that out and was headed to Justice. After Summers name came up in our conversation about having something explosive on the President, you must have put two and two together."

Pepper blew out another plume of smoke and while standing to his feet removed a silenced PPK. Pulling back on the slide, he chambered a round and walked over to look out the window.

Friends did not miss the loading action, and he objected, "Now look fellows, there has to be a sensible path from here." Right hand up in a surrendering gesture, he deftly reached into his left coat pocket and pushed the speed dial button on his phone. He said forcefully, "It seems that it is the time for me to go." Then he said it a little louder, "Yes, it's time for me to go."

When he did not rise, George gave him a quizzical look and Pepper turned from the window. It was in that second that Pepper's head exploded, sending a plume of red mist and brain matter into the streaming sunlight filtering through the window. The door burst open with a loud crack. George stood only to catch two shots in the forehead from a black-clad tactical jumpsuit with FBI stenciled on the side of his helmet.

Friends made no attempt to stand or even raise his hands. He did remove a handkerchief from his back pocket and disgustedly wipe some of the brain matter and blood from the side of his face. As more armed men flooded into the room, he finally announced, "Congratulations. You have just killed the

300

leaders of this little insurrection. Need I remind you that I was never here."

Chapter 40   Virginia Beach, Virginia Monday

It had taken all of Monday morning for Charles to make it back to Rudy's. Fortunately, the little cash which remained in his wallet was enough to pay for a cab and a sandwich at a sub shop nearby. His rental car was where he left with the unfortunate bonus of a yellow parking ticket flapping under his windshield. Charles crumpled it up and threw it in the passenger seat. He did not plan on being in Virginia Beach that long and didn't plan on returning anytime soon. He found the charger for his phone and plugged it in. He started to make a call but decided that he still had some work to do. He exited the car and crossed the street to the Tyler Rose. It appeared to be vacant and conveniently the door leading to the living quarters was unlocked. Charles guessed the low-crime rate in Virginia Beach was to credit for this good luck, but more likely Tyler had just forgotten to lock the door. It was a 46-foot Ocean Alexander Classico with two staterooms and a downstairs galley. Charles figured the impressive trawler cost at least a half million dollars. He was tempted to check in at Rudy's to see if Carly was working, but he wanted to get a look at the boat for anything that might have been left behind by Tyler.

As he went through the cabin door, he noticed the large sitting area amidst the teak trim and furnishings. Nothing seemed to have been disturbed, Tyler was evidently a neat tenant, or it had been cleaned recently. On the countertop was a small set of binoculars. Charles put them to his eyes and looked out the dockside windows. He had a perfect view of Rudy's. Setting them down, Charles made his way through the kitchen and into the master stateroom. The king size bed was unmade, the seat hanging somewhat unruly off the end, and apparently missing a blanket. There was a swipe of blood at the end of the bed, but that could have been from one of Tyler's assorted injuries. A satchel with some loose clothing was tossed in an upholstered side chair. Charles picked up some shirts and shorts and dropped them back into the satchel. On the bathroom counter rested an overnight bag with a tag still attached. It contained a toothbrush, travel-sized tube of toothpaste, saline, and a ream of floss. Apparently, Tyler understood proper dental hygiene. There was no deodorant which made Charles wonder if the boy ever sweated. There was no razor either, but Charles

302

found a used razor in the shower. A small box of condoms was nestled unopened in the front pouch of the travel kit. A tube of super hold gel was resting cap side down on the counter. Two used towels which lay on the bathroom floor implied that Tyler had stayed for at least a couple days. Charles checked the trash can only to discover some to-go boxes with only remnants of the meals and some bloody gauze dressings. On the floor next to the door were a head bandage and an ankle support of some kind. Opening the closet doors, he found a couple more changes of clothes, all with the tags still attached.

He moved to the guest stateroom which was undisturbed. Towels in the bathroom were in place and the closet was empty. Stepping back into the bedroom, Charles checked the night table. A pen, which rested up against the lampstand, could have been there prior to Tyler's visit, or he may have used it to write something down. Charles pulled both pillows but was unrewarded. The second item, television remote lay on the night table next to the bed. Instinctively, Charles flipped on the television. Instead of a television station, the screen showed a closed-circuit view..., of where? It was a picture of the master stateroom. Charles studied the angle of the video and then moved back into the master stateroom and searched the ceiling for a camera. There it was cleverly hidden in what would appear to be a standard smoke alarm. Charles went back into the guest stateroom and examined the remote. Looking back into the closet, he found the video setup, that he had not noticed in his previous inspection. He pressed play and moved back into position in front of the television. The video showed Charles walking into the master stateroom, looking around and searching the trash cans and the side table. "Motion activated camera," Charles said to himself.

Charles hit stop and four panels opened on the screen. Moving in a little closer, Charles could see a couple of shots which were of Tyler. In one, he was propped up on the pillow, evidently watching television, naked. The next panel one showed Tyler walking from the bathroom, naked. Charles thought, *this kid has some type of clothes allergy*. Charles moved the pointer to the next one which looked like Tyler was diving into bed. He was clothed this time, in the same clothes that Charles remembered from their meeting at Rudy's. He pressed play. The screen came to life complete with a very loud accompanying sound causing Charles to scramble to find the mute button. Tyler was, in fact, moving quickly toward the bed, but had evidently misjudged the landing ricocheting off the end of the bed to the floor and out of sight of the camera. The next person entering was a surprise to Charles because it was himself being pushed into camera view and collapsing on the bed. Into the view of the camera floated a silenced weapon pointed at Charles. A second man who Charles thought he recognized from the bar from the previous day quickly moved in front of the camera, picking up Tyler and throwing him onto the bed next to Charles. He moved back out of the camera shot to reveal Tyler lying next to Charles, who had rolled onto his back and inched up on his elbows with what seemed to be a concerted effort. Watching the video with fascination, Charles realized he had muted the sound and quickly brought the audio back up.

"Mr. Hansford, tell me about the Senator's death." It was the familiar melodic tone of the Gray Hair, but the man infuriatingly was just out of the cameras' view.

A second voice said, "I think he is out."

Gray Hair said, "See if you can put some life into him."

The second man moved into the screen, pulled Tyler up by the shirt and delivered a full slap to his face.

Tyler said, "Okay, Okay." He then began unbuttoning his pants.

Gray Hair said condescendingly, "Mr. Hansford, I am not here for a blow job. Stop undressing."

But Tyler had already stripped off his pants and was working on his shirt.

Charles looked over and slurred, "Tyler, you are not wearing any underwear,"

Tyler responded with another repetitive, "Okay, okay. I can do this."

Gray Hair said sternly, "Mr. Hansford, stop taking your clothes off. Harry, stop him from doing that."

This time Harry stepped forward and unleashed a vicious open palm blast that snapped Tyler's head to the side. Tyler went limp, sprawled on the bed and it appeared that his eyes rolled back in the sockets.

Watching the video, Charles grimaced at the brutal hit and sat on the corner of the bed.

Gray Hair said caustically, "Maybe next time you can let up a smidgeon instead of knocking the little shit out of his mind."

Charles again noticed the accent. It must have been Ukrainian or Russian or maybe it was Austrian as Charles had suspected before.

"Sorry," the second man said sheepishly.

Gray Hair moved forward, but his face was blocked by the second man who seemed to be unwittingly keeping the older man from being photographed. "So, it is Mr. Reynolds, is it? And you are some kind of reporter. And it seems that you had some inside information about the Senator who was killed. I would like to know what you know."

Mesmerized by seeing himself on the television, Charles punched up the volume of bit to hear his response. What came out was a drunken slur that was an indistinguishable string of pig Latin. Unexpectedly, both Gray Hair and the other man broke into laughter. On the bed, Charles threw his head back and began laughing as well. It was several moments before everyone composed themselves. It was Gray Hair that spoke next in that calm voice. "Seems that Mr. Reynolds can't handle his liquor." Both men had given another chuckle or two before Charles spoke. Again, it was a muddle of sounds and words that might be that of an insane homeless person. It was then that Charles just collapsed backward, staring up at the ceiling.

Harry asked, "Should I slap him?"

"No, Harry. I don't think that would serve our purposes very well. But we can't question them here. Let's take them to the hotel. If we can get them in unnoticed, we will let them sleep it off and maybe we will buy some time to get something useful out of them. Wrap up the gay boy in a blanket and gather up his clothes."

Calling back to someone in the main cabin, Gray Hair said, "Mark. Harry is going to need help carrying Mr. Reynolds and the boy out to the Tahoe. Do you two think you can get them out of here without anyone seeing you?"

There was an audible "Yes."

"Good, I will pull the Tahoe around as close as I can get. I will be waiting, so don't take too long. And make sure that no one is watching."

Mark came into sight of the camera and could be seen with some effort hoisting Charles over his back. Charles immediately recognized the man as being the third occupant of the bar in Rudy's Ruckus. It was clear that the three had doctored their drinks and followed them to the boat. Harry could be seen wrapping Tyler up with a blanket from the bed and raising the boy over his shoulder. With amazing dexterity and strength, he reached down and scooped up Tyler's pants before exiting. The video stopped and went back to the original scene with Tyler flying toward the bed.

Charles stood on his tip toes and ejected the memory stick from the video recorder. As he was exiting, Charles caught a glimpse of a stack of magazines ruffled from a pile in a basket by one of the dinette chairs. Lifting the stack of magazines allowed a small spiral notebook to drop out. Quickly flipping through, he could see that Tyler had been trying to recall everything that was said in the bathroom in which the Senator was murdered. It seemed to be the same dialogue that Tyler had recounted to Charles at Rudy's. In other words: nothing new. He slid it in his pants pocket and exited the Tyler Rose.

Chapter 41   **Miami, Florida**   **Monday**

Sam was sleeping in Charles' guest room while almost a thousand miles from Miami, Charles had returned to his rental car. Retrieving his phone which was still charging, Charles placed a call to Sam. After multiple rings, the call went to voice mail, but before he could leave a message, Sam was calling back.

As soon as Charles pushed the send button, he heard Sam's voice. "Charles?"

Charles sighed at Sam's tone. It was a mixture of apprehension and weariness. Charles said softly, "Yeah buddy it's me. You, okay?"

"Well, I have been better," Sam said in a hopeless voice. Then in a rapid regurgitation said, "I was worried about you. Where have you been? I have been calling since yesterday. It has been...," he looked at the clock, trying to do the calculations in his head but giving up said, "It's 2:00 o'clock on Monday and I have not heard from you since you left on Sunday."

"Sam, I am so sorry. I was tied up and my phone ran out of juice."

Sam parroted Charles, "I was tied up and my phone ran out of juice." Angrily he continued, "I was run off the road, shot at and beaten up by FBI agents, or at least we thought they were FBI agents. Jerry said that I did not have to go this morning and he is going to call me back, but I am still not going to make it back for class tomorrow. I was supposed to go back to school today but had to stick around to go to talk to the FBI. Oh, my lord Charles, this is a mess, just an unbelievable mess."

Charles felt a surge of guilt as he rushed to figure out how to tell Sam how sorry he was for all the trouble his old friend had undeservingly been subjected. "Sam. I am so sorry. This was my entire fault."

Somewhere outside the noise of a large engine rumbled to a stop. Sam stood from the bed which had been where he was sleeping when Charles first called. Everything was quiet again and Sam sat back down on the edge of the bed relieved.

"You know Charles, at this point I don't even know what to say," Sam said disconsolately. "I spent three hours at the emergency room getting my cheek stitched up. And they almost called the police because I slipped up by mentioning the wound on my neck from the gun fight the night before. They said by law they had to report any gunshot wound to the police."

Before Charles could respond, the doorbell jolted Sam. With a rush of adrenaline, Sam said softly, "Someone is here!" There were a couple bangs, or more like thuds, on the porch causing Sam to glance toward the back door as a possible escape route.

Charles' said emphatically, "Don't answer it!"

It was quiet again and Sam was already moving into the front of the house. He whispered, "I just have to see who it is."

Charles pleaded, "Sam, just let them go away."

Covering the speaker on the phone, Sam gently creased the blind on the front window looking out onto the porch. The engine of a Federal Express truck roared to life, and the vehicle sped away.

Letting the blind close, Sam let out a breath that he did not even realize he was holding. "It was just Federal Express."

Charles exhaled as well and massaged his temples with his free hand. "Yeah, okay it is all right. I am expecting some boxes from newspaper." Charles paused for a second, "Just not this soon."

Slowly shaking his head, Sam said, "Charles, all of this has just really got me spooked."

Charles said, "Yeah, something is off."

The doorbell rang sending causing Sam to jolt in the air. "What the hell!" Sam said in a stifled scream.

"Don't answer it!" Charles warned again.

A voice from the other side of the door called, "Mr. Huckleberry? Are you in there?"

Sam said angrily, "That damn kid!" Sam moved to the door, aggressively turned the locks and handle, and yanked the door open.

Covering the phone tightly with hand, Sam growled, "What in the hell do you want?"

Devin took a step back. "Whoa there, Mr. Huckleberry. I was just bringing over a package that my mom signed for earlier today."

"They just delivered it you little prick."

"They just delivered those boxes," he said pointing to three boxes stacked next to the door.

Sam angled his view to take in the boxes. He took a calming breath.

"Say mister, did the police arrest you for going to a nude beach?"

"The police did not arrest me!"

"Okay sure, well anyway the envelope is for Mr. Charles. So, I can bring it back later. He's coming back, right?"

"Just give it to me," Sam rumbled while opening the door wider.

"Whoa mister, what happened to your face? Did the police do that? Isn't that police brutality or something? How many stitches did you get?"

Devin handed the overnight envelope, then immediately reached down for one of three boxes that were sitting next to the door. "I had better bring these in, cause you don't look like you should be doing any heavy lifting." Within mere seconds the boy had pushed through the door, box in hand.

Holding the express envelope, Sam was speechless and just backed up enough to let the boy come through the doorway.

Setting the box down inside Devin said, "You know Mr. Charles is a really nice guy and I hope he is coming back. Did I mention that I mow his grass?"

Extending the phone to the boy, Sam said, "Here, he is on the phone. Why don't you talk to him?"

Devin said, "Oh hi Mr. Charles. I brought over a package that Mom signed for this morning. I think Mr. Huckleberry was passed out and did not hear the doorbell.

Sam just glared at this impertinent boy.

Devin continued his conversation, "They needed a signature so I told them my mom would sign for it." He listened. "Okay, I won't call him that anymore." He listened some more. "A doctor huh." Devin looked over at Sam then quickly away. "Yes sir, I sure will, he does not look so good. You know the police have been here several times. I think your friend was arrested for going to a nude beach."

"Give me that phone," Sam yanked it out the kid's hand.

Devin stood for a moment wide-eyed, but then quickly said, "Let me get the rest of these boxes for you, Dr. Jackson. Mr. Charles said that I should look after you; you are his very best friend."

Sam's glare moved from the boy hauling in the last of the boxes to the phone. "Thanks a lot Charles."

Smiling, Charles said, "Hey, Devin is a good kid. Just let him help you, okay. It will be good for him."

Resignedly Sam said, "Yeah, okay the kid can help."

Devin was stopped halfway out the door and turned with a huge smile. "Mr. Charles says I am the best beer fetcher there is. You look like you need a beer!" He bolted past Sam toward the kitchen.

Sam's eyed narrowed. "Yeah, I could use a beer, kid. And get yourself one too, you have earned it."

Charles said, "Whoa there Huckleberry, don't give the kid a beer!"

Sam went over to the couch and plopped down. Calling out to the kid, "You know I was just kidding right?"

From the kitchen, ignoring the question Devin called out, "Mr. Charles likes a lime in his beer. Do you want one?"

"A lime will be fine," Sam called back. Devin did not answer.

To Charles, Sam said, "He knows I was just kidding."

Charles laughed and said, "Well, maybe, but he can be a bit presumptuous."

Sam said, "Charles, are you okay?"

Charles looked at himself in the rearview mirror. "Yeah, I am okay. I have had about as much fun as you have had. I will have to tell you about it."

"Did you meet with the kid?"

Charles said, "Yes, I did. And he got me into as much trouble as I have gotten you into."

Devin returned to the living room with a bottle of beer, dressed with a perfect slice of lime protruding out the spout. After handing the beer to Sam, he scooped up the remote and dropped down on the couch next to Sam.

Eyebrows raised and just staring at the kid, Sam said with a convicting tone, "Charles, you knew Haulover Beach was a nudist beach, didn't you?"

This caused Devin to look over with one eyebrow raised. Sam pointed to the door with a warning look. Devin put up both hands in surrender and returned his eyes to the television.

Charles said sincerely, "Sam, I am really sorry about that."

"No, you are not."

"Yes, well sort of sorry. I am sorry that it caused so much of a problem. It was a stupid prank."

Sam said, "You know Ms. Nosey Neighbor knows."

Charles gave a little laugh and said, "Oh shit, I will never hear the end of that."

Devin looked over with a critical eye, but quickly decided not to say anything.

"Charles, I would like to hang around till you get back, but I need to get back to Houston."

"I understand completely. Just lock the door and I will be back tomorrow or the next day."

"What else do you have to do?" asked Sam.

"This is all about the Senator's murder. And it was a murder. The boy saw it happen."

"And how do you fit in all this?"

Charles exhaled and started his engine. "They, whoever they are, seem to think the Senator sent me a package. That is why they were at my house. They also searched my Washington apartment."

Sam looked over at the delivery that had just been made.

"Charles, you just received three big boxes and an overnight envelope. Tell me these aren't the packages."

Charles asked, "No those are probably from my office. Do they all have the same return address?"

Moving over to the boxes, Sam skimmed the tops, moving them side to side for a view. "Yeah, it looks like they are all from the Washington Bureau. You have two heavy ones, one light one and the overnight envelope. You need me to open them up?"

311

Charles said, "No, it's just some stuff from my Washington office."

Sam said, "The overnight envelope is marked Urgent and Confidential."

"Yeah, that's okay. It's just work stuff. I will get it when I get back to Miami."

Sam looked over at Devin, who was taking in a Monster truck rally on one of the sports channels. Fearing that the same people would come looking again, Sam asked, "But what if the package they are looking for is in one of these boxes?"

"Sam. I was expecting boxes from the office. It is just odd that they would be delivered today."

"Okay, what about the envelope?"

Charles sighed realizing that Sam was not going to be satisfied and had a legitimate reason to be scared.

"Okay Sam, I know what are in the boxes. It is my personal stuff from the Washington office. They...," he paused. "Sam when were the boxes shipped?"

Sam pulled the delivery manifest. "The boxes were shipped on Saturday."

"What about the envelope?" Charles asked.

"Looks like Saturday as well. I didn't know they could ship Saturday to Monday."

Charles was running the conversation that he had with Stanton through his mind. "Open the letter and see when it was dated."

Sam pulled the tab and unfolded six pages of paper. "This is dated Saturday as well. Wait Charles, this is a termination letter. You were fired?"

This caused Devin to look over, but quickly returned his attention to the television.

"Yeah, Stanton fired me, but he said it was because I was arrested with Tyler for sexual deviancy. He called me this morning."

"Sexual deviancy?"

Charles said, "Well that is what he said, but it is obvious that he had already fired me right after the Summers press conference."

"I am just confused," Sam said while shuffling through the papers. "There is a severance package letter, a termination letter, a non-compete addendum, a resignation letter and several pages of company policy. They are asking you to resign here, but this one says that you were terminated. Who gives severance to someone arrested for being a sexual deviant?"

Charles said, "Well, I was never actually arrested. Look this was already in the works."

"Charles, now I am the one who is sorry. I had no idea."

"Ah, don't be. When I write this story about Tyler Hansford, I will have the papers knocking down my door...," he paused, "along with the FBI."

"What can I do to help?"

Charles said, "I need a home phone number. Inside one of the boxes, there should be a book called The Cleaning."

Sam began futilely trying to pull off the tape from one of the boxes. He turned to Devin, "Devin, get a knife from the kitchen and come here."

Devin was off the couch in a flash, returning with the paring knife with just a trace of lime on the blade. He handed it to Sam, who looked at the remains of the lime, sighed and wipe the blade on Devin's trousers. Devin gave a toothy grin. Sam split open one box and gave the knife to the boy. To Devin, Sam said, "Open those two."

With expert dexterity, Devin sliced open the remaining two boxes. Following Charles' instructions Sam said, "We are looking for a book called The Cleaning."

With all the contents of the boxes being pulled and stacked to the side, Devin finally held up the book in triumph. "The Cleaning, by D.C. Reed. Never heard of him."

Shaking his head, Sam said, "Never heard of him either."

Devin asked, "Okay, now what?"

"Now what?" asked Sam.

"Open it. There should be an address book in there. I need a home number for Sam Orenstein." Charles said.

Sure enough, when the novel was opened a carved-out space tightly held a little black book. Devin handed it to Sam, who thumbed through and located the number. While reciting it, Devin had retrieved a brown paper envelope. Sam looked over and said, "Devin, we found what we were looking for, so you can stop going through Mr. Charles' stuff."

Devin shrugged and said, "Okay, it just looked interesting. It said personal and confidential."

"Yeah well, we found what he needed, thanks," Sam said in a dismissive tone.

Devin stood and started back to the couch. "It has the name of the guy you were talking about earlier."

This caught Sam's attention. "Wait a minute, what guy?"

Devin turned around said, "Mr. Charles said that his boss fired him right after the Summers' press conference."

"Wait a minute," drawing the phrase into an accusation. "You have been listening to this entire conversation," Sam said reproaching Devin.

Devin gave a little guilty shrug.

Through the phone Charles could be heard asking, "What did he say about Summers?"

Devon answered directly in a louder voice. "I said there is an envelope with here that has personal and confidential, and it is from that guy you were talking about earlier. And Mr. Charles what is a sexual deviant?"

Sam interrupted, "It is what you are going to be if you keep listening in on other people's phone conversations."

Devin gave a little frown.

Charles said, "Open the envelope, Devin."

Sam said, "Open the envelope, Devin."

Devin gave that goofy smile and using the paring knife to slit the top.

Sam and Devin were looking at a brochure folded in half.

"What is in it?" Charles asked expectantly. By this time, he had pulled off road at a small pull-off overlooking the Atlantic Ocean.

Sam puzzled, "It looks like a sales brochure for some kind of voting machine."

Devin looked disappointed at the find, handing the brochure over to Sam. Turning back toward the kitchen, Devin said, "I am going to get another beer. Want one?"

Chapter 42   Miami, Florida   Monday

It had been a couple hours since the discovery of the brochure by Devin. Charles seemed equally disappointed not knowing how a sales brochure could possibly be incorporated into this enigma of events. Neither Sam nor Charles could figure what could be so important which would cause a U.S. Senator to clandestinely send a sales pamphlet to Charles. He decided that there must be a hidden message in the brochure that they were missing. He asked Sam to take a picture of all four sides with his phone and send it to him. Charles was going to drive back to Norfolk and get a room before heading to either Washington or coming back to Miami. He wanted to try to catch up with Tyler and he needed to see if the FBI could lift the fingerprint from his satchel.

Devin, having heard his mom yell his name from across the street, had headed back home with an admonition from Sam to not say anything to his mother or Ms. Wendell about the events of the day, especially the beer. To avert any questions about hanging out at Mr. Charles' house all afternoon with the Huckleberry, Devin had exited the back door, jumped the back fence and came around another neighbor's house. His presence was shortly replaced by Jerry, who stopped by to check on Sam.

Jerry said, "Looks like you are off the hook. My FBI contact said that McQueen and Parrish took off for Virginia this morning. They evidently had bigger fish to fry."

Sam's head had begun to ache again, and he was feeling like another nap. He asked, "So they were FBI agents after all?"

"Yeah, they are big time FBI. They are on some special task force that reports directly to the Director of the FBI."

Sam grimaced. "Great, so this might not be over."

Jerry answered with a casual, "Nah, I think they realized you were just in the wrong place at the wrong time. They were more interested in finding Charles. Seems they think he has some inside information about the Senator's death."

Sam contemplated this and said, "Well he did interview the witness, but I thought the kid was back with the FBI."

315

"That is probably why McQueen and Parrish went racing back to Virginia."

Sam said, "This whole thing is so surreal. I get invited to speak in place of someone, who I now realize was the Senator, who was murdered. The group that invited me to speak is somehow suspected of having the Senator killed. That makes no sense."

Jerry was scratching his head. "We would have to know more about the Senator and the reasons for him being killed to make any sense of this."

Sam said, "Tyler Hansford is the key because he saw the man who killed the Senator."

"Well, the FBI will figure it out. I mean this is going to be priority one. A U.S. Senator just doesn't get bumped off every day. They will track down this friend of yours in the dissident group. It sounds like they are the ones responsible.

Shaking his head, Sam said, "I just don't see George Jones or George Love killing anyone. I mean he was a really easy-going guy. He was not a killer."

"Hard to say, Sam. He was pretty sneaky in how he finagled you into speaking."

"Yeah, I suppose. I would sure like to talk to him again. I bet he knows exactly what is going on."

Jerry said, "Sam if I were you, I would head back to Houston and hope that no one ever mentions this whole event again. You will probably be able to read about it in the papers when Charles breaks the story."

Sam's phone chirped. Jerry moved around the coffee table and picked up the phone. "It says Stan."

Sighing, Sam said, "Yeah, I need to answer that. Can you hand it to me?"

Punching the call button, Jerry extended the phone to Sam's uninjured side of his face.

"Stan?"

"Hey, Dr. J," Stan said haltingly. "You are not going to believe this."

Taking the phone, Sam asked, "Believe what?"

"Well, Dr. J, I showed up today to feed Sylvester."

"What happened to Sylvester?"

"Sylvester is fine."

"Stan, what is wrong?"

"It's the house."

Sam sat straight up and winced at the pain rushing to his cheek. He had a quick visual of Tom Cruise sliding across his wooden floors in his underwear, but it was Stan's face which wore the sunglasses. "You had a party, didn't you?"

There was a pause. "Well yes, I did, but I promise I cleaned the house, and it was just like you left it."

Sam was dubious of this, but at the moment, his face swollen and aching; he was not interested in interrogating Stan. "So, Stan, what am I not going to believe?" His anger was evident in his voice, while he prepared for the latest event to add to his calamitous weekend.

"Dr. J, someone came in last night after we left and trashed the entire house."

"Stan!" Sam said as if a parent accusing a teenager.

No, I'm Dr. J., it wasn't me. Well, the light globe above the kitchen table was me, but not the rest. That light fixture is really low. You ought to think about raising it some."

"Stan, just tell me what happened."

Sam could hear voices in the background. "Stan, who is there?"

"Oh, sorry Dr. J. That's a police officer. Like I said, you had a break in.

Sam heard a separate set of voices. "Stan, who is that?"

"Oh, that's the Fire Marshall."

"Stan! What the hell is going on there? Is my house on fire?!" Now Sam had a visual of Project X in Houston and a low-flying helicopter dousing his house with dry foam fire extinguisher.

"No, no, no. No fire. But it is good that this all happened, because the wiring in this place is not up to code and with the walls torn up the way they are, there were some exposed wires. The police suggested that I should notify the fire department. Good thing Dr. J., this could have been a real disaster down the line. Did you have this place inspected when you bought it?"

Fifteen minutes later, Sam had popped a second dosing of Tylenol and started in on a beer. In complete detail, Stan covered the illegal entry through the patio door and the room by room dismantling of drawers, closets, air ducts, walls, and furniture.

"Stan, I am going to try to get a flight out of here tomorrow."

"So, I will need to cover your Tuesday class?" Stan said with a little more enthusiasm than Sam would have preferred.

Grudgingly Sam said, "Yes. How did the test go for the Monday classes?"

"Everything went fine Dr. J. The Dean stopped in. He seemed a little surprised to see me, but I covered for you."

Sam let out a barely audible "Shit."

"No Dr. J., everything is copasetic. I told him that I wasn't sure why you had to leave, but I thought it might be a family emergency."

Sam grimaced. He should have sent an email to the Dean's secretary Hazel. She would have covered for him, but not after the fact. He sort of forgot and sort of just counted on getting by without telling anyone. This was supposed to be a quick trip and he really did not want anyone to know that he was using a graduate assistant to cover his class while he was out earning extra cash. Now he was sure to have to either come clean or propagate a lie. "Dammit George Jones!"

Stan said tentatively, "Excuse me, were you talking to me?"

Sam took a deep breath to allow the anger to subside. "No Stan I was not talking to you. Everything will be fine. Thanks for taking care of the house for me. I will talk to the Dean when I get back."

"Good, good. He said he was going to check in with you when you got back."

Sam could barely suppress a "That is just great!"

Chapter 43   **Norfolk, Virginia**   **Monday**

During his trip from Virginia Beach to Norfolk, Charles had made a reservation over the phone at a local hotel. During his drive, Charles held the small notebook over the steering wheel reading over and over again the entries by Tyler. He saw the acronym AIG along with the names Pepper and Rivers. In quotes was the sentence, 'Friends ought to know better than to try this strong-arm tactic.' Tyler had written a description of the man: six-foot, white, nice suit, Amedeo Testoni boots and too much gel. There were some notes from the internet on drugs that killed instantly followed by syringe and pancuronium bromide and potassium chloride. On the next page Tyler had written, Justice Department and newspaper reporter. Next to the newspaper reporter, was scribbled news conference and Charles Reynolds. The Washington Bureau office number was there just above where Charles' cell phone was scribbled. *At least that made sense* thought Charles.

Checking in upon his arrival in Norfolk, Charles had called to extend his rental car contract. He wasn't sure if he was going to be going to Washington or Miami, so he just decided to hold pat with the rental. He also placed a call to his old benefactor, Sam Orenstein.

"Sam, it is Charles Reynolds.

"Charles, good to hear from you. Are you in Washington?"

"Not exactly. I am in Virginia on a story."

"That's good to hear, I was worried that Stanton would fire you as soon as he sat his ass down in my chair."

Charles laughed. "He did."

"Seriously?"

"Seriously, but that is not while I called. Well, it is sort of why I called."

"I am going to have a story to sell. It is going to be a keeper. I am needed a place to publish it."

"Tell me about it."

For the next thirty minutes, Charles explained Tyler's story. Orenstein peppered Charles with questions and it was just like when Charles was starting out as a cub reporter having to justify and substantiate every detail.

Charles concluded the story, "The only thing that I can figure is that while working on one of his committees, Summers found out about something illegal that someone important did not want to come out. The AIG connection could be it."

Orenstein said, "It could have been, I guess. He uncovers the plans of the AIG, plans to expose them and they snuff him to protect those involved. I mean it sounds like you had some pretty heavy hitters at the dinner party. And you said Summers sent you a brochure on a voting machine. That has got to be important, or he would not have sent it to you, What's the company name?"

"VoteTech Enterprises."

"Well, I have not heard of them, but that does not mean much. Let me do an internet search here. Well, it looks like ES&S is the big dog with about 50% of the total electronic market. There are four companies which dominate the market, and the rest of the market is split up among a dozen or so companies. Maybe the company was going to steal a state election for the governor's race or something, but I can't imagine how they could get away with it on a large scale."

"Do you see VoteTech?" asked Charles.

"No, no VoteTech. Let me search the company name." Charles listened as Orenstein clicked away. "Nothing comes up which tells me that they are not a public company. Is there a location on the brochure?"

"I don't know Sam; I am looking at pictures on a phone which are really tough to see."

"Tell you what, let me do some checking. When I get something, I will call you back."

"Thanks Sam. Sorry to cut short your retirement."

"For you Charles, I am happy to do it. And when you figure this thing out, I will have a list a mile long of newspapers that will beg you to come work for them. Stanton will be the biggest idiot in Washington for getting rid of you."

When he finished his call to Orenstein, Charles wanted to look over Tyler's notebook again, but instead opted to take his satchel to the FBI to get a fingerprint ID on Gray Hair, as well as check on Tyler if he had not already been transferred to the D.C. office. When he met with the FBI, Charles knew the video would be his ace in the hole in case they did not believe him. But he wanted to hang on to the video if possible; it would be the coup de grâce for the story he was going to write. Parking in a four-story parking garage, Charles had arrived at the FBI office just before 5:00 o'clock. Upon arrival, he asked for the agent in charge of the Tyler Hansford transfer and had immediately been placed in an interrogation room. Still hanging on to his satchel, Charles nervously patted his pants pocket with the video drive. He was drumming his fingers on the table when Agents McQueen and Parrish entered the room.

Parrish said, "Mr. Reynolds, I am Agent Parrish and this is Agent McQueen. I am glad you decided to turn yourself in."

Sarcastically McQueen said, "And meeting us here in Norfolk, quite thoughtful."

Charles gave an amused look. "Not sure what you mean by that, but I do have some evidence that may help identify a man that kidnapped me and Tyler Hansford."

McQueen stepped forward. "What kind of evidence?'

"My satchel has a fingerprint of a man who kidnapped and interrogated Tyler and me at a hotel in Virginia Beach."

McQueen cleared his throat. "Oh yes, the gray-haired man. We heard about that story from the office staff here. Evidently the Virginia Beach Police Department delivered quite the description in the case file when Tyler was picked up. We were just going over it when you, of all people, just walk in the door. It sounded more like you were caught in a dalliance with the Hansford boy and needed a story to get out of a jam."

Charles let out an impatient sigh. "If you will dust the satchel, I think you will get a good print. This guy went to a lot of trouble to kidnap both Tyler and me. It was clear that he was going to get whatever information he could and then he was going to kill us both. It was quite fortunate that a maid interrupted his plans."

Parrish said caustically, "Well we will get to that, but there are several areas that we need to explore first. How exactly do you fit into the American Independence Group?"

Charles just looked befuddled. "Who?"

Parrish said, "Oh come on Mr. Reynolds, you and your friend Sam Jackson had dinner with a domestic terrorist organization just two nights ago, and you expect us not to know?"

McQueen said, "Yes, we had a discussion with Dr. Jackson down in Miami. He was quite forthcoming about your role with AIG."

Parrish added, "A group that we think is likely to have killed Hank Summers."

Wide-eyed Charles said, "You are full of shit! Sam Jackson had no clue about AIG or even who the people were at the dinner. The only AIG I know of is the insurance company. I have no idea who killed Hank Summers, but I would like to find out as much as anyone."

Parrish said, "But somehow, you seemed to be the first to know that Summers had been killed."

Leaning forward Charles said, "You guys seem to be missing the point here. I am an investigative reporter. I do not go around killing U.S. Senators or associating with terrorist groups. I report on events, not create them."

McQueen asked, "So how did you know that the Senator was murdered?"

"I did not know. A confidential informant, who was correct I might add, told me going into the press conference that it was not a heart attack."

Charles internally grimaced for mentioning the timing of the tip he received from Ellen Cochran. Sure enough, McQueen made eye contact with Parrish, stood, and left the room.

Appearing to take Charles' concern earnestly, McQueen set the satchel down, removed a handkerchief and picked it back up. He nodded toward Parrish. "I will get this checked out."

"Well. Mr. Reynolds, your contact at the press conference, should be easy enough to sniff out with all the cameras that were at the press conference."

Charles chided himself again but felt confident that he was off camera when he spoke with Ellen Cochran.

"So, what did the Tyler Hansford tell you?"

Charles said flatly, "Probably what he has told you."

With apparent disgust, Parrish said, "Mr. Hansford is refusing to speak to us."

Charles felt a momentary inexplicable sense of pride. "Well, good for him."

Parrish stood up and pushed the table toward Charles bumping hard against his chest.

Charles sucked in a breath and said, "You do realize that I am a nationally syndicated reporter, right?"

"That's funny; I heard you are a fired syndicated reporter. A soon to be disgraced by the revelation of a sexual affair with a boy thirty years younger than you are."

Charles took exception, "He is not thirty years younger than I am."

Parrish smiled knowing that he was finally getting to Charles.

Charles continued, "We did not have a sexual relationship. He called me and I was questioning him."

Parrish smirked. "That's funny too. Do you usually question your sources when they are naked?"

Charles stood up. "You know, this farce of an interview is over. You are wasting your time and my time. I have a legitimate lead in this investigation. Run the satchel for the print. You will find at least someone that you should be questioning instead of haranguing me for something that you know is bogus."

McQueen returned to the room not looking happy. He made brief eye contact with Parrish, which Charles interpreted as a lack of video on the press conference meeting between Charles and his informant.

McQueen spoke. "Mr. Reynolds, you were acquainted with an Ellen Cochran, were you not?"

This caused Charles' heart to jolt, but he managed to show no reaction.

Parrish asked, "Could this have been your inside source prior to the press conference?"

Charles said blandly, "I have lots of contacts and sources."

McQueen said hoping to strike a crucial blow, "Do you know that Ms. Cochran has been found dead?"

This rocked Charles. He could not hide the sadness and shock. McQueen gave a slight smile of satisfaction. Parrish stared intensely at Charles. "Mr. Reynolds, I know that you have had your share of harrowing escapes and you are a well-recognized reporter, but you are playing with people's lives and people are getting killed. Just confirm that Ellen Cochran was your source, and we will see if there can be a scenario where you are not the one held culpable for anyone else's life."

Then Charles remembered that regular interrogation tactics did not preclude the authorities from lying to a suspect. "Prove it," he said.

"Prove what?!" McQueen said.

"Prove that Ellen Cochran is dead." Charles watched and their reaction told Charles that they were bluffing. They had made a lucky guess, knowing that she worked for Summers, and they had obviously reviewed everyone who was in attendance at the press conference. And it almost worked.

McQueen stepped in and placed his face just inches from Charles. "Reynolds you are dangerously close to being charged with impeding a federal investigation into the death of a U.S. Senator."

Anger consumed Charles' face. "You will have to keep guessing about my sources and I would suggest that if you lie to me about someone dying again that I once cared about, you will not like the newspaper story when it comes out with your tactics. Now, get the hell out of my face. Run the satchel for a fingerprint, or I will take it to some other authority who is interested in finding out who killed Summers."

McQueen pulled a tissue from a box sitting on the table and picked up the satchel. Parrish stood. "Just take your seat, Mr. Reynolds, we have someone else that wants to talk to you." Both men left the room, shoulders back and with faces red with anger.

Five minutes later, Tyler Hansford was escorted across the office by Agent Parrish. Opening the interrogation room door where Charles sat, Parrish said, "Now you two don't get any gay ideas. The blinds are to remain open."

Charles stood as Tyler entered the room. The boy looked like he had not slept in days. His hair was in disarray and his gate had been reduced to a shuffle similar to a prisoner chained at the feet. When the door was closed, Tyler shuffled over to Charles and embraced him with a long hug. Charles looked over his shoulder to see several people in the office gawking at the sight. Charles was tempted to flip them the middle finger but resisted. Tyler finally let go of the embrace and sat down.

Charles said softly, "How you are doing Tyler?"

"Oh good. The FBI is mad at me."

"I can imagine. Why won't you talk to them and why did they bring you to me?"

Tyler smiled. "I told them I would only talk to you. And you came!"

Charles gave a weary smile. "That explains a lot."

Tyler took both hands and gave an enormous scratch of his head which left his hair looking somewhat like Red Skelton.

"Tyler, you just need to describe the man who killed the Senator, and you will be fine. The FBI will protect you."

"No, no, no. You don't understand."

"What don't I understand?" asked Charles.

In a quiet voice, Tyler said, "I saw the killer."

Stunned, Charles said, "Well that's great. Just tell them who he is!"

Tyler was rocking back and forth and shaking his head.

Charles was confused. "Why?"

"He does not think I saw him, but he is here."

Jerking his head up, Charles looked out the glass window into the office. "In here? Now?"

"Not now, but I saw him go into the bathroom as I was coming down the hall."

"Here? In this building?" Charles asked incredulously. "You saw the killer?"

Tyler had tears in eyes as he was nodding his head.

"Do you know his name? I mean look out there, can you point him out?"

Tyler said, "I am scared to look. He may be there and know that I know who he is."

"Tyler, you have to look. There has to be a dozen or so agents out there. They are not going to let him do anything to you. You have to identify this man so we can have him arrested."

Charles was looking out into the open floored office space. There were several men, but they all seemed to be tending to computers or reports. Parrish had one leg straddled over a desk talking to another agent that Charles had not met. Charles saw McQueen come in and say something to Parrish. They both looked toward the interrogation room. Charles said,

"Tyler you are going to have to look. Look out there and tell me if you see him. He may not even be there."

"Are they looking this way?" Tyler asked.

"Yes, hold on a second and I will tell you when to look."

McQueen and Parrish were joined by another man who looked like he was perhaps in charge of the office. They all stared at Charles as he stared back at them.

"Now?" Tyler asked pitifully.

"No wait."

Two more agents came in together and Charles watched as Parrish and McQueen finished a conversation. McQueen draped his jacket over his shoulder and felt his pants pocket. He pulled out a set of keys and then a cell phone before giving one last stare at Charles and Tyler as he left the room. Parrish was still engaged in conversation with the man in charge.

"Okay, now Tyler, they are not looking."

Tyler quickly looked up and scanned the room.

Parrish and the man in charge both looked toward the interrogation room. Tyler quickly turned and placed his head on the table.

Charles said in disbelief. "It is one of those two?"

Tyler said with his voice cracking, "No. he's not out there."

Charles said, "Here they come."

"Don't tell them Charles. You don't know who you can trust. Please!"

Charles closed his eyes and said, "Yeah, maybe you are right."

Chapter 44   **Norfolk, Virginia**   **Monday**

Opening the interrogation room door, Parrish said, "Gentlemen, this is Special Agent in Charge of the Norfolk field office, Ken Sheraton."

Sheraton, an average sized man with unusually dark eyes and a bad comb-over, moved over to Charles and extended his hand. Charles decided to make nice and gave the man a winning smile. Tyler did not make eye contact and did not return the man's effort to shake his hand.

Sheraton pulled back his hand gave a tight smile. "I understand you guys have had a rough couple day. Mr. Hansford, I also want to say sorry for your loss."

Tyler raised his head long enough to give a glaring look at the man before returning his eyes to the table.

Sheraton cleared his throat before saying, "We have received orders to transport Tyler to the Washington FBI office to be placed in protective custody. Mr. Reynolds, if you feel that you are in danger, we will place you in protective custody as well and make sure that you get back safely to Miami."

Without looking up, Tyler whispered a pleading, "Charles."

"I am staying with Tyler," Charles said firmly.

Sheraton looked at Parrish for guidance.

Parrish said, "Mr. Reynolds, I understand you have a vested interest in Tyler, but I only have orders to transport Mr. Hansford."

Tyler said, "I won't go."

Sheraton let out a frustrated sigh and Parrish just shook his head in disbelief. Finally, Parrish said in a fatherly tone, "Tyler, we want you safe. It would help if you talked to us now. We can't help you if we don't know who to protect you against. It is because you are not talking that you are going to have to go to the D.C. office. So, you can avoid that if you just tell us what you saw."

Charles said, "Tyler, it might be a good idea to get you safely out of here."

"Will you go with me?"

Charles let out a long breath. "Okay, how about this. Agent Sheraton provides you with a bullet proof vest and I go along with you till we get to the D.C. FBI office. We get you into protective custody where no one can get to you."

Eyes wet, Tyler looked up at Charles and raised his hands in despair. "They are going to kill me."

Parrish had lost his patience. "You are in the custody of the FBI," he growled. "We will not let anyone get to you."

Tyler looked at Charles with the sorrowful eyes of a man was being led to the gallows. He wiped his eyes with his shirt sleeve and said, "Whatever."

Twenty minutes later, Parrish was escorting Tyler and Charles down a back set of stairs leading to an underground parking garage. A dark colored panel van, with FBI, emblazoned on the driver's side door was backed up with its back doors open revealing two long bench seats facing each other. Tyler inched along at a snail's pace, occasionally being prodded by Parrish to move a little faster. Through the back door, Charles was loaded first, taking a seat on the right side of the van. He could see that McQueen was already positioned in a high-backed driver's seat and had his phone to his right ear, apparently keeping a vigilant watch out the left side of the van for anyone who looked threatening. McQueen glanced into the rearview mirror but did not turn to welcome his new guests. Parrish helped Tyler up into the van and then on to the left bench seat across from Charles. Tyler sat downcast, studying the floor with a blank stare.

McQueen said very softly into his phone, "Okay, they are loading now, and we are plus one for some reason. I repeat plus one."

Parrish hopped out the back of the van, closing the double doors with a one-two solid thud. He came around the passenger side, pulled himself aboard and buckled up.

McQueen said, "It will be just a minute until the escort car pulls around."

Parrish said, "I didn't know we were going to have an escort."

McQueen said, "Yeah just extra precaution. He just called to say he would be here in a minute."

Charles was studying McQueen's profile. He was a handsome guy for sure. He had strong features, made more striking by the dark suit. For the first time, he noticed the man's hair. It was heavily gelled. Charles' gaze dropped down to his foot on the gas pedal. Charles asked, "Say McQueen, what kind of dress boots are those?"

Not turning in his seat and ignoring the question, McQueen said curtly, "Reynolds, I guess it is your lucky day that you are able to go with us on a little road trip."

Ignoring what seemed to be an unnecessarily sarcastic tone, Charles persisted, "Are those Amedio Testoni boots? Those are nice."

Charles shifted his gaze toward Tyler, who was already leaning forward in an effort to see the man in the front seat. Moving to all fours, Tyler unsuccessfully craned his head up to get a look at McQueen, who was intently studying his side view mirror. In the front passenger seat scanning the parking garage, Parrish also seemed oblivious to Tyler. When a dark sedan pulled up behind the idling van, Parrish said, "Looks like the escort is here." From the newly arrived vehicle, the driver side door opened allowing a man wearing sunglasses, an FBI logo jacket, and baseball styled hat to exit. McQueen said, "Let me see what he wants." Hastily he opened his door and moved around to the back of the van. Tyler sat back on his bench and tried a swift look between the back of the seat and the driver side door.

Mildly irritated, Parrish said, "Let's just go." He sighed and powered down the window, sticking his head out. He was about to yell out for McQueen to get back in the van, but upon hearing that the back door being checked and then being unlocked, Parrish swiveled around in his seat. Looking first at Tyler and then at the rear door, Parrish was startled when he sensed someone had approached his open window. Genuinely aggravated, Parrish turned back to his right and asked coarsely, "What the hell is wrong?"

With his silenced PPK, the man calmly shot Parrish between his eyes with two quick shots. At such close range, Parrish's head could not contain the force of the bullets. Brain matter sprayed across the front seats; the jolt felled Parrish sideways onto the middle console like a Minnesota pine. Reacting to the man at the passenger door, Tyler had started toward the back door, only to reverse toward the front of the van when the back doors were yanked open. Wasting no time, McQueen shot two silenced nine-millimeter rounds, striking Tyler in the back. The impact of the shots and Tyler's momentum caused him to stumble forward, landing between the front seats, atop the slumping body of Parrish.

"That's what I should have done in the bathroom when I had a chance," growled McQueen.

McQueen shifted his attention and his aim toward the right of the van. Charles, who had lunged along the narrow side of the front passenger' seat and the headrest, was gripping the gun hand which had just killed Parrish. Rising up on the back bench seat, Charles had been able to use his weight and leverage to wrench the shooter's right hand down over the inside edge of the door. However, this sudden movement had caused another silent spit of the gun; the shot passing dangerously between Charles' legs, striking the bench seat below, sending a few strands of stuffing up through the haze of gunfire.

The gunman let out a cry of pain as Charles maintained his grip and continued to push his gun hand awkwardly downward. The assassin had stood on the doorstep railing, but this seemed to cause Charles' body to shift further into the crevice. He had also tried to open the door, but it was locked, and he could not reach the door latch with his free left hand. This left the option to take a swing at Charles with his left hand, but he was squeezed so tight through the window, he only managed to ram his hand into the door trim.

Charles had heard the second silenced pops, and he immediately knew that it was McQueen. Charles also did not need the evidence of Tyler falling on top of Parrish to know that he was going to be McQueen's next target. Charles tried to envision using the gun which he was currently struggling to control, to somehow shoot McQueen in some sort of under the arm movie shot. But his body seemed inextricably in the way and letting go to get into a better position did not seem to be a healthy option. Still, he had to consider that McQueen was going to shoot him at any moment. In fact, which is exactly what McQueen was preparing to do. Like a deer caught in a trap awaiting the final bullet to put him out of his miserable existence, Charles tried in vain to look back over his shoulder to see from where the final shot would come but could not locate McQueen in his peripheral vision.

McQueen remained standing street level at the back of the van trying to decide how best to place his next shot. He did need to act quickly so they could get as far away from FBI headquarters as possible and find a place to set up a scenario that would have left his partner shot in the head. After adjusting his aim a couple times to properly line up the struggling target, McQueen squeezed off two eight-foot shots into Charles mid back. Like being stung with a two-pronged branding iron, Charles felt the bullets impact his back and let out a scream of pain. The momentum of the bullets jolted him forward causing his head to collide with the door frame, and his body dropped like a squished sack of flour between the high back seat and the door. The unconscious Charles had released his grip on the shooter's wrist, but now the shooter frantically tried to free his gun from the wedge formed between the door and Charles' lifeless body. McQueen jumped up into the back of the van, bringing his weapon up for a head shot on Charles. Another deafening bang reverberated from the van and McQueen stumbled backwards out the open back doors, thudding onto the parking garage floor. Tyler, who had managed to recover Parrish's service weapon now, turned the gun on the attacker still struggling for his gun through the passenger side window. The latest shot caused the man to instinctively try to duck, but his arm was trapped in a vise, and he could not suppress a bitter cry of pain and frustration. Now, his attention shifted to this petulant boy who continued to be an irritant which would not go away. The two finally made eye contact as the gunman stopped his struggle to free his arm just for an instant. Tyler recognized the man, whose hat had been knocked off in the struggle and sunglasses sat askew on his face. Tyler aimed the gun and with another deafening blast, shot Gray Hair between his cold blue eyes.

Epilogue   Houston, Texas

Earlier, Charles had given a blow-by-blow account of his adventuress in Virginia Beach, Rudy's, and the events which followed in Washington DC FBI Parking garage. Now, Charles Reynolds was seated comfortably poolside, sipping on his third Shiner Bock. "Clubbo, the house looks great."

Sam was exiting the patio doors with his own beer and took a seat.

"Thanks. The cleanup was not that bad, and the electrical work was completed just a couple days ago."

"Well, you have done a great job and this pool..., the pool is fantastic!"

"With another week or two of 90 degree heat I may actually be able to go swimming." Sam enjoyed a pull from his own bottle of beer.

"So, you have made it thru Spring Break, and everything is Kosher with the university?"

Sam laughed miserably, "Well, the Dean called me on the carpet for missing class without following proper procedure. He was appeased when I offered to contribute my speaking honorarium to the School of Business. And somehow the nude beach event did not catch his attention."

This caused Charles to break into a full laugh.

Sam even laughed a little. Shaking his head as if to try to rid himself of the memory, Sam said, "In the end, he only issued a warning – mostly because you gave me a mention as some sort of hero, which I was not – in your article.

"Yeah well, you got a lot of bad things that you did not deserve, so why not get some undeserved attention."

Sadly, Sam responded, "Nothing like the attention that George Love and Pepper Wallace received."

Charles said solemnly, "Yeah, I figured that you heard about that."

Sam closed his eyes. After a moment, he took a deep breath and exhaled. "I really liked George. When I saw it in the paper, it made me sick. I just tried to forget that I ever knew the man, 'cause the fallout...," he paused, "I can't even imagine. I am certainly not going to bring it up at the next faculty meeting. If the Dean made that connection, even tenure might not cover me."

Thoughtfully Charles said, "Looking back, it makes sense with what Tyler had told me about the names that Summers' killer had mentioned in the bathroom. I really never made the connection with Pepper and Rivers until I saw the report. I knew that the name Pepper rang a bell but did not put it together. Pepper Wallace was a huge benefactor of Florida State. I may have actually met the guy at an alumni event, but I am not sure."

Sam said, "And no one has heard about what happened to Rivers?"

Charles said, "Evidently not. It was obviously another alias, but no one was able to identify who he was."

"The story of you cracking the Senator's murder and the election fraud was all over the news, but there are still several loose ends that I don't understand."

Charles nodded in agreement. "It was a puzzle for sure. It appears that the President has survived the voting scandal that ensued, but I don't think it is over yet. He made a big deal about removing the interim tag from the current director of the FBI, Russell Epstein; right after the Assistant Director Rick Uhler was thrown under the metaphorical bus. Probably some type of political leverage or payback, but it was rumored that Uhler had some inside information on AIG and did not reveal it."

Eyes wide, Sam asked, "But can he just fire some bureaucrat and totally ignore the rigged election?"

"Apparently, but you probably saw on television that a Congressional hearing was launched headed up by a guy named Mike Pemberton and Brad Hutchins. No surprise, Hutchins seems to be real chummy with the President, early reports are that the vote count was not significantly affected *enough* to invalidate the election. The President, of course, claimed he had no knowledge of the vote fraud."

Sam ventured, "So it was the election equipment brochure that was the key?"

Charles said, "It was the brochure that led me to the company that produced the election machines that were used in three states. Predictably, these were the swing states that just happened to be critical electoral vote states. Those machines were manufactured, assembled and designed by a company owned by a multi-billionaire named Casey Friends. Of course, he is claiming that if there were any discrepancies in the vote counts it was simply computer error."

"Could it have made a difference, these machines?"

"Oh yeah. The margin of victory in the three states which used those voting machines was so close that the electoral count could have been completely reversed."

"Meaning that the President probably lost the election."

333

Charles put up both hands while closing his eyes. "I know it sounds like a conspiracy."

Sam asked, "And this Friends guy. You did not recognize his name? Isn't he like a zillionaire?"

Charles was nodding his head, "I certainly should have. According to Tyler, the Senator told the assassin that friends ought to know better. I just assumed that was a figure of speech, but somehow Summers figured out that Friends was behind the bathroom confrontation. This is probably what got the Senator killed."

Sam asked incredulously, "Then how is Friends not being tied to the murder of Summers?"

Again nodding, Charles cynically said, "Friends of the President I suppose get a pass. McQueen and Freeman won't be contradicting the story since they are also dead."

"And who was McQueen?" asked Sam.

"McQueen was an FBI agent, but he was likely on someone's payroll along with Walter Freeman. Epstein released a report that both Freeman and McQueen had some tie to AIG. Freeman, the infamous Gray-Haired man, in addition to kidnapping Tyler and me, was also the likely culprit who ordered the search of our houses and your escapades at the beach. Now that George Love and Pepper Wallace are dead, we get whatever story they want us to get."

"But Freeman has no ties to the President?" asked Sam incredulously.

Charles sighed. "He was rumored to have visited the White House, but everyone has been mum. The President offered up the White House log of visitors – no Walter Freeman. Since he is dead, it seems that the President is once again the Teflon man."

Sam put a finger in the air to backtrack in the conversation, "Back to the shooting in the basement parking lot, the news said that you and Tyler were both wearing bullet proof vests that saved your life. How did you know to wear vests?"

"We did not know. It was just a fortunate turn of events. I have to take credit for suggesting that Tyler wear a vest, but it was Parrish that insisted on me wearing one too. It hurt like hell, but the vests worked."

Sam asked, "Not to be insensitive, but why didn't McQueen shoot you in the head instead of the vest?"

334

Charles gave a slight laugh, "That was the really fortunate part. He could not have known we had on vests. McQueen knew that Tyler could identify him as Summers' killer. He was conveniently somewhere else every time Tyler was in the room. But Tyler had gotten a glimpse of him in the hallway and was trying to convince us that the killer was somewhere near. McQueen left early to set up the transport before I suggested the bullet proof vest to appease Tyler's fears about being transported. Those vests are so thin. They fit under regular shirts with hardly a trace unless you are really looking for them. When we got off the elevator McQueen was already waiting in the van, and fortunately was determined not to look back when they loaded us up. Since he was worried about Tyler recognizing him, he never really gave us a good look."

Again backtracking, suspiciously Sam asked, "But the news said that the election scandal had to do with a group called AIG trying to get rid of the President. It does not make any sense that they get him elected in the first place?"

"That's where it takes one of many strange twists or perhaps turning fiction into fact. The President's talking heads, and, therefore, the sycophant press, have claimed that the AIG wanted to get the President re-elected because he was their best chance of the states achieving secession, but when the election fraud was threatened to be revealed, they had to cover it up."

"And that whole group at the Miami dinner were part of the AIG, and they were trying to create the meltdown which would cause some states to secede? That is just hard to believe."

"Without a doubt they were working on something. It is debatable how extensive or organized it would have been. My sources tell me that the financial crisis was averted when Brazil, Russia, India and China withdrew the plan to replace the dollar as the world reserve currency."

Sam asked, "How does that all fit in?"

Pleading ignorance, Charles said, "I have no idea, but I thought you as an economist, could shed some light on that."

Sam ventured, "I know that it would have been devastating to the economy but figuring out how someone could instigate the process or reverse it is inconceivable."

Charles jibed, "And, by the way, you were an active part in their plan."

"Yeah well, I had to do some real convincing that I was not a part of any group and just an accidental dinner guest. You know the lady named Sarah. The one who arranged my travel. The one that I was so hot to meet after my speech in Miami. She was the one who turned my name over to the FBI?"

Eyebrows raised, Charles asked, "How did you find that out?"

Sitting up a little in his seat, Sam said, "She called and sort of offered an apology after your article came out."

Charles drank from his beer and said, "I still don't know how they knew I was at the dinner, but I suspect that there was a traitor in the AIG who was feeding information to the FBI. My best guess is that it was Friends."

"Wait a minute. You mean that Friends was playing both sides?!"

Charles breathed out heavily, "Well, it could be a story that I need to follow up with. The work of an investigative reporter is never done." Charles wiped the sweat from his drink with a napkin and tossed back another swig. He continued, "The Secessionist plot, if there was ever one, fell apart when the Governor of Texas passed it off as a political stunt of which he had no prior knowledge."

Sam sat there dumfounded, shaking his head. "It is strange times that we live in. So, what is happening with Tyler?"

"Tyler is a Nuevo celebrity out to clean up corruption in politics. He was even invited to the White House, which he refused. He has decided that he is no longer gay and is booked for the coming year on the talk shows."

"Seriously? You would think he would want to go back into hiding." Sam stopped and after a second thought asked, "How do you stop being gay?"

"I have no idea," laughed Charles. "But it seems to be working for him. He has a book deal too."

After another pause in the conversation, Sam asked, "How is Devin? You know I started liking that kid."

"Oh, he is doing great. Jerry Collins nominated him for the kid version of the Meritorious Service Award. He got a new bike, and he had the satisfaction of knowing that Ms. Wendell was totally pissed off that something good came out of my mess. Made my day as well."

"Ms. Wendell! I had almost forgotten about her. What a hoot!" Sam laughed.

"She is a piece of work. She filed a public nuisance complaint as soon as I returned to Miami but dropped it when she found out I was fired from the Miami Express."

Sam smiled. "Think she will refile when she finds out that your boss rehired you?"

Charles said, "She might, but I have not decided about that yet."

Evident surprise in his face, Sam asked, "What are you going to do?"

Charles pulled another swallow of beer. With a sliver of a smile, Charles said, "The Times has offered me a column and will allow me to stay in Miami."

"The Times!" Sam said enthusiastically. "That is fantastic!"

"Yeah, I am going to take a couple weeks off and see how I feel." Taking a look around the pool area and then back to Sam, Charles earnestly said, "I just wanted to come check out this incredible house and..," he paused, "mend any fences with you."

Sam was laughing and shaking his head. "No need. It will give me six semesters of stories to tell in my classes. Hell, it may even last me for the rest of my career."

"Well, I am truly sorry that you got roped into all that happened."

"Seriously Charles, it is not like a lot of exciting things happen in the life of a college professor. It was sort of ..., he thought for the word, "exhilarating."

Charles said with no hint of deception, "Excellent, cause I am going to need some help flushing out Friends and tying him to the President."

Sam started to protest, but realized that Charles was just pulling his chain, just like he had done for their entire friendship. They both broke into a long mutual laugh. After a few moments, Sam asked, "Where do you go from here?"

Charles stretched and signed, "I am headed back to Virginia Beach."

Nodding, Sam asked, "More follow-up on the story?"

"I guess you could say that. I have my second date with a young lady named Carly."

Sam asked, "The young waitress who served you the drinks?"

Charles only gave a confessionary smile. Sam's surprise gave way to amusement.

Sam lifted his beer bottle to clink a toast to the irrepressible Charles Reynolds.

The End

For other D.C. Reed novels, visit
http://cbwpublishing.sharepoint.com/Pages/default.aspx
Or purchase through Amazon.com

The Cleaning – Politics Can Get a Little Dirty (2009) by D.C
Reed is the first novel which introduces Charles Reynolds to
the world. When Chars Reynolds, Miami investigative reporter,
gets a hunch about an auto accident that claims the life of U.S.
Senator Mike Robertson, he unwittingly puts himself on the hit
list of two powerful organizations: the Chicago Mob and the
Freedom Organization.

Deadly Trifecta (2010) by D.C. Reed follows Charles
Reynolds, award-winning investigative reporter across the
country in a puzzle of related events. When Charles helps out a
former girlfriend straighten out a problem with a city
bureaucracy, he unknowingly threatens a plot to attack a
strategic military base in Tampa Florida, as well as expose an
insider's deal to buy gambling boats in Florida and casinos in
Arizona.